*So here was my sentence on this Day of Judgment! With blankness before my eyes, I had no distraction as I saw my many misdeeds.*

*My in-laws used to laugh at my ignorance and make snide remarks about the "shiksa" Jeff married—until Sheila married a Hindu and shocked them into mournful silence. But before then, they used to grin and exchange looks whenever I asked a question.*

*Provided I didn't trouble to entertain them or feel troubled by their lack of responsiveness, my in-laws were very easy people to have as house guests. They were as quiet as shadows and just as undemanding; like shadows, something you noticed every now and then and could either attend to or ignore without consequence. They were fully self-contained.*

*The enormity of our undertaking overwhelmed me. The move to Jerusalem became dwarfed by the thought of taking another couple's child to become a part of our family: one father, one mother, one son, one daughter...and now one little swarthy-skinned mongoloid. I prayed for a miracle because I saw this as a tragedy.*

*None of the other people on the bus paid any attention to the men or their Uzis, and my alarm turned to relief as they paid the driver and slipped their gear under a seat. Would I ever grow used to seeing Israeli soldiers on busses and in the streets?*

*There were so many new rules to learn. In Tucson, we considered ourselves Orthodox, but our Bayit Vegan neighbors underlined how far from truly observant we were. When we were invited to Shabbas lunch the previous week, I found pre-ripped toilet paper in the bathroom. Was this yet another rule or ritual peculiar to Jerusalem?*

*Memory has a way of editing. Knowing this, I feared returning to Tucson, which in Israel had taken on an Eden-like attraction. I was dazzled by the beauty of Tucson upon our arrival. I'd expected culture shock going to a foreign land, but I was surprised at how strong it was on our return to the familiar.*

# T'SHUVA

a novel

by Carolyn Keiler Paul

Strawberry Hill Press

Strawberry Hill Press
3848 S.E. Division Street
Portland, Oregon 97202

Cover by Ku, Fu-sheng
Cover sketch by the author
Typeset and designed by Wordwrights, Portland, Oregon


Manufactured in the United States of America


**Library of Congress Cataloging-in-Publication Data**

Paul, Carolyn Keiler, 1951-
      T'shuva : a novel / by Carolyn Keiler Paul.
         p.   cm.
      ISBN 0-89407-115-7 (trade paper)
      1. Americans—Israel—Fiction.  2. Jewish women—Fiction.
I. Title.
PS3566.A82617T77    1996
813'.54—dc20
                                                      95-37125
                                                         CIP

It would be a misrepresentation to take sole credit for this novel. Over the several years I've worked on it, many people offered encouragement and concrete suggestions that I feel have enhanced and improved the story.

Many friends read earlier manifestations of the manuscript and told me what they liked—and what they didn't. These include my husband David Paul, Joyce Williamson, Chana Yahalom, Janice Cohen, Barbara Beasley, Bob Kaufman, Katy Clay, and Dorit Hovav.

My sister Barbara Keiler, a prolific novelist herself, critiqued the work, as did award-winning author Mary Betty Underwood, and my cousin Robert Avrech, a screen-play writer.

Thanks are due fellow members of my writing group in Portland, Oregon. Linda Davidson, Stan Funk, Pat Landers, Dody Orendurff, Mary Schoessler, and Alan Stone have given my prose the line-by-line scrutiny that has taught me a great deal about how a reader construes what I attempt to communicate. Likewise my writing friends in Boston: Louis F. Williams, Jackie Herskovitz, and Dorothy O'Connor.

Also helpful were the many reference librarians I called upon at the public libraries in Tucson, Portland, Boston and Brookline.

I was fortunate to get the input of a few people in the book-making industry: Jeremy Kay at Bartleby Press, and at Mesorah Publications, Judi Dick and Rabbi Moshe Lieber, who also did me the invaluable service of checking the story for accuracy regarding observant Jewish practice. I'm very grateful to Joseph Lubow of Strawberry Hill Press for his editorial incisiveness. And the largest measure of gratitude goes to my publisher, Jean-Louis Brindamour, who has exceeded my expectations in so many ways.

For David, whose wisdom and goodness inspire me.

T'SHUVA is the Hebrew word meaning an answer or response, a return, repentance. A Ba'al T'shuva is a formerly non-religious Jew who becomes observant. T'shuva also refers to the period around the Jewish New Year when all Jews are called to renew their commitment to God.

The blowing of the shofar (ram's horn) on Rosh Hashanah is a call for t'shuva. According to the Rambam, better known as Maimonides, it is as if the shofar were saying, "Awake, sleepers, from your sleep! Arise, slumberers, from your slumber! Scrutinize your deeds! Repent with contrition! Remember your Creator!... Peer into your souls, improve your ways and your deeds...." (*Hilchos Teshuvah* 3:4)

# Part I.  B'Midbar (In the Desert)

# One

It was like a blink, only the blink didn't end. We'd just risen to our feet for the final sounding of the shofar, and I stretched and yawned. Then something happened in the synagogue. Suddenly I was blind.

So here was my sentence on this Day of Judgment! With blankness before my eyes, I had no distraction as I saw my many misdeeds. I thought of the time one Saturday I forgot it was Shabbas and scribbled "napkins" on my shopping list, and another time I accidentally spread cream cheese with a meat knife and then only rinsed the utensil in tepid water before replacing it in the meat drawer. What about gossip? I found it as hard as the next person to resist a good story, especially about someone I didn't like. If only I could see again, I'd re-*kasher* all the silverware in boiling water. I'd plug my ears and mind my tongue.

Most of the congregants broke off in the middle of the prayer. Drifting more gradually to silence were a couple of scratchy voices belonging to men whose glaucoma and cataracts had already clouded their vision, who relied on memory more than sight to say their prayers, for whom it mattered little whether or not we had light.

A couple of snickers intruded on the quiet: a chuckle at the straggling voices, or at the undignified way in which Rosh Hashanah services had come to a halt. Or perhaps it was the comfort of discovering that, if it was Divine judgment, at least we were all equally distressed. Surely I drew relief in finding I wasn't the only one in the dark.

If a congregation is a flock, in the next few minutes ours behaved like sheep. My eyes adjusted; I could make out silhouettes shifting aimlessly in the dim synagogue, and many people sat down with a tired sigh. The general attitude seemed to be to let someone else figure out what should be done.

There was a rising volume of whispering. Two women near me discussed the timer, an energy-saving device set to automatically shut off the lights after sabbath and holiday services. One woman laughed at the lack of foresight in whoever had set the gadget for a time too early, the other complained about the lengthy service running so much later than expected. I was a little disappointed to learn that the darkness could be attributed to something as mundane as a timer.

The blackout wasn't an act of God in the obvious, miracular sense, not like the ninth plague of darkness which afflicted Egypt, or a less fantastic phenomenon, such as an eclipse. After all, it was Thursday, September 8, 1983, the first day of the Jewish year 5744—that many thousands of years since God created everything. Our little outage was far from cataclysmic. The others around me seemed to welcome the power failure as a diversion, a break in the protracted service. But I didn't share their amusement. To me, it was a sign nonetheless, a very literal foreshadowing.

A few less devout individualists groped their way to the back and out of the building, intent on getting home to lunch now that the show was apparently over. A shaft of bright Arizona daylight sliced into the dark at the rear of the men's section as the door opened. Then the wedge of brightness shrank to nothing and was followed like thunder after lightning by the thump of the closing door.

Perhaps spurred by a concern that the milling herd might follow those who left, the men on the small central platform began to confer in earnest. I readily identified Mr. Schneider, the cantor, by his white, high-domed holiday skullcap and long white satin robe, both of which glowed vaguely in the dimness. Though he attempted to hush it, his baritone carried, and I could clearly hear him say, "So what can we do? We can't continue like this."

The rabbi was also dressed in a white robe but distinguished from Cantor Schneider by his greater height. He bent over the railing, his shadow merging with that of someone on the other side. When he straightened again, I perceived the shaking of his head. "No, Harry, I can't let you do that," I heard him say. "I can't allow a Jew to violate the laws of the holiday. But it's not an altogether bad idea." Then he addressed the tiny octogenarian who spent most of his time attempting to keep the synagogue running smoothly. "Mr. Liebowitz, do you think we could find a *goy* outside who could turn the lights on for us?"

"There's that woman next door," Mr. Liebowitz answered in a high-pitched wheeze.

"So go already and see if she's home," coaxed Mr. Schneider. There was a long-standing animosity between the two men. The cantor, as a professionally trained vocalist, tended toward the temperamental artist. (He was retired from a synagogue in Brooklyn. His services here at Young Israel were offered gratis, since our congregation could barely afford the rabbi.)

"She don't like for us to trouble her with the shul's business," Mr. Liebowitz whined, the shadow of his head sinking as he descended from the platform. "Prob'ly can't do nothing anyway since it's on the timer. But okay, I'll go ask her." He shuffled down the aisle to the back. "I'm going," he repeated.

"Mr. Liebowitz," called Rabbi Danziger. He was a young man,

uncertain as to how he fit into the politics between Schneider and Liebowitz. Often his peacemaking efforts earned the disdain of both. "Maybe you can ask her to bring a flashlight so she can see what she's doing."

Mr. Liebowitz grumbled, "I should tell her to bring a flashlight, no less. Now prob'ly she'll be charging the shul for the use of her batteries."

I stood by the partition to the left of the men's section. Our daughter Ronnie, finding incipient adolescence utterly exhausting, had collapsed on the seat behind me, her legs giving out only seconds after the overhead illumination.

Adam was beyond me on the other side of the partition. I concentrated on his short, chubby shape rocking back and forth on the balls of his feet, his hands braced on the back of the seat in front of him. As I watched, he increased in velocity. The man seated in front of him, no doubt suffering from the rhythmic impact of our son's thrusts, turned and said "Shush!" though the boy was soundless. Jeff told Adam to sit down.

These laws about what we could and couldn't do—what sense did they make? Certainly the non-religious world thought we were insane. On Shabbas and Yontif, all our holy days, our days of "rest," we found ourselves waking early and walking to synagogue, a distance more comfortably traversed by car. We couldn't turn on or off any electrical appliance but we could turn water on and off; we couldn't adjust the air conditioner but we could open or close a window. We were supposed to sing songs of praise, but we were prohibited from playing an instrument. (And didn't one of King David's psalms describe playing the harp on Shabbas?) It was very hard to extrapolate from a known law to an unknown situation because the rules were so complex and convoluted.

Jeff tried to explain it all to me. According to him, the proscribed "work" could more accurately be defined as "acts of creation." We were supposed to emulate God, who ceased from creating on the seventh day. But the rules were hardly clearcut. Rabbis spent their lifetimes deciding about the minutest nuances of what might or might not be done. They consulted scientists for clarification regarding technology. And they didn't always draw the same conclusions. For example, that bit of Mishnah about the Shabbas candles we were supposed to read in our prayer books each Friday evening: it was full of Rabbi This says this but Rabbi That disagrees. If learned men had so much trouble deciphering God's laws, how could I be faulted for making a few mistakes?

Just as Mr. Liebowitz reached the rear of the men's section, a clean, pleasant light fell into the synagogue from behind me. A happy "Ahh!" rose simultaneously to everyone's lips.

An outsider, no doubt much brighter than the prayer-groggy congregants in our synagogue, might question why it took so long for someone to conceive of opening the heavy drapery that covered the windows over the two women's sections flanking the synagogue. I turned to see who was clever enough to think of this simple solution and then show the initiative to act upon it. As the drapes drew open and the increasing light made it easier to discern what before were only outlines of humanity, I was surprised (and proud) to see Ronnie reaching up to work the pulls. How had she found the resources to push her leaden body off the seat to execute her idea? Had a Divine Spark jolted her out of inertia?

Mr. Liebowitz stopped and turned toward the daylight which relieved him of his unpleasant mission to our Christian neighbor. With uncharacteristic speed, he crossed to the other women's section and stretched his skinny arms up to reach the loop of cord which opened the drapes on that side.

The midday September sun glared through the south-facing windows, justifying the use of the curtains on a day when we had artificial lighting. Mr. Liebowitz shuffled back to the central *bimah*, climbed up the two steps, riffled through his prayer book, and, panting slightly, announced, "Gentlemen, please stand and turn to page two-ninety-seven for the sounding of the shofar."

Everyone stood. Jeff poked Adam, who had settled trancelike on the seat beside him. Under the guidance of Mr. Schneider, who dropped all his cantorial flourishes in a nod to expediency, we began the prayer again.

I prayed with more fervor than usual in a self-conscious attempt to show God I really meant it this time. I felt there must be a reason for the lights going out. Timer or no, I believed God wanted us to stop and reflect. Up until that moment, I had recited the ritual as a matter of form, without any conviction. Now I remembered what it was all about. These were the days when our fate for the coming year was being decided; the blowing of the ram's horn was a call for *t'shuva*, for all Jews to repent their wicked ways and return to God. I thought if I prayed doubly hard, maybe when my fate was sealed, I wouldn't have "lights out" next to my name.

When we got to the place where we were forced to stop before, I imagined a certain expectancy in the air, an extra alertness to see if we'd make it beyond that point this time. The moment passed; there were no further interruptions. The service concluded with the singing of the "Adon Olam" and we filed out, wishing each other "*Shanah tova tikka-tevu*"—may you be inscribed for a good year.

Ronnie slouched and squinted in the brilliant sunlight; Adam disappeared up a tree. After greeting some women I saw only on holidays, I joined Jeff on the gravel where he talked to Marty Fisher, who was also with the University, and Ed Zlotnick, who was worth millions in land he bought on speculation when he first came to Tucson in '67. Neither of Jeff's friends came to synagogue regularly; they had some catching up to do.

While they chatted, I watched the rabbi and his family making their way through the congregants to the corner. Before crossing Tucson Boulevard, the rabbi's wife Naomi turned around and called for her son to come. She saw me and waved.

The men were still talking. I amused myself studying their faces. For all his money, Ed was one of the homeliest men I'd ever seen. Though he was not overweight, he looked flabby and unkempt, his face flaccid, his hair rested on his head like an ill-fitting toupee. Next to him, Marty was gorgeous; in spite of his shapeless nose and swollen lips, he had an athletic, trim look about him.

But I found Jeff attractive. He hid the pock marks left by acne with a neatly trimmed beard, and his *kippah*, the skullcap his mother crocheted and which he wore daily, covered the thinning dark hair on his crown. The buttons of his shirt strained just a little around his middle, but this added to the impression that he was a man of appetites: this and his hairy, muscular forearms, the shape of his throat at his open collar, his relaxed, animated mouth which twisted into the most appealing smile, and his narrow, mobile hips conspired to make him look virile. In fact, it was the pursuit of satisfying that particular appetite years earlier which had led him away from Torah long enough to connect with me, a nonpracticing Jew in those days.

"Where's Finkel?" asked Ed. "I didn't see him in there."

"Didn't you hear?" Jeff replied. "They moved to Colorado over the summer."

"Finkel? I mean Jim Finkel, a little chunky, his father-in-law's a shrink here in town."

Hadn't I just promised to plug my ears against gossip? Yet I grinned at Ed's description.

"Yeah, I know who you mean. They moved, it's been a month already, hasn't it, Cyn?"

"Last July," I said, itching with sweat. I didn't like being called "sin." Jeff tended to abbreviate names and places. For example, as far as he was concerned, we were standing a couple of yards from Tucson Bull, and there were all the standard ones: oj, pj, libe (where he studied), the U (where he worked). His sister Sheila became She, which led to unfortunate locutions, such as "I see we got a letter from She." And so Cynthia became Cyn.

"Has it been that long?" he asked me.

"Don't you remember? Their farewell *kiddush* was the Saturday after the Fourth of July."

"That's right. What a memory my wife has!"

"So what's he doing up there?" asked Marty. "Where is he? In Denver?" (Marty's wife was busy smiling at Harry Bass in the shade of the synagogue porch.)

"No, I think it's Boulder. Cindy?"

I turned my attention back to him. "Yes, it's Boulder. Jeff, come on, hon. The kids are getting restless."

He tore himself away. "*Shanah tova*," he called to the two men. "Come on, kids. Where's Adam?"

"Up there." Ronnie pointed to a sneaker poking from the foliage of a tree in front of the synagogue.

"Adam!" Jeff shouted. "Come down here this minute!"

There was a crunch on the gravel as our son sprang to the ground. We started walking home, Adam in the lead.

"How did you do that?" Jeff bellowed when he saw the tear. Adam must have caught his one good pair of slacks on a branch. I shared Jeff's chagrin but had come to accept injuries to flesh and fabric as intrinsic to rearing a son. Besides, I should have stopped Adam on his way up.

"What?" asked Adam.

Ronnie perked up. "Ha, Adam, I can see your undies."

"Shut up! You can *not!*" Just the same, he craned his head around to check. A little white peeked through the navy blue polyester where one side of the patch pocket had ripped away. He began to walk backwards, facing us and holding the pocket in place in case his classmates should see him as we made our way past the schoolyard.

Though I didn't actually sigh, my voice was laden with resignation. "What do you plan to wear tomorrow?"

"Tomorrow I can wear shorts," Adam suggested.

"You know you're not allowed to wear shorts to shul," Jeff answered, his face frozen in a cold scowl in spite of the heat.

"What? Oh yeah. Second day of Rosh Hashanah."

"And don't forget, dummy: this year, after Yontif we go right into Shabbas," his sister reminded him. "That makes three days in a row."

"Aw, do we really have to go? I can't take any more." Sweat rolled down his cheeks.

"Watch where you're going, you'll get run over," Jeff said.

Adam turned to cross the street, still holding onto the pocket.

We walked under a cloudless, dazzling blue sky, the daylight insinuating itself everywhere. The only shade sat in small pools around the base of palms and orange trees, like dirty undergarments slipped down legs to the floor. To me, this was what made southern Arizona a desert: not the scant flora nor the lack of rain, but the lack of shade. Therefore, all the more ominous that our problem a few minutes earlier had been too much shadow, too little light. In spite of the glare, I felt an overbearing gloom.

Though not a superstitious person, I searched for a manifestation of the calamity I predicted in synagogue. It gave me a different perspective on Adam's ripped pants, which seemed comparatively trivial. Part of me wanted to blow up the rip to proportions equal to the foreboding, so I could say "that (the rip) takes care of that (the premonition of disaster)" and forget about it. But I knew the rip was not enough.

While I was weighing in my mind all these heavy thoughts, while we waited to cross Sixth Street and as we made our way to Ninth, Jeff was scolding Adam for his disobedience (we had told him a dozen times not to climb in his synagogue clothes), his irresponsibility, and his stupidity. It seemed to me Adam started shrinking, but it could have been from the heat. No doubt it was more the heat than Adam that irked Jeff. And it was finally the heat that shut Jeff up. We walked the last two blocks with nothing but the drone of three fighter planes from Davis-Monthan Air Force Base to cut through the shimmering stillness. At last we turned up the walk past our cactus garden.

I unpinned the housekey dangling from the neckline of my dress. (Another one of those "no work" rules: no carrying, even something as small as a key, outside an enclosed area. Actually, on holidays that didn't fall on the sabbath, carrying was okay, but the habit of pinning my key onto my synagogue dresses—so that I wore it instead of carrying it in my pocket—was so ingrained that I'd pinned it on this day as well.) As I redid the catch of the safety pin, I had an idea. "It's okay, Jeff," I said, quietly out of respect for the heat. "I can safety pin his pocket up temporarily."

"Can you?" I could see Jeff didn't like the idea of Adam getting off so easily. "It'll look lousy."

"No, it'll be fine if he's very careful and doesn't climb any more trees." I looked meaningfully at Adam. Then, unlocking the door, I led the way out of the sun into our air-conditioned house.

# Two

On Monday, we were back to our weekday rhythm. After breakfast, Jeff and Adam pedaled off on their bikes to Sam Hughes Elementary, where Adam was in the fourth grade. Jeff continued west on Third Street, reaching the Optical Sciences Center on campus within a few minutes.

Taking advantage of the bright, cool morning, I went out to the backyard and hung laundry. Then I washed the dishes, took something out to defrost for dinner, and did the crossword and the wordseek in the *Daily Star* before driving circuitously to drop Ronnie at Mansfeld Junior High, then heading out Speedway to my job.

I worked at the Kopy Kat, the photocopying place next door to the Karpet King. It was an incredibly dull job, sticking people's originals in one of the mammoth machines, setting the number of copies, and pushing the button to start the automatic process, then tallying the cost for the customer and making change. The biggest challenge of my day was to refill the paper tray, which sometimes jammed. Beyond that, I sought stimulation by culling pleasantries into conversation with the customers waiting on the other side of the counter. The nineteen-year-old girl who worked beside me was friendly enough but lived such a limited existence, a couple of sentences a day sufficed to inform me that: a) she was still seeing her boyfriend ("Duane came over after work last night") and b) she was well ("I didn't know if I was gonna to make it today; it's that time of the month, you know, and I'm like..."). The pay barely compensated for the boredom, but I couldn't be too choosy when I was only willing to work the hours the kids were in school.

Still, I liked to go to work. It was better than not working. I needed a routine, a little push to get me out of bed each morning. Back in New York—when Ronnie was first born and I let my maternity leave drift to months and my boss finally called to say he couldn't hold my position open any longer—when I was unemployed for the first time in my adult life, I got into very bad habits. Or rather, I got out of all my good ones. I'd blame my indolence on the midnight feedings or the lousy weather. It wasn't the pregnancy which gave me my matronly figure but the post-partum lazing around in housedresses and noshing through the long hours. Not that I didn't like motherhood, and Ronnie was a good companion: cute, bright, testy, and precocious. I was just very undisciplined about myself.

When I started having to wear maternity shifts to cover my spreading backside, when friends started tactfully inquiring when I was due, I decided in a sort of backward-reasoning way that I'd better quickly get pregnant again and produce an excuse for my girth. Poor Adam, but that was why I decided to have him.

It was a unilateral decision: Jeff frowned on the use of contraception, seeing it as a form of onanism—spilling of seed in vain. Of course, he was brought up quite differently from me. He was raised in an Orthodox home, so he felt bound by practices that I had difficulty assimilating. When we first started seeing each other, I was drawn to him by the calm and strength his religion gave him. I wanted that confidence too, that sense of being a part of something larger than just myself and my egocentric concerns and desires. Before I met Jeff, my Judaism meant little to me. It was just a label, an attribute no more special than my eye color or the last name I exchanged for Jeff's. But I began to feel a pride in belonging to a group so tenacious, it had survived through the millenia. I wanted to be actively involved, I wanted to do something to contribute to that survival. So with Jeff's name, I took on his lifestyle, his rules, his belief in God. In some things, though, the old, pre-Jeff me asserted itself. Having a dozen babies was one such issue. We accommodated each other by avoiding discussion. It was a tacit agreement between us that if I chose to limit the size of our family, it was my business and my responsibility, and if I chose to increase our number, he didn't want to be informed that I'd stopped using what he didn't want to know I was using in the first place.

I managed to control my weight through the second pregnancy, and then, between nursing Adam and chasing after his active sister, I managed to get back in shape.

The move to Tucson did away with the externals that were keeping my weight down. Ronnie entered school, reducing my exercise in proportion to the hours she was away. Also, Tucson being less urban, I started going shopping behind a steering wheel instead of a stroller. Before I could do too much damage to my waistline, I enrolled two-year-old Adam in a nursery school and reentered the job market.

It didn't work. Second Street School was an unusual place, with its spacious yard and assorted pets and unconventional values. Here was a private school which fostered open-mindedness, which challenged both the children and staff to be creative, to discover their own solutions, even when the byproduct of such experimentation might be messy. There was a quiet acceptance of each child and adult as an individual. But it was just these features I found so attractive that intimidated Adam. The new environment of Tucson was about as much newness as he could handle, and within a month, he was a preschool dropout.

I stayed home with him and tried to get organized: joined a play group, took him to moms-and-tots swimming classes at the Y, to story hour at Himmel Library. By the time he was four, he'd had enough of me and went back to Second Street School, and I took a series of part-time jobs that at least gave me a daily destination other than the kitchen. The idea was to keep busy.

▲    ▲    ▲

I stopped off at Rincon Market on my way home from work, pulling into the carport roughly the same time as Adam on his bike. After putting away the groceries, I fixed him a snack, myself lunch. We sat down together for a few minutes, and he told me what happened at school: how the hamster got out of its cage and ran down the hall, and the real reason he got a thirty on his spelling test. ("It wasn't fair, Mom. The teacher says she announced it, but I didn't hear her.") The public elementary school was less successful than Second Street had been at meeting the needs of my dreamy boy.

After refilling his belly, he ran out to play. I took down the laundry and caught up on some reading. Ronnie came home about four, complained about the long walk home, then stomped off sullenly to do her homework. The transition to seventh grade was hard for her; she missed the security of the small elementary school.

Jeff got home from the lab about five and as soon as he'd washed up, we sat down to eat.

"Yum, yum, spaghetti!" Adam said.

"No meat sauce?" Ronnie whined. "I hate spaghetti without meat sauce."

"How come you didn't make meat sauce, Cyn?" Jeff asked quietly, trying hard not to sound too critical. He'd told me on other occasions that spaghetti wasn't one of his favorites either. "You know Ron won't eat worms without meat sauce."

I'd made a dairy meal because it was preferable not to eat meat before using the ritual bath, but I didn't feel like announcing in front of the kids I was scheduled to go to the *mikvah* that night. "We'll have meat tomorrow," I promised.

Jeff must have guessed something from my hesitation, or maybe he realized a couple of weeks had passed since we began our period of separation, because he said, "Oh!" and caught my eye. His mouth widened and stretched, causing his beard to gather and bristle a bit where his cheeks contracted. His look made me feel desirable.

"What, Daddy?" Ronnie asked.

"Okay, Ron, let's see: Mom grated cheese and this tomato sauce smells good." He almost appeared enthusiastic as he spooned some on top of his pasta.

▲   ▲   ▲

Naomi Danziger, the rabbi's wife, opened the door at the rear of the synagogue. She was always cheerful and nearly always pregnant; now she was growing large with her third child. I was a bit in awe of her and her amazing energy. In addition to running the *mikvah*, she and her husband entertained often, having guests for Shabbas meals and hosting frequent get-togethers at their house. I looked forward to my monthly visit to the ritual bath as an opportunity to get in a few uninterrupted minutes of conversation with this busy woman.

Of course, the main reason I was anxious to use the *mikvah* was that after dunking in the small pool, Jeff and I could resume our physical intimacy. The submersion removed the spiritual impurity imparted by menstruation. Not that having a period was shameful or evil; the "unclean" status had something to do with death, a missed chance at procreation.

I'd once heard a man explain the practice of family purity as a conspiracy among women to avoid their husbands, but that comment only reflected poorly on him, not only his adversarial attitude toward women but also his lack of finesse as a husband. Why would any wife want to avoid a sensitive, loving mate?

Jeff had a cup of herb tea waiting for me when I got home. My hair and the insides of my ears were still damp; I smelled of the chlorinated *mikvah* water. Jeff watched me as I sipped my drink, then, lifting his own cup, winked over the brim.

▲   ▲   ▲

Later that night, Jeff's gentle nuzzling nudged me out of a dream. "Oh, did I wake you?" he asked innocently when I rolled to him and opened my eyes.

"What is it, sweetheart?" I mumbled, my mouth not awake.

"Nothing. Go back to sleep. Do you mind if I just hold you?"

"No." I smiled. It would be one of those nights of little rest. That half month of abstinence between the onset of my period and the visit to the *mikvah* always whet his appetite. My nonreligious friends asked me about those two weeks of separation, questioning why we observed them, but to me they constituted the sweetest sort of deprivation, knowing that when they ended, Jeff, as attentive as a bridegroom, was unable to leave me alone.

"You're so gorgeous," he murmured.

"Especially when the lights are out and you can't see me," I teased.

"No," he protested. He slipped out of bed and switched on the light in the adjacent bathroom. Climbing back in next to me, he propped his cheek on one bent arm so he could look down into my face. "That's better," he said, his dark eyes catching the light. "You have such beautiful cheeks." He stroked my short, brown hair away from them. "So round. And your chin: I like the way it comes to a little sharp point. And your forehead is so broad and flat and smooth."

What he described by omission was that my features were less prominent than the spaces between them, my yellow eyes widely spaced, my nose like a button, my mouth as small as a moue. I looked kittenish.

"And I love the way you're shaped," he continued. "So full and round and womanly."

"It's called fat," I informed him.

"No, I love the way you look. Not one of those skinny scrawny things. You're like those last grapefruits on our tree last month, so full and ripe and sweet."

"And rotten," I added impishly.

That did it. The romantic whisper disappeared. "They were not! You are not!"

"Remember when we first bought the house and Adam kept bringing in the grapefruits he found on the ground?"

"Yeah," he embellished, "this kid waddling in in his diapers carrying these big grapefruits in both hands and reaching up to put them on the kitchen counter and us saying, 'Thank you, Ad, good boy, Ad,' not noticing 'til about the tenth grapefruit that there's ants crawling all over the place. He was so cute when he was little."

"So was Ronnie."

"Ron cute? You gotta be kidding: she was a tiger. Ferocious. There were some days I was so glad I had the excuse of going to the U, just to get away from her. She exhausted me."

"What happened to her?" I asked.

"Eh, I guess it's just adolescence. Maybe she exhausted herself too."

"Remember the time she threw up all over Larry and Gloria's new rug?" I recalled.

"Hey, that was too much. 'Daddy, I don't feel well...blech!' They never invited us again, did they?"

"No."

"Kids are the true litmus test of friendship," he said. "Trouble is, they grow up. We should have a couple more and see who'll ask us over." His smile showed off his teeth, perfectly straight with just enough gray fillings to make them look real. That was as close as he'd get to telling me he wanted more kids.

I felt two were plenty. "Maybe we better get some sleep," I suggested.

"You want me to turn off the light?" He scratched his beard and yawned.

"If you want."

Instead of standing to get the light, he reached for my full, womanly roundness. "I do have to show up at work tomorrow," he complained. "So do I. Look, don't look at me. Who started this, anyway?"

▲   ▲   ▲

For Succos, we put up our little slat-roofed shed on the back patio and covered it with palm fronds from our own trees. The walls were decorated with Adam's elaborate, juvenile drawings of fighter jets and battleships, and with travel posters of Israel. The weather was so dry and mild, we were able to eat all our meals out there—even breakfast. There was something special about eating outside in the early morning: the cool, fresh air, the oblique, increasing sunlight, the novelty, a certain intimacy.

We were lingering over our emptied plates in the dusk one evening when the phone rang.

"Hi! It's Naomi. How are you?"

"Fine."

"You sound out of breath. I can call again later if this is a bad time."

"No, no! It's a good thing you called or I might never have found the motivation to leave the table. It's so pleasant out there."

"Yeah. Hasn't it been great? I can't remember a Succos like this. Let me quickly tell you why I called and then you can go out again. I was thinking it would be nice to make a special *kiddush* on Sh'mini Atzeres this Thursday. Sort of a farewell to the shul's *succah*. I thought maybe some different salads, or even a *kugel* would be nice. You think you could help me prepare the food Wednesday morning?"

"I'd love to but I have to work."

"Oh."

I was flattered by the disappointment I heard in her voice. "You know what: I'm going to take the day off."

"No, you don't have to do that. I can get someone else."

"Look, Naomi, I'm already taking Thursday and Friday off. They don't care, they save money on the days they don't have to pay me. I'll tell them tomorrow I won't be in on Wednesday either."

"You sure? That would be great. I really appreciate it."

I was glad to receive Naomi's gratitude. As a formerly unreligious Jew, I felt a little insecure about my place in the Orthodox community. My in-laws used to laugh at my ignorance and make snide remarks about the "shiksa" Jeff married—until Sheila married a Hindu and shocked them into mournful silence. But before then, they used to grin and exchange looks whenever I asked a question. They never let me live down the time I wanted to know whether, if I were preparing a chicken for dinner and then was to sit down to a dairy lunch, I had to somehow *kasher* my hands. This faux pas was shared with every distant relative they'd discovered in the New World, so that at family gatherings, all eyes turned to me to see what other entertaining mistakes I might make.

   At one family feast we attended, at a time when I'd finally got the basics of *kashruth* under my belt, they played a trick on me, offering me ice cream after a meat meal. I smiled and said "no thanks"—then stared agape when they brought out bowls of frozen white-and-brown dessert for everyone else. Big joke: it was non-dairy ice cream. After they had their laugh, my mother-in-law went back to the kitchen for my portion.

   That was why Naomi's acceptance was so important to me. I felt as though I'd finally made it, that I was an observant Jew after all.

# Three

We didn't have that last *kiddush* in the *succah* because of the rain. It came down heavily for the next several days. Whole streets turned into shallow rivers, and by Saturday, when we ventured out, wading through ankle-deep water to synagogue, we found Mr. Liebowitz was the only other person to brave the weather. So we turned around and went home again. The following Monday, all the schools were closed. We sat around in bedroom slippers sipping cocoa and playing Monopoly with the kids. The flooding and mudslides made national news: nearly every relative on the East Coast called to ask if we were all right. Except for a little dampness on the carpet where the rainwater had seeped under the door, we were snug and dry. When Naomi was finally able to get back to the shul later that week, she found all the food we'd made had spoiled.

Jeff's parents arrived the next Sunday, a beautiful, warm autumn day. We drove out to the airport to meet them. It was a cute little airport, although renovations threatened to turn it into the anonymous clone of any municipal terminal: two wings to a handful of gates were under construction.

There were a pair of display cases, one full of model airplanes, the other a mineral exhibit. The latter was a mini-museum the children pored over, pointing to the lavender amethyst crystal, the milky quartz, the chunk of green copper. Upstairs was a game room where uniformed men on leave from Davis-Monthan played pinball and drank cokes.

Jeff, nervous not to keep his parents waiting, got us to the airport half an hour before their plane was due. Being Sunday, the terminal was particularly quiet. The gift shop was closed. Not that I wanted to buy anything, but it was a place to waste five minutes examining the ceramic lizards, the colorful duck-billed hats with TUCSON printed on them, the tiny pots of baby cactus, chocolate bars, newspapers, magazines, roadrunner tie clips, string ties, tiny brass boots, and ashtrays shaped like cowboy hats. After looking at the rocks in the glass case, this was our kitsch museum.

Adam spent some time examining the case of plastic airplanes, telling us which models he would buy if the gift shop were open. Ronnie strolled a little way down the hall, took a seat under a mural of children's drawings credited to a local preschool, and stared apathetically out the window at takeoffs and landings of tiny privately-owned airplanes.

"Come, Adam," I called over my shoulder as I followed her. "Let's watch the planes." I wasn't feeling too well. My period was late and I was tired and bloated. I sat down heavily next to Ronnie.

Jeff took the seat on her other side. "Hey, Ron." He patted her on the knee. "You wanna play Ghost?"

"Boo," she answered without turning her gaze from the window, without turning up the corners of her mouth.

"Ha. You want me to start?"

No reply.

"Okay, F," Jeff said.

"F," she said indifferently.

"Yeah, that's what I said. What do you say?"

"F."

"F-F?" He smiled crookedly at me across the path of our daughter's vision. Her eyes didn't flicker.

"Uh-huh," she grunted.

"I challenge you."

"Ffff...." She sounded like a balloon deflating.

"That's not a word!" Jeff's chuckle was infectious and I joined him.

Not even a glimmer of a smile from our straight-faced comedienne. "When are they gonna be here already?" She sighed.

Jeff flipped his hand palm upward and checked his watch, which he wore upside down, the face against the inside of his wrist. "Just a few more—Ad, get out of the way!" Adam, his nose pressed against the glass, stood directly in line with the wide broom a man in coveralls was pushing along the tile floor.

At last we could saunter in slow motion out to the gate, which was reached by walking under open sheds along the tarmac. We waited another five minutes in the shaded heat before the plane taxied into view. We watched a staircase being rolled up to the door of the newly arrived jet, and then, finally, the big door in the side of the plane swung open and a stewardess stepped out onto the wide top step. Handsome young men in blue blazers assisted old ladies down the stairs, helped parents traveling with small children carry folded strollers and diaper bags. When we first arrived in Tucson, we were greeted with this courtesy. I believed I'd come to the end of the world, some remotest corner in which impersonal, cruel efficiency had yet to make an inroad.

"Grandma, Grandpa!" shouted Adam, running out to meet them.

They looked old and feeble.

Of course, I tended to underestimate Jeff's parents. They couldn't possibly be as frail as they looked, having both survived Hitler's concentration camps. But if that experience toughened them, it also aged them in a peculiar, uncanny way. They seemed to wear an ancient patina, a crust impervious to further suffering. Their shield also warded off any pleasure, as though happiness were only bait in which a barbed hook was concealed. That was how they viewed Sheila, their beautiful, bright, obedient little girl. Some perverse joke of God's, giving them this child to comfort them in their old age. They felt bitterly betrayed when she fell in love with a foreigner. Chad, the tall, dark, strikingly handsome Indian who ran the New York branch of his family's import-export business, was unable to soften them with his charm and modesty, his culture and grace. He was not Jewish and therefore they rejected him outright. Their daughter of twenty years was dead to them. And their desire to smile died with her.

Joining the children in the southern Arizona sun, Jeff leaned over to hug the pale, impassive pair. They stood stolidly squinting into the brilliant daylight. Ronnie took her grandmother's hand, Adam, his grandfather's, and slowly the children led them into the shade where I waited.

"How was your trip? Everything all right?" Jeff asked. "You get your special meals?"

"Yes, yes," said the man, impatient with the unimportant questions.

"Wait," said my mother-in-law, letting go of Ronnie's hand. She unclasped her pocketbook and searched inside. "Here," she said, bringing out two plastic cups containing citrus sections and handing one each to the children.

"They're still frozen," Adam noted with a laugh.

"I don't know how they expect you to eat that," the woman complained.

"Mom," Ronnie whispered to me, thrusting her cup into my hand. "Here, I don't want this."

Holding the half-thawed fruitcup, bothered by the sticky syrup that had seeped out and coated the container, I awkwardly embraced Jeff's mother. I glanced around in search of a garbage bin.

"You're looking well, Cynthia," my mother-in-law stated flatly.

I felt puffy. "Thanks, Mom." I didn't return the compliment.

"Come. Let's get your luggage and go home. I bet you're tired." Jeff clapped his large hands together, trying to generate enough snap and enthusiasm for us all.

I worried how we'd fit six people into our car. The kids were getting too big to sit on laps.

It was an annual event, Jeff's parents' visit. I sometimes wondered why they came. They couldn't possibly find sleeping on the twin couches in the family room too comfortable, and the kids were in school and Jeff and I at work all day. They took a daily walk around the quiet residential streets or over to Safeway on Broadway Boulevard. The rest of the time, they sat virtually silent doing nothing I could discern.

But they kept coming; each fall they spent two weeks with us. Most elderly New Yorkers preferred to visit Tucson in February, when they could benefit from the midday sunshine radiating therapeutically to bake arthritic bones. But Jeff's parents came instead at a time when New York was at its best, with brisk, clear days, deep blue skies contrasting with golden autumn leaves. October was probably the only time I grew homesick for the East. But then, my in-laws seemed oblivious to the seasons.

Or perhaps they were less indifferent to their passing than they appeared. Perhaps the deadness of winter was comfortable, since they already knew how to numb themselves to the cold. But autumn, the season of dying, might still pull at poorly healed scars for them. It was the letting go, the confrontation with nature's message that all living things, no matter how impoverished, still have something more to lose.

Intuitively I sensed their covert clinging to things they claimed to have long ago discarded. I thought they must be like Jeff and me, who, in preparation for our move to Tucson, had decided to rid ourselves of extra baggage. With self-righteous proclamations, we heaped piles of useless paraphernalia in the center of our apartment living room with the intention of throwing or giving everything away. There were unflattering college sweatshirts, infant-sized dresses, maternity tops, old letters and papers and paperbacks, back issues of *Physics Today*, seashells from forgotten beaches, keys to doors we no longer had the right to open. The following morning, on our way to the kitchen and breakfast, we both cast guilty glances in the direction of the diminished pile. Two weeks later, in our new home, we furtively unpacked our little caches—Ronnie's first pair of shoes, the tattered clipping of a letter-to-the-editor I once wrote, Adam's teething ring, Jeff's boyhood stamp collection, a map of Central Park—and stowed them on top shelves of closets, where they remained untouched except for our Passover cleaning each year. Yet, we knew they were there, salvaged bits of our past which we brought with us to our new life. In the same way, for all their stoic posturing, Jeff's parents were surreptitiously keeping alive a little of their past.

I arrived home from work one day to find them in the living room leafing through a picture album. They almost smiled at the photographs: Taken on one of their visits to Tucson, Adam, then five, sitting awkwardly on his grandfather's lap, his grandmother in the next vinyl-web chair, the grapefruit tree and the clothesline in the background. Another showed proud eight-year-old Ronnie straddling her first two-wheeler. I cringed when I saw the one of me with an idiotic grin and waving with a hammy bare arm. (It must have been the plump Jewish matrons who decided that out of modesty a woman must cover her upper arms and thighs. Over time, I'd adopted much of the Orthodox dress code, not because of peer pressure or growing faith but simply because shorts and sleeveless blouses looked so bad on me.) There was the picture my father-in-law took, slightly off center and out of focus, of the four of us, Jeff showing off with a child on each shoulder.

They flipped the page and came to the ones we took the following spring, when we had flown to New York for a visit. A few showed a family gathering in their apartment. Relatives stood around the linen-covered table set with silver and crystal and china for the upcoming Passover seder.

Then there were the pictures taken later that week, during our visit with Sheila and Chad and their baby girl. Tamara must have been over a year already, but she looked much younger, a tiny thing, diminutive even when compared to her small cousins. Her flat cheeks and slanted eyes and straight dark hair added even more foreignness to her racial mix of features, her mother's large, dark blue eyes, her father's light brown skin. Objectively, if I could divorce myself from the implications of her features, the child looked beautifully exotic.

My mother-in-law stared a long time at the picture of the grandchild she'd never met, then shook her head and sighed. Her "Such a shame," seemed to mean much more than "Isn't it too bad." She meant also that she was ashamed, that her daughter should be ashamed.

Her husband expressed less sorrow and embarrassment, more indignation and disdain. "A mongolian idiot. It's the work of God," he muttered, implying that he felt his daughter got what she deserved.

I flushed, angry at him and also uncomfortable because I too shrank from the child. The pictures didn't show her strange, loud grunts, her unfocused eyes wandering in different directions, her drooping head bobbing on its weak neck, the drooling tongue hanging out of her mouth and dripping saliva on my silk blouse. I tried to be brave that visit. I fixed a stiff smile on my face and pretended to like the baby though I was overwhelmed by her inadequacies. She had to be handled so carefully—no bouncing on the knee, no boosts in the air—and she responded so little, so late when I tickled her belly. I could have counted to sixty before she produced a grimace and a single shriek.

But in spite of my own rejection of the infant, I never allowed myself to believe she was sent by God as a way to punish her parents. As we stared at the picture of the unfortunate child, I hated my father-in-law for his smugness in thinking he understood God, for his self-righteous belief that his spurning of Sheila and her marriage was vindicated by the product of the union. I was tempted to tell him that by his reasoning, he himself certainly must have sinned grievously, considering all the sorrow God had visited upon him in his life. But I held my tongue, not so much out of care for his feelings, but because I was aware that if I spoke, I too would be guilty of passing judgment.

The moment passed, and with it, my rage. It was difficult to hate a man I pitied. He had lost so much—his first wife and children and his parents during the war, and now Sheila. I was fond of Sheila. When I came into the family, she was the only one of Jeff's family who made me feel at all welcome. At the time, she was still very young, ten years younger than Jeff and me, and still in junior high school. She was awkward and yet demure, overly polite, soft spoken, docile. She continued to be the ideal, unreal teenager during an era of adolescent rebelliousness and alienation. It was a shock when six years later, in '76, she brought Mr. Chadrepadhivan to her parents' thirtieth wedding anniversary. But quiet, obedient people, finding it impossible to rebel in the little things, sometimes show their defiance in a grand gesture. She sprang him on everyone without warning, walking into the party in our apartment with her stunning stranger.

Chad...well, when I first met him, I had a good-looking, good-natured husband with a Ph.D. and a promising future (he had just been offered the assistant professorship at UA) and two gorgeous babies, but I admit I did look at Chad with more than idle curiosity. Whereas Jeff was attractive in a beaten-up, familiar way, Chad was handsome in a princely, perfect manner: erect and neatly groomed, his white teeth against his dark, well-shaped lips, his beautifully formed, straight, thin nose, his soft yet lively dark eyes, his wavy black hair. He was mature and relaxed and poised in a situation that would unbalance any other person, and he knew how to say precisely the right things in his soft singing voice.

At the time, we lived in the cramped one-bedroom apartment we could afford on Jeff's postdoc. The place was cluttered with kids' stuff—crib, highchair, toys, boxes of disposable diapers—and hundreds of books—technical, juvenile, English lit, and otherwise. The living room furniture bore traces of every imaginable excretion and the walls badly needed two coats of paint. But Chad, perhaps sensing my embarrassment over the shabbiness of the place, complimented me on its comfort and homeyness, asked about the wall hangings—some framed Art Deco posters that were in vogue at the time—and later came over with a paperbound volume of poetry he had found amid the haphazard collection on the bookshelves. It was something by Theodore Roethke I had picked up in my undergrad days. His elegantly slender finger was inserted to hold his place.

Opening to a poem cycle that described the world from a small child's perspective, he smiled so gently I didn't feel threatened by his charm. "Ah, Cynthia, these are wonderful. I have just now been reading them to your daughter Rhonda, and I believe she understands them better than I."

I quietly fell in love.

But he didn't single me out. Unruffled by the hard stares Jeff's family cast his way, he spoke modestly, respectfully to anyone who responded positively. My parents were also guests. Priding themselves on their broad-mindedness, they were delighted to spend the afternoon talking to Chad about business, the ballet, and his home town of Bangalore.

Before she and Chad left, Sheila asked me to come with her to the bedroom. Amid the coats piled on the bed, she confided how serious she was about him and asked what I thought. I was unsure. Though I was by then closer to Jeff's Orthodoxy than my parents' nonobservance and would theoretically frown upon a mixed marriage, I was very sympathetic. I brought up sinister possibilities, pointed out the great difference in their ages, insulted her by insinuating that at a very naive and unworldly nineteen, she alone could not sustain the interest of such a man. I told her not to be hasty. But underlying my words were warmth and understanding. I was both jealous and vicariously joyful.

About a month after we arrived in Tucson, Sheila called to tell us she and Chad had just wed. When Jeff called his parents later that same day, they informed him that they were in mourning, they were sitting *shivah*.

It was hard for Jeff, torn between his disapproval of intermarriage and his love for his sister. He needed help to find a way to excuse her, and I had some influence. I told him it wasn't for us to play God and spurn Sheila. "None of us are perfect: we've all done things against God's Law," I argued. "Look at King David. For his adultery with Batsheva, he should have been stoned to death. I'm not even talking about how he connived to get her husband killed. But his merits saved him. His love of God, his beautiful psalms, his mercy toward Saul, all his goodness must have mitigated the punishment due him. Let's remember Sheila's merits before we pass judgment." He wouldn't come out and say he forgave her, but he didn't discourage me from writing to her, and he always read the letters she sent back.

We didn't see Sheila and Chad often because of the vast distance between our homes, but we did keep in fairly close contact. Sheila depended upon us as her only link to family. She would write long, touching letters in which she described her marital happiness and asked indirectly about her parents. Sometimes I read her "happiness" as a stubborn determination to justify herself, but I also sensed that Chad truly did give her nothing to be unhappy about. When they visited us in '78, a year and a half after they married, there seemed to be no friction at all between them. On the contrary, they were still moony-eyed. Jeff too must have been aware of it, because their presence stimulated romantic behavior in him—kisses on the nape of my neck as I brushed my teeth before bed, special smiles directed at me across the dinner table, the gift of a small, leather-bound copy of Jane Austen's *Sense and Sensibility* he picked up in a used book store.

They came in March. In April they spent a month in India. In December of that year, Chad called to tell us Sheila had given birth to a baby girl. We unfairly attributed the hesitancy of his enthusiasm to disappointment that the child was not male. However, when we spoke to Sheila a couple of days later, after the karyotyping had shown positive for trisomy-21, we understood. The infant had Down syndrome. She was retarded, had a defective heart and poor muscle tone.

    With the added responsibilities of motherhood, Sheila had less time to write to us, and we gratefully withdrew from their lives, unwilling to share all their heartbreak. There were visits to all sorts of specialists, therapists, "early intervention" stimulation programs. Luckily, Chad had the funds to cover the expenses—flights to Boston to a pediatric ophthalmologist, adaptive equipment, massages and other experimental treatments. Before Tamara turned two, after that one time we saw her in New York, she underwent open-heart surgery. It was a success, Sheila wrote hopefully, we read skeptically. Tamara gained weight and strength. Soon she was able to sit unassisted. By her third birthday, she was taking her first steps and uttering intelligible syllables. They kept sending us snapshots. In all of them, Tamara looked beautiful, but I knew the pictures lied. I found excuses not to fly to New York and failed to invite the Chadrepadhivans to Tucson again.

    The most recent picture showed a dark-haired, round-faced girl pushing a doll stroller. I could tell it was taken in a New York park by the distinctive hexagonal gray paving tiles. I could tell she wasn't too steady on her feet by the high-topped white leather shoes she wore and the way she seemed to lean against the stroller for support. I knew that the open-mouthed smile hid an over-sized tongue which protruded from an always open mouth, that the pretty oriental slant to the dark blue eyes was one of the stigmata of her retardation.

    Without a word, my mother-in-law closed the album and replaced it on the shelf. I wondered if she wanted me to tell her about Sheila and her family, but I decided against saying anything. What more was I willing to tell her beyond what she'd already learned from the pictures? Perhaps she wanted to know if the stress of raising a handicapped child had been divisive to the marriage. It was a question of my own, and I searched for its answer in Sheila's letters. But I found no evidence to support this possibility. If anything, they appeared to be bound more tightly together by the burden they shared. In any case, I didn't feel comfortable to talk about Sheila with my in-laws. There was always a strangeness, a hole, in our conversations. Unlike with a truly dead child, about whom one could reminisce with the bereaved family after a suitable interval, Sheila's name was never mentioned between us.

    Provided I didn't trouble to entertain them or feel troubled by their lack of responsiveness, my in-laws were very easy people to have as house guests. They were as quiet as shadows and just as undemanding: like shadows, something you noticed every now and then and could either attend to or ignore without consequence. They were fully self-contained.

    Weekday mornings and evenings, cars drove up by our house to take my father-in-law to synagogue for the daily *minyans*. On Saturday they walked with us to shul. On Sunday we drove them out to the Saguaro National Monument and ate lunch among the cacti. Most visitors were impressed by the giant cactus, but our guests that day expressed nothing, barely aware of the splendor of the desert and the mountains around them. Adam brought them rocks and saguaro ribs to examine as they sat slowly chewing at the picnic table. Ronnie carried over the yellow fruit of a prickly pear, held gingerly between thumb and finger. They nodded and took another bite.

I saw my mother-in-law knitting long strips in ugly clashing colors—avocado green, maroon, brown, metallic pink, rust orange—and in different weight yarns, some wool and some synthetic. Before they left, she presented Ronnie with an awful, odd-shaped afghan for her bed. I braced myself for my daughter's unswervingly honest appraisal. I myself was at a loss for an appropriate adjective that wouldn't be too pejorative.

The grandmother had already turned her back and was returning to her things in the family room, unconcerned with our reactions or opinions. My eyes followed the retreating figure, hard and lumpy under a shapeless dress. Bristly gray hair poked out where her brown wig curled up at the bottom; ankles clothed in opaque stockings bulged above the stack-heeled black lace shoes.

Ronnie was staring at the thing spread out on her bed, shaking her head, a disgusted twist to her lips. "Isn't that too much? Really punk." She burst past me to catch up with the little woman walking away. "Grandma! Thank you, I love it. It is so cool!" She hugged the woman warmly. I was left feeling there were dynamics to their relationship I had not previously observed.

Adam, too, appeared to be enthralled by their undemonstrative, unobtrusive presence, sitting with them on the back patio, accosting them with rambling accounts of his day or detailed descriptions of his dreams.

There were outside issues disturbing me during the time my in-laws visited, things that made me both irritated with the presence of two extra people in my house and at the same time grateful to them for being so undemanding. In fact, in ways they were helpful: I had no patience to listen to Adam's fantasies, unable to concentrate, too distracted by my own thoughts.

One problem was that I walked into the Kopy Kat the day after my in-laws arrived to learn that my nineteen-year-old co-worker had either quit or been fired, though no one would give me a straight answer. Not that it mattered, really: it came to the same thing, that either I maintained a brisk pace or I'd have to listen to the complaints of those waiting to be served. The one thing I had enjoyed about the job had been that it was so mindless, I could chat amiably with the customers. Now the chitchat had to stop, not because my silence could actually increase the speed with which the copier made a hundred, but because the impatient people in line believed my talking slowed it down. My supervisor implied there would be a bonus for me for being a good sport during this rough spot. To show he too was a good sport, Jon left his offsetting machine to come up front and help on the occasions when things backed up and potential customers were leaving for our competitors.

Another major worry, but more nebulous in nature, was the continuing wait for the onset of my period. The sanitary napkin I carried in my purse in readiness was getting linty. Once I actually grinned at abdominal discomfort, thinking, "Here it is at last," mistaking in my eagerness flatulence for cramps. The obvious implications of my failure to bleed were not lost to me, but I wanted desperately to deny this possibility. After all, I was going on thirty-seven, I had a daughter who was bat mitzvah already, and as bad as my job was, I didn't feel up to exchanging it for a routine of breastfeeding and diapers. Perhaps it's the stress on the job, I tried to convince myself, and the two strangers in the house. Perhaps I'm going to have a very early menopause. The fatigue and weakness are from working so hard. The queasy stomach is just nerves.

Jeff was oblivious to my state of body and mind. He avoided my body, greatly inhibited by the presence of his parents in our house. Otherwise he would undoubtedly have become aware of our prolonged period without separation. He ignored my mind, not deliberately, but because he tried so hard to focus on his aging parents during their brief stay. By the time we had a few minutes alone, he was too emotionally washed out to be very receptive to my worries. When I mentioned that I was doing the work of two at my job, he only complimented me on my stamina. As for the other worry, I didn't even mention it, knowing he would consider it a blessing.

On Sunday morning, two weeks after their arrival, we drove Jeff's parents to the airport. Again we arrived too early—his parents were packed and dressed by six and stood around anxiously, muttering, "Maybe we should call a cab," until we finally got into the car. When they checked in and learned how long it would be before their flight left, they told us not to bother waiting with them. Of course Jeff insisted we would. The minutes ticked by as tension slowly built and then gave way to boredom. The children ran races up and down the corridor, Jeff spoke to his parents of useless things about airplanes, and I spent the time trying to calculate how late I really was.

# Four

"Congratulations, Mrs. Roth. Let's see now, according to this, you're just about two months along," said Dr. Freedman, referring to the cardboard chart provided by some pharmaceutical firm. I knew this was impossible, having been to the *mikvah* less than six weeks before, but I also knew from past experience that obstetricians had their own way of counting. I sat on the examination table, sagging behind the crisp disposable gown, a white sheet draped over my lap.

"I don't see how...," I began.

He smiled apologetically, as if he were personally to blame for my predicament. "Of course, no method is absolutely foolproof."

Was he implying I was a fool?

He shoved his hands into the pockets of his white coat, pulling it taut across his well-rounded middle. His puckish face looked kindly, fatherly, though he was nothing like my lanky, urbane father. "Look, it's not so bad," he tried to joke. "You're married, you're in excellent health, you're financially secure."

"Just what I need," I grumbled. My mind drifted back to Rosh Hashanah and my sense of impending doom. So, God, I thought, is this Your idea of a little irony? Instead of visiting death upon me this year, You're going to saddle me with a little extra life?

"Why don't you get dressed and we'll talk in my office." He closed my folder and carried it out of the examination room with him. What secrets had he scribbled between the covers? What did he want to keep from me? But he was right: if he had left my chart behind, I would have peeked inside and tried to decipher the notations. Why was I made to feel like a thief when stealing a glance at my own medical records?

I dressed in a rage, then entered his office, a comfortable room, pleasant and impersonal. I slipped into a leather-and-teakwood chair.

After a few minutes, Dr. Freedman came in, walked around the massive desk, and sat down. He flipped open my folder and picked up his fountain pen. (I wondered if he favored such obsolete instruments in the operating room.) "So. You were born in forty-seven. That makes you"— he whipped out another drug company figure-it chart—"thirty-six." He looked up for confirmation. I nodded. "How old is your husband?"

"Also thirty-six." I watched his hand and the scratchy pen.

"Any history of heart disease, diabetes, dizzy spells...?"

I shook my head.

"You *are* healthy."

I grimaced.

"This is your third pregnancy?" Again his eyes flicked up, this time for my nod. "And the others were uncomplicated and carried to term?"

"My daughter will be thirteen when this baby is born."

He smiled and looked up. "There are women who go on to have babies when they're already grandmothers."

"I know. My mother is one of ten. My grandmother was pregnant at her oldest daughter's wedding."

"Really? So maybe it runs in the family."

I opened my mouth, then shut it again. Unable to think of an appropriately droll comeback, I settled for a sigh-laden chuckle. I could have told him that, overwhelmed by all the aunts and uncles and cousins who peopled our childhood, I escaped to Arizona and my sister chose to remain single and childless.

"We should set up an appointment for the amniocentesis." He glanced at his desk calendar. "Any family history of birth defects or retardation?"

I swallowed. I'd heard the insertion of the needle hurt. "Let me check with my husband first."

"If you like. He's with the University, isn't he? We could arrange it during the Christmas break if you'd like to have him with you."

I eyed the point of his pen, poised and waiting for my go-ahead.

"I don't know how he feels about amniocentesis," I blurted out.

"Oh?" The pen returned to idle on the blotter.

"It's just that..." The tissue I'd helped myself to in the examination room was turning into a wadded ball in my sweating palm. "I don't think he believes in abortions."

"And you?"

"I don't know," I admitted.

"Do you have reason to fear you'd need one?"

"Why do the test if there's no fear?" I replied.

"True." He waited, alert to what I might add.

Finally, focusing on his smooth, clean nails, his one hand resting patiently on top of the other, I got it out: "My niece has Down syndrome."

"Oh." He nodded, looking sympathetic and sober. "Your husband's side or yours?"

"Jeff's."

"How old is she?"

"I guess she'll be five in December."

"No, I mean, how old was your sister-in-law when she had the child?"

"Oh. She was only twenty-one."

"Really? That's unusual. How's the child doing?"

I shrugged.

"You're aware, of course, that only in rare cases is this condition hereditary."

I nodded though I hadn't been aware of this.

He considered. "I think under the circumstances we should go ahead and schedule that test, just so you can enjoy the rest of your pregnancy with some peace of mind."

"I'll have to let you know," I repeated.

"As you like," he said, clearly annoyed with my hesitation. "It's a highly standard procedure. We do them all the time."

"Yes, I know."

He scribbled on a pad, pulled off the top sheet, and handed it to me with the closed folder. "That's just a prescription for Natalins. Which doesn't mean you should stop eating well. Have Kathy out at the desk make an appointment for you for one month." He stood and I did too. "And you'll give me a call in a week or two so we can set up an appointment for that test."

"Yes."

He came out from behind his desk and extended his right hand. I had to shift the crumpled tissue to the hand with my purse and the folder before I could take it.

"Good luck, Mrs. Roth." He smiled and winked. "Don't worry so much. It isn't good for the baby. You'll manage."

I sensed him watching me as I went to the receptionist. That was as far as he'd trust me with my own medical records.

▲  ▲  ▲

After dinner, after Adam and Ronnie disappeared to watch TV in the family room, I cleared my throat. "Jeff," I began.

"I can tell from the tone of your voice you want me to wash the dishes."

"No."

"No?" He raised his eyebrows and flashed his toothy, lop-sided grin.

I hesitated, then smiled crookedly too. "No, you can wash the dishes if you want to, but first I have something to tell you."

"You've been fired," he guessed.

"No."

"You forgot to release the parking brake until you were halfway home."

I shook my head.

"I give up."

"I'm pregnant."

It took a second to sink in. Then it broke out all over his face and quickly spread throughout his system. "Are you kidding, that's great! What are you so serious about? I thought you were dying of cancer or something. But that's great, that's really terrific news. I can hardly believe it."

He pressed me tightly against him, his strong biceps squeezing me. Eventually he slowed down. He was forced to notice that I wasn't contributing to all the exclamations; he had to acknowledge that his shoulder was growing damp where my face was buried in it. "Hey, Cyn, what's the matter?" he asked gently.

"I don't know," I sobbed.

"I don't suppose those are tears of joy."

I shook my head, my hair catching in his wiry beard.

Holding my shoulders, he pushed me away and looked at my averted face. I refused to meet his eye. "What is it?"

"I guess I just hadn't planned on it, that's all."

Still holding me at the shoulders, he bent his knees to get face to face with my drooping head. "Hey." He smiled tentatively. "Hey, don't you know by now there ain't no such thing as planning something like that? I mean, you just have to take what comes in these things. I mean, God forbid, there are people who try for years and years and years to have a baby, and there are others who have them fifteen months apart, boom boom boom. That's just the way it is. It's not for us to decide. It's not in our hands."

I had always believed it *was* in my hands. After all, I was in charge of the contraception. After so many years of believing that I had some control over my life, it was hard to accept the confusingly contradictory doctrines of Free Will and Divine Omnipotence, that I had the right to choose the course of my life, but God had the right to cancel any of my plans. It was at times like these, when God seemed to intervene, that my faith was seriously shaken. I wished He'd go mind His own business, I wanted Him to leave me alone. It was different when one day followed fairly predictably after another: then it was easy to go through the motions of the rituals, to be religious. Reciting blessings before eating and *bentching* grace after, lighting sabbath candles and ceasing all work for the next twenty-five hours, yes, sleeping with my husband, no, observing the period of separation—this was easy for me once I got the rhythm of it. I could even accommodate a few variations—a fast day, a *bris*, a festival, a burial—small syncopations in the general flow. But when something major and unexpected took place, the music ground suddenly to a halt.

Like the time we saw Tamara. Not when she was born: though I was saddened by the news, it all seemed so remote, so very far away. But when I actually saw her, when I actually held her, I was forced to change how I perceived myself. I had to face my own squeamishness, my own prejudices—and I used to think that, like my parents, I had none. I had to admit I wasn't the Universal Mother, the Woman Who Loved All Babies. I found myself cursing God for creating such an offensive creature. And in the next breath, thanking Him for blessing me with two healthy, whole children. Then I felt guilty.

It seemed to me life had been a lot easier before I burdened myself with religion and a conscience. If it weren't for my nominal espousal of what Jeff had just stated—that God was in charge—I might have quietly gone off and got rid of the unwanted pregnancy. Intellectually, objectively, I believed abortion was better than bringing an unwanted child into the world. But I knew that I wouldn't actually be able to go through with one. To me, it would be playing God. To me, it went against the nature of things.

There was a moment in Dr. Freedman's office when I welcomed the idea of carrying a defective fetus. Then, I reasoned, an abortion would be justified. But when the moment passed, I saw my faulty logic. There was really no point in going for the test, because even if the results came back positive, I'd be forced to accept this further blow as God's will too. Even if I carried an unhealthy fetus, even if I were pregnant with something so messed up, the most extreme anti-abortionist would consider it moral to terminate it, even then I couldn't elect to end the life that grew within me. Who was I to judge matters of life and death? Who was I to decide a child was unfit to be born? In a land where it was unlawful to discriminate against the handicapped, how was it ethical to discriminate against a handicapped fetus?

So there I was, pregnant and with no apparent escape.

Why did I balk at the idea so violently? Because I was so set in my ways that I couldn't tolerate the little adjustments an infant would force on my schedule? Because of the sleepless nights and demanding days? Because, though I had reveled in the exertions of labor with Ronnie and Adam, now I dwelled on the hurt and exhaustion, the afterpains of recovery after the adrenaline had worn off? Because I feared I too might have a mongoloid? All these were factors, and then there were silly thoughts about needing to buy a bigger car, and replacing all the maternity clothing and the crib we had given away, thoughts of hard engorged breasts and sticky sweet milk leaking through my blouses, and scuffing around the house for days on end in slippers and muumuus, thoughts about smiling at my baby and getting no smile back, raising a dull, feeble child who would never be independent, or worse still, a misshapen, sickly thing that would constantly drain, drain....

Yes, but this was only part of it. It was also the feeling of being out of control. I was angry. I felt cheated. When I became pregnant before, I had made a conscious decision. And then I had the fun of anticipation, the secret blushing thoughts of wondering if that night had been *the* night, the illusion of participation in the moment of creation, feeling at that instant the Divine Presence blessing our union. I'd been cheated of all that this time.

And I worried that this baby was being cheated too. I wasn't rooting for it from the outset. Even if I grew to love it, I would always know that I had once despised it.

Jeff could never share these feelings of anger and guilt since he never planned to have a baby or planned not to have one, since it never occurred to him that he should try so grossly to manipulate his fate, since he hoped with *every* marital intimacy that he might have created a new life. And so this too nettled me, that I couldn't even share with him my disappointment at having "missed" the conception.

However, Jeff's enthusiasm and delight acted as a salve to my raw nerves and dark ruminations, a boon to my morale. He immediately set to pampering me, helping to put out breakfast, taking on many of the household chores. ("Hey, Cindy, what are you doing with that vacuum?" "What do you think, dum-dum? I'm going to clean the carpet. Somebody's got to." "Hey, let me do that." I gladly stepped aside.)

He also took to proudly broadcasting my "condition" to the immediate world. Word spread so fast that by the next Saturday, Marty Fisher and his wife Melanie made an unexpected appearance at synagogue just so they could look me over and confirm the rumors. Was I really so old my pregnancy seemed out of the ordinary?

Late one afternoon, Burt Roberts from Optical Sciences called asking for Jeff.

"He's not home yet. I'm expecting him any minute. You want me to have him call when he gets in?"

"No, it's not important. I'll catch him in the morning."

"Okay."

But before I could hang up, he surprised me with: "By the way, is it true?"

"What?" I asked, already guessing.

"That the Roth family is expecting an addition?"

"I guess so." I felt myself smiling, embarrassed and pleased and enjoying all the attention.

"When?"

"Next June, I guess."

"Well, congratulations and all the best."

"Thanks."

I was still sporting a goofy grin when Jeff walked in a few minutes later.

At work, line or no line, I slowed down. If I continued to be so efficient, why should they pay the salary of someone to help me? By midweek, a young man joined me behind the counter and I could relax. (Of course I never got the bonus Jon had promised.) Norman was a skinny, pimply Pima Community College student and we got along fine. He was willing to take on twice as many customers as I did, and all I had to do was look the other way when he Xeroxed a page from one of his library texts. I refused to feel bad about abetting his petty thievery; it was not my job to police my co-worker, and I couldn't afford to let him get fired. Besides, I felt Jon owed me something, so I let Norman collect and pay me back with extra minutes sitting in the folding chair in the corner. It all seemed equitable enough to me.

The kids' reaction amused me. One morning, when Adam asked me to get him more orange juice right after I'd sat down, Jeff announced, "Hey, listen, you two. You're not to make your mom jump up a dozen times. She has to take it easy."

"Why?" asked Adam.

"Because she's gonna have a baby."

"Neat!"

Ronnie rolled her eyes up to the ceiling and groaned. When I was pubescent, I too found any evidence of my parents' sexuality mortifying.

"Where you gonna put it when it's born?" asked Adam.

"I hope not in my room," Ronnie offered.

"Why don't we wait and see when the time comes," Jeff suggested.

"Depends on if it's a boy or a girl, right, Dad?" Adam decided.

"I'll just die if that thing screams all night," Ronnie stated.

"I think a baby would be neat," said her brother. "Then, since I'll always have more homework than him, *he'll* have to take out the garbage."

"Not for a couple of years, though," Jeff pointed out. His cheeks inched up with a grin.

"What makes you so sure it's gonna be a him?" Ronnie stirred her cereal around in her bowl until the milk swished up the side and onto the table. "My luck, it'll be a girl and I'll have to share my room with it. The whole place will probably start smelling of stinky diapers."

"Don't forget the stinky spit-up," I added.

"Gross." She got up to get a paper towel.

Adam started laughing, spluttering sodden cereal from his mouth. "Hey, after the baby's born, I'm gonna bring Paco and Darren over and gross them out. I say, 'Gee, what smells so good? Maybe my mom's cooking something,' right? And then I show them the garbage pail full of old diapers. Then I say, 'You wanna hold the baby?' and the kid spits up all over them." Fourth grade humor.

Ronnie put a corner of the towel in the spilled milk and watched the liquid spread up into the absorbing paper. Without looking up, she said, "All I want to know is if you expect me to baby-sit for the thing whenever you feel like it. Because I plan to charge a dollar an hour. A dollar and a quarter if I have to change my plans."

"Such as?" I asked.

"Such as if I was going to a movie with my friends."

"That sounds reasonable to me," said Jeff, trying to straighten out the corners of his mouth.

"That's not fair!" shouted Adam. "She gets all the jobs. Why can't I baby-sit too?"

"Don't worry. You'll both get a turn to baby-sit," Jeff reassured them. When the kids left the table to brush their teeth, he squeezed my hand. His face was more than smiling, it was transcendent. "Oh, Cindy, it must be so thrilling to have a baby growing inside you. A little like God, creating life. I'm sure I've mentioned this to you before: women are on a higher spiritual plane than men. Maybe it's procreation that puts them up there."

▲    ▲    ▲

And so my misgivings began to melt into a sweeter expectancy. By late November, the time of my next appointment with Dr. Freedman, I had mellowed considerably. Reconciled to the loss of my waistline, I was wearing a newly purchased maternity shift. Jeff, always anxious to participate in my pregnancies, came with me.

Though I was glad of Jeff's involvement, it was embarrassing to lie there with my hem pulled up to my hips and the doctor's gloved hand probing my uterus as he chatted with him standing at my shoulder. After having Jeff with me through two deliveries, I didn't know how to tell him not to join me in the examination room. But my discomfiture was perhaps more an index of my self-absorption: both of them treated my nakedness as natural and healthy, neither was lewd or disrespectful. After Dr. Freedman finished the physical, they discreetly ignored me as I pulled my clothing back in place, intent on discussing the medical applications of the new laser technology. Instead of appreciating their delicacy, I felt neglected, like the forgotten centerpiece, as conversation flew back and forth over my head.

In the office, sitting in a chair with my skirt pulled back down, I felt the return of the dignity and equality I'd imagined had been slighted during the examination.

Dr. Freedman looked at my chart and said, "I think we were off by a couple of weeks the last time I saw you. Your uterus today is more the size of a ten-week gestation."

"By my calculations that makes more sense," I agreed.

"That means we'll have to push back the date of the amniocentesis by two weeks. Let's see, that puts us into January."

"What's this?" Jeff asked.

"Dr. Freedman," I said, "I decided against having the test."

"Oh?" He looked surprised.

"What's this?" Jeff asked again.

"Amniocentesis," the doctor answered. "It's a standard procedure by which we take a sample of the amniotic fluid—"

"Yes, I know. Why do you want to do it?"

"Because of your wife's age. She's now in the high-risk age group."

"When you say 'high risk,' what exactly do you mean?"

"Well, I don't have the exact figures," he replied as he rummaged through the papers on top of his desk and then in one of his drawers, "but roughly speaking, women over thirty-five have a higher risk of—oh, here it is." He skimmed a sheet with numbers before handing it to Jeff. "That's the statistical breakdown for birth defects by age group."

"Thanks." After a brief glance, Jeff looked up. "But what I want to ask is, let's say you do the test and you find out there's something wrong, then what?"

"Then you may elect to terminate the pregnancy."

"Meaning abortion."

"That's right."

Jeff turned to me. I flinched.

"There's really no point in doing the test," I said.

"Unless there's something that could be done to correct a condition?" Jeff asked the doctor.

"In utero? No, not at this time. Maybe in a few years, with the use of lasers, perhaps." He smiled. "But for now, that's all in the theory stages."

Jeff nodded, then looked at me. "What do you think, Cyn? I don't see any point to it, do you?"

I shook my head.

"So." Dr. Freedman opened his drawer again and pulled out another sheet. "I'll ask you to sign this," he said, handing me the paper. When I started to read it, he explained, "That just says I've discussed the testing with you and you have, with full knowledge, refused it."

Was he really afraid I'd sue him if I gave birth to a child with some problem? I signed it and handed it back.

"So." He attached the sheet to my file. "Unless you have any further questions...?" He raised his eyebrows and waited expectantly. We both shook our heads. "Then we'll see you in another month." He handed me my closed chart. "We'll be closed the last week in December, so you can make it for early January."

▲   ▲   ▲

The next couple of days went smoothly. I no longer felt queasy and was grateful to finally be moving out of the first trimester. I enjoyed eating for two. I enjoyed the attention people were giving me. We spent evenings in El Con Mall, pricing cribs and carseats and smiling at pretty babies in arms and strollers. I accepted the inevitable and abandoned myself to the pleasures of it.

Some form or card I had filled out at the doctor's office put me on the mailing list of *American Baby* magazine. My first issue came. I thumbed through the articles—how to bathe a baby, advice from a pediatrician, tips from other mothers. It all seemed so anachronistic. I'd already been through all this. That era was over; I felt old and jaded. Poems about the sweet, soft perfection of a newborn: I knew what a perfect terror the kid would soon grow to be.

I seemed to be on everybody's mailing list. A catalog arrived with dozens of pictures of incredible nurseries. One room all done up in ducks: a quilt appliqued with yellow ducklings, wooden ducks glued to the wall and crib, tiny ducks all over the frilly curtains and wallpaper. Similarly, a clown motif, umbrella motif, alphabet motif, all in sumptuous color reproductions. My nausea returned.

"What's that, Mom? Can I see?" I handed the brochure to Ronnie. "Oh, isn't that cute! Are we gonna do this?"

"Yeah, sure, in whose room—yours or Adam's? Or maybe I should turn *my* room into the nursery."

She smiled. I actually got her to smile. Or was she smiling at the pictures in the catalog?

I walked down the hall to my room for my afternoon nap. On the way, I peered into Ronnie's messy nest—the punk motif, I thought, including the authentic ugly afghan—and then Adam's—the junk-lot motif, complete with scale-sized handprint wall patterns and scattered random toys.

It was not an altogether undesirable experience, this jaundiced tour through modern baby-making. I found it all refreshing and entertaining, a step out of the rut I was in. I began to look forward to changes in my body and in the texture of my life.

▲     ▲     ▲

One Thursday evening, Jeff took me to the movies. We went to see an Australian film at the New Loft, the "alternative" cinema, Tucson's equivalent to the Thalia in New York. Before the movie, I visited the ladies' room. It was a small, dark lavatory with walls papered in old movie posters. When I wiped myself, there was a touch of color on the toilet paper, but the lighting was poor, and when I wiped a second time, the paper was clean. I pretended I hadn't seen what I saw—it was down the toilet already. I allowed myself to believe that the second wipe canceled out the first. As I returned to my seat, I decided not to share my doubt with Jeff. What for? He couldn't do anything about it, but he'd try to by insisting I quit my job and lie in bed all day. Later that evening, back at home, there was another small brownish stain.

After work Friday, I found three small dots in my underpants. I put on a clean pair. Saturday morning, there was a large, pale pink stain. I told Jeff.

"What! You should have told me right away. What do you think it means?"

"Maybe it means nothing," I suggested hopefully.

"Call Dr. Freedman."

"It's Shabbas."

"I know, but this might be a matter of life and death," he said. Any Jewish law can be violated in order to save a life.

"I don't think so. It's such a little drop, it can wait another day. Besides, what can he do about it?"

"I don't know but I think you should call." When I still hesitated to pick up the phone, he did. "What's his number?" he asked impatiently.

"It's seven-thirty. He won't be in yet," I said as I leafed through my phone book.

"That's okay. I'll leave word with his answering service."

The phone rang ten minutes later. "Don't answer it," Adam shouted as he trotted down the hall. "It's Shabbas." His eyes bugged when he got to our threshold and found his father lifting the receiver to his ear.

Jeff hung up. I looked at him expectantly. "Wrong number, dammit," he said.

"How come you picked it up, Daddy?"

"Go get yourself some breakfast. Is Ron up yet?"

The next call was the doctor. He told us to meet him at his office at one-thirty.

"How will we get there?" I asked. The office was out on Wilmot, five miles to the east.

"We'll have to drive."

"I don't like this. Really, it could have waited 'til tomorrow."

Jeff wouldn't let me come with them to services that morning, afraid the exertion of the walk would stimulate further staining.

"But I want to pray," I protested.

"We'll pray for you," he said. "For you and the little one."

While they were gone, I lay in bed willing my body to hold onto the new little life, asking God to please make sure everything would be all right.

When they got home, we rushed through lunch. Jeff barely finished the post-meal *bentching* before standing and urging me to come with him.

Leaving the kids behind, I reluctantly got into the passenger seat and let Jeff drive me down Broadway. It felt so strange, riding in a car in broad daylight on a Saturday afternoon. In my life prior to Jeff, this would be no cause for concern or reflection, but for the past fourteen years, observance of the sabbath had been increasingly a part of my personal repertoire. Riding in the car on Shabbas made me feel like we were naughty children sampling a shot of schnapps when the grownups stepped out. I even imagined dizziness, the sense of doing the forbidden was so intoxicating.

Dr. Freedman had me drink several cups of water so my full bladder would push the uterus up beyond the pelvic girdle. Then, in this uncomfortably bloated state, I lay on a hard table with my belly exposed. He squirted K-Y Jelly over my abdomen and ran his ultrasound microphone back and forth, searching for a positive sign.

"There's a mass in her uterus," he said. "You see this, Professor Roth?" I had an oblique view of the screen. He was pointing out a denser area to Jeff. "But it isn't large enough. Not nearly as large as we should be seeing with a fourteen-week gestation, and I can't find a fetal heartbeat. There should be a heartbeat at this point."

"Remember, last time you said we miscalculated," I said, lifting my head up from the table. "I'm not fourteen weeks along yet."

He sighed and studied the screen some more. "Even for twelve weeks it's awfully small."

I refused to share his pessimism. "Maybe my fetuses develop at a different rate than the norm. I gave birth two weeks late with Ronnie, and ten days late with Adam."

Dr. Freedman shook his head. "This seems to be far beyond the parameters of what's normal."

"Should she take it easy, Doc?" Jeff asked.

"I'm afraid it won't make any difference."

On the ride home, my head grew muddled with conflicting emotions. As valiantly as I'd strived to reconcile myself to the pregnancy, some small resistance had failed to die, and with the possibility of spontaneous termination, it swelled up with relief. On the other hand, I was genuinely sorry that things looked bleak. And another doubt wove itself into my confusion: what if I didn't abort, what if I carried to term some half-cooked freak?

The staining stopped after our Saturday visit to Dr. Freedman. For a whole week, there was nothing. We smiled and foolishly told each other it was all an aberration, that now I'd settle down to grow a nice, big, heart-thumping fetus. We even made disparaging remarks about the medical profession with its fancy equipment which didn't show everything, the practitioners who didn't know anything. Still, there was a hesitancy in our jubilation, a quiet waiting, a sense of life hanging in balance.

Later in December, the staining began again. I had just been around the corner to mail a birthday card to our niece; as I let myself back in, I felt a dampness. This time it was not so tentative, and it grew into a flow in the next couple of days. On December 22, the day before Tamara turned five, I had cramps. Jeff was spending the evening at the lab, the kids were watching TV. The contractions intensified and became rhythmic. I marveled at how much an animal my body was becoming, sweating over its beastly function, unintelligent, unthinkingly bent on expelling the small interloper without the slightest qualm. I called Jeff at work. While he was rushing home, I called the doctor and left a message with the answering service. Shortly after I hung up, I felt a flush of warm water gush out of me and ran to change my underwear. Clumps came out with the flowing blood.

As I bled through pads and rags and my clothing, Jeff drove me past old houses, his headlights illuminating untended yards returning to a wilder state, the overgrown weeds frozen in winter death. The route seemed circuitous in comparison to the strong directedness of my body.

I lost all sense of time, only vaguely aware of the car stopping, my walking in a daze through the emergency entrance at St. Joseph's, being led immediately to a cubicle where I stripped without even waiting for the door to close. People, reduced in my perception to the polyester uniforms and permanent-press tunics they wore, asked questions, prodded my private parts, asked more questions: "Are you sure you're pregnant? Was this verified by your doctor? When was your last menses? How far along are you? Have you passed any tissue?"

"Jeff, hold my hand," I insisted, catching his eye, becoming a person again for an instant before returning to my instinctive birthing. This was not strictly "kosher," his touching me when my bleeding should have indicated a period of separation, but I needed him, I needed the strength and love he gave me, the "humanness" he gave me. Gripping callus and knuckles, I turned my attention, my concentration, once more to the center of the universe my abdomen had become. It was not even that I was egocentric: the birthing process was so central that my self was forgotten, my ego evaporating to a thin atmosphere of no concern to the core body. I was larger than life—a bear, a rhinoceros, some gross, lumbering creature—indifferent to the people around me, to my naked-ness, my exposed, blood-smeared thighs. I focused only on the amazing mechanism of spewing forth, the building, building to a climax as my uterus tried to rid itself of a troublesome irritant. I felt as indifferent as a stupid beast to the sudden cathartic expulsion of bloody tissue: the glob of dark placenta and the small form of a tiny body, almost human. Indifferent to all that, I experienced only the release, the sudden all-encompassing relief, the utter exhilaration of a well-coordinated mecha-nism functioning smoothly. Following the great exertion came the endorphin high, the happy tingling fatigue in every muscle. I was an organism which had worked as a whole, worked in a unified, concerted effort. A quiet replaced the violent action of a minute before, a quiet and peace and euphoria seeping into all corners of my being. I lay back on the table and relaxed.

Dr. Freedman arrived later, after they'd rolled me upstairs. I stoically submitted to all his poking and prodding. Jeff at my side tried to distract me with jokes when all I wanted to do was focus all my consciousness on this new assault to my uterus, the scraping away of the last remnants of clinging tissue. Whereas before all outside sensations were subordinated by the tremendous, overriding, primitive rhythm of my organs, now it was painful and unbearably annoying.

Eventually Dr. Freedman was satisfied that I was clean inside. I recuperated in a cold room, chilly under a white sheet and bedspread. Jeff left me to call the children at home.

Finally I was told I could get up and get dressed and go home. The back of my dress was wet where Jeff had rinsed out the blood.

It was late. The streets were dark and empty. Except for Jeff's occasional "you feeling okay?" it was quiet. I sat in the car after he turned off the engine, waited for him to lock his door and walk around to unlock mine, too exhausted to resist his help as he guided me through the house, to our room, to the bed. He helped me undress, made sure I was settled before going back to lock up and turn out the lights.

I lay in the bed, so broad and low and warm after the strange beds I had lain in that evening. I felt weak, submissive, and grateful. "Thank You, God," I whispered before falling asleep.

# Five

I stayed home from work for several days to convalesce. It was already Christmas vacation, or winter break, or whatever euphemism the Tucson Unified School District used as an excuse to close the doors of the city's educational institutions for sixteen days, so I had company when I would have preferred solitude.

The significance of my miscarriage seemed totally lost on Adam, who apparently viewed the change in plans with no more remorse than a ballgame canceled because of rain. Ronnie suffered, she quietly mourned. However, her sorrow didn't include me: *she* was the one to be pitied for the loss of her sister. The fetus became hers. She even chose to assume its femininity to heighten her bond to it. I became the imperfect body which had destroyed her baby. But she was willing to forgive me if I'd undo the unfortunate by actively pursuing another pregnancy; she suggested she might draw consolation from the appearance, with minimum delay, of another young sibling. Jeff shared his daughter's wishes. He hinted about my fertility, demonstrated a willingness to pamper me, mentioned how attractive he found me with enlarged belly and swollen breasts.

Neither Jeff nor I had told our families about the pregnancy. We didn't want to get the grandparents excited until after the first three unsure months were past. But when my parents called, I felt the need to tell them about the loss.

"Oh, Cynthia, we're so sorry!" my father moaned long distance.

"Would you like us to come out and be with you?" my mother asked on the extension.

If they hadn't offered to come out, I would have resented their indifference. As it was, my immediate reaction was defensiveness: why did they have to come and poke around in my business? I impugned them with ungenerous motives, envisioning them deriving vicarious satisfaction from being close to me during my "hour of need," reasserting themselves in the role of "most intimate relatives." Thinking of them hovering made me squirm. "Thank you, but that's not necessary," I answered tersely. "Jeff and the kids are all between terms, so I have more than enough people fussing over me."

boy. They didn't find what they were looking for and came back to Brooklyn before Jeff started school. But he returned. Between his junior and senior years in college, he went again, spending the summer on a kibbutz. This was shortly after the Six Day War; the country was in a state of euphoria. He came back sunbaked and fired up about the Jewish homeland. It was his doing that we were on the Aliyah Center's mailing list.

▲    ▲    ▲

A smiling, fresh-faced young man sat across the table from us in the kitchen of what was once the Volks' house before it was bequeathed to the JCC. One of the first questions we asked him was about compulsory military service in Israel. Back in the late '60's, Jeff had enrolled in a doctoral program less from a desire to pursue his field than to avoid the draft and Vietnam. Though his pacifist ideals became muddled when he thought of Israel's self-defense, he still harbored an antipathy to guns and combat.

The Israeli offered this logic: "You will be coming on a permanent-residents visa. This way you do not lose your U.S. citizenship. You are not yet an Israeli citizen. Therefore, you do not serve in the army."

"But we want to become Israelis," I insisted.

"Yes, you will become," he replied. "After three years, you automatically become."

"Then I'll be drafted?" Jeff asked.

"But you'll be forty by then," I reminded him. "They wouldn't draft you at that age, would they?"

The man shrugged. "Don't even think about it," he assured us.

We asked him about employment, housing, education, learning Hebrew. Everything was simple according to him. Everything would be taken care of. We were not to worry about anything.

Jeff, in spite of his rosy recollections, was skeptical: it was improbable that everything in Israel should be as easy as the young man promised. He took the initiative to write and call any friend or acquaintance with Israeli connections. Instead of resigning from his professorial position, he decided to apply for a sabbatical from the University, arguing that it didn't hurt to leave his options open. By the end of the month, he'd sent out letters to every Israeli university, institute, and research lab, both private and government run.

"We could always go live on a kibbutz," I suggested.

But toiling in the fields didn't appeal to him anymore. "Anyway," he said, "the man from the Aliyah Center said I shouldn't have any trouble getting a job in physics." Optics was a "hot" field.

Predictably, Adam greeted our plans with enthusiasm and his sister sulked. "We'll have to learn Hebrew," Ronnie complained.

"Yeah, well." Jeff waved away her objection. "You'll be speaking fluently in less than a month," he predicted.

"You didn't learn to speak Hebrew when you were on the kibbutz," she pressed.

This had always baffled me: how was it that he could read and recite Hebrew from his prayer book yet be unable to converse in the language? He explained that *davening* wasn't the same thing, that modern Hebrew had a different vocabulary and pronunciation. "Just because you can sing 'Frere Jacques' doesn't mean you know French," he had pointed out. But now he minimized the difficulties. "I could have," he insisted. "I was supposed to. It's my own fault I didn't. I hung around with all the American kids too much. Anyway, kids pick up new languages like that." He snapped his fingers.

"Didn't you tell me everyone in Israel speaks English?" I asked, my own anxiety increasing.

"Yeah, sure."

Adam perked up. "Yeah? How come?"

"Because it's a good language to know. Also 'cause the Israelis love America."

"Yeah," Adam agreed. "We send them money and weapons." He picked up an invisible gun, sighted along the barrel, and sprayed us with imaginary bullets and the saliva which accompanied his explosive sounds.

Light-weight letters with beautiful stamps began to appear in our mailbox. A couple of places expressed interest in Jeff. We put the house on the market.

At *kiddush* after Saturday services, we talked to Rabbi Danziger. He shook his head. "I'm worried about you. I don't think you should go."

I was surprised and annoyed. "But it's the land God gave us. Every Jew belongs in Israel."

"I don't know," he answered. "I've seen some religious people lose their faith there."

I refused to believe him. "On the contrary, it should be easier to be a practicing Jew. All the stores will sell kosher meat, and everything will be closed for the Jewish holidays. Jeff won't be the only one wearing a *kippah*. We finally won't be a minority."

"What can I say? I obviously can't talk you out of it, so I guess I wish you luck."

"What's this?" Mr. Liebowitz interrupted, his voice cracking. "You can't go. We need you for the *minyan*."

"Where are you going?" someone else asked.

"To Israel," Mr. Liebowitz informed everyone. "The Land of Milk and Honey, no?"

"That's wonderful."

"I hear everything is terribly expensive there," offered another person in the cluster growing around us.

"It's a hard life. He's right: you can't live on an Israeli salary."

"The Israelis do," Jeff countered.

Ed Zlotnick had made one of his infrequent appearances at synagogue that Shabbas. "What, are you crazy?" he asked, his steelwool hair making him look a bit like a madman himself. He lifted off his *kippah* and tried to resettle it on his bushy mane. "The Israelis don't want you there. They want you here where you can make a mint and send them fat contributions." Ed made semiannual trips to see a daughter from his first marriage who was studying medicine in Haifa.

"They're all feeling guilty," Jeff stated on our walk home. "If we move to Israel, why can't they? But they don't want to; they're comfortable and settled here. So they have to say it's impossible. In fact, it probably is impossible and we probably are crazy."

"But...?" I smiled, waiting for a punch line.

"But nothing," he answered, chuckling. "But we're going to do it anyway."

Ned and Mandy Petersen, who lived two doors away, stopped by to ask us about the "For Sale" sign that appeared in our cactus garden.

"It sounds so exciting, going to live in a country that's both foreign and yet your homeland," said Mandy, adjusting her large tinted glasses on her freckled nose.

"You going to live on one of those kibbutzes?" asked Ned. "That's what I call the real pioneer life. I can really get into that."

Mandy, smiling broadly, shook her head slowly. "The Middle East! I've always wanted to see that part of the world. Arab markets, the Old City, Bethlehem. So much history."

"It's the Cradle of Civilization," Ned embellished.

Mandy nodded. "Here, something built at the turn of the century is considered old. There, you can actually walk on the streets Christ walked on."

I didn't have the heart to tell her that was not in the least the reason we were going there.

▲ ▲ ▲

At 4:30 one morning, we were awakened by a call from Jerusalem. Jeff tried to be coherent. After he hung up, he turned to me. In the light of the bedside lamp, his eyes were still sleepy but his smile looked wide awake. "I was just offered a job."

"What!" I sat up. "Where, Jeff?"

"JCT. That stands for Jerusalem College of Technology. I gather the name is bigger than the place. But they do good work. One of their profs had a very decent paper in *Phys Rev*; that's how I heard of them."

"That's wonderful, Jeff! How much are they paying you?"

"I have no idea. This guy I just spoke to, I think he said his name is Litansky. I should write that down; he's the big wheel there." He looked in the night table for a pen and paper. "Anyway, he says salaries are all government regulated but he figures that since I'm an assoc prof here, I'll get an equivalent appointment there."

"Great!"

"The only thing, Cyn. He said JCT is just starting up—only been around a couple of years—so they don't have a lot of funds. He said they're getting a government grant to pay for me, something from the Absorption Ministry. He said they'll pay for up to two years. After that, we'll have to see."

"But once we're there, you can look around."

"Exactly."

"And besides, once they see you, they'll offer you something permanent."

"It's nice to be married to a woman with so much confidence in me!"

▲   ▲   ▲

On March 15, we celebrated our anniversary. There were no kosher restaurants in Tucson, unless one considered the few tables set up at Feig's, the kosher butcher and deli. We'd sometimes go out for a beer, or to a coffeeshop which had disposable cups. The University had concerts and plays, and we went to movies. But that night, when the kids were settled with the baby-sitter and we backed out of our driveway, we decided against all our usual evening-out activities.

"Why don't we just take a drive," I suggested. So Jeff drove up Tanque Verde into the foothills.

As he maneuvered the winding roads, Jeff said, "Did you really think we'd ever be celebrating our fourteenth anniversary?"

His question surprised me. "Of course! I wouldn't have married you if I thought we were going to get a divorce."

"I didn't mean it like that. Of course. Me too." He glanced at me before continuing. "Cindy, I depend on you in ways I can't even begin to tell. Do you know that, Cyn? I really do. I know I don't take the time to tell you this enough, but I really do." He rubbed his free hand through his beard. His eyes watched the road, but I could see he was looking inward. "No, I guess what I'm really trying to ask you is: did you have any idea fourteen years ago what you were getting yourself into? Did you really think this is where you'd be at this point?"

I peered through the windshield. It was dark everywhere except the couple of yards ahead of our high-beams. "I'm not a prophet, Jeff. How could I see into the future?"

"Yeah, but when you were a young woman, didn't you sort of plan out your life? When you married me, didn't you say to yourself something like, 'I hope we have x number of kids and live in a mansion, or a houseboat, and I want an exciting job bossing everyone around'?" His laugh-lines crinkled around his eyes.

"Are you saying I'm too bossy?" I asked, matching his smile.

"I'd better not answer that."

"I thought you told me we can't decide those kinds of things. I thought you said God decides about whether we have kids, and things like that."

"Yeah, up to a point. But I also believe you have to do something toward having those kids if you want them. You can't just sit around waiting for life to happen to you. You do stuff, sometimes aimlessly, sometimes with a direction. What was your direction? Where did you want to be at this point in you life?"

"I don't know. I don't think I was as directed as you. I'm not like you with your years of grad school and your passion for your field. I majored in *English* at Hunter, not exactly very goal-oriented. After college, I just took the first job that came along."

"And the first husband that came along?"

"But I didn't do too badly with that first job." I grinned. "Or, for that matter, with my first husband either."

"Your *first* husband? How many you plan to have?"

"I guess I have just sort of let life happen to me. Maybe it's just that I'm more open-minded than you!"

He laughed. "Define open-minded: hole-in-the-head."

"Ha-ha. Besides, I don't really think you had it all planned out so perfectly. What made you marry me? I would have thought you'd have married a girl with a religious background."

"Yeah, but you were so much sexier."

After so many years in a monogamous relationship, so many years of practicing a religion which frowned on promiscuity, thinking about my past indiscretions made me uncomfortable. Or maybe it was just that now I was the mother of an adolescent daughter. "Hmm. That's not how it usually goes. My mother warned me that men fool around but then when it comes time to marry—"

"Yeah, I know. But it didn't work out that way. I got stuck on you." Something about his grin made me think he too was embarrassed about his premarital transgression. "Yeah, I was raised to be a good boy and marry a nice, religious girl who'd know as much about running a Jewish home as me. But I have no regrets, Cyn. Really." His eyes shifted toward me, then away. He grew pensive. "Life's full of surprises, though, isn't it. Who ever thought we'd find ourselves in Tucson, of all places? And this last pregnancy. I was so worked up about it and then it just sort of disappeared." His eyes glistened in the dark. "When I first met you, who'd've ever expected that now you'd be a religious woman, that you'd be off to settle in some far-off country with this ornery old man and your two brats?"

"Whose kids are you calling brats? Whose old man are you calling ornery?" I joked, but I could see he really wanted me to respond to his doubts. The answer was no, at age twenty, or twenty-two, I didn't know who I was, let alone who he was and how living with him would change me. I never in my wildest dreams thought that now I'd be keeping so many troublesome ancient laws or that I would want to move halfway around the globe. "I guess we'd be bored to tears if we could really see our lives mapped out ahead of time."

"Either bored or terrified." Jeff pulled over onto the shoulder where we could glimpse the city lights below. He turned off the headlights and the engine. "The valley's pretty, isn't it." Then, opening his seatbelt, he pivoted toward me, his elbow propped on the steering wheel. His smile was gentle, his dark eyes glowed softly in the unlit car on the unlit road. "Hey, I've got a gift for you."

"A gift! That's not fair, Jeff. I thought we said we weren't going to give each other anything this year because it would just be another thing to pack." I felt bad I had nothing for him.

"It's okay. A practical gift, and small." He reached over to open the glove compartment, then handed me a box. "Here. Hope you don't mind: I didn't bother to wrap it."

The box was long and thin and imprinted with "Crown Jewelers." It was so uncharacteristic of Jeff; he never gave me jewelry. Getting my engagement ring had been a big production because it was such an alien act for him. He'd been to a jewelry store ready to purchase whatever he could afford on his teaching fellowship, unaware that rings came in sizes. He had no idea what size my finger was or how to find out, and eventually I went back with him. He wanted to get one with an elaborate setting—it was really beautiful, but not at all practical, and certainly beyond what he could afford. There was something so endearing about his helplessness. I thought that I was a liberated woman to the nth degree because I was the one being pragmatic and unsentimental. "I'll scratch you with it. I'll get mugged in the subway. We'll have to pawn it in order to pay the rent."

I glanced at my ring. I'd ended up with a much more subdued design. And in time, my husband too had become more subdued and practical.

His anniversary gift was supposed to be practical. Maybe it really was a can opener, some other tool that would fit into such a box. But Jeff wasn't the kind of practical to play a practical joke.

I carefully eased the cover off, lifted away the long piece of cotton, and found a bracelet: a sturdy gold chain encrusted with diamonds, though I immediately assumed that these were well-done imitations. What possessed him to buy such a thing? I was dazzled, greatly flattered. And at the same time, I was mildly annoyed. I always considered our bank account joint property. What business did he have to spend so much of our money on something so frivolous, especially at a time when we might need that money to help in our move? "I thought you said your gift was practical," I said, trying very hard to keep the irritation out of my voice.

He was beaming. "Oh, Cindy, I love you. You haven't changed at all from the wonderful girl I married." He wrapped his arm around my shoulders and gave a squeeze. "Listen to my logic. The Israeli economy is a mess, terrible inflation, and there's all sorts of bureaucratic red tape regarding monies. Remember I read to you about it being illegal for Israeli citizens to have foreign bank accounts, and I was worried about what's going to happen to our U.S. savings when we're naturalized in three years? So I did a very Jewish thing. What have our ancestors done to survive fluctuating economies and political instability? They've bought diamonds, right? This will be our insurance, our little something extra in case of a financial disaster. And you"—he hugged me again—"are the most wonderful wife who is entrusted with wearing our family fortune."

It took a minute to digest Jeff's speech. And then I laughed, because I was now truly flattered—not because Jeff wanted to give me beautiful things but because he saw me as so integral to our joint welfare. I hugged him back.

He broke from my embrace. "Put it on, Cyn." He helped me clasp it, then held my hand out to look at it. "Pretty nice, huh?"

I admired Jeff's investment in our future twinkling at my wrist.

▲   ▲   ▲

I drove out to the airport with Adam to pick up my parents. I had yet to mention our plans to them: I didn't know how. I didn't want to trivialize such a momentous decision, yet I didn't feel like presenting it in heroic proportions. When we turned in at the driveway, my mother, spotting the realtor's sign, asked, "What's this?"

"We're moving," Adam replied, already releasing his seatbelt, the buckle making a ping against the door. "Hey, Mom, would it be all right if I go to Paco's house for a while before dinner?"

"Your grandparents just arrived."

"Do you mind, Grandma and Grandpa? I won't be long. The thing is, I just remembered we have a test tomorrow and I didn't bring home my math book."

My parents laughed. "Go," said my father. "We'll visit later."

After Adam jumped out and onto his bike, my mother said, "So what's this about a move?"

I stalled in answering her, concentrating instead on getting out of the car and helping my dad lift the suitcases from the trunk. We deposited them in the family room.

My mother flipped one open to take out the things that would wrinkle. As she hung her dresses and my father's slacks in the closet in the corner of the room, she asked again. "Do you have anything in particular in mind or are you just getting a feel for the market?"

"No, actually, we were thinking of moving to Israel," I said offhandedly.

My father looked up from the return airline tickets he'd been fussing with, his eyebrows stuck halfway up his forehead. My mother also stopped, a hanger poised in the air. The constellations of beauty marks on her arms came to a halt, as though my news could make the Universe stand still.

Deciding to soften the blow, I equivocated. "Jeff's been here for seven years already. He's due a sabbatical."

"Oh!" Both of them relaxed considerably, willing to believe what they wanted to believe, regardless of whether it contradicted what I said before. "So it's just for a year," my mother clarified, greatly relieved.

"Then why sell the house?" my father asked.

"Well," I extemporized, "it's a headache to own a house long distance."

"Of course," my mother agreed. "You have to worry about break-ins. And what if the plumbing went?"

"You could rent it out," my father suggested.

"That can be a headache, too."

"What do you think, then?" my mother probed. "When you get back, you'd look for another place?"

"I guess so." I was a bad liar. I sat down on one of the couches.

"Maybe you could use something a little bigger, now that the kids are growing up."

"And with a swimming pool," my father added.

My mother forced a stupid grin. "It's really so exciting!" she decided, hanging her bathrobe. "Imagine: Israel!"

"What about the kids?" my father asked.

"What about them?"

"You're taking them with you?"

"Of course, Dad!"

"But what about their schooling?"

"They have schools there," my mother said.

"It's a rough part of the world to be taking children," he qualified.

"The Israelis love children," I answered, pretending not to get his meaning.

"Remember when those terrorists held the school children hostage?" he said pointedly. "Adam and Ron could stay with us for the year."

My mother's eyes flicked toward him, her lips pressed together. She obviously didn't share his enthusiasm for spending generous amounts of time with the grandchildren.

"Look," I said, impatient with the same arguments I myself had posed over the previous weeks but now had dismissed. "There are bad people all over the world. The police come around to all the public schools here to tell the kids about child molesters. They say one in every four girls will be molested before she reaches adulthood."

"They tell the kids that?" my mother asked.

"No, just the parents. The point is, no place is safe anymore."

"My God, is it that bad?" She looked upset. She had a new worry to mull over.

▲     ▲     ▲

We ate dinner at the bigger table in the dining room. Sticky rice was scattered over the carpet by Adam's seat. It was a nuisance, always having to keep the house neat in case a realtor wanted to show it to a prospective buyer.

"What a beautiful bracelet you gave Cynthia for your anniversary," my mother said in a tense, affected voice. Whenever she talked with Jeff, she tried to suppress her New York accent in deference to his erudition. This was ridiculous since Jeff's Brooklynese was more pronounced than hers.

"Isn't it nice?" he agreed.

My father said, "The University must be doing good business this year that you can afford that, and the trip to Israel, and the move to a bigger house when you get back."

Jeff glanced at me. I hadn't had a chance to warn him about my lies. "Yeah. I guess so."

"Where in Israel do you think you'll be for your sabbatical?" my mother asked.

"It looks like Jerusalem."

"Isn't that where the Technion is?" my mother asked. "I'm pretty sure that's where Sid and Bea's nephew is," she informed my father. I didn't know Sid and Bea. I could see she was already making a list of strangers I should contact in Israel.

"The Technion's in Haifa," Jeff told her.

"What's the name of that big university there?" asked my father, wrinkling his brow.

"Hebrew University?" Jeff suggested.

"Yeah...." My father frowned, unsure. "Name me some others."

"There's the Weizmann Institute, but that's in Rehovot."

"Weizmann. Yes, I think that's the one. There was a big article in the *Times* about some breakthrough they made in microbiology. Did you hear anything about that?"

Jeff shrugged and grinned. My father thought someone with an advanced degree in physics should be inquisitive enough to want to keep abreast of a discovery in microbiology sufficiently important to make *The New York Times*. Jeff thought my father was a well-read fool.

"Were you planning to spend your sabbatical at Hebrew University?" my mother asked in her stilted voice.

"No, actually, I think I'll be with a smaller place called Jerusalem College of Technology."

My father nodded. "Ah, yes. They have a very fine reputation."

"Really?" Jeff shot me his listen-to-this-joker grin. "I didn't think they had very much of any reputation. The school's only been in existence a few years."

"Wait, isn't that the place which teaches religious studies also?"

That wiped the smirk off Jeff's face. JCT was the only place we ever heard of which granted its graduates both a rabbinic and an engineering degree. "Yes," Jeff stated soberly. "They study Talmud in the morning and science in the afternoon. Interesting combination."

"Will you be teaching, Jeff?" my mother asked.

"I think so."

"Do you know enough Hebrew?" my father asked, sporting Jeff's cast-off wiseguy grin. The two of them: overgrown boys with their male posturing!

"No. I guess I'll have to teach in English. Everyone knows English there."

"Really? That's not what I heard. I heard that things have changed and now you really need to know Hebrew to get around."

"I'm going to learn Hebrew in one month," Adam bragged.

▲     ▲     ▲

It was always like this when my parents visited. I had a theory as to why Jeff was so critical of them. He probably had more to talk about with my dad than he did with his own father. Rather than feel guilty over it, he went out of his way to make sure he didn't enjoy his father-in-law's company.

Why didn't my father like Jeff? The psychology books would probably say it was an unavoidable, universal antipathy: fathers hated their sons-in-law because they were sleeping with their daughters, some Freudian nonsense like that. Surely too simplistic an explanation. Of more significance was the innate masculine trait of rising to a dare, and Jeff surely challenged my father. There were the substantial changes I made with regard to religion thanks to my association with Jeff. (To my parents' thinking, Jeff and I were as much a mixed marriage as Sheila and Chad.) They weren't happy we lived so far away and they got to see their only two grandchildren infrequently, also Jeff's fault for having a profession with few job openings.

And why didn't I get along better with my parents? They really weren't bad people. They hadn't had the benefit of a formal education, but they were intelligent and worldly. Though unreligious, they were moral, they were kindly and ethical in their dealings with others. And it wasn't only the normal personality clashes that every child, no matter what age, has with her parents. No, the main reason I couldn't stand having them around was because I was caught between them and Jeff. When they were gone, life was easier for me, there was less tension. Their presence unbalanced the peace I sought to maintain in our household. Rather than quarrel with Jeff, whom I had to live with year round, I took it out on them, thus violating the commandment to honor one's father and mother. The guilt Jeff was trying to avoid was shifted onto me.

In spite of our minimal efforts at hospitality, my parents enjoyed their two weeks in the Tucson sun. My mother's skin soon turned as brown as her moles. Each evening, my fairer father rummaged through the medicine cabinet in search of something to soothe his sunburnt nose and red shoulders. They swam in the pool at the University's Student Union and visited all the city's museums, which were pretty rinky-dink compared with the treasures back East. When the kids got off for spring break, they rented a car and took them on day trips to Bisbee and Tombstone, Nogales on the Mexican border, and the giant telescopes at Kitt Peak.

Characteristic of my reaction to whatever my parents did, instead of rejoicing over their resourcefulness in finding things to do, I resented all the fun they said they had while I was at the Kopy Kat. Yet the thought of taking off a few days from work and joining them on their outings made me shudder.

Surprisingly, the children never fully corrected my parents' misconceptions as to the permanence of our move to Israel. Ronnie, who was still casting dirty looks at my flat tummy, was especially noncommunicative on the subject, which she considered yet another grievance, to displace her after we had denied her a baby. As for Adam, my parents considered him too much a dreamer to be taken literally as he described the grenades he'd throw into terrorist nests when he was old enough to be in the army.

We were preoccupied with our plans. The days slipped by until I distractedly placed them on the plane that returned them to New York.

# Six

Jeff received official word from Jerusalem College of Technology that the funds were coming through for his employment by them. A few days later, he was formally granted a leave of absence with half pay from the University of Arizona. Then we received a solid bid on our house. It was considerably lower than what we thought the house was worth, but the market was exceptionally bad, with mortgage rates running close to sixteen percent. We decided to accept the offer, reasoning that God might be angry with us if we let greed stand in the way of our going to the Promised Land. We made reservations for a September 3 flight to Ben Gurion Airport via Los Angeles, applying for special new-immigrant rates through the Israel Aliyah Center. Since as immigrants we were each entitled to take three large suitcases, we looked into buying inexpensive luggage and began sorting through our possessions in earnest. Ed Zlotnick, who planned to visit his daughter in Israel, offered to find us an apartment near the JCT campus.

▲　　▲　　▲

The telephone started ringing as we sat down to our Friday evening meal. After six rings, it stopped. Half an hour later, it rang ten times. A few minutes later, it rang again.

"It's probably someone trying to sell us life insurance," Jeff joked. "They always call around dinnertime."

"Uh-oh!" Adam hit his forehead with the heel of his hand. "I just remembered. I told J.J. to call me, and I didn't tell him we don't answer the phone on Shabbas."

"Oh, brother," Jeff groaned. "That damn thing'll probably be ringing all day tomorrow."

It rang again. And again. When it rang at 10:30, I grumbled, "Doesn't that kid ever give up?"

"Doesn't he have a bedtime, is more like it," Jeff said. We were getting ready for bed ourselves.

When it rang twenty minutes later, Jeff picked it up.

As he listened, as he replied in monosyllables, his face drained of color. He disconnected and strode to the kitchen.

I chased after him. "What is it, Jeff? What is it?"

He was riffling through the Yellow Pages, his other hand poised in front of the wall phone.

"Jeff?"

The phone off the hook, he punched in numbers, then waved me to be quiet. When he talked into the receiver, he began pacing between the kitchen counters and pulling his hair. From what he said, I gathered he was looking for plane reservations.

After three such calls, he sat down heavily in a chair and stared at a challah crumb on the table.

I tried once more. "What is it?"

"Sheila."

"What? Jeff, tell me!"

"She's in the hospital. Critical condition."

"What!" Chills prickled at the side of my neck.

"They were driving up to UConn for the Memorial Day Weekend. Friends up there, the Guptas. That's who called. Just outside Storrs they collided with a truck. Chad's dead."

"Oh my God!" I collapsed in a chair and shared his wide-eyed shock.

"I've got a flight out in a few hours."

"Oh my God!"

"Better pack." He sighed and heaved himself out of the seat. "The kid's okay. She was strapped in in the back. The Guptas have her. The police found their name and address with the maps in the car. That's how they knew to contact them."

In our dark bedroom, he pulled out shirts, underwear, and pajamas from his drawers and dumped the haphazard assortment into a valise. He took a pair of slacks from the closet and rolled them up before stuffing them in on top. "Well," he said as he zipped the bag closed. He stretched out on top of the covers but neither of us slept.

Before dawn Saturday morning, he boarded a plane to New York. He changed planes in LaGuardia and got to the hospital late Saturday evening. Sheila died shortly after he arrived.

While Jeff was sitting in airplanes and airports, I spent the sabbath noshing nervously and screaming at the kids. It seemed grossly inappropriate for them to giggle and squabble when their aunt was dying. By the time Jeff called, I was hoarse and had consumed every cookie and cracker in the house.

Jeff recited his plans in a dry, precise voice. I could only say "okay" across the thousands of miles of telephone wire. He told me the Guptas were certain Chad would want to be cremated, and Jeff accepted their wishes. He chose to give his sister a Jewish burial and had already called a physicist friend in New Haven to help him make arrangements there.

"I'll fly in for the funeral," I said.

"That's not realistic."

I felt offended. "She was my sister too. I felt closer to her than to my own sister," I insisted.

"I'm burying her tomorrow, Cyn. Even if you got a flight out in the next two minutes, you wouldn't be here in time. After the funeral, I'm taking the kid back to Brooklyn with me to sit *shivah* at my folks' place."

"But they already sat *shivah* for Sheila," I objected.

"That's their problem."

"Why don't you come home and sit *shivah* here?"

"I think my parents need me right now."

I needed him, too. "I'll fly out and be with you."

"What about the kids?"

"I could bring them with me. School lets out in about a week, so they wouldn't miss anything."

"No. I don't think so. It'll be too crowded at my folks'. I don't think it's a good idea."

"We could stay with my parents," I suggested.

He said nothing. I let it drop.

"What will happen with Tamara?" I asked.

"Yeah, there are a lot of things that need taking care of. There's their apartment to close up, too. The Guptas have been in touch with Chad's family in Bangalore. You know," he added, "she was pregnant."

"Huh?"

"Sheila. She was four months pregnant."

After he hung up, I sat a long time on the edge of the bed, my eyes fixed on the phone on the night table but not seeing anything. When the numbness began to thaw, I wept. Chad would soon be reduced to ashes. I would never again hear his soft, melodious voice, his charming words. I'd never again enjoy the visual pleasure of his beauty. That was bad enough.

But Sheila's death was unbearable. I suddenly missed her so sharply, I ached. How could it be that one minute she was driving along anticipating a pleasant weekend with friends in the country, a baby on the way, looking forward, happily planning for the future, and in the next minute, she was twisted in misery and pain, with no future at all? Death itself wasn't tragic; it was the hope and joy that made life's termination sting. All our striving, our planning and scheming, had the same ending. To think we could control our destiny was an illusion. Would our plans to move to Israel meet the same obstacle? Would we ever board the plane? Would we ever land at our destination? I could cease to exist at any moment.

Later that night, I contemplated suicide. No, of course I wouldn't take my own life, and not only because it was forbidden. It was just that it seemed so appealing—to simply end it all instead of living constantly with the possibility of death. I wanted to exert control over my life, to at least determine the time of its ending. I wanted to flee from my body, uncomfortably distended from all the refined carbohydrates I'd stuffed into it during the course of the day.

Early the next morning, I felt better. A chill breeze from my open window played over my limbs where I'd pushed off the covers. The peaceful stillness reassured me. Life seemed precious at that hour. I languidly rolled over and reached across the bed but found emptiness where I'd expected to find Jeff. This jolted me out of my drowsiness; I woke abruptly. In violent reaction to my late night despondency, I was consumed with a fierce desire to get to Israel before I died.

Still unshowered and undressed, I jumped out of bed to pack one of our large suitcases with winter clothes. The activity made me feel as though I were doing something constructive toward reducing the miles between me and my goal.

Ronnie had spent a lot of her infancy in her Aunt Sheila's lap, so she was subdued and contemplative for the next few days. These were the first people she'd known who died. Adam was also withdrawn, but the mood stemmed less from mourning his aunt and uncle than from missing his father. He looked forlorn as he rode off alone to school each morning. Meals were strangely quiet without Jeff's criticisms of Adam's failure to use his fork or close his mouth while chewing. I tried to pinch-hit but my nagging lacked Jeff's animation and style.

Jeff called from Brooklyn each night. The first time I spoke to him after the funeral, I could tell the stunned aloofness he possessed the day before had been replaced by hot grief. We discussed the details of the burial, Jeff hiccuping around sobs. I heard the suffering in his wavering voice, no longer flat and wooden but low and resonant. With subsequent calls, we had fewer and fewer details to deal with. Our conversations became stilted as we avoided painful subjects. There were spaces that echoed in the night-rate telephone connections, holes in the fluff of our chatter.

"Mark Rodman stopped by this evening."

I had to remember who Mark Rodman was. He had gone to high school with Jeff. I recalled being introduced to him at our wedding but could no longer conjure up his face. "That's nice. How is he?"

"Okay."

I paused, waiting for him to say more. When he didn't, I said, "I'm glad he's okay."

"His father died two years ago."

"Really? That's too bad."

"Yeah."

After a few seconds, I asked, "What did he die of?"

"Heart attack."

"How are your parents?"

"Okay. How are the kids?"

"Okay."

I wished I could be brilliant. I wished I could say something eloquent that would cut through the swaths of protective padding we wrapped around ourselves, something beautiful and incisive which, like a pointed laser, could focus on the pain and cauterize it. If it were physically possible, if Jeff were not so far away, I would have squeezed his hand and that would have been almost as good, but while he was in Brooklyn, our only means of communication, of touching, were the words and silences, and I was inept.

After the seven days of *shivah* had been observed, Jeff was able to start tying up loose ends. Chad's brother had flown in from London (where he managed another branch of the family business) and that Sunday and Monday, they went together to their lost siblings' apartment and met with a lawyer who helped sort out what assets had been Chad's individually and what reverted to the import emporium. A trust fund was set up for Tamara. Insurance claims were filed. The bulk of the Chadripadhivans' furnishings and effects would be disposed of in an estate auction.

Grateful for all these details to discuss with Jeff, I overlooked the central, crucial issue.

After a longer than usual silence, Jeff broached this subject. "Cyn, remember how a few months ago you thought you were going to have a baby?"

This seemingly irrelevant question unbalanced me. For a second, I thought he was going to tell me that Sheila's unborn fetus was being kept alive in a jar and would I be willing to offer a surrogate womb. My next thought was that he was going to ask me to replace his sister's life by getting pregnant again. A third possibility was that we were at last getting into the philosophical heavies of life and death. My miscarriage too was a death.

"How would you like to have another little daughter?" he asked.

"What do you mean?" I stammered.

"What I mean is, I've now spent more than a week with Tam—"

At the mention of the girl's name, I felt as nauseous and dizzy as if I were once again in my first trimester. Before he could finish, I blurted out, "But Jeff, we're leaving for Israel in less than three months!"

"So?"

I could think of nothing to say.

"Cyn, listen to me. I know what you're thinking. I know. Believe me, I know. We've never talked about this, but I've always known how you felt. Let's face it, I felt the same way. But now—well, listen to me. Are you listening?"

I nodded dumbly.

"First of all—how to convince you?—first of all, she's human. She's not just a thing, a monster or a nightmare or whatever. I mean, she's a real little person with a personality and feelings. And the thing is, she's kind of likable. I mean, she's cute. For example, the way she brings my father a book and asks him to read it to her—"

"She can talk?"

"Yeah, sure. I mean, not perfectly. Like a baby, sort of. But you can understand her."

"Why don't your parents keep her? It would be good for them."

"Yes, it would be good for them. Only, they won't. They're too old and inflexible. It's too painful for them to have her around because they never forgave She. What can I say, they just won't. I was hoping when I brought her here, but it isn't working out."

"What about Chad's brother?"

"He's not even married, Cindy. And the grandparents in India, well, there are problems there, too. Besides, the way I see it—I've been thinking a lot about this—Tam is Jewish. Her mother was Jewish so she's Jewish. It's as simple as that."

"She should be raised as a Jew instead of a Hindu, is that what you're saying?" I couldn't keep the sarcasm from my voice.

"Well, if you want to put it that way, yeah, she's a Jewish soul. You never want to lose a Jewish soul."

"She's sure to make a great contribution to the Jewish cause," I remarked.

"She will," he answered. He sounded sincere. "She does. She's a sweet, affectionate little person. I've really grown to like her."

I inhaled the smell of drool. I was tired. Wasn't Jeff tired too? It was well past midnight in New York. "Look," I suggested, "why don't we sleep on this, and we can discuss it further tomorrow."

"No, I think it's important we decide about this right now. I'd like to think about flying home already, and I can't until this is resolved. As it is, I doubt I'll get home for Shavuos."

"I forgot. When is it?"

"It starts tomorrow night."

"What about an institution?" I suggested gingerly, blushing as though I'd used a four-letter word.

"Come on, Cyn. How would you feel if you were a little kid with limited understanding and both your parents suddenly disappear, and then you're stuck in some big, impersonal institution with a lot of other kids who aren't too nice, and too little staff to get any kind of individual love and attention? How would you feel?"

I refused to answer such a stacked question. To point out that institutions must have improved since the Willowbrook scandal was to enter into petty fighting, an argument of semantics and sophistry.

"Look, Cyn," he said more gently. "We can always institutionalize her. If all else fails, we have that option. But let's at least give it a try. Okay? Please?"

I tried to match his tone of calm reason. "Under normal circumstances, sure, why not? But right now? It isn't even fair to her. We'll be so busy packing and getting ready, we'll have no time for her. And then what do we do? Transplant her again and take her to Israel with us? She'll have just got adjusted to Tucson—if we're lucky—and then we want to schlep her halfway around the world to a totally new place with different customs and a different language?" My voice was rising. "You say she can express herself a little in English. What is she going to do where everyone is speaking Hebrew?"

"I guess she'll have to learn Hebrew, too," he said good-naturedly.

"Be realistic, Jeff!" A lump of frustration was forming in my throat. I felt overwhelmed.

After a pause, he said, "Let's take it a day at a time, okay? The first thing to do is to find Tam a home for right now. Why don't we say these next three months are a trial period? If it really looks like it won't work out, we'll find some alternative for her before we leave. In the meantime, we've bought her some time. Who knows, maybe some long lost relative will come forward with an interest in raising her. Maybe we can find someone to adopt her. Okay?" When I didn't answer, he repeated, "Okay? A couple of months isn't asking that much, is it, Cindy?"

I recognized his cajoling for the trap it was. Once I committed myself to taking that first step, it would be hard to go back, to change directions. "I really want to go to Israel," I whined. "I don't want to postpone going there. Besides, we've already sold the house," I threw in, immediately sorry I did. Only a month before, selling the house had seemed a major consideration, but as we discussed the future of the one who hadn't died, it became trivial.

"Do you think God will welcome us to our new home with open arms if we can't find it in our hearts to give a little girl a home?"

"Okay," I muttered, resigned. I feared the ease or difficulty of our forthcoming venture hinged on my acceptance of a retarded child. Why God chose to saddle us with this new burden just as we were trying to reduce to a minimum our baggage was unknown to me, but I accepted that somehow it was His intention we take on Tamara. Perhaps this, at last, was the blow I had predicted in synagogue on Rosh Hashanah. Our fate was decided on that day. We only had the free choice of rising to the challenge or bungling it.

# Seven

I had trouble falling asleep that night. The enormity of our undertaking overwhelmed me. The move to Jerusalem became dwarfed by the
thought of taking another couple's child, a stranger really, to become a
part of our family, our neat little foursome, our ideal American-dream
unit: one father, one mother, one son, one daughter...and now one little
swarthy-skinned mongoloid. I prayed for a miracle because I saw this as
a tragedy.

After hours of restlessness, I abandoned the bed and pattered
through the night-still house. I attacked the ice cream in the freezer but
gagged on the sweetness at the unaccustomed hour. Sitting down in the
family room, I leafed through periodicals, too tired and distracted to
concentrate on reading anything. Pages and pages of perfect, cherub-faced
babies—I had picked up one of my complimentary, unsolicited *American
Baby* magazines. Which made me think of the phantom baby of mine that
would have been born just around this time. The irony of life. I
wondered how Ronnie would feel, now that we were in fact presenting
her with a little sister right on schedule.

Bored with the advertisements for new improved Luvs diapers and
Nuk nipples, disgusted by all the gushing enthusiasm over the noble
station of motherhood, I tossed the magazine aside. Opening the drawer
of the end table, I pulled out a deck of cards and set out a game of
solitaire on the coffee table. When I came to the ten of hearts, I had to
chuckle, compromising my foul humor. Adam—it must have been Adam
—had drawn a smily face in one of the red spots. Oh well, motherhood
was not without its little surprises and rewards.

I had dozed off on the couch when the phone awakened me. It was
a quarter to five. "Hello, Cyn? This is Jeff. I just wanted to let you know
I got reservations for a one o'clock flight out of Kennedy. We should
arrive about five p.m. Tucson time."

"I'll meet you."

"You sure? We could take the Stagecoach." What a too-cute name
for the airport limousine.

I missed him. We'd never been apart for so long. "No, I'll be there.
I want to meet you."

When I woke again, it was full, brash daylight, the cicadas were shrilling, Ronnie and Adam were fighting in the kitchen, and I felt as hung over as if I'd spent the previous night carousing. My nose and eyes had that stuffy, swollen feeling, as though I'd been crying. My head ached, and all the muscles in my arms and legs felt crampy. As I staggered off to the bathroom, I debated whether or not to call in sick.

"I'm leaving now, Mom," called Adam. As he mounted his bicycle, he broke into the little ditty about no more pencils, no more books, no more teacher's dirty looks. I checked the calendar. I'd forgotten. It was the last day of school for them. The reason Tucson schools closed the first week in June escaped me—something about it being too hot to study. It seemed to me sitting behind a desk would be less sweat-producing than running around outdoors, but the Board of Education evidently felt it had justification for closing down for three long months each summer. It took the entire month of September to teach the kids to sit still again, and another two months to review all they'd forgotten. Then they wondered why local kids scored lower than the national average on standardized tests.

Looking at the calendar reminded me that the next two days were Shavuos. I pulled my splitting head together, splashed cold water on my eyes, and decided to make it to work after all since I'd be out the next two days. I made a mental note to stop off at Feig's on my way home to pick up some frozen cheese blintzes. After all, what would Shavuos be without blintzes? An amusing little thought twinkled in the thickness of my brain: I wondered if Tamara had ever tasted blintzes. I wondered if she'd like them. I also wondered if she'd like flying in the airplane, then remembered that in her short life, she'd been in more planes than I had, having flown to doctors in Boston and relatives in India. Not only had she more than likely eaten blintzes, she'd probably tried foods I didn't even know existed. The thought humbled me.

I realized with a start that this might be my last day at work, unless I could convince Ronnie to baby-sit Tamara every morning. But Ronnie was already signed up for the sports program offered by the University. What about Jeff? He wasn't teaching summer school. Let him take care of Tamara if he was so fond of her.

After spending a half-asleep morning at the Kopy Kat, I drove to Fifth and Rosemont for the blintzes. As was bound to happen with only one kosher delicatessen in town, I met someone I knew. Hope Wolfe often came to the get-togethers Naomi and Rabbi Danziger hosted during the year. I hated Hope because she already had five children yet managed to keep her twenty-two inch waist. In fact, she always dressed impeccably, a remarkable accomplishment considering her youngest two, an infant and a toddler, were constant companions. The baby sat like a doll in a plastic infant seat propped in Hope's shopping cart, the two-year-old clung to her skirt. "Hi, Cynthia," she greeted me. "I hear you're going to Israel."

"Yes. In September." I tried to match her smile in spite of my weariness.

"You look pooped. It must be a lot of work, all that packing."

"Yes," I agreed.

"What're you doing? Renting out your house 'til you get back?"

"We're selling it. We're not coming back."

"That's what you think," she said with a good-natured grin.

Disconcerted and annoyed by her doubt, I blurted out, "Did you know Jeff's sister and brother-in-law died in a car crash a little over a week ago?"

"Oh yeah, I did hear something about that. Isn't that awful? Who told me?"

"Naomi?"

"I don't think so. Maybe. Anyway, please tell your husband we're very sorry to hear about it."

"Thanks. I will." I considered mentioning that we were taking in our niece but decided not to go into that. I paid for the blintzes and a package of frozen chicken legs that were on sale. "Goodbye, Hope. *Hag same'ach.*"

"Yes, you too. Have a good holiday, and do send our regards to your husband."

Adam was waiting for me when I drove up the driveway. As I parked the car, he called, "Hi, Ma, I'm going to the library. I'll be back at five."

"Wait a minute!" I stuck my keys in my handbag and climbed out. "Don't you want a snack?"

"Nah."

"Here." I held out the bag of frozen food. "Carry this into the house for me. I have something to talk to you about."

Reluctantly, he set his kickstand and took the bag, fidgeting impatiently as I locked the car and unlocked the kitchen door.

"First of all," I said as I put away my purchases, "your father is coming back today."

"He is? Neat! That's great." For the first time in ten days, he smiled. "When's he getting in?"

"We'll pick him up at five. That's why I had to talk to you before you ran off to the library." I paused and looked at Adam. "He's bringing someone with him."

"Yeah? Who?"

"Your cousin. Tamara."

"Yeah? That's neat. I'll take this apple with me to eat on the way. What time should I be home?"

"I don't know." I shrugged at his nonchalance. "Four-ish? We should leave here about four-thirty to allow for traffic."

"Okay. See ya, Mom." He stopped a second at the door, reached into his back pocket, and removed a folded yellow envelope. "I almost forgot. Here's my report card."

"You sure?" my dad asked. "Remember how depressed Mom was when she miscarried?"

I didn't remember. I was barely two at the time. "I don't feel so bad," I said.

"You never get over it," my mother stated. "I still sometimes wonder."

"It's always hard," my father concurred. "Even though you hadn't been planning for it, your body was all geared up and now it has nothing to do. Your hormones and everything."

"Look," I said, "you're supposed to come out here in the spring, aren't you? Let's stick to our original plans."

"Whatever you say, honey. We just want you to know we're here if you need us."

About a week later, as though my father's words had left a post-hypnotic suggestion, I suddenly *did* feel bereft. Maybe it was hormones. I still didn't regret losing the fetus, and I really didn't want to replace it with another. But when the kids returned to school and I returned to work, I felt myself chafing against the dimensions of my life. I grew impatient with the status quo after the couple of months of expecting something new. My world seemed to contract with my shrinking abdomen. The sameness tasted stale. I wanted a change.

A letter came from the Israel Aliyah Center. "Our representative will be in your area at the Volk Jewish Community Center in Tucson on January 17." We had received similar letters before; as always, I threw it out, then went out to the back yard to take down the laundry.

But while I pinched clothespins and caught the falling sheets and undershirts, my mind returned to the form letter. The quality of the duplication was crude—nothing like the beautiful copies I made at work. It must have been run off on a mimeograph, or an antiquated photostat machine. The dates were filled in with a pen. When I brought the clean wash in, I fished the letter out of the garbage to take another look. That it wasn't slick appealed to me. It made me think of Zionist pioneers singing as they reaped wheat grown where there had once been swampland.

My restlessness stirred and settled on this possibility. A move to Israel would tap all the reserves of energy nature had set aside for the procreative process. It was 1984: as the world shuddered superstitiously, waiting to see if George Orwell's fiction would become reality, I imagined God whispering in my ear to come live in the land He promised to Abraham. I saw Him hovering over me, just as I'd pictured my parents in that position, but instead of irritating and enervating me, He imbued me with strength.

It took little effort to rouse Jeff's interest in meeting with the Israeli representative. His parents, in search of distant relatives, or a less alien life than as refugees in New York, went with him to Israel when he was a

I watched as he hopped on his bike and rode off. The report card was typical: C's and B's and a comment that "Adam is a bright, creative boy who could do much better work if he'd pay attention."

He returned just as Ronnie was getting home. "Did ya hear, Ron?" he hollered, his voice echoing under the carport. "Dad's coming home."

"I know," she said in a bored voice. I wondered how she could: I hadn't told her yet, too distracted as I drove her to school in the morning to say anything.

"He's bringing Tamara with him," he mentioned, ignoring her feigned indifference.

"So what?" She walked into the house ahead of him. "Hi, Ma."

"Hi, Ronnie. You have your report card?"

"Do you believe it? They don't trust us to bring them home so they're mailing them. How do you like that for a vote of confidence?"

"It doesn't matter, Ronnie," I consoled her. "Next fall you'll be going to school in Israel."

"Yeah, it doesn't really matter. I don't have to see any of their creepy faces ever again." She dumped her notebook and pen on the kitchen table and peeled a banana. "So where's Tamara going to sleep?"

"I hadn't thought of that," I admitted.

"We could put her on one of the couches in the family room," she suggested.

"I don't know," said Adam, shaking his head. "Maybe she'll roll off and hurt herself."

"You think so?" I asked. "She's five and a half already."

"But she's retarded, Mom," Adam insisted. "She probably has to sleep in a crib. I once saw this thing on TV about a hospital, you know?, and they had little fences around all the beds, even for the grownups."

"Well, we'll just have to see," I said with growing concern. Where would I find a crib? There wasn't enough time before sundown and the onset of Shavuos to go to Sears. "Why don't you two get washed up and we'll head off. Daddy's due in forty-five minutes."

Their plane was delayed. We had a full half hour to wait after arriving at the airport. We passed five minutes in the gift shop and several more playing Geography. Ronnie and I groaned when Adam said "North Dakota." Alaska-Arizona-Argentina-Alabama-Andorra-Austria-Australia-Atlanta-Armenia-Albania. Breaking the chain, I said "Arkansas."

"What does that end with, Mom?" Adam asked. "W?"

"S."

"Oh." He thought. "South Dakota."

The game ended when we ran out of A-places.

I carefully avoided talk of Tamara. With her arrival imminent, there was no point in fretting over speculations of what she'd be like. The fatigue my lack of sleep produced earlier was replaced by a high-strung alertness. When I stopped in the ladies' room to run a comb through my hair, my eyes looked rounder than usual, yet the dark rings beneath them belied their wide-awake openness.

The first thing I noticed when I saw Jeff descending from the plane was that his beard looked longer, the thinning hair around his *kippah* looked shaggier, his shirt wrinkled, his slacks stained. Then he saw me and his lips twitched up. I rushed to him and threw my arms around his neck. I blocked out everything—the people pushing past us, Tamara still clinging to Jeff's hand, Adam jumping up and down, Ronnie turning away in embarrassment and the recognition that she was right this wasn't proper modest-Jewish-wife behavior, the evening heat, our impending plans, everything—just concentrating on the strength of his one unencumbered arm around me, the reassuring pressure of his body against mine, the tangy smell of a man who'd sweated in airplanes for eight hours. When we finally returned to this world and pulled apart, I found that I was weeping. I dabbed at the wetness on my cheeks.

I squatted down to say hello to Tamara. She had changed a lot since the last time we met. She was solid and sturdy on her chubby little legs. She no longer thrust out her tongue, though her lower lip jutted just a little, as if she were on the verge of crying. Was she jealous of sharing Jeff with the rest of us after having him all to herself the previous week? Or did she find my face frightening? I'd forgotten her strikingly deep blue eyes; the color was lost on Kodak film. The folds at their inner corners had become less pronounced with the development of a small but definite bridge to her nose. She was a truly handsome child, in spite of the flatness of her cheeks, in spite of the stigmata of her condition. She didn't look like the kids in *American Baby*, but she was pretty in her own way. I had an impulse to hug her, but the urge was checked by her shyness and my own awkwardness. I simply said, "Hi, Tamara. I'm Aunt Cindy."

"Hi," she said unsmiling, eyeing me.

We walked back along the covered walk to the building and the baggage claim. Tamara soon permitted Adam to take her other hand, a squat, broad-fingered little mitt. Adam accepted her; he took for granted that he should love her because she was his cousin. She accepted him in much the same way. Though I doubt she understood that he was a relative, she seemed to recognize his nonjudgmental and direct openness and responded to it. Ronnie, like me, approached Tamara with more complexity; it would take longer for us to find our way through the maze of our feelings.

In addition to his small bag, Jeff lifted a large suitcase and a carton off the carousel. These contained all of Tamara's clothing and a few of her toys.

"There was so much stuff, Cyn," Jeff told me as he drove us home. The children were playing a nonverbal giggly game in the back seat. "All sorts of educational toys and equipment, like for instance, a little trampoline and a special tricycle with straps to hold the feet on the pedals. And then all sorts of beautiful stuff, like china dolls and music boxes and a set of carved elephants with real ivory tusks. Oh yeah, and an enormous dollhouse. And their piano. If we were staying here, maybe I would have shipped some of the stuff to Tucson, but with our plans, especially with us trying to pare down what we bring overseas, it didn't make sense. Still, it seemed a shame to leave everything."

"What'll happen with it?"

"It'll all be sold in the estate sale and go into her trust fund. I guess we could always replace a lot of the stuff once we get settled."

"Our own children might resent her if she has so many fancy things," I pointed out, feeling a bit resentful myself. I never thought I had to provide my kids with riches—not that I could have even if I wanted to —but now I felt defensive. "To some extent, if Chad and Sheila wanted to raise her to be a little princess, that was their business, but if she's going to live with us, she'll just have to accept our standards."

Jeff laughed at this. "Really, Cindy, Tam could care less. She's the least materialistic person I've ever met."

As if in proof of his statement, Ronnie called my attention to the toys Tamara was systematically removing from the carry-on bag in her lap and distributing between the other two, joining in their boisterous laughter. Adam was holding some barrettes, a doll, and a couple of books; Ronnie had a silver-handled brush, some crayons, and a gold bangle. I eyed the bracelet, fingering my own. "You won't believe it, Mom," said Ronnie. "I just said to her, 'Can I see your bracelet,' and she goes, 'Here, take it,' and gives it to me."

"Put it back on her wrist," I insisted.

"But, Ma, she said I could have it," Ronnie protested. "I'll give her one of mine when we get home." Ronnie had a drawerful of costume jewelry.

"I think you should give it back to her. She's just playing. In fact, give her back all her things now. Both of you," I added.

"Okay," said Adam agreeably. He had no use for the doll, the barrettes, and the baby books.

When we got home, there was little time before we had to light candles and start the holiday. We carried in the luggage and set up, turning on the lights we wanted on for the next two days. I turned the back coil of the stove on low, since cooking was allowed on Shavuos but turning on a fire wasn't. Jeff adjusted the thermostat for the air conditioning. Ronnie and Adam ran off to change their clothing for synagogue.

While we were running around getting ready, our newcomer was forgotten. When we gathered in the dining room for candlelighting, she was missed. "Wait, where's Tam?" Jeff asked abruptly as Ronnie prepared to strike the match.

"I thought she was with the kids," I replied.

"But you told us to go get dressed," Adam whined.

"Never mind who was supposed to be watching her. Let's just find her," Jeff said.

We ran around disorderly, bumping into each other in the hall, each in turn opening the same closet doors and kneeling to peer under the same beds, each calling, "Tamara, Tamara, where are you?" After several fruitless minutes, Ronnie ventured into the kitchen. "Hey, Ma, Dad, come here," she shouted from there. "The door's open."

We assembled quickly and stared. Such a commonplace sight—the door open to the carport—yet it filled me with dread. After an endless instant, Jeff formulated a plan and mobilized us. He would take the car, Adam was to check the alleys on his bicycle, Ronnie was to run east, I west down our street. We all scurried off.

I trotted along, scanning our neighbors' yards. Soon I reached the corner. Though not a main street, Plumer was busier than most streets in our neighborhood. At first I surmised that it would intimidate her, that she wouldn't cross it, but when I didn't see her to my right or my left, I remembered that she came from New York, where she must have crossed many more impressive avenues than this two-lane byway. Ninth Street didn't run directly across Plumer, but broke and picked up a few yards to the south. Or maybe she turned right and ran down the alley, or up to Eighth Street. Maybe she turned left and left again and was heading east on Tenth. I wished I could split myself in pieces to explore all the possibilities.

I got to the northwest corner of Ninth and Plumer and looked down into the sunset trying to see the silhouette of a small child. How fast was she? How far could she get? Running desperately, I tried to calculate how many minutes we had left before it would be too dark to see. My panting fanned my imagination, blowing up pathetic pictures of Tamara curled up all night behind a garbage pail in an alley, or trotting oblivious before the on-coming headlights of a car, or being snatched up by an evil man with a warped character. To quell my alarm, I began to pray, making bargains with God, promising to be more attentive and more responsible if only He would give me another chance with Tamara. My eyes swept to the right and to the left, searching.

A horn tooted. I turned to see our car. Jeff pulled up to the curb and reached over to unlock the passenger door.

Totally winded, I gasped, "Did you find her?"

"Not yet. Hop in. She couldn't have got this far."

The sun dipped below the horizon. Long shadows reached back to the east. As though they pointed the direction, Jeff made a U-turn and headed back to the house.

Out of breath and miserable, I sat silently beside Jeff. As we neared our driveway, we saw Adam turn in. Before Jeff could shut off the engine, I sprang out of the car, shouting, "Any luck?" to Adam, then fumbled to open the kitchen door. "Where's Ronnie?"

"I don't know. I didn't see her."

I raced into the house, to the phone, and called 911. "I'd like to report a missing child. She's five but short, has dark, straight hair, dark blue eyes—what was she wearing?" I asked Jeff as he came in.

"I don't know. A dress, I think."

"You're a lot of help," I snapped at him. "Her name is Tamara," I told the woman at the other end of the line. I hesitated to say she was retarded. It bothered me to think of a statistician working out how much more the handicapped cost the taxpayer based on extra police searches. I also worried the woman might weigh with less importance Tamara's disappearance: "Oh," I imagined her saying, "just a dim-witted kid. No point knocking yourself out about it." On the other hand, I realized this information might be vital to her discovery. I said, "She's five but she looks and behaves a bit younger."

After hanging up, I went into the living room and took down the photo album. The police would want to see her picture. I pulled out the one Sheila had sent to us in April—a pretty little child standing between her two handsome parents. I started crying.

Jeff had followed me into the room. "Stop it, Cyn," he said. "She'll show up. She couldn't just evaporate into thin air."

I opened my mouth to share my fears with him, but through the window I saw Ronnie run up. "I found her," she was screaming.

Jeff threw open the front door in time to see Adam leading the little girl up the sidewalk toward us. "You see, I told you," he said to me.

I pushed past him through the door and down our front walk, then leaned over to look Tamara in the eye. She didn't look upset, frightened, remorseful. She didn't look relieved either. "Hi," she said, smiling. She recognized me.

"Where have you been, Tamara?" I felt my tears drying in the cooling twilight.

"Go for a walk," she explained. She had a deep voice for such a small person.

"I found her walking down Wilson. She was practically at Sixth Street," Ronnie embellished.

My eyes still linked with Tamara's, I stated, "You were a very, very bad girl to go out by yourself. You must never do that again." She stared back at me, her face revealing no particular expression, except perhaps curiosity. "Do you understand, Tamara? You are not to leave the house by yourself. That was a very bad thing to do. You scared all of us terribly." My voice caught around a lump in my throat.

Her eyes shifted, settling on my hand. "Mommy," she said, and I realized I still held the photograph. I showed it to her. "Mommy, Daddy, and me, Tamara," she chirped as she pointed to the people in the picture. She seemed very pleased, grinning broadly, showing a mouthful of tiny, crooked teeth. Then she looked at me sharply. "I want my mommy," she demanded. Her lower lip jutted, her chin began to tremble.

"Oh, Tamara." My own mouth stretched into a contorted smile as I tried not to cry. "Your mommy is dead," I said softly. Dead. Did that word mean anything to her? I reached my arm out to her, wrapped it around her narrow shoulders, and drew her to me. Her fine hair tickled my cheek. "I'll be your mommy," I whispered too quietly for anyone to hear.

# Eight

The policeman arrived about ten minutes later. Even though we had already located her, he asked us questions for his report. It soon came out that we weren't her parents, and he began looking at us suspiciously. He asked Tamara who we were, but she just stared at him through dark eyes.

The officer glanced around the house. Surely he thought it strange we didn't turn on the lights in the dusk-dark living room. Seeking illumination, he walked into the dining room, and it didn't take him long before he spotted the box of matches lying open by the candles on the side table. "You shouldn't leave those around," he commented.

"Yeah, well, we were just about to light candles when we noticed she was gone," Jeff said, but he took no steps to remove the potential danger. Whereas before it was okay to drive and telephone because "saving a life" overrode the observances of the holiday, now that Tamara was safely home, the prohibitions were once again in force. To touch kindling after Yontif began would be a violation.

Obviously annoyed with our apparent indifference, the officer picked up the box, closed it, and carried it into the kitchen. There he spotted the rear burner glowing on the range. He immediately strode over to it and shut it off, once again warning us of the dangers of leaving an untended fire.

"It's our holiday, officer," I tried to explain. "We aren't allowed to turn appliances on or off until the end of Shavuos." I hoped he'd understand and turn on the stove again so we could cook during the next forty-eight hours.

Of course it was a mistake to go into our Orthodox practices with him: under the best of circumstances, people had difficulty understanding why we couldn't just flick a switch or turn a knob.

Jeff pointed to the box of defrosted blintzes and my frying skillet on the counter and said, "We were just about to cook dinner when we realized Tamara was missing. We dropped everything and ran to look for her." This explanation wasn't true: we hadn't planned to make dinner until after we returned from synagogue, but to the non-Jew, perhaps it sounded more plausible. Jeff added, "We were all very busy. I guess that's how she slipped out without anyone noticing."

The officer seemed to understand about the frenetic quality of evening domestic activity. But though he no longer suspected gross negligence on our part, he didn't comprehend our need to leave the stove on. The burner remained unlit. I mentally sorted through the refrigerator, trying to think what to serve for dinner instead of the uncooked blintzes.

Just as it looked like the policeman would finally go, we hit another obstacle: he asked Jeff to sign his report.

"Oh." Jeff eyed the filled-out form. "I'm really sorry, sir, but I can't. You see, we don't write on our holiday."

"You can sign it for us," I quickly added.

The man scowled and shook his head. At the door, he eyed the "For Sale" sign and asked us, "Where are you folks headed for?"

Before Jeff could think of a way to evade the question, Adam piped up with, "We're moving to Israel."

"That so? You planning on taking her with you?"

"We don't know yet," Jeff replied.

"That's right, you don't know," he agreed portentiously.

It was too late to go to services. Jeff was upset: it was the first time he missed saying *kaddish* for Sheila.

Though the events of the previous hour completely removed my appetite, the kids were famished. As I fixed them cheese sandwiches, Jeff worried. "You know, Cyn, those CPS people are sometimes a little over-eager to take a kid away. Remember that article you showed me?"

Granted, it was in a sensational tract full of paranoic speculations about insidious government plots, but after reading of the Child Protection Services taking children away from loving parents based on the reports of spiteful neighbors, I took great pains not to scold my children in public lest my actions be construed as child-abuse.

"You think the CPS will pay us a visit, Cyn?"

"I don't know."

"Why d'ya have to call the police? We found her, didn't we?"

"I know. I should've waited. I just got scared with it getting dark outside and not knowing where she could be."

"We better be really careful with her. Don't let her out of your sight."

Tamara liked the cheese sandwiches. If Shavuos was supposed to be a feast day, she certainly made the most of muenster and mustard on rye. As she finished her dessert—the ice cream I'd been unable to eat the night before—she began to yawn.

"I bet she's really tired," Jeff noted. "I know I am."

"It's three hours later in New York," I remembered. "Do you have enough strength to help me make up the couch in the family room? Ronnie thought Tamara could sleep in there."

"Uh-uh. What if she wakes up in the middle of the night and decides to take another walk?"

"So what do you suggest, Jeff? Where should we put her?"

"She's just a little thing. Why can't we stick her in with one of the kids for the night?"

"In my bed? With me? No way!" Ronnie interjected.

"Something smells," Adam added.

Tamara wasn't toilet trained. With all the excitement, she hadn't been changed since their stopover in St. Louis. Jeff walked her to the bathroom, then got a clean disposable diaper from her suitcase, which was still standing unpacked in the hall. She was cooperative as he lay her down on a towel spread across the tile floor and ripped open the tapes of the sodden Pamper.

"Where did she sleep at your parents' house?" I asked from the doorway.

"I put a cushion from the couch on the floor."

"How about the sleeping bag? I can spread it out on the floor in our room," I offered.

"Good." He taped the fresh diaper closed. "You wanna hand me her pj's?"

I fumbled around in her bag in the dim hall looking for something I'd never seen in the jumble of clothes. "It's warm," I said, giving up. "She can sleep in her undershirt."

"What undershirt?" He pulled her dress over her head to reveal a bare chest. A red scar ran just left of the sternum, a souvenir from her heart surgery.

I went into Adam's bedroom and found a T-shirt in his drawer. Bringing it into the bathroom light, we saw it was his UA one with a picture of the mascot wildcat on it. "Tiger," Tamara identified the big cat, quite pleased to be wearing such decorative apparel. I slipped it over her head and it fell to below her knees. She pulled out the front and looked down to admire the ferocious beast.

The tradition on Shavuos was to stay up all night studying Torah, but Jeff and I barely stayed awake long enough to tuck in each of the children. We were awakened during the night by Tamara. She slipped in under the covers between Jeff and me. In keeping with our monthly periods of separation, our bed was actually made up of two twin-size mattresses pushed up against each other, and she started out lying right on the crack. Curled into a fetal position, thumb in mouth, she poked her knees and elbows into my side. During the night, I edged away and she edged closer; until I had to lie on my side to fit on the sliver of mattress remaining to me. She rolled over and cuddled her backside into my belly, and we slept quite peacefully that way until the morning.

The next day we went to synagogue. It being a new experience for Tamara, she spent a lot of time trotting around exploring the place. She especially liked climbing up and down the two steps to the central *bimah* and pulling on the men's prayer shawls.

Some men gave her dirty looks and Jeff intervened. But just as he got her to sit down on the seat next to him, the old man behind them tapped her teasingly on the head. She turned and kneeled to watch him as he dangled his shawl fringes in front of her. She reached out for them. He smiled encouragingly. When she succeeded in grabbing a handful of the strings, he yanked them away and scowled at her.

Then there was the man who beckoned her with a crooked finger and offered her a candy. After sucking it awhile, she grew tired of it and put it down on a seat, returning to the man to get another. When another man sat down on the sticky sucker, he complained to Jeff.

I didn't know quite how to respond when my handful of neighbors in the women's section offered words of praise or criticism. "You should make her sit here with you." "She's so cute!" "Children don't belong in the synagogue. It's too hard for them to sit still." "It's good to bring them when they're young." "Why don't you take her out to the back where she can play?" "Let her be. Nobody minds her noise."

I agreed with each one of them in turn but resented anyone telling me what to do. I had even more trouble dealing with their curiosity. Each woman wanted to know who she was, how long she was staying with us, and why she didn't resemble us, though no one was forward enough to ask the last question outright.

I overheard Mrs. Miller whispering loudly to hard-of-hearing Mrs. Weissman. She speculated that Tamara had a Japanese father. That would explain the short stature, the darker skin, the slant of the eyes, the straight, dark hair. When she saw me glaring at her, Mrs. Miller smiled at me and added, "A beautiful child, isn't she."

Halfway through services, I took Tamara out for a walk. Three blocks away was Second Street School. Lots of little kids ran around the yard. Several, only wearing their underpants, sat in a mud puddle, as pink and contented as a litter of piglets. I held Tamara's hand tightly: I sensed her eagerness to join them. Other children were taking turns watering a vegetable garden, with an occasional accidental spray in the direction of classmates. A third group, dressed in man-sized T-shirts, painted the brick wall of the schoolhouse in vivid colors. The school was still the free-wheeling place I remembered.

A young woman approached us. Reminiscent of a flower child of the '60's, she was dressed in a flowing batiked garment and Birkenstock sandals. "Hi. Can I help you?"

"Yes. My name is Cindy Roth. My son Adam went here a few years ago."

She nodded, waiting for me to continue.

I shouldn't have been making arrangements on Yontif, but I was there already and anxious to find a program for Tamara. "This is our niece. She's staying with us for the summer, and I was wondering if she could come here."

"Sure. No problem." She leaned over to smile at Tamara. "Hi. My name is Chelsea. Who are you?"

Tamara jammed her thumb in her mouth and stared at the tiny silver bells hanging by a piece of yarn around the woman's neck.

"Tamara, tell her your name," I coaxed.

Chelsea straightened and said, "Why don't we go into the office so I can get you an application and the medical forms."

Could it be that simple? Sheila had written us long, angry letters describing the difficulties she had convincing preschools to accept Tamara. In the past year, Tamara had been relegated to a special kindergarten class in the public school. Fearing a misunderstanding, I said, "Uh, you know she has Down syndrome."

Chelsea nodded, apparently unconcerned.

"It's still okay?"

"Oh, sure. We have no problem with that."

"She isn't toilet trained yet," I confided.

"That's all right," she said, winking at Tamara. "Maybe when she sees our little toilets, she'll want to use them."

Tamara smiled back around her thumb.

We went to a cluttered cubicle in the building to get the forms. Because of the holiday, I couldn't fill out the application nor pay a month's tuition, but Chelsea said I could bring everything Tamara's first day at the school.

"Then it's all right if I bring her here the day after tomorrow on my way to work?"

"Sure. There's only one thing."

Oh no, I thought, here it comes.

"Well, it's really up to you," the woman said, "but maybe she'd be happier in more casual clothing. I mean, it doesn't matter to us, but we can't guarantee she'll be going home as clean as you brought her."

I looked down. We were dressed for synagogue. Tamara's pale blue dress was laden with frills and lace. I laughed.

▲   ▲   ▲

The laugh was on me, though, when later that day I sorted through Tamara's clothing and couldn't find a single T-shirt or pair of sloppy shorts. Oh well, I decided, let her get the fancy stuff dirty.

It was a relief knowing Tamara had someplace to go each morning. Both Ronnie and Adam were signed up for Sports-O-Rama at the University. I could go to work and Jeff could spend the summer playing in his lab if he wanted.

▲   ▲   ▲

The next many days were a period of adjustment for us as a family. In one sense, it was easier having Tamara with us than a temporary visitor or a child whose parents might object to our methods. She ate what and when we ate, she went where we took her. We didn't feel inhibited by her: at home, we continued to observe only the most casual modesty and in general ran the household in our usual informal, haphazard fashion. I never felt embarrassed to wipe her with a towel that already had dirty fingerprints on it; I never apologized to her for serving leftovers.

On the other hand, unlike a guest, she had no departure date. As a newcomer, we often treated her too politely. We tended to look the other way when she went through our things or rearranged the bookshelves. "It's okay," Adam would say as she pulled open all his drawers in search of the wildcat T-shirt. We averted our eyes at the table as she mushed her fingers through her food. We allowed her to establish permanent sleeping quarters in the middle of our bed. (Jeff and I were forced to rendezvous in the family room.) We were apt to say yes to more requests than could feasibly be indulged on a regular basis. There were too many trips to Himmel Park, too many pushes on the swing, too many hours in the wading pool while I sat in the hot afternoon sun worrying about all the things I still had to do to prepare for our move.

Quite naturally, she liked having life revolve around her. On Sunday, she staged a sit-down strike when we felt we'd spent enough time standing in front of the Atari games in Safeway. Her protest was rewarded by Jeff's lifting her and carrying her out, her squeals of delight warning us she was sure to sit down again the next time.

Also, though we were less likely to admit this, we were prone to indulge her out of pity. Rare were the moments I looked at her without thinking, "Poor little retarded orphan." When Ronnie said "Mom," Tamara looked around for a face that wasn't there; when Adam called, "Daddy's home!" she wept to find Jeff at the door instead of Chad.

Just the same, all the time and attention we initially lavished on her was not ill spent. Our pampering must have been some comfort to her. Also, I grew to know her, to feel comfortable being around her. If we were too polite to discipline her properly, she too was polite, remembering to say "please" and "thank you" more consistently than any of the rest of us. I liked her cheerfulness, her readiness to be easily pleased. Her open, guileless approach to life was a refreshing change from Ronnie's ennui and Adam's dreaminess. Little things delighted her: ants crawling on her leg when she sat in the park, a squirt from the hose at Second Street School, the discovery that Big Bird was on our TV set too.

I grew fond of her, the way she nestled into my lap for a bedtime story, the way her stubby hands gently stroked the hair on my arm, the way she giggled irresistibly when I tickled her, the way she called me "Mommy-Cindy" because "aunt" didn't appeal to her. I still had times when I focused on her differentness—the flatness of the back of her head, her somewhat awkward gait, her primitive speech, her low, guttural voice —and I drew back, repulsed by her failure to be normal. I'd compare her to Ronnie, stretching out into a gawky adolescent, and I'd secretly prefer Ronnie's funny-looking face to Tamara's pretty but alien one.

Ronnie started taking over with Tamara. She finally had the little sister she suddenly longed for after my miscarriage. But Tamara was better than any infant I could have produced because she was both more capable and more patient, a willing doll anxious to comply with the tedium of Ronnie's ministrations. Each evening after dinner, Ronnie liked to bathe her, then practice making French braids in her damp, wispy hair, bribing Tamara to sit still by letting the little girl push the buttons on her pocket calculator. Fascinated by all the delicate dresses of expensive fabrics, with smocking, embroidery, and lace inserts, Ronnie coaxed Tamara into allowing frequent clothing changes. On Tamara's first Shabbas with us, she tried on six different dresses.

Tamara spent her afternoons in the wading pool at Himmel Park. I couldn't encourage Ronnie to sit there in my stead; she was still too young to hanker after the lifeguards. Yet there was something peaceful about those afternoons by the pool, little oases in an otherwise hectic time of packing and preparations. I sat there wearing a giant straw hat (which the occasional gust would swoop off my head and deposit in the chlorinated water), my skirt pulled above my knees and my bare feet planted in the tepid bath. I'd stare at the dancing patterns of sunlight on the rippling surface and become mesmerized, a feeling of tranquility descending over me in spite of the shrieks and splashes of the score of tots around me. Tamara tended not to mix with her peers, instead sitting near my feet and amusing herself with quiet play, saying, "Look, Mommy-Cindy," as she whooshed the water through her chubby fingers, as she tried in vain to catch the elusive reflections.

As the daylight hours decreased, so too did the number of days before our flight. It became apparent we were stuck with Tamara and Tamara was stuck with us. We applied to legally adopt her and set out to get another discount plane ticket to Israel. Having previously made trips overseas, she already had a passport. The idea of bringing Tamara to *Eretz Yisroel* appealed to my romanticism. I nurtured the thought that in God's eyes, she was as Jewish as any other Jew.

In early August, a letter arrived festooned with colorful stamps on a crinkly thin blue airmail envelope. The return address was Bangalore. The Chadripadhivan family offered to take Tamara if we felt the present arrangement was inconvenient.

"Well?" Jeff asked me after reading the letter.

Here was the out I had prayed for two months earlier. Yet I felt let down instead of elated. "I guess I've grown accustomed to the inconvenience," I admitted. The truth was I might have relinquished her if I felt

I could still see her often, get a hug every now and then, watch her develop. But Bangalore might as well have been the moon. I didn't foresee ever going there, especially after we got to Israel, where we'd be closer but our budget would be too tight to allow for frivolous tours of Asia. We dispatched a cordial letter of refusal to India and completed the adoption process.

In our last weeks in Tucson, I distanced myself from our life in the States. I regarded politics and local news as a visitor, uninvolved. The fights in synagogue between Cantor Schneider and Mr. Liebowitz no longer concerned me. Neighborhood complaints of University encroachment didn't affect me. Even the heat didn't bother me because I viewed it as only a temporary discomfort. I was in Tucson for only a brief period. If only I could maintain this attitude throughout life, always view myself as a temporary resident, a tourist, a short-term visitor in this world, realize the futility of getting aggravated by petty annoyances, power plays, and the misdeeds of my fellow tourists!

I mentioned our plans to a frequent customer at the Kopy Kat. She reached her arms across the counter to hug me. "Oh, I love you," she said. "In our church back home in Mexico we believe that when all the Jewish people have returned to Israel, the Messiah will come back. I wish you the best of luck."

The last days passed quickly. We sent out a large check for one month's rent and two months' security to hold the apartment Ed Zlotnick found us close to the Jerusalem College of Technology. We closed the deal on our house. All our books were placed in cartons and hauled off to the post office with the hopes they'd be delivered to the apartment in Jerusalem. I quit my job and spent my mornings packing a final time the fifteen suitcases we were entitled to take on our El Al flight. Everything that didn't fit was placed in our carport for a yard sale one Sunday. We sold all our appliances, our furniture, our car. (I tried to sell the ugly afghan my mother-in-law made, but Ronnie caught me at it and stuffed it into an already engorged suitcase.) What we couldn't sell was picked up by the Beacon Foundation for their thrift shop. There were farewell parties, and a *kiddush* in our honor after services on our last Saturday.

We woke an hour before dawn on Monday, September 3, 1984. (This happened to be Labor Day—while our patriotic neighbors flew their flags, we were flying away, expatriating ourselves.) With all our lamps disposed of, we had to dress by the overhead lights in bathrooms and kitchen. We stuffed our sheets and pajamas into the last open suitcase, locked the door to our empty house, and climbed into the Stagecoach airport limousine as the driver tried to stack all our luggage inside and on top.

Feeling pangs and qualms and anticipation, we rode down the dark streets of Tucson. Tamara was the most awake of us, turning her head right and left to look out the windows. Then she noticed me and said excitedly, "Go on airplane, Mommy!"

I was groggy and nervous and thinking of a dozen other things, but I caught the significance of my new name.

# Nine

True to form, we got to the airport an hour early. It was nighttime deserted. All but one of the ticket counters were closed. The lone agent took our bulging suitcases with a smile and a groan and wished us a good trip. I wondered if he understood that he was launching us on an act of disloyalty to the United States, that our one-way tickets meant we had no intention of returning to his, to *our* native land.

We found seats in the empty terminal and ate some of the odds and ends I had pulled out of the refrigerator before leaving our house for the last time. The children were unusually quiet. Adam and Tamara amused themselves by ripping open cigarette butts they found in ashtrays and sprinkling the last bits of shredded tobacco on the floor. Ronnie picked at a piece of masking tape on her carry-on bag. Jeff checked the tickets and our passports yet another time.

The flight to L.A. via a domestic airline was short and painless. We made our way to El Al in the International Terminal and sat for another couple of hours. During that time, a young woman asked me to come with her. She was wearing a short, tight skirt, a plastic laminated ID with her photo clipped to her shirt pocket, and carrying a walkie-talkie with a rubber antenna. Escorting me behind the ticket counter, through a locked door with a sign that said "Authorized Personnel Only," through several narrow corridors (stopping occasionally so she could chat in Hebrew with other El Al employees), and down a flight of stairs, she ultimately brought me into a large, hot, exhaust-filled garage. This was the result of our admitting when we checked in that we had not had our luggage within sight at all times.

I was to open each of our fifteen giant suitcases and cartons to check that nothing explosive had been slipped into any of them. When I complained to the El Al woman about the magnitude of the task, she shrugged and said, "I am not going up in the airplane so why should it concern me? But for you, yes, you should be concerned. I should think you should want to make sure that it is safe."

Amid a huge heap of bags, I found those which contained virtually all our worldly possessions. As baggage trolleys and trucks beeped me to get out of the way, I dripped sweat and heaved suitcases, unclasped and unzipped each of the crammed bags, buried my hands up to my elbows in clothing, linen, framed pictures wrapped in towels, plastic bags filled with spools of thread or bottles of shampoo or bobby pins, my fingers searching for something unknown. Finding no unfamiliar object, I stuffed everything back in and struggled to yank the zipper closed again, cursing silently as I bruised my shins, ripped my fingernails, soiled the dress I had to wear until we reached Jerusalem.

The woman stood not far from me, eyeing impassively the jumble of things we had deemed worthy of taking with us into our new life, marking each piece as I finished with it.

Through all this strenuous search, I also had to deal with my pocketbook, which kept slipping down off my shoulder until I placed it on the floor between my feet. With my bracelet buried inside, I was ever conscious of it, regardless of how unlikely that it would get snatched in this security garage.

The cartons with our dishes and pots were taped shut and there was no sign of tampering, but my security officer was a thorough woman.

"So what does it matter to me?" she repeated. "But it should matter to you."

"How will I tape them back closed?"

She shrugged.

I reopened the suitcase where I'd felt a roll of tape and scissors. We both heard the ticking.

"Hah! What is this?" She pulled me away, at the same time talking into her radio.

"It's just our alarm clock," I tried to explain. We'd parted with all our appliances, including the clock that had been on our night table for years, knowing none of our electrical goods would work on Israeli current. The wind-up ticker dated back to my adolescence. One of those sentimental artifacts that had spent its entire time in Tucson in a box up on a closet shelf.

We waited near the door to the staircase, several feet from the pile of our suitcases. Two men arrived, dressed in protective gear, and she pointed them to the location of the ticking with the rubber antenna of her transmitter. They approached cautiously. One called out something in Hebrew to her, she shouted back over the noise in the echoing garage. Finally, they removed the offensive item from the mess they'd made of the bag's contents. They carefully peeled away the swaddling of pajamas Jeff had worn the previous night. After examining the clock, they tossed it back into the bag and walked away. As they passed us on their way to the stairs, they stopped to talk a minute to my companion. She grinned, then laughed, so perhaps not all they said was official.

I returned to the suitcase and shoved everything back in. I cut open, searched, and retaped the cartons. The security woman marked all our luggage and I was permitted to go upstairs.

▲    ▲    ▲

Finally our flight was called, and we were subjected to further security checks. We were shoved by people rushing to get ahead of us in line, as though the jumbo jet would take off before all of the hundreds of passengers had boarded. People complained angrily as we accidentally bumped them with our heavy, swollen carry-on bags.

Again for security reasons, our plane was parked out on a remote airstrip. El Al officials herded us into what they called tenders, special "space age" buses that transported crammed humanity to the jet. "Like the cattle cars," Jeff muttered, the comparison with his parents' ordeal at the hands of the Nazis adding to my agitation. The few seats in the bus were all taken by the time we squeezed in. Barely able to keep his own balance, let alone protect Tamara from getting trampled by the passengers standing against her, Jeff thrust her into the lap of a stranger who had claimed one of the seats. The woman looked less than pleased, but she was Israeli, with a reputation for loving children to maintain. She forced her bright red lips into a smile and produced nonsense syllables (or was she speaking Hebrew?) and jostled Tamara aggressively on her knees. Tamara responded by arching her back away from the woman's cushioning bosom and chomping on her thumb.

Every seat in the 747 was taken, but few people sat. The aisles were crowded with standing passengers, each visiting with a long-lost or new-found friend. Working our way through this confusion, we found our seats—three together, two right behind—and settled in. A stewardess, in search of a way to fit even more people on the jet, asked me to hold Tamara on my lap and relinquish her vacated seat. But the thought of twenty hours in this cramped position was unbearable. Jeff produced the ticket to prove we were entitled to the fifth seat. Well after the scheduled time of departure, the overladen plane took off.

Tedium was punctuated by stopovers in Chicago and Amsterdam. We didn't bother to get off the plane since passengers were required to remain in isolated rooms, sealed off from possible attempts to breach security. Meals arrived at strange hours, but who knew what time it was as we crossed ten time zones?

At 2:00 a.m. by my watch, I plugged in my complimentary earphones to watch the movie *Educating Rita*. I could only make out half the dialogue due to the accents and the poor quality of the headset. Michael Caine smiling drunkenly in the British Isles added to my total disorientation.

In the seat next to me, Tamara was curled into a ball, sound asleep. Adam was staring out the plastic window at a black sky. I twisted around to see Jeff and Ronnie sleeping, awkwardly leaning against each other in the seats behind me. I couldn't get comfortable. I couldn't doze off for more than a couple of minutes before a spasm in my neck or a disturbance in the aisle woke me again. I passed the time eating and watching the nonsense on the screen: with the movie now over, some mediocre Israeli pop singers dressed in shiny costumes made a big show of posturing with their microphones while Disco dancers shimmied around them.

To me, conversation in an airplane was difficult, the white noise of the hissing air system and the popping of my ears from unequalized pressure all but deafening me. But our fellow passengers seemed unaffected. They continued to block the aisles, their mouths in perpetual motion. It was almost impossible to make my way to the lavatories, and then there was a line with a fifteen-minute wait. When my turn finally came, the cubicle was littered with sodden towels, and all that was left of the toilet paper was the cardboard tube. Luckily there were still some facial tissues I could use. Later, when Tamara needed changing, I decided against taking her to the toilets, instead performing the maneuver in the narrow seat. I fretted over our dwindling supply of clean diapers.

It was just before sunset on Tuesday, September 4, and I was exhausted. Over the public address system came an announcement, first in Hebrew, then in English, that we were about to make our final descent. This was followed by recorded Israeli folksongs. My fatigue and indifference disappeared. "Havenu Shalom Aleichem" became the sweetest song when, as I looked across my children, the wing dipped, revealing the sun-dazzled edge of the Mediterranean and the lush green of the fertile plain. When the Israeli national anthem played, a hard lump formed in my throat and I had to blink back the tears. I was a Jew returning to my homeland after a two-thousand-year exile. My allegiance was with Israel now. "Hatikva" was my song, my anthem. *Hatikva*, meaning "the hope," became emblematic of my dream about to be realized. All our efforts of the past months culminated in this happy reward: to come to the Jewish homeland, to finally belong. My weariness vanished along with my headache, the cramp in my calves, the crink in my neck. All at once, I was young again, young and fresh and grateful beyond reason to be landing in my country at last.

We spent a long time waiting to be processed in an upstairs suite of rooms in the air terminal. There were a few others from our flight: a young, single woman whose mother lived on a kibbutz, an older man coming to Israel with his pension, others more nondescript. No one was particularly friendly. The hour grew late; still no Israeli official arrived to complete our paperwork. A silent rivalry developed as to who had rights to be served first.

A sluggish, stout woman, holding some sort of mop, wearing a blue dress the shape and material of a lab coat and what resembled bedroom slippers on her stockinged feet, shuffled over to the children and offered them small bags containing a few candies. She then escorted the children into a small office which incongruously contained a television. She turned it on. Adam and Tamara sat on the floor, Ronnie in the one chair, and watched the news, mesmerized and uncomprehending. I stood at the door a minute, making sure they were okay. Israeli news looked a lot like a stagier, less polished version of American news, but maybe it was the lack of communication to add import to his facial expressions which made the emotive commentator appear so silly to me.

Back out in the larger reception area, the blue-clad woman set out a coffee urn and a tray of small, unappetizing cookies. She made no gesture to indicate these refreshments were meant for us, so no one touched them but the woman with the Israeli mother. I nodded at the worker as she pushed her mop along the smooth floor and she responded with a gap-toothed grin.

Eventually, a bureaucrat arrived, glanced at the children (who had abandoned the TV for the cookies), and beckoned us into his office first. We beamed, the others glowered.

The woman with the Israeli mother tried to intercept, spewing Hebrew at the slouching official.

He was a little man, skinny with a sunken chest and wrinkled, tanned face. He wore a colored sports shirt open at the collar. As he listened to her, he pulled a loose cigarette from his chest pocket and lit it, then shook his head no as he shook out the match. "Please," he said to us, indicating chairs for us to sit in. The other woman said something else, he nodded, and she left.

While sucking on his cigarette, he unfolded and examined our documents. I felt like a fool as I smiled at him: I had no idea what the Hebrew said. For all I knew, he might have read, "Cynthia Roth is a supercilious character, but since she's Jewish, we have no choice but to let her in." I thought of a German woman I used to see in New York, the agreeable grin forever fixed on her face, the stupid nodding as children teased her and used obscene language. Now I was an ignorant immigrant.

He studied Tamara. "This is not your child?" he asked. He found her name on the passport. "Ha-dra-pa—this name is different, as is her complexion and features."

"No, she's our daughter," Jeff stated. "We adopted her last month." He showed him the papers.

"Ah." The man inhaled on his cigarette as he looked these over. "But she is not Jewish," he concluded.

"Yes, she is. Her mother was my sister." Jeff took out a letter he had asked Rabbi Danziger to write for us listing each of us and declaring his assurances of our Jewish lineage. Then Jeff offered him the death certificates, but the man grew impatient and waved these documents away.

Balancing his cigarette on the edge of his desk, he took up a pen, asking us again for our names, ages, destination. He scribbled our replies down on a scrap of paper, then took another drag before typing his information into a word processor. We experienced a modern-day Ellis

Island: in modern Hebrew there is no "th" sound, so we became what was pronounced "Rott," said with a throaty "r." I became "Sintia." Jeff reverted to his Hebrew name of Yosef; Adam had the emphasis shifted to the second syllable. Rhonda and Tamara came out sounding almost the same in the new alphabet, with the exception of the guttural "r's."

We were entitled to a free trip to our apartment, compliments of the Absorption Ministry. A muscular young man accompanied us downstairs and helped us locate our belongings. He placed the luggage on three carts, then pushed two as Jeff teetered behind the third. We walked through customs without the inconvenience of having to open the bags again. There were still people from our flight standing in line to be inspected. Evidently the wait down here equaled our wait upstairs.

Outside the terminal, the night was balmy. Every inch of pavement, and often also the dirt around the palm trees, was filled with people—the newly arrived and those who came to meet them. Even if I were inclined to fall on my face and kiss the blessed earth, it was physically impossible.

A thin little man with a beard and a felt hat emerged out of the masses. "Professor Roth," he called, approaching us. "I am a student at the Jerusalem College of Technology. Professor Litansky asked me to meet you. I'm terribly sorry I have no motor." He spoke with an English accent.

Jeff took a hand off his cart to shake the student's hand. I suffered a moment's embarrassment when I offered my hand also. He wouldn't touch a woman, even in such a casual way. I should have known better.

"How were you able to identify us in this crowd?" Jeff asked.

"In actual fact," the young man admitted with a smile, "you weren't the first family I approached."

"I think we're supposed to get complimentary transportation to Jerusalem," Jeff informed him.

The student talked at length in Hebrew with the large man with our luggage. After a delay, we were directed to an old, beat-up Volkswagen van. The Russian immigrant driver, a short, powerful man in his fifties, struggled to stuff our bags into the back and under our feet. Tamara was forced to sit on my lap, where she soon slumbered. I felt the warm dampness of her soaked diaper seep through the skirt of my wrinkled dress. Ronnie sat atop a jumble of carry-on bags; Adam was pressed against me on the bit of seat that remained after our dish carton was placed next to us. After another short delay, three more bags were shoved into a space already full, and the retiree we had met upstairs joined Jeff in the single front passenger seat. The JCT student, unable to ride with us, handed Jeff the apartment key and promised to meet us there. After securing the doors, the driver climbed into his seat, honked away the people standing in the road, and we were off to Jerusalem.

As bags shifted and pressed into me with the changing velocity of the van, I tried to look out the windshield at the nighttime landscape.

The noise of the engine and the whistling draft from an open window drowned out the conversation emanating from the heads which obstructed my view. I told myself, "This is it. We've made it. We're here," unwilling to admit to myself my disappointment in seeing only asphalt and ordinary arc lights that could have been a highway in any other place. I romanticized the awkwardness of my perch, likening the disregard for safety and comfort to the hazardous journeys the pioneers of the late nineteenth and early twentieth century had made to come to the Land of Milk and Honey.

The van began to slow and strain as we made our ascent to Jerusalem. I caught glimpses of a steep embankment to our right and clusters of lights. As the road veered to the left, I saw the variegated ground cover spell out Hebrew letters. Jeff, his shoulders folded inward like a sleeping bat's, twisted around to call, "That says 'Yerushalayim.'"

Then we were on a bustling, night-lively boulevard. Trees and bushes grew in front of multi-storied, white stone buildings which reflected back the bright streetlights. Small cars and big buses wove from lane to trafficked lane.

Finally I was satisfied that things looked foreign: the city was too crowded and active for Tucson, too small and verdant for Manhattan, too hilly for Brooklyn. I lurched as the road followed the contours of the land; vistas of dark valleys dotted with light flashed beyond the windshield.

After discharging the older man somewhere, we continued to our apartment. We turned off the main boulevard onto an equally busy avenue, then left the hubbub behind for quieter residential streets. At last the driver stopped and the engine was silenced.

Our JCT student was already waiting at the entry to our building, leaving me in awe of the public bus system which delivered him more quickly than our nearly direct transportation.

I woke the children. Our legs, deprived the past hour of proper circulation, collapsed beneath us as we clambered out of the truck. Jeff and the student helped the driver unload the van as I stood stupefied beside the children. The entry was an open, terraced garden which extended under the jut of the building rising above us. It was planted with all sorts of unkempt green things and flowers, and a light drizzle heightened the scents they gave off. The night air was heavy with jasmine. Intoxicating.

The overhead light was on a timer, automatically switching off after half a minute. The children soon located the glowing button that when pressed produced the light. Tamara scrambled up on the ledge of the planter adjacent to the post in order to reach it, then giggled teasingly as she prolonged the intervals of darkness. Adam ran to another button on the wall next to the entry door and confounded her game.

"No, no, no!" she shrieked. "I do it!"

"What's all that noise?" Jeff asked, coming around the van carrying a carton, which he set down by the curb. "Hey, Cyn, can't you do something about it?"

It didn't seem fair that in addition to the luggage, he should also have to deal with the kids. I tried to rouse myself. "Tamara, please be quiet," I said with little effect. "Adam, you're a big boy. Let her push the button."

"Hey, Ad, come here and help us with these carry-ons."

That worked much better. Adam bounded over to his father and around to the back of the van.

Finally, the driver slammed the rear doors shut, climbed into his seat and slammed his door too, then rattled off into the night, leaving behind a peaceful stillness.

"Fortunately, *baruch Hashem*, you have a lift," the student informed us.

"What does that mean?" Adam asked.

"*Baruch Hashem*?" Jeff said. "Even you know that much Hebrew. Literally, 'Bless the Name.' Thank God."

"Oh. Why'd you say that?" he asked the student.

"Well, because we thank Hashem for anything that makes our lives a bit easier. You've heard people say '*baruch Hashem*' when you ask after their health." Adam shook his head. "Haven't you, then? To acknowledge His hand in their good health?"

"We were living in Tucson," Jeff explained. "How many Orthodox Jews do you think there are there?"

"Ah, then they don't say that where you come from? Oh dear, too unfortunate." He seemed sincerely distressed, but then he brightened. "Well then, but they do say it here," he assured us. "You'll finding living here a great improvement."

"And what's a lift?" Adam asked.

The elevator was a joke, though we didn't laugh since the alternative was to carry the fifty-pound suitcases up three flights of stairs. It was the size of a stall shower. It had a mottled glass door that swung open, adding to the impression the contraption belonged somewhere other than a lobby. The student and Jeff took many trips to get our suitcases upstairs. I sat down on the low garden wall.

"Cindy, come on," Jeff called as he held open the glass door. "Don't you want to see the place?"

I walked across the slippery-wet polished stone toward the entry and elevator. "Children," I called. Adam jumped down from the planter ledge he'd been using as a balance beam and skipped to his father. Zombie-like, Ronnie followed him. Tamara continued to kneel by a planter, poking her finger into the rich, moist soil. With a sigh, I went back to pull her away with me.

We squeezed into the space left beside the last two cartons, then rose slowly but smoothly. When we reached our floor, the door remained closed. The motor stopped humming and the light went out.

Panic overtook my fatigue as I contemplated how long we might be trapped in the black box.

After a minute, the student opened the door, reactivating the light and the motor. "Oh, there you are," he said amiably. "I was wondering what became of you."

"The elevator broke down," Adam explained with delight.

"What! No, really, did it? How odd. However, it appears to be in working order now. Oh, I see: you actually thought it'd stopped functioning? Didn't you realize you have to push the door open when you reach your floor?" He returned to his task of sliding suitcases from the landing into the apartment. "Go in," he encouraged me. "It's a really super flat."

We could barely enter with all our bags clogging the hallway. Climbing over them, I went past the kitchen and peeked into three tiny bedrooms and a strange-looking bathroom. A larger room was cluttered with couch, armchair, shelves, a table and chairs, and the majority of our luggage. Beyond the windows I saw a balcony, beyond that, the building across the street and, to the left, the night sky extending to distant city lights.

I made my way back through the hall to the kitchen. The overhead light glared on a tiny refrigerator, a funny little stove on wheels, two deep sinks set in a high counter of stone-hard material.

"Isn't it a super kitchen?" the student enthused. "Look: you have all the appliances. Not all flats are so well equipped."

Each cabinet bore a word written on a strip of tape. "What does this say?" I asked him.

He read the scribbly Hebrew for us: "The ones on this side say *beser* and over here you have *halav.*"

"Meat and dairy," Jeff translated for me.

"There you go, you're all set then. All you have to do is move in." It was nice to know we didn't have to *kasher* the kitchen.

There was a small table hinged to the wall. On it someone had set large, heavy plates laden with salads and hard boiled eggs, fruit and sliced bread. Next to this unexpected feast lay a piece of paper. It was a note from Professor Litansky's wife. "Shalom," we read. "Welcome home."

# Part II.  B'Aretz (In the Land)

# Ten

"Come on, Cyn, get up. We have to enroll the kids in school and register with the police and check into which medical insurance we want. I want to look into getting that subsidy on the rent and there's something we have to do to get our tax credit on the kids. And I won't even mention that we need to go shopping. We could starve."

My body rebelled: fatigue made me nauseous and leaden. "Can't we do all that later?"

"Come on. It's morning already."

The bed felt lumpy; it smelled different. I opened my eyes to the bright daylight filling an unfamiliar, close room. Its slight dimensions were encroached upon by the addition of an entire wall of floor-to-ceiling cupboards. The beige formica doors of the closets latched with the twist of skeleton keys, all jutting from their keyholes. The door to the hall, painted shiny white, contained a pane of patterned glass, and the handle was a long, gracefully curved lever instead of a round knob. I became aware of smells of plants and soap and cleansing agents sweet and fruity and queerly unlike what I was accustomed to. My stomach churned with excitement at how very far we had traveled; it clenched with homesickness over how foreign everything was.

Maybe Jeff felt as peculiar as I did and coped by keeping busy. Perhaps he used his list of errands to distract him, to occupy his thoughts so he couldn't dwell on the unsettling feeling in his gut. Or maybe he was running on adrenaline, rushing to keep up with the accelerated rhythm of his system before gravity and friction slowed him down.

I squeezed sideways around the bed and went to sit uncomfortably on the odd contours of the plastic toilet seat. Another slick white door with glass inset led off the bathroom. I'd failed to notice it during my hasty tour of the apartment the night before. The door opened to another terrace. This struck me as bizarre: the thought of Juliet making her famous soliloquy out beyond the bathroom was ridiculous enough to make me smile, softening the tension in my face. However, I was not in the land of Shakespeare, nor even a land which could claim his works as its second-hand heritage. To further detract from my romantic notion of balconies, this one contained a small washing machine, a plastic bucket, and plastic cord running back and forth across the ceiling. Held by brackets to the outside of the balcony wall were more lines of thin wire. Looking down at the swaying treetops beneath these four parallel clotheslines added to my queasiness.

Before sitting down to the breakfast of leftovers from our supper, I decided to collect and launder the sweaty, soiled clothing we shed the night before. Making my way through the apartment, surveying the sea of opened suitcases, the disarray of the strewn contents, I began mentally compiling my own list. I felt overwhelmed by the things I had to do before I could feel at home in this strange place. Forgetting my original plan, I leaned over and began lifting out piles of clothing. "Ronnie, here, take this into your room."

"Where should I put them?" Unable to locate a hairbrush, she tugged a finger through tangled locks.

"I don't know. Pile everything on your bed for now."

Jeff came out of the kitchen just as I handed Tamara another pile for the girls' room. "What are you doing, Cyn? Come on. Get dressed and eat something so we can get out already."

"But it's such a mess."

"Leave it. We'll unpack later. I just remembered I have to get to the bank and convert some dollars. Also, we only have one diaper left." He disappeared into our bedroom.

I quickly gathered together the balled up socks and discarded underwear and sneaked back to the bathroom terrace to start the laundry. The washing machine was a funny little thing, but so were the appliances in the kitchen. The instructions on it were in another language—French, I guessed, judging from the way it filled my mouth when I tried to pronounce a few words. The inside of the washer looked all wrong: its narrow drum lay on its edge, with a trapdoor to put the clothing in opening in the curved cylindrical wall. I shoved the clothes in, poured in some white stuff from an open blue-and-white box, and turned the dial to number 1. I was reassured by the sound of water running. This was followed by a click, a grumbling as the motor turned the drum, then another click, another swish-swish-swish as the drum again rotated, another click. Jeff called. I made my way to the living room in search of something to put on.

After dressing, on my way to the kitchen, I checked in on the churning machine. It swished merrily one way, then back again, then, with another click, came to a stop. The numbers went up to 8; the dial was at number 3. I opened the lid to take a peek, shut it again, and turned the dial to 4. Nothing happened. Impatient, I turned through 5 and 6. Then I went to eat.

I downed some bread and butter, an egg, leftovers from the night before. Jeff dressed Tamara in the kitchen so he could further enumerate the things he wanted to accomplish. He stopped in the middle of putting on her shirt to jump up and show me the cabinets over the sinks. "Did you see this, Cyn? Isn't this clever?" Inside, instead of shelves, there were plastic dishracks. "You stack your wet dishes in here, they drip directly into the sink, you don't have to take up valuable counter space with messy drying racks which, by the way—remember in New York?—attract roaches, and you just close the door and they're out of sight. Isn't that a great invention?"

I thought the dishwasher was a great invention, but I had to admit that drying racks over the sink were innovative.

Tamara began flailing her arms and grunting under her shirt. Wisps of hair waved above the neck hole. Jeff sat back down and pulled the shirt on.

"What should I do with the bracelet today?" It was getting to be a burden, worrying about it.

"Let's think. You don't want to wear it?"

"Is it safe?"

"In Israel? Oh, yeah. This isn't New York." His voice was muffled when he leaned over to put on Tamara's shoes. "I didn't think you should wear it on the trip because we were in too many crowds, and what with our sleeping on the plane, and then I didn't know whether we had to claim it or anything. I don't know how much I trusted that immigrations guy."

"He was okay. He took us ahead of everyone else."

"That's only because he didn't want the kids running around and whining. Okay, Tam, you're all set." He sat up again.

"I don't know. I think the kids are going to be our greatest asset in Israel. More than the bracelet, more than our U.S. dollars."

"Yeah, I know: Israelis love children. I've heard that. We'll see." Full of nervous energy, he collected the dirty dishes and brought them to the sink. "On second thought, maybe you shouldn't wear the bracelet after all. They'll wonder why they need to give us subsidies if they think we're rich Americans."

"Okay. What should I do with it, you think?"

"I don't know—the bottom of a drawer? The corner of a closet?"

I nodded as I swallowed the last of my milk.

"Good. You're finished. Go hide it and then let's go."

"Should I just keep it in my handbag?"

"Then you have to worry about your bag."

I nodded again and ran to our room. I removed the jewelry from my pocketbook and opened one of the built-in cupboards. Of course, it was empty except for a couple of wire hangers. Above the pole was a shelf, also empty except for a balled tissue and a dead fly. I wrinkled my nose, then rethinking the usefulness of the tissue, placed the bracelet behind it. If anyone broke in and riffled through our stuff, he'd never think to look in such an unpromising place. I could take the skeleton key. No, as the only cupboard without a key, it looked suspicious. I replaced the key, grabbed my bag, and ran into the hall.

"It's put away all right? Good. Let's go."

"Oh, Jeff, just one more thing. Let me just go hang the laundry."

"What!"

"It'll only take a minute."

"Can't you do that later?"

"It'll get all wrinkled." I raced into the bathroom before he could waste more time arguing with me. As I approached the door to the terrace, I was discouraged to hear a click and a swish-swish-swish. The dial was back at number 3. "Ronnie! Adam!" I shouted.

"Where are you, Ma?" Adam called.

I ran back to the hall, where they all converged. "Who's been fooling around with the washing machine?" I asked.

Four pairs of innocent eyes stared back at me. "I don't even know where the washing machine is," Adam pointed out.

Jeff sighed. "What's the problem?"

"Maybe it doesn't shut off automatically," I thought aloud. "Maybe it'll just keep going through its cycle."

"Come on, Cyn," he whined. "It's after eight. Let's go already."

I walked through the bathroom, followed by the other four. The dial was now inexplicably at 7 and whirring. "What is with this thing?"

"Do you know how it works?" Jeff asked.

"I just assumed it worked like a regular washer."

"You can't assume anything," he commented, scratching his beard.

Tamara sat down on the stone tile floor and pulled off her shoe.

"Tell you what," Jeff suggested: "let's just unplug it for now, and we can figure it all out when we get back. Why did you get involved with this now, anyway?"

Just then, the dial rotated to 8 and, with a click, everything came to a stop.

"It's finished." Grinning triumphantly, I opened the lid and poked my hand into the drum. The metal felt hot.

"Don't do that now," Jeff begged.

"Just one or two things. Just my dress so it won't wrinkle." I located a bit of the flowered hem and began tugging it gingerly from the tangled, steaming mass. A coiled rope of fabric emerged, bringing with it an odd pair of socks and Jeff's undershirt. My heart sank. The dress was hopelessly creased. I shook it out and, to my amazement, the buttons flew off, the plastic having cracked from the heat. "Add buttons and a steam iron to the list of things we have to get right away," I said quietly, my eyes burning.

Jeff wrapped his arm around my shoulders. Sniffling and blinking, I turned my back on the discouraging mess. "You're right," I said to Jeff. "This can wait 'til later." I stomped off to the front door, anxious to escape the claustrophobic mayhem of our new domicile. Adam and Ronnie paraded out behind me. Jeff followed as soon as he retied Tamara's shoe and grabbed the envelope containing our documents and funds.

As we waited for the elevator, Tamara discovered the echo in the stone landing. "Eee," she shrieked, then listened. "Eee," she repeated, giggling.

A door squeaked open on a lower landing, then slammed shut. "Muzzle her," Jeff ordered, and Adam slapped his hand over Tamara's mouth before she could let out another squeal.

The elevator came. Ronnie pressed 1. We exited on the first floor but couldn't find the street. "What about these steps?" Adam asked. He ran downstairs, then shouted up, "Hey, you guys, come on down. I found the front door." We filed back into the elevator and pushed the button below the 1. This took us to the ground level.

The neighborhood, situated on a hill a couple of miles southwest of the Old City, was called Bayit Vegan, meaning "house and garden." It was considered a nicer area, though not what one would expect to find in the magazine with the similar name. On either side of the narrow curving road, white apartment buildings rose above bits of cultivated earth. The vegetation was profuse. Overgrown flowers shared space with scraggly weeds and vines. Coming from the Sonoran Desert, the abundance of wet green delighted me. Closer inspection revealed trash between the foliage; still, there was a clean, fresh look about the place. In a deep blue sky, the sun dazzled without glaring: the tall buildings and filter of flora rendered the light more peaceful than Arizona brilliance.

Contradicting the lush beauty, the strong scent of onions prickled my nostrils. The well-organized wives of Bayit Vegan were already preparing the large, midday meal before leaving for their work and morning errands.

A young man dressed in a white shirt, black suit and fedora, a scant beard sprouting from his soft, boyish cheeks, walked along the sidewalk across the serpentine street.

"Hello," I called out.

He stopped but ignored me, instead resting his eyes on Jeff.

"*Efo beit-sefer?*" Jeff asked.

The young man replied in Hebrew.

"*Anglit?*" Jeff tried.

"Yes, a little." The man nodded and waited.

"Can you tell us where the school is?" Jeff asked again.

"Yes, you must to follow along in the same direction as you are at this time walking, perhaps several meters. When you come to the footpath to the right, you proceed up the hill to the Hida. Before the Sfardi shul you find the path; you know where is the Sfardi shul? Never mind, if you miss, you must come instead to the stairs a short distance beyond, they likewise take you up to the Hida. This is better, perhaps: you find the school directly at the top. For the boy, it is beyond. You are better to ask another." Rumbling warned him to glance to his left. A bus came tearing around a blind bend, and he raced to the bus stop to catch it.

We followed the winding street until we found a paved path that went off to the right. "This must be it," Jeff said.

"Maybe we should go to the stairs," I suggested.

"Nah, we may not find them." Jeff turned up the hill.

Jasmine tumbled over the wall separating the path from the building to the left—was this the Sephardic synagogue? As we climbed the path, we looked over the wall into a flower garden: rosebushes, dahlias, and dwarf fruit trees were being groomed by a robust man with brown skin and gray, curly hair. He looked up from his labor and grinned at us, showing blue eyes and a gold tooth.

"Excuse me," Jeff called over the wall. "Are we going in the right direction for the school?"

Still smiling, he shook his head and shrugged.

"*Beit-sefer*," Jeff tried.

He shook his head again.

We continued to climb. The Hida, it turned out, was the name of the street we found ourselves on. Street names in three alphabets— Hebrew, Arabic, and the one I could read—were written on blue tiles embedded about ten feet up on the walls of corner buildings.

I asked directions of a plump woman, her head covered in a kerchief, who was pulling a child out of the backseat of her car. She told us in perfect (American) English, "You go down this way, oh, I don't know, a few hundred feet, maybe, and the school will be on your right. Actually, the entrance is on another little street off the Hida, but I don't know what it's called. Actually, it's not really a street. I have seen cars on it, but it's not meant for traffic. To get to the boys' school, you take that path up to Hapisga and turn left. You know where Hapisga is, don't you? That's the main street. Cross the street and turn left. Down the hill on your right you'll see the boys' school. The entrance is around the corner. You can't miss it."

"How long have you been here?" I asked.

"Seven years. When did you arrive?"

"Last night."

"Oh! Yesterday? That's great. You'll love it here. Don't worry: it's confusing at first, but before you know it, you'll have no trouble getting around."

I shared her smile. "What's this?" I asked, pointing to the large one-story house in front of us.

"This is Gan Sarah. A preschool. She's very good but it's always full. You have to sign them up when they're still in here." She patted her round belly.

"You don't think there's any room for her?" I asked, lifting Tamara's hand in mine.

"I'd be surprised, but it doesn't hurt to ask. Come."

Following the woman and her child up some steps to the door of the school, Tamara and I were introduced to Sarah, an older woman, who, as predicted, told me there were no openings.

We came to a fenced-in schoolyard with empty soft-drink bottles tossed in the tall weeds. A basketball court was paved with cement squares, many cracked or partially missing. "How could you dribble on that?" Jeff commented. As we made our way around a garbage bin, two stray cats leaped out and disappeared in the underbrush. Stone steps led to the front door.

A small man in a beret sat on the ledge by the doorway. A large gun rested in his lap, but otherwise, he looked benign. Smiling at the children, he nodded and pointed up inside the entry.

The stairwell was filled with activity: homely, thin, dark-haired girls clad in plaid skirts and unmatching polyester blouses ran up and down chattering loudly. Childish murals covered the pastel-colored walls. My energy flagging, I paced myself to Tamara as she climbed one uneven step at a time.

On the next floor Jeff had already found the small room that served as the office. The secretary was telling him, "Wait. The headmistress she will come." She directed us to sit on a wooden bench in the narrow corridor.

I glanced at the notices tacked to the bulletin board near me. They were all in Hebrew. I felt humbled by my illiteracy.

The headmistress spoke fluent English, though her accent indicated it wasn't her mother tongue. Everyone, students included, referred to her as "Miriam." She shook her head about Ronnie's lack of Hebrew, suggested we get a tutor for her, then sighed and said, "Well, children learn so much faster than we adults do, no?"

She led us up another flight, then waited panting at the top until Tamara and I caught up. Down the hall was the eighth grade classroom, where I recognized the girls from the staircase. The room was austere, containing none of the educational decorations—posters, mobiles, bookshelves filled with colorful bindings—that I had taken for granted in American classrooms. A piece of corrugated cardboard nailed to a wall had the girls' compositions and drawings pinned to it. The chalkboard was a plank of wood painted such a faded green, it was difficult to see the white writing against it. One small metal closet leaned askew against a wall, its open door displaying meager supplies. However, the teacher had a warm smile. Putting her arm around Ronnie in welcome, she had the girls greet their new classmate. We left her amidst a chorus of "Shalom, Ronnie."

Downstairs, Miriam asked, "How old is your other girl? She is too young for us, no?"

"She's five and a half," I said, greatly encouraged by Miriam's unconcern about Tamara's handicap.

"Speak to the headmaster about the kindergarten when you take the boy over. For kindergarten we still have them mixed, girls and boys."

Adam and Jeff ran ahead as I dragged Tamara up the next hill. At the top was Hapisga, a broad, heavily-trafficked street. Losing all the altitude we'd gained, we followed the road down to the boys' school. Boys in sandals and shorts shouted and darted around the dusty yard and through the dingy corridors. Others sprawled on the floor, engrossed in a game played with slips of paper which flipped over in the breeze created by the clapping of hands. A tile mosaic decorated the wall next to the office, a spacious suite compared with Miriam's cramped quarters. Once, the boys' building might have resembled an American elementary school.

The headmaster tried conversing with Adam in Hebrew. Adam's failure to reply made him grimace. "Wherefore have you not gone to the absorption center?" he asked. "Then you would come here knowing already how to speak."

Why hadn't we? We thought we knew better. We wanted to avoid being isolated in a ghetto of new immigrants. We wanted to plunge right in to the Israeli mainstream.

The man shook his head. "It would be better he should go first to an *ulpan* where he will learn to speak. However, you may bring him here in the morning and we shall see." His frown indicated pessimism.

We asked him about Tamara.

"He you must talk to the psychologist about."

"She," I corrected automatically.

He was writing something on a scrap of paper but looked up. "What is it?" he asked impatiently.

I smiled, a bit embarrassed. "I just said that Tamara is a girl." I thought she looked obviously female.

"Of course." He checked what he'd written down before handing me the paper. It had the six-digit telephone number of the Psychology Bureau. Then he shook Jeff's hand and ran out to talk to one of his teachers by the mosaic wall.

We joined him in the lobby. Was he speaking with Adam's teacher?

At last he noticed us. "Excuse me? There is something else?" he asked, his voice louder than necessary.

"We wondered where Adam should go—" I started.

"In the morning. In the next morning you bring him here." Turning his back on us, he resumed his conversation with the teacher.

Once again, we surmounted the hill of Hapisga. At the top, we found a Bank Leumi, where we were directed to stand on a line. When it was our turn, the woman listened to our request to open an account and said, "You must first to speak to him," and pointed to another line.

Eventually, everyone in front of us had been helped and we sat before a stoop-shouldered, pimply man who told us to open two accounts, one for shekels and one for dollars. He chain smoked as he filled out forms. In the middle of our transaction, he stopped for a coffee break. When he finally presented us with forms requiring our signature, we had no idea what they said. "It's okay, it's okay," he assured us, his hand trembling as he mashed out another butt in his ashtray. "It is nothing out of the ordinary. Everybody has to sign."

After we signed, he sent us back to the line we had mistakenly stood in originally, now to withdraw shekels from our newly opened account. The teller exhibited the particular Israeli talent for doing many things at once: she spoke on the phone and counter-signed a check another teller presented to her as she counted out our paper money.

It was already early afternoon. We recovered Tamara, who was asleep on the floor in a corner, only a minute before the bank locked up for an afternoon break.

School was due to let out. Leaving Adam and Tamara with me on the front steps of the bank, Jeff ran around the corner to get Ronnie. He had all our passports and money; I watched anxiously for his return.

A flood of girls flowed up to Hapisga. Sticking out like a piece of flotsam amid the sea, Jeff appeared, coming back with Ronnie.

We asked directions to the closest market, and several girls with earnest faces conversed in Hebrew, discussing which one to send us to. They finally all pointed across the street. "He speaking English," one girl informed us. We crossed recklessly through the steady stream of traffic, discovered a driveway between tall pines, and looked down the steep path. "You think this leads anywhere?" Jeff asked.

As we descended, Ronnie, flushed and verbose, described her morning. She handed Jeff a mimeographed sheet listing in Hebrew all the texts she needed. "They wrote down the place where you can buy them," she said, pointing to a scribbled address.

"You mean we have to buy your books?" I asked.

"Yeah. Also, you have to pay an office fee. Here." She handed me a halfsheet with tiny Hebrew print and oddly formed numbers inked in.

"Office fee?"

"Yeah. To pay for paper supplies and copying costs and stuff," she explained.

"I thought you were supposed to be getting a free education," Jeff commented. "What if a kid can't afford to pay?"

"I don't know." She didn't seem to care.

Halfway down the hill, we found an unassuming doorway in the basement of a residential building. Empty milk crates were stacked outside. "You think this is it?" Jeff asked me.

I looked down the hill. The driveway twisted around trees and between buildings. There was no sign of anything more commercial.

A man emerged through the dark doorway and pulled down a metal shutter.

Jeff approached him. "Do you speak English?"

"So-so." He straightened and looked Jeff over, playing with a padlock in his hand.

"Is this a store? Do you sell food?"

"*Ken*. Yes. Only unfortunately I just now go home to eat my meal. I open again at four hours."

"In four hours?" Jeff asked.

"No, no, no. Here." He held out his wrist to Jeff and pointed to the four on his watch. "Four," he repeated. "*Ad* four *le shevah*," he added, pointing also to the seven.

"From four to seven?" Jeff asked.

"*Ken*, yes!" The man smiled broadly at Jeff's comprehension. "How long you here?" he asked conversationally.

"Permanently," Jeff bragged. "*Ani oleh hadash*," he added, the phrase meaning "I am a new immigrant."

"*Nachon? Tov me-od!*" (I knew "*tov*" meant "good.") "But I ask you: how long here?" The man stressed his question by pointing to the ground. "When you come?"

"Just now," Jeff answered, puzzled.

"*B'ruchim haba'im*—you know what means this? Welcome! From America? You come from New York? I was once in New York. Big city. Buildings so big." He pointed up. "Is too big, no? Is better here, *nachon*?"

"Yes!"

"I am sorry I must be closing now. My wife, she is looking for me. You come back later." He leaned to lock the metal shutter. "Shalom, shalom." Leaving us, the shopkeeper ran down the path.

Jeff turned to me. "Now what do we do? We haven't got a thing to eat."

"I'm hungry," Adam complained. He rubbed his protruding middle.

"Well, no use just standing around here," Jeff said, and we hiked up the driveway.

On Hapisga, we noticed noisy school boys congregating outside a shop two doors down from the bank. We crossed over and waited our turn to be served.

It was a dull, dark little room with shelves and counters full of newspapers, bottled drinks, and candy and gum in unfamiliar wrappers. Next to the cash register, circular pretzels covered with sesame seeds were stacked on an upright wooden dowel. A freezer in the corner contained ice cream. We bought five pretzels, five ice cream sandwiches, two bottles of beer and three small sealed plastic bags of chocolate milk. I asked the woman behind the counter how the children should drink the milk. She pierced the bags with skinny plastic straws and handed them back, never parting with her scowl.

The children found drinking from a bag amusing. The woman scolded them, so we left the store, dribbling a trail of chocolate milk to the doorway.

A low wall abutted the shop. We joined the school boys sitting there and ate our carbohydrate-laden snack. The woman came out of the store, shooed and shouted at the boys, and took a well-worn broom out to sweep up their litter before pulling down her shutter and locking up.

Behind us, beyond the wall, was a garbage-strewn vacant lot, and below that, the uneven basketball court of Ronnie's school. From out of windows of the residential buildings edging the open space, clothing flapped on lines in the hot, sunny breeze. The traffic on Hapisga dropped off to a trickle and the children disappeared.

We retraced our steps back to the apartment along empty streets and paths. The soothing sounds of children's voices, of cutlery clinking against porcelain, drifted from the open windows. The air was soft and warm, the shadows of trees and buildings cool. I felt drowsy.

Opening the door on the chaos of our possessions jarred me. Jeff, too restless to sit still, said, "Look, Cyn, maybe I'll leave the kids here with you and go down again to investigate."

Avoiding the laundry, I emptied a suitcase and transferred all the things in the cartons to the kitchen cupboards. Adam napped. Ronnie looked at the pictures in old magazines left behind by the landlord or his previous tenant. Tamara soaked her last diaper and trotted through the rooms with a kitchen towel pinned around her bottom.

Jeff returned at five laden with thin plastic bags full of assorted odd things: a large, unwrapped loaf of bread, a thin paper bag with six loose eggs in it, tiny cans with pictures of fish on the label, cup-sized white plastic containers with pictures of cows and houses, sealed plastic bags of milk, dry cellophane-wrapped tea biscuits, and a few sorry-looking pieces of fruit, loose and crushed under the other items. A large white bag, devoid of pictures or writing, contained disposable diapers. The left-side tape on each diaper was defective. We used masking tape to fasten one on Tamara.

"I've spent all our money," Jeff told me as he helped me unpack his purchases. "I'm going back up to the bank to cash some more dollars. There's so much to tell you, but not now. There's a *makolet*—that's what they call the grocery stores—just down our street, but he's a louse. He hates Americans. You know how much bread costs? I think it was about ten cents. And I've already been to the college, but I'll tell you about that later. I'd better run now and get to the bank before everything closes again. Maybe I can pick up Ronnie's books for her. I found out the place is just across the street from the bank. And once I'm up on Hapisga, maybe I'll stop in at that other *makolet*. What do you think? Did I get everything you wanted?"

I glanced at the strange food lying on the table and didn't have the heart to tell him the truth. "Yes. I'll try and put some dinner together while you're gone."

"Hey, kids, you wanna come with me? Where's Adam?"

"Asleep."

Adam appeared, groggy but ready for adventure.

"Good. Hey, Ron, you can read that later." He squatted to tie Tamara's shoes. "Cyn, you coming?"

"What about dinner?"

"Yeah, you look wiped out. Why don't you take it easy here while we're gone? Lay down for a nap."

Lie down, I thought, then cautioned myself against getting testy about grammar. I'd heard much worse earlier in the day and had considered it a boon to be able to communicate, even if in this coarser form of English.

"Okay, kids. Everybody ready?"

I looked over the three children, their shirts untucked and spotted with chocolate milk and ice cream and grime, their unkempt hair matted with sweat. I forced a smile. "Have fun. I'll see you later."

The door shut on them. I heard the elevator come and carry their voices away.

Back in the kitchen, I opened a can and found pieces of oily, smelly fish inside. The cups contained cottage cheese and watery yogurt. Silently weeping, I rinsed and cut a bruised tomato, a shriveled, smelly cucumber. I regarded the unappetizing food I placed on the plates, my own plates brought all the way from another world, as unkosher, unclean. Shrunken and unwholesome, the fish, the vegetables defiled my plates.

After slicing the bread, I wandered around the quiet apartment, tripping over the clutter on the tile floors, feeling desperately lonely and heartsick in the ebbing afternoon light.

Eventually I reached the front of the living room, the sliding glass door to a terrace. I opened it and stepped outside.

A cool evening breeze made the treetops below me sway and sigh. Shadows lengthened and covered toy-sized parked cars and miniature children playing downstairs. From the branches the voices of a million birds bedding down for the night blended with the children's shrill jump-rope rhymes and the calls of a mother to her son: "*Shmuli, bo!*"

The drooping potted plants on the balcony added the scent of their soil to the evening air, the evergreens, flowers, and weeds. From the corner of the terrace, I could see out across the valley. The lights of the few streets traversing that open space blinked on, accentuating the increasing darkness.

My head filled with the words of psalms, jumbled and out of order but full of beauty and passion and poetry. I breathed in deeply. I determined to love this land.

# Eleven

The next day, after depositing Ronnie and Adam at their schools, Jeff, Tamara, and I hopped on one of the buses that tore so recklessly through Bayit Vegan. The bus was crowded. We had to stand, though an old woman sitting by us held Tamara around the waist.

A sharp turn threw me into the arms of a bearded, black-frocked passenger. I apologized and quickly righted myself, remembering that the JCT student wouldn't even shake my hand. But the man didn't seem upset or offended by my contact. Maybe because it was accidental.

Minutes later, I suffered a second jolt. When the bus stopped, two young men wearing khaki climbed on toting submachine guns. *Terrorists!* I thought. I began praying for redemption.

None of the other people on the bus paid any attention to the men or their Uzis, and my alarm turned to relief as they paid the driver and slipped their gear under a seat. Would I ever grow used to seeing Israeli soldiers on buses and in the street?

I glanced around. Men with untrimmed beards and hats wore dark suits, no ties, their white shirts buttoned to the collar. The women had on thick stockings and jogging shoes, their hems pulled below the knees, their hair covered in kerchiefs tied over wigs. Though the morning was already warm, the women wore cardigans or cuffs to the wrist. Empty plastic baskets were slipped up their forearms, and they studied shopping lists on scraps of paper.

In the back seats sat young men in tight pants. They had rolled up the short sleeves of their colored shirts to show off tan, well-formed biceps, and gold chains adorned their exposed necks. They wore no head-covering; their hair was dark and thick, their cheeks shaven. Unlike the other passengers, they talked loudly and laughed, often draping an arm around the shoulders of a friend or resting a hand on the next man's thigh. I liked their relaxed camaraderie.

We rode to the city center, a congested, noisy, exciting little cosmos. There we sought out the government agencies, sprinkled at random within the old stone buildings throughout the area, often at addresses other than the ones we were given. Each agency was in a different building, in a different street. Sometimes one office didn't even know of the existence of another. We got lost on winding streets and alleys. We climbed up flights of stone stairs, rode down crowded, creaking elevators, waited on long lines, filled out forms we couldn't read. We answered questions asked in broken English and interrupted midstream by incessant phone calls. I wondered if immigration to other countries was so complicated. Did newcomers to America have to deal with this much bureaucracy?

All the offices we passed through somehow resembled the Bayit Vegan schools: utilitarian, sometimes cluttered, old, worn. In spite of the ubiquitous mopping, the bureaus all gave the impression of griminess, as though everything were covered with a film of gray. Only the cheerful sunlight filtering through streaked windows brightened the dreary interiors. Rarely, but nevertheless sometimes, the dim bleakness was relieved by an array of potted plants, though the disposition of the bureaucrat with a garden was not noticeably softened or sweetened by his greener environment.

Thus, in the next few days, we registered with the police, applied for a new-immigrant housing subsidy, and arranged for our monthly child allowance (a rebate on the automatically withheld income taxes). We visited the four national health plans and finally chose one for no better reason than that the head doctor in the main office was from England and we could make ourselves understood.

When Jeff had visited JCT, he was informed of the Science Ministry's reluctance to forward his stipend to them, so we visited that office also. We were assured Jeff would get his grant, and the man we spoke to further encouraged us by saying that of course Jeff would receive the standard associate professor's salary. When we asked what this was, he said, "I can't be certain. It fluctuates with the economy. You should probably be getting something like two-hundred thousand shekels."

It was such a big number, I didn't bother to do the mental arithmetic of converting into dollars.

Our grins made him uncomfortable. "That's per month," he clarified.

And I'd thought the enormous number was a per annum figure! What was this we'd been told about Israeli salaries?

But Jeff scowled. "What? That can't be right."

"Maybe two-hundred and fifty. As I say, it changes each month."

"Six-hundred dollars," Jeff said quietly.

"No, it will come out closer to seven hundred, I think," the man said. He shrugged. "This is Israel, not America."

Tamara slowed us down. She was cooperative, never complaining about the exhausting treks or the boring waits, but her rapid steps couldn't equal Jeff's strides. We hastened to get her placed in school. When we called the number of the psychologists the headmaster had given us, we were told we had to come to their office. Before the end of the week, we made our way down a steep hill from King George Street.

In an old building with twelve-foot ceilings and endless shallow stairs to the second floor was the Psychology Bureau. Still panting from our climb, we presented ourselves to the receptionist, a woman who wore her straight, dark hair in a boyish cut and tweezed her eyebrows into thin lines. "Everyone is leaving already for the *Shabbat*," she told us. "Come back on Sunday."

▲   ▲   ▲

That afternoon, our phone rang for the first time. I picked it up and said hello.

"Shalom, Mrs. Rott, this is Pertsa Litansky. I am calling to see how you are doing."

It took me an instant to realize who she was. Jeff had already met her husband at JCT and made a point of thanking him for the food his wife had left for our arrival. Now I also expressed our gratitude.

"Oh, it was nothing. I already know. My husband told me."

"Well, it was really very nice. We were so tired and hungry. We would've had nothing 'til the next day if it weren't for you."

"It's nothing."

"I have all your dishes put aside. How should I return them to you?"

I didn't know where she lived. In fact, it would have been polite for me to call her as soon as we found the meal she left, but I didn't have her phone number.

"Oh, don't worry about the dishes. I don't need them. Why don't you keep them for awhile?"

"I'd be afraid something might happen to them. It's really very nice of you, but we've already unpacked all our own dishes."

She sighed. "Okay, then. I'll have to stop by for them sometime. I must go now. We are expecting our son home from the army this *Shabbat*. Let me know if there is anything else we can do. *Shabbat shalom*." And she hung up.

▲   ▲   ▲

Shabbas in Jerusalem was a new experience for us. The most marked difference was that the whole city observed it to a greater or lesser degree. All the stores shut by Friday afternoon. Offices closed. Buses stopped running. Though nonobservant people lived in our neighborhood, Bayit Vegan was considered a religious area and special preparations for the sabbath included putting up barricades in the streets to prevent the flow of traffic on the day of rest. In our building, the elevator was turned off. Lightbulbs to burn through the night were screwed in on each landing since we couldn't press the buttons that operated the timed overhead lights.

I started preparing our Friday evening meal. In Tucson, I used to make chicken soup, but the *makolet* didn't sell meat, and we had yet to find our way to a butcher. I put carrots, celery, onions, and small, dirty potatoes in the sink, planning to boil them in chicken bullion. When I turned on the water to wash them off, barely a trickle came from the faucet.

I panicked. Years before, reading *O, Jerusalem*, I'd been riveted by a description of the siege of the city in 1948, and especially of the difficulties arising from the scarcity of water. In Tucson, I learned to respect this resource, taken for granted in so many other places. Now I feared the scant flow was a manifestation of either a drought or a hostile attack. We'd been too busy taking care of the petty arrangements of our relocation to pay attention to larger, communal concerns. In search of information, I knocked on the door across the landing.

A woman dressed in a housedress, stockings, and slippers, her hair covered with a kerchief, opened the door. "*Ken?*"

"There isn't any water," I reported with alarm.

She stared at me impassively.

"English?" I asked.

"*Lo.*"

"I live over there." I pointed impatiently to the open door of our apartment.

"*Ken. Shalom.*" She grinned. "*B'rucha haba'a.*"

I'd heard the phrase before and inferred it to be friendly. "Shalom," I replied, smiling. Reassuring myself that she wouldn't be so calm if Jerusalem were under siege, I took the time to be neighborly. "I'm Cynthia Roth."

"*Ani Rivka Gorovitz.*"

"Shalom, Ani," I greeted her.

She scowled. "Rivka!"

"Excuse me. Hello, Rivka." She seemed satisfied, so I continued, "There's something wrong with the water."

"*Ma?*"

"Water." I pantomimed turning the tap, then shrugged.

"Ah, *mayim!*"

"Yes! *Ken!*"

She asked a long question.

I stared at her in bewilderment.

She took me by the arm and led me into my apartment. I turned the faucet and pointed to the thin stream.

"*Ach. Eyn mayim.*" She laughed. "*Hayom Yom Shishi.*" Seeing my blank expression, she smiled again. "S'okay," she said. "*Kol beseder.*"

"But what's the matter?"

"*Bo'i,*" she said, again taking me by the arm.

I followed her out onto the landing and down a flight. On the second floor, she knocked on the door of the apartment beneath ours.

The door was opened by another woman, similarly clad in housedress and kerchief and holding a dust rag.

After considerable discussion in Hebrew between my neighbors, the second woman turned to me. "So you are the Americans. How are you finding everything?"

"Yes, hello," I said. "I'm concerned because we have no water."

"Oh, that." She snorted. "Every Friday this happens. It is due to everyone making preparation at the same time for the *Shabbat*. Too many people use the water at once."

"Oh!" I smiled in relief. "Thank you. I feel so much better. I thought maybe—"

"Excuse me, but I have no time to talk now. I have to make my preparations. You must tell your children to be quiet from two to four. Every day I am disturbed from my rest from they are jumping on my head. We will talk another time. *Shabbat shalom*." Then she turned away from me and continued her conversation in Hebrew with Rivka.

After a minute of being ignored, I made my way back upstairs to my vegetables. With patience, I filled the pot to make my soup.

▲   ▲   ▲

There were synagogues all over, about one a block, and we were unsure where to pray. We wandered into a large synagogue on Friday night and felt self-consciously under-dressed wearing casual summer clothing. The other women wore long sleeves and high collars; the men had on dark suits and felt hats. The following morning, we tried the Sephardic shul by the path to the Hida, but in spite of the friendly welcome we received, the small room was hot and crowded, and we didn't recognize any of the melodies. We left. Someone on the street suggested a synagogue on Hapisga where "all the Americans go." It was less friendly.

During the years of my growing religious observance, I became accustomed to the Shabbas service. I looked forward to Saturday services in Israel, believing at least in this setting I'd feel at home; the familiar prayers would be a common denominator between me and my foreign neighbors. Instead, I found I couldn't follow the all-Hebrew prayer book I picked up at the door. The Torah reading was meaningless without an English translation to read at my seat. Many of the prayers I looked forward to singing were either said silently, eliminated, or sung to different tunes. I spent the entire service flipping through the book in exasperating ignorance.

Another radical change in the service was the speed in which it was completed. In Tucson, morning services began at nine and ended close to noon, followed by a generous *kiddush* and socializing. In Bayit Vegan, the services began at 8:00, and by 9:30, people were already sitting down to a heavy meat meal at home. As newcomers, we were asked to an early dinner by a family on the hospitality committee: their son had been dispatched to our door earlier in the week to extend the invitation. When we called our hosts to confirm, there had been a lot of confusion over the time they wanted us, but indeed they did want us at this early morning hour. Jeff and I found it difficult to do justice to the challah, hot soup, fish, *cholent*, pot roast, salad, and two desserts, but our children ate with appetites grown large after a week of canned fish, yogurt, and limp vegetables. Our hosts explained that with only one day off each week, they had to keep a tight schedule which allowed time for naps, catching up on reading, and visiting with friends. By eleven, our hosts made it clear they wanted us to leave.

▲   ▲   ▲

"Mom, I have to talk to you," Ronnie said on our walk home.

"What is it?" I hung back to join her, letting Jeff take the lead with Adam and Tamara.

"It's driving me crazy, Ma," she said. "You have to find somewhere else for Tamara to sleep. She has this awful snore—"

"She snores? I never heard her snore."

"Well, not exactly a snore. Sort of a whistling sound coming from her nose."

"Maybe she's a little congested. I think I'm also allergic to some of the stuff growing around here."

"It's not only this noise she makes. She's always getting into my stuff, and this morning she climbed into my bed."

"She likes to sleep with someone."

"Well, I don't. My bed here is small enough as it is. She jabbed me with her elbow. It really hurt. And another thing: she has bad breath."

"Oh, yeah, I really have to do something about that. I've just been so busy the past few days. I keep meaning to take her in the bathroom to show her how to do a good job of brushing her teeth. Maybe you could teach her. I'd really appreciate that."

"She has no respect for my stuff, Ma. She takes pens off my desk and writes on my papers. Yesterday she put my panties over her diaper. I don't want them anymore. You can just throw them out."

"Don't be silly. I'll wash them."

"No, forget it. I don't want to wear them anymore."

"Did she really put them on herself?" I mused. "That's good. I didn't know she could dress herself."

"Ma-a, listen to me. You're not listening to me. What are you going to do about it?"

"Remember when Adam was a baby? He also found all your things irresistibly attractive."

"Yeah. But that was a long time ago. I didn't have any real good stuff back then. I didn't have any homework papers to destroy."

"You know what, Ronnie? When you were a little girl, you used to get into all my stuff. As soon as you could crawl, you went straight for the bookcase and yanked out all the books, and you weren't too kind to the pages. You were also fond of dumping out all the stuff in my bottom drawers and crumpling the leaves on the philodendron, which was having enough trouble surviving in our New York apartment, especially considering I kept forgetting to water it."

She didn't laugh. "You should've stopped me."

"And fast. I couldn't keep up with you. No sooner did I discover one catastrophe than you were off to create another."

"If I were you, I'd have put me up for adoption."

"Don't think I never considered it," I joked.

She grew solemn. "I don't suppose Aunt Sheila ever considered putting Tamara up for adoption."

"I don't know," I said, matching her tone. "Look, Ron, I know she can be a pain. It's just that she's still a baby in many ways. You eventually grew up, right? She will too. It's just going to take her a bit longer."

"Yeah, Ma."

"And in the meantime, do yourself a favor and don't leave too much temptation in her path. Put away your things and stick the stuff she can ruin out of her reach. You can have a shelf in one of my closets."

"Yeah?"

"Sure. I'll make room for you." I begrudged giving away my precious storage space, but if I couldn't give a little, how could I expect Ronnie to?

▲    ▲    ▲

Saturday night, after we made *havdallah* to mark the end of the sabbath, I confronted the large pile of laundry. Once again I knocked on the door across the landing. "Can you help me, Rivka?" I asked when the door opened.

She smiled.

"Come." I led her to the washer on the bathroom terrace.

"Ah," she said, followed by a question I couldn't understand.

When my words and pantomime elicited no more than a bewildered grin, I brought out the dirty clothing and started to fill the machine. Then I pointed to the dial, made an exaggerated shrug, and guided her hand to the dial.

"Ah," and more Hebrew verbiage. She scratched her head under her wig and considered, then turned to 4 and smiled at me.

"Last time, too hot." I blew on my fingers and shook my hands, trying to demonstrate the last word.

She frowned. "*Hom?*" she asked. The water filled in the washer.

"Hot, hot!" Remembering the word for sun, I said, "*Shemesh.*"

Her frown deepened and she shook her head. Giving up, she looked into the drum before closing the trap door and the lid. "*Kol b'seder,*" she assured me.

"Thank you."

"*Shalom, shalom. Shavu'a tov,*" she said in parting.

Half an hour later, the machine clicked off. The clothing was clean and cool to the touch. I hung what would fit on the lines overhead. Before breakfast the next morning, I swallowed my fear and hung the rest on the closest line beyond the balcony wall.

▲   ▲   ▲

Sunday took getting used to. It was truly the first day of the week, with business as usual. Ronnie and Adam returned to school and Jeff, Tamara, and I returned to the Psychology Bureau. The receptionist directed us to benches, where we waited for people who turned out to be unavailable, on vacation, or unable to speak English. "Anyway," she informed us after another wait, "this is not the right place. You need to go to the Ministry of Education." This was in a building several blocks away.

We got there just as everyone was leaving for a two-hour lunch break. Realizing Ronnie and Adam would soon be coming home, we took the bus back to Bayit Vegan having accomplished nothing. When we came back the next day, it turned out the only man who could help us was in *Melu'im*—the army reserves, where all Israeli men disappeared for a month out of each year. We were standing in the dark passageway outside his office wondering what to do next when a woman carrying coffee in a thick glass made her way past us. Then she turned back to us. "What is your problem? Perhaps I can help."

We told her we needed to see the man who wasn't there.

"Why are you coming to see him?" She listened to us and shook her head. "I do not understand. We do not deal in such cases. You must go back to the *Sherut Psychologie*. There is no one here who can help you."

Our goodwill eroded on the walk back up King George Street and down Hillel and up the hundred stairs.

"This is impossible!" Jeff shouted at the receptionist, who responded by raising her thin eyebrows into two perfect semicircles. "First you make us wait for days and then you send us somewhere else and now they send us back to you. No wonder people leave this country. I've never seen such frustrating inefficiency. I want to speak to someone right now. I don't care who, but it better be someone who can help us."

The receptionist turned her back on him and talked into the phone.

A minute later, a stout middle-aged woman appeared and led us to her office in the back. She was the bureau director.

"I am very sorry of all this mix-up," she said congenially. "Unfortunately, we have now a very busy time with the end of vacation and school just beginning."

Tamara found a doll and two trucks in a corner. She crawled quietly along the floor, pushing a truck before her. Jeff glowered at the woman from a chair. As he said nothing, I began, "It's difficult for us, being new immigrants and not knowing the language. We have so many things we have to take care of before he starts work, and it's hard to have to drag Tamara with us wherever we go."

"Yes, this I understand," she commiserated. "Unfortunately, the only psychologists available right now have no English. Your girl have no Hebrew. How can they evaluate?" She shrugged. "It is impossible."

Jeff sat forward. "You mean to say she can't go to school until she knows Hebrew?"

"Oh, no, no! Ruti will be back from vacation directly after the *hagim*. She will test the girl as soon as it can be arranged."

"Not 'til after the holidays?" Jeff moaned. "That means she won't start school for another month at least. What do we do with her until then?"

"You do not work?" the woman asked me.

"No, but I wanted to take Hebrew lessons. Eventually, I was hoping to work. I understand there are lots of jobs for people to teach English."

"Yes, here everyone wishes to speak English. And you must go to your *ulpan*," she agreed. "This is very important that you should learn." She shrugged again. The end of her shirt rode up over her fat waist. "I agree it is no good the girl should sit at home. I wish I know of a solution."

"You speak English," Jeff commented. "Couldn't you do the evaluation?"

"Oh, no, that would be impossible." She tugged the end of her shirt down again.

"Why?"

"My English, it is not so good. Furthermore, I am not a psychologist."

"But you're the supervisor," Jeff pressed. "And your English is just fine."

"Couldn't you just place her temporarily, until she's tested?" I suggested.

The woman pursed her lips and tilted her head first to one side, then the other, as she weighed the possibility. She asked us to leave the room while she talked and played with Tamara. After calling us back in, she phoned a few of the special education programs in the city.

There were no openings. She laughed. "So anyway she needs to go to the neighborhood school until there is an opening. I will call the *ganenet*—excuse me, the kindergarten teacher—to arrange it."

"She was mainstreamed before we came here," Jeff pointed out, "and she did very well."

I wasn't so sure she did well, but she certainly didn't do badly during her two months at Second Street School.

"Yes, I understand it is very popular in your country, with some degrees of success." She stood and walked us down the hall. "Here we are not set up for it. Our teachers have no special training, and we have no support services. The therapists will not come to Bayit Vegan. Maybe hopefully it will be all right at least until an opening become available at a more appropriate setting. I will call you after I speak with the teacher of the *gan*."

"How soon will that be?" Jeff asked.

Her smile seemed to say Jeff could be gruff and pushy, but she was in power. "Just as soon as I speak to her I will let you know."

▲   ▲   ▲

Days passed. Our cartons of books arrived at the post office, but the postman refused to deliver them. Jeff and I took turns carting home the boxes, one at a time, on our collapsible luggage wheels. Some of our books were damaged in shipping—spines broken, pages dog-eared. Our poor old friends! We placed them gently on the bookshelves in the living room.

Jeff began to spend a part of each day at the college. While he was gone, I wandered around Bayit Vegan with Tamara, trying to familiarize myself with the winding streets, trying to find better sources of food.

The *makolet* off Hapisga consisted of three small basement rooms where basics were lined up on wooden shelves. Flats of thirty eggs each were stacked in a corner behind the cash register, and plastic bags of fresh milk were generally sold out of the crates they were delivered in. Sometimes the bags leaked. At home, we emptied our milk into a jar.

A few doors down from our apartment, there was a larger store where merchandise could be purchased at reduced rates. It was run by a five-foot tall, chain-smoking proprietor who darted around shouting at customers and his sluggish pregnant daughter behind the cash register. Fruit flies hovered over the tables of produce. The shelves displayed stale cookies, jam, candy, soup mixes, cans of fruit and fish, bright-colored drinks in plastic bottles, paper products, ceramic cups, thermoses, and toilet seats. Jeff dubbed the establishment "the crazy place" because we never knew what affordable commodity we'd find there. This was where we bought Tamara's diapers. They were always defective but half the price of those sold elsewhere.

I found a butcher on Hapisga beyond Adam's school. Even the government-subsidized chicken was expensive enough to deplete my supply of shekels, sending me back to the bank. Now that we had accounts, I only needed to stand on two lines: one to transfer funds from our dollar account to our shekel account, the other to withdraw shekels from that account. We didn't want to transfer too many dollars to shekels because of the outrageous inflation.

While I stood on the bank lines holding Tamara's hand, my mind drifted, replaying all the day's transactions. I tried to project myself into the Israeli perspective. Would someone used to running down to the *makolet* in her block every day find it equally difficult to get used to weekly visits to my Safeway in Tucson?

I finally got up the nerve to take a bus without Jeff. I kept worrying that I'd get lost and no one would be able to speak English and I wouldn't have enough money to get back home. I was behaving like a 37-year-old baby. But when I learned of a supermarket in Beit Hakerem, a neighborhood just north of us, I had motivation. First I thought of walking—anything not to deal with the buses—but didn't think Tamara had the stamina to go that far. On Thursday, after taking care of the household chores and hanging out the laundry, we went down to the bus stop. It was late enough in the morning to find a seat on the bus. Someone told us where to get off.

The supermarket was large and well-stocked, and as crowded as the Daitch-Shopwell near the apartment where Jeff and I had lived in New York. Though I couldn't guess what many of the packages contained, quite a lot had English on the label. One whole aisle featured loose breads, and I picked out one with seeds. I found mayonnaise, peanut butter, boxes of breakfast cereal, pasta, frozen vegetables, cheeses, ground beef, fresh fish, Jaffa oranges, cans of olives, and sandwich cookies. I felt giddy.

The checkout sobered me. There were no prices on anything in my cart: each item had a sticker with a multi-digit number and throughout the store were charts which listed the price corresponding to each number. By this clever system, prices could be raised in pace with the inflation without the impossible task of retagging each item on the shelves. But I couldn't begin to figure out the costs. It required excellent eyesight and a double conversion, from sticker number to chart number, from that which represented shekels to dollars. I estimated that in Tucson my cartload would come to thirty dollars.

After ringing up our items, the cashier pointed to an incomprehensibly large sum on her register. The number contained more digits than I could count. She quite impressively recited the total, but in Hebrew, which didn't help me. An older man behind me in line translated the number with an English accent. I owed more than sixty thousand shekels.

I emptied my wallet, then trusted the cashier as she figured out what I could afford and helped herself to the money on my open palm. We left many delicacies behind. As it was, I could barely carry the four plastic bags of our purchases. One of the handles ripped as soon as we stepped out of the store.

I was too burdened to hold Tamara's hand and a stranger helped us cross Sderot Herzl, the main boulevard, to get to our bus stop.

A woman at the bus stop, observing my bags of groceries, commented, "Why didn't you have them deliver?"

"I couldn't afford it."

"It's free. Didn't you know? Free delivery is the least they can offer, considering how dear everything is in there. You'd do better to buy your produce at the *shuk*." Like the man at the checkout, she had an English accent.

"Where is that?" I asked.

"Mehane Yehuda. You know, the big open market."

"Just by Jaffa Road on the right as you go into town," another woman explained.

I knew where that was. On our rides home from the government offices, the buses always stopped a long time a few blocks after we crossed King George Street. Crowds of women and men, usually old and squat, dressed in dark, calf-length skirts and seedy, baggy trousers, would climb on carrying heavy plastic baskets of fruit. They left the baskets in the aisles, forcing other old men and women to step over the bundles. The stop was on a narrow, snaky section of Jaffa Road with ancient buildings opening directly onto the slim margin of sidewalk. The buses bottle-necked there. The bus drivers honked the pedestrians who spilled out onto the street. Everything—the people, the stone buildings, the buses crawling along—looked weary in the baking sun.

The mystery of the place hadn't been enough to lure me, but after my experience at the cash register in the supermarket, and my success in using the bus, I thought I might look into this less expensive source of nourishment for my family. I thanked her for her suggestion before hoisting my purchases and Tamara onto a number 39 bus. Another bag handle broke.

Somehow, we got home. As I put away the food, the phone rang. It was the placement woman from the Psychology Bureau. I could barely understand her: I had become dependent on all the nonverbal communication that took place in face-to-face encounters. The technologically inferior phone didn't help. Though we were fortunate to have one, as installation cost money and months of waiting, the quality of sound reproduction was poor, there was additional static, and quite often the line would go dead due to a faulty connection in the jack. I held the receiver with one hand, the plug in place with the other, leaving me no free hand to copy the name of the *ganenet*. Luckily, it was easy to remember: Rivka, like my neighbor across the hall.

"So she can start tomorrow?" I shouted into the phone.

"*Ken*. No, wait. Tomorrow it is *Yom Shishi*. Better you should start her in the beginning of the week."

"Okay. On Monday, then. I mean, Sunday."

"This is good. I will have to ask of you one other thing: the *ganenet*, she would like that you should stay with Tamara in the classroom until the girl knows what she is to do. A month, maybe two. I know you are not working so I tell her you will come."

"Okay," I said, glad enough to have Tamara finally going to school. My *ulpan* would have to wait.

# Twelve

On Friday morning when Jeff and the older children had left, I put on Tamara's shoes and collected several plastic bags with handles. In two days, she'd start school and I'd be stuck sitting in the classroom with her; this was the last day for weeks I could explore. After getting money at the bank, we crossed Hapisga and boarded a bus for town.

Half the people in the bus got off when we did, at the *shuk*. Following them, we found ourselves on a street perpendicular to Jaffa Road. The way was closed to vehicles; people filled the space from one curb to the other. We were soon caught up in the thick stream of shoppers flowing between tables laden with produce, candy, and fish. Afraid Tamara would get trampled, I lifted her onto my hip and tried to make my way out of the bustle and din of bickering and bartering.

Strings of bare bulbs cast a weak light under the awning covering the clogged street. Not noticing something underfoot, I tripped forward, bumping into a woman and causing her to overturn her basket. While leaning to gather rolling turnips and onions, she screamed and shook her fist at me. I drew back. Tamara's weight unbalanced me and I fell, landing hard on my backside, Tamara sliding into my lap.

Knees and feet and shopping baskets knocked into me. I tried to stand up but couldn't right myself with Tamara in my arms. Two soldiers with long guns loomed above me and shouted something in Hebrew. Unable to hold back the tears, I glared back at them in silence, too cowed by their boots and lean muscles and weapons to voice out loud what was raging inside.

One of them leaned over and helped Tamara to her feet. Clumsily, I got up off the pavement, and the soldiers passed on. My skirt was damp and stained where I'd sat on a squashed tomato. My coccyx ached.

No longer concerned about getting soiled or further bruised, I shoved my way to the side, tugging Tamara along behind me. We made our way to a side alley, even dimmer than the main market but less crowded. From the doorway to a men's toilet came the strong smell of urine and this mixed with the odor of rotting garbage in cardboard cartons piled four feet high in a corner.

We passed a cave-like opening in a wall where a man with hands black with polish repaired a worn shoe on an old sewing machine. When he was finished, he picked up its mate and added them to the other dark shoes lined up on a flattened carton lying over the dank floor. All of them were stretched out into shapes suggestive of the bunions and old twisted feet they had encased. Behind his sewing machine the cobbler found the next pair. With pliers, he yanked off the heels, then opened a pocket knife to cut new ones from a sheet of rubber.

Tamara pulled me away. She was drawn to a different stall where the darkness of the interior was brightened by sparks from a soldering iron. A collection of somewhat rusty hardware, small appliances, and a metal tea kettle lay on a rough table. I shook my head, wondering who would want such unattractive junk. I felt like we'd crossed some time zone into an earlier century.

Another alley took us past a butcher. Plucked chickens, looking long and scrawny with their necks and feet still attached, lay in forlorn white heaps on a counter. Others, yet to be beheaded, hung on hooks suspended from the ceiling. It seemed disrespectful, these dead creatures so displayed.

In contrast, there were shops that sold dry goods in primary colors: cheap toys, plastic basins, buckets, and bowls, shirts.

One alley led to an uncovered market, and I felt relieved to be out in a more open space, even though it had begun to drizzle. Bins of nuts and sacks of grain lined the sidewalk in front of open store fronts, blocking entry. In the space behind, aproned men reached down cans and boxes for their customers in the street. There was a shop displaying pastry in its window, but after what I'd seen of the *shuk*, I questioned the level of sanitation used in the bakery. Standing nearby, a woman sold toothpaste, transistor radios, combs, and sneakers from her cart. Men hawked underwear out of the back of a truck. Rubbish and collapsed cartons lay in the gutter.

We came to a small, crowded shop with tables of vegetables extending onto the sidewalk. Women filled dirty plastic bowls with small cucumbers or potatoes or bell peppers and handed them to the shop-keeper. A cigarette dangling from his lips, he'd take the bowl and put it on one side of a scale, then arrange kilo and half-kilo weights on the other. As the buyer pulled shekels from her purse, he emptied the container into a small paper bag, then, in a single movement, flipped the bag while holding the top corners, thus folding it closed.

Finally I got up the nerve to step up to his table and pick through potatoes with the other women. Tamara held the bowl he handed to us. When it was nearly full, I reached it to him and pulled out a bank note from the wallet in my pocket. His cigarette ash fell into the bowl. When our potatoes failed to balance with the kilo weight, he reached over and picked up two more, putting one, then the other in the bowl until the scale tipped in my favor. He only charged me for one kilo, which pleased me.

At another stand, I bought oranges and bananas. Before we reached the bus stop on Jaffa Road, my bags were heavy with a chunk of halvah cut from a block I hoped hadn't been handled or sneezed on, and a plastic tub with "choco" on it. It only cost four hundred shekels, worth about a dollar, and contained a sticky, sweet, brown confection I thought might taste good on ice cream or as frosting on a cake. Not that I knew where to buy a cake mix or ice cream.

When Ronnie got home from school that afternoon, she pounced on the tub. "Oh, Ma, this stuff is so great. The girls at school eat it on bread for lunch. Can I have a chocolate sandwich for tomorrow? Oh, wait: tomorrow's *Shabbat*. Can I have one on Sunday?"

How could Israeli mothers send their children to school with such unnutritious fare? Chocolate sandwiches, indeed! I was ranting, she was arguing, until I stopped myself. I didn't have the strength to fight every battle. It was her body, her complexion—let her eat whatever she wanted. But she'd have to make her own lunch. I wasn't going to be a party to it.

Triumphant, she left the kitchen. I pulled the top off the container and sampled a little "choco" on the tip of my finger. It tasted good, like the stuff of hot fudge sundaes. Definitely more palatable than slimy canned fish or runny yogurt, and cheaper than the cheese at the Beit Hakerem supermarket. But for lunch?

I dumped the potatoes into the sink to wash them before putting them in the chicken soup. Mold grew on one of the potatoes the shop-keeper had added.

▲   ▲   ▲

On Saturday afternoon, we had visitors. Our neighbor from across the hall knocked on the door. I smiled. "Shalom, Rivka."

After a string of unknown words, she said, "*Rega ehad*," and went back in her door. She returned a minute later with a man and a cake on a plate. "*Shelach*," she said, presenting me with the cake. She pointed to the man and said, "*Zeh Uri*."

"*Shabbat shalom.* Come in." When they still stood at the threshold, I waved them in. I wondered if her husband's name was Zeh Uri or simply Uri. When she'd introduced herself the week before, I made the mistake of taking the first word she said for her name.

They followed me down the hall to the living room. Jeff was sprawled on the couch reading *The Jerusalem Post*, the English-language paper. He jumped up and tucked in his shirt. "Hello."

"Jeff, this is Rivka Gorovitz and this is Uri."

Jeff shook the man's hand. He nodded at Rivka. "*Shabbat shalom.* Sit down."

"I learned a new Hebrew word," I said. "This is *shelach*." I displayed the cake.

The three stared at me, then laughed. "*Lo, lo*," explained Rivka. "*Zeh ugah. Ha ugah shelach*." She pointed to me. Then she took the plate back as she said "*sheli*," then handed it back to me, saying "*shelach*" again.

"For me?" I asked.

"*Ken. Tov me'od.*"

Pointing to the cake, she said, "*Ugah.*"

"Cake is *ugah*?" I asked.

"You got it," said Jeff, smiling. Rivka nodded. I felt my cheeks flush.

For the next half hour, Jeff and I did our best to entertain the Gorovitzes. We served them their own cake. I offered them fruit, which they smiled at politely but didn't touch. After adding a lot of sugar, they drank our tea. Conversation was impossible, though many words were said, accompanied by grimaces, grins, and gestures.

Another knock on the door announced the arrival of a wife and professor from Jeff's college. They spoke some English and spent their visit translating back and forth. They also took cake and tea. Before peeling a banana, the wife asked, "Where do you get your fruit?"

"At the *shuk*," I announced, proud of my accomplishment.

"Oh." She put the banana down uneaten.

"Is something the matter?"

She explained that in Israel, fruit too could be unkosher. "You must only buy from a shopkeeper you know observes the Levite tithe." Rivka nodded agreement. In Israel, the ancient law of putting a part of the crops aside had to be observed. "In the *shuk* you do not know. Some of the shopkeepers do, but some do not. The supermarket is okay, and all the shops in Bayit Vegan. Unless you know the shopkeeper in the *shuk*, it is best not to take a chance."

There were so many new rules to learn. In Tucson, we considered ourselves Orthodox, but our Bayit Vegan neighbors underlined how far from truly observant we were. Unlike the other women, I didn't cover my head with a scarf or wig, feeling my short brown hair was far from immodest. At least I conformed somewhat in dress, having abandoned jeans when my hip measurements deemed them unflattering. When we were invited to Shabbas lunch the previous week, I found pre-ripped toilet paper in the bathroom. Was this yet another rule or ritual peculiar to Jerusalem?

After our guests left, I mentioned it to Jeff.

"Oh," he said. "Do you rip toilet paper on Shabbas?"

"I always have."

"Oh," he said again. "You're really not supposed to."

"But we always did in Tucson."

"Yeah, I didn't know you were. I guess I never told you about that rule. Look, don't feel bad about it. Nobody keeps all six hundred and thirteen *mitzvahs* of the Torah. Everybody makes mistakes."

"But you never filled a little bag with ripped-up toilet paper."

"Nah, I never bothered. I just use tissues. Gee, I guess I better tell the kids about that. I never thought about it."

On the other hand, whereas carrying as much as a housekey on Shabbas was unacceptable to us in Arizona, no one in Bayit Vegan seemed to know about this prohibition. I was shocked to see the righteous transporting pots of *cholent*, babies, and bottles of wine on Saturday. "Tell me this, Jeff: how come we see people here carrying all sorts of stuff on Shabbas?"

"They tell me there's an *eruv* around the city."

"A what?"

"You know, a fence. Just like you can carry within the confines of your home, so they make the whole city enclosed so you can carry anywhere within it's borders."

"You mean there's a fence all around Jerusalem? I don't remember seeing a fence as we entered Jerusalem two weeks ago."

"What're you looking for? Something with white pickets?" He laughed, obviously amused by the vision of a whole city surrounded by a wooden fence. "No, Cyn, I think it's a thin wire strung around on the utility poles."

All the small differences unbalanced me. Once again, I felt as insecure as when I used to visit my in-laws as a newlywed. I never knew when I'd make a religious faux pas.

▲   ▲   ▲

The following morning, when I prepared Adam's sack lunch, I made an extra cheese sandwich. (Ronnie was standing there next to me, glopping chocolate on her bread.) I preened Tamara and set out with her and the sandwich for the two-classroom annex in front of Adam's school. Pacing myself to Tamara's short steps, I arrived at the dusty, weedy schoolyard barely winded. But my breath was soon knocked out of me as a big boy, turning to see if his pursuing friends were gaining on him, ran headlong into me. Without even glancing at me, he leaned over to scoop up his fallen *kippah* and ran off, simultaneously clipping the skullcap to his hair. I stared after him, waiting for an apology, but he never acknowledged me.

The *gan* was in a low building with a fenced-in yard. We entered the wrong door and were told we should go to the classroom next door. No one was there except a sour-faced woman sitting at a low table. She shook her head when I asked her if she was Rivka, then returned to her task of cutting colored paper.

When I began to leave with Tamara, she called gruffly to me.

I looked back at her, then continued to the door.

Raising her voice, as though volume would increase my comprehension, she shouted something else I didn't understand. Then, with fingertips drawn together, she shook her hand at me and growled, "*Savlenoot!*"

Between the gesture and the unpleasant expression on her face, I decided she was being rude and turned my back on her.

With a sigh, she pushed her large, tired body out of the child-sized chair and lumbered past me across the threshold and into the other classroom. She came back with the same woman who had pointed out Rivka's classroom.

This woman, more petite but equally slovenly in a faded housedress, apron, and slippers, smiled at me shyly and said, "She want I tell you wait, Rivka come in minutes." She held up ten fingers. "Maybe—" She withdrew one hand, leaving five fingers.

"Thank you," I said gratefully.

"*Tov.*" The bear from Rivka's room smiled. She pushed past me again to enter the *gan* and waved me in. "*Shvi,*" she ordered, pointing to a tiny chair. Then she went out to a back porch where she shouted at the screaming children in the yard. Returning to her chair, she repeated, "*Shvi!*" and demonstrated that I should also sit down. She picked up the scissors and colored paper again.

She was cutting out dozens of rectangles with an oval at one end. "*Nerot,*" she identified them. "*Shel Shabbat,*" she amplified, and I suddenly connected with the final words of the prayer I said each Friday evening at candlelighting: "*ner shel Shabbat*"—sabbath candles. She showed me the candlestick shapes she'd already finished. I smiled. An art project with a Jewish theme: I had always cringed when the kids came home with cutouts of Christmas trees and Easter bunnies.

The woman continued her skillful snipping. Something about the way she carried herself made me judge her age past menopause in spite of her black hair and unlined skin. Her dull, brutish face hid a softness that gradually revealed itself to me. She asked me something.

"I wish I could understand," I said, blushing. After all, it was my shortcoming and not hers that we were unable to communicate. "As soon as Tamara is settled in here, I'll be able to go to an *ulpan.*"

She understood my last word and smiled and nodded encouragingly. She asked something else. I understood her last word—America.

"Yes."

"*Lo tov b'Amerika,*" she commented, shaking her head and frowning. "*Zeh tov yoter b'Yisroel.*" She smiled.

Though unsure what I was agreeing with, I nodded.

She asked me something else, pointing to Tamara, then holding up her fingers and looking to me to confirm whether she should hold up four or five.

"How old is she?" I guessed at her question. "She's five-and-a-half. Almost six." I held up five fingers, then the pointer of my other hand. "Almost. In December, six," and I emphasized with the six fingers.

"*Ken?*" She looked surprised. "*Hamish v'hetzi?*" She held up five fingers, then one to which she added a chopping gesture with her other hand.

"Yes, yes!" I nodded.

"*He k'tana,*" she observed, indicating height with the flat of her hand held out at eye level.

"*Ken. Katan,*" I said, remembering the word for small.

"*K'tana,*" she corrected me, smiling. "*He k'tana. Hoo katan.*"

She lost me.

A pretty woman dressed in a flared cotton skirt and red, brimmed hat entered and smiled apologetically as she gave some explanation for her delay to the scissors-wielding woman. After receiving a reply, she turned to me and introduced herself as Rivka, and then prattled on in Hebrew.

The other woman stopped her and told her I spoke no "*Ivrit.*"

"Oh." Rivka turned back to me and said haltingly, "I no English." (I prayed she meant "I know English," but when nothing more was said, I was forced to make the other interpretation.)

"I am Cynthia Roth," I said slowly. "This is Tamara. The woman from *Sherut* Psychology told me Tamara should come to *gan.*" I waited to see if anything registered.

She looked intently at me. After a moment, she blinked. Then she shrugged and looked abashed.

"*Rega,*" the other woman said, accompanied once more by the gesture I found offensive. Rivka continued to smile wanly, unperturbed by her aide's shaking hand. The large woman heaved herself out of the chair once more and went for our translator in the other room.

Meanwhile, some of the children drifted back into the classroom and, happy to find Rivka back, bothered her with questions and complaints. Nodding politely to me, she turned her attention to her pupils.

After several exchanges between the teaching aides, the *ganenet,* and me, I was shown a small chair in the corner near the toilets.

Tamara, somewhat bewildered but happy to be around children and toys, wandered quietly through the room. Compared to the classrooms of the older children, it contained a wealth of materials: blocks, plastic dolls and animals, trucks, a play-house corner, picture books, even a little wooden cabinet with a velvet curtain containing a small Torah scroll. On the shelf in front of it were a charity box and candlesticks.

Thirty rambunctious five-year-olds entered through the back door and looked Tamara over before running into the washroom to clean their hands ritually by pouring water over them with plastic cups. They took their lunch satchels from pegs on the wall and sat down silently at the tables, awaiting the recital of the blessing.

When most of the children had finished washing, I stood and took Tamara by the hand to the lavatory to do the same. We were squirted by two children playing at the sink. Tamara received a few more unfriendly glances. When the rest were finished, I helped her wash at a puddly sink, then dried her hands on one of the damp terrycloth towels. I handed her her lunch bag and told her to go sit down.

All the seats were taken, the few spare chairs disappearing as Tamara approached a table of seated children. Rivka yelled something at a child, who pulled a hidden chair out from under the table, then pushed his own seat close to his neighbor and as far as possible from the place designated for Tamara. She sat down and ignored the obnoxious boy.

The children recited the blessing and began eating. I saw the aide distributing drinking water and offered to help her. She smiled and readily handed over her tray of plastic cups.

▲   ▲   ▲

I spent many more days in the *gan*, watching to see what activity the children were engaged in and directing Tamara to join them. When I saw a way I could help out the two adults, I did. They in turn offered me a glass of tea when they made one for themselves.

Once during lunch, they both needed to step out of the classroom at the same time and left me in charge. I wondered whether I should feel annoyed that they were taking advantage of me or honored they trusted me. I wasn't sure how to supervise the children, ignorant of their customs, classroom rules, and language. When they started giggling and acting silly to test me, I found scolding them in English was reasonably effective. A few gazed wide-eyed at me and said, "*Ma? Ani lo mevina*," but I knew very well they understood me at least as well as I understood them. In fact, I was probably learning Hebrew almost as quickly as if I attended an *ulpan*.

Most of the time, I sat in my corner, somewhat of a curiosity to the children, who called me "*imma shel Tamara*"—mother of Tamara. A couple who knew some English asked me questions about her, about her short stature, her dark skin, but never about her mental slowness. Others brought me things to look at, or copied my accent when I tried a few words in Hebrew.

I observed Tamara. She participated in everything with a minimum of help, though she approached the activities at a more primitive level than her classmates. She liked lining up the toy trucks or dressing up in the doll corner. The picture books weren't as attractive as the ones she had at home but she leafed through them. Though at school there seemed to be an understanding that the blocks were off limits for girls, Tamara watched the boys build towers and roads and imitated their structures later, back in the apartment. Though her pictures came out sloppier than the other children's, she liked pasting up the shapes of construction paper the aide cut out each day.

She squirmed—just like the other kids—during the half hour they sat in a circle and the teacher discussed the Torah reading of the week or something about the observance of the sabbath or the upcoming holidays. I could only make out every tenth word myself and pitied Tamara during that break from play.

Twice a week, the music teacher came with her accordion and rhythm instruments. Tamara responded enthusiastically, taking her turn to shake a rattle or ding the triangle, getting up to dance with the other children. The music teacher grew fond of her, telling me, "In this she does very good. Music is the universal language, *nachon?*"

After lunch the aide pulled the curtains and turned on the classroom television. (I found it amazing the Education Ministry could finance color TVs for all the *ganim* but was so stingy with basic supplies for the older grades.) The Israeli children's shows were awful: the acting was emotive, the voices exaggerated sing-song. I was mildly amused to see some Sesame Street muppets on *Rehov Sumsum*, but Tamara would beg me to take her home when it came on. Perhaps she felt betrayed that even these old acquaintances had reverted to the foreign tongue.

The other children excluded Tamara. Some just avoided her; others were hostile. Chairs were pulled out from under her, toys grabbed away. She was teased and derided. I didn't need to know the words to guess at the intentions. They were also rough with each other, but Tamara was picked on much more than the rest.

Whether she was truly unaware of their nastiness or deliberately ignored them, she effectively took away the pleasure the others would have derived if she allowed their cruelty to provoke her. She cried when she fell due to one of their pranks, but she didn't fight back or even glare at the aggressors. Once I scolded a group of girls who were faking sneezes that sprayed saliva in Tamara's direction, but for the most part, I tried not to interfere. I couldn't force the other children to accept her.

I wondered how much of her handicap in socializing with her peers stemmed from the everyday presence of "*imma shel Tamara.*" She rarely came to me. I felt superfluous in the classroom, folded into my little chair in the corner. I brought stationery with me and sent Rosh Hashanah greetings and our new address to everyone in my address book.

▲   ▲   ▲

I came to "Chadrepadhivan" in my list of addresses. Gee, I thought, forgetting for a moment, I haven't heard from Sheila in a long time. The realization that I wouldn't sent a spasm through me. Two dark-eyed girls looked at me. "*Ma at osa?*" one asked, jerking in imitation. The skin around my lips tingled. When would I ever get used to the idea? How could I have forgotten, when her daughter stood only yards away, a constant reminder? But it was too shocking, that Sheila was dead was too shocking. The two girls edged away as I stood, spilling my cards from my lap, and stumbled to the washroom to splash water on my stinging eyes.

▲   ▲   ▲

On September 26, the day before the New Year, we learned too late we should have been hording food in preparation for Rosh Hashanah, which once again fell on the two days before Shabbas. The difference to us this year was that, unlike the supermarkets in Tucson, everything was closing down for three days. On the day before the holidays, we ran from one shop to another grabbing up the leavings that remained on the shelves. We were further hampered by the inflation, which was at its peak, going from a little over 300 shekels to the dollar to about 450 during our first month in Israel. We understandably didn't want to convert more dollars than necessary but then didn't have enough money to pay for our purchases. Twice that day we had to run to the bank and stand on interminable lines.

Thus we entered the New Year. In synagogue, standing in the thick of perspiring women behind the heavy curtain (resenting being so blocked off from viewing the service), trying in vain to follow in my prayer book, I thought of the previous Rosh Hashanah, when the lights went out and I took this unusual incident as an omen for a tumultuous year.

But before I could mentally enumerate all the upheavals of the past twelve months, Tamara tugged on my hand and said, "Go peepee."

Hoping that perhaps finally she was gaining sphincter control, I rushed out of the sanctuary and searched for a toilet. I found one behind a wooden door down the hall. I carefully pulled down her diaper, she made a little, and I wiped her (with a handful of ripped-up toilet paper). I refastened her diaper with the masking tape and flushed.

When we opened the door, I discovered to my embarrassment a man waiting to use the lavatory. We had been in the men's room. How was I to know? I couldn't read the sign.

Back behind the *mehitzah*, I prayed fervently for a year of health and peace and ease. And I prayed to God that I would adjust, that I would some day feel less alienated.

# Thirteen

"So what do you think?" asked Jeff as he sat down beside me.

I looked down between the metal bars supporting the terrace railing. One of those boys playing a noisy game of tag in the street was Adam. Though it had rained during the day, now the evening sun reflected off the windows across the road. I turned to Jeff. The light caught all his pores and acne scars. "You look tired," I said.

He nodded, then took a sip from his coffee cup.

"It's hard," I admitted. Tears burned my eyes. To acknowledge the difficulty was painful. I had thought that if we came to live in God's given land, He would smooth our way.

After a pause, Jeff asked, "You sorry we're here?"

"Well, it'll get better," I reassured myself. "One month is too short to tell."

He scratched his scalp, then patted down his thinning hair and replaced his *kippah*. "I think I'll have to get another job. The college really has no money."

"Why are you worrying about that now? That's two years away."

"They have to reapply for the government funds each year and there's a good chance they'll be turned down."

"You mean after this year?"

"Yeah."

"But why? You're doing your job."

"Just the way it works. The government says to JCT, 'Support him yourself if you like him so much.' And the college can't afford to support me. They want me to support myself with grants. I don't know where to apply. They mentioned some joint U.S.-Israel grants, but the competition is fierce. And the grants would only take me through another year or two. Scrambling each year for funding: I can't live like that."

"Before you got tenure at the University of Arizona, it was sort of like that."

"Yeah, I know, and I hated it. I don't do well with that kind of insecurity. Besides, I was younger then. With each year, it gets harder for me to find another job. I was thinking: maybe I can get something in industry."

"If you think you'll be happier, Jeff."

"I don't know. Everything's so difficult here. Absolutely nothing is simple. Not knowing the language makes it ten times worse."

"I thought at least synagogue would be familiar," I added to his complaint. "I can't even find my place in the prayer book most of the time."

"Why don't you take one of our *siddurs*?" Jeff suggested. "At least they have English in them."

"You mean to services?" The idea took getting used to. It was prohibited to carry a prayer book on Shabbas back in Tucson. I sighed. "I don't think it would make that much difference. I don't even recognize the prayers most of the time."

"I know. I lose my place, too." He watched the children shouting in the street. "How much longer do you think you'll have to sit with Tamara? It would be nice if you could start going to the *ulpan* with me."

"You're much more advanced than I am. I'll never catch up." I swished the coffee remaining in my cup.

"Sure you will. You'd be surprised how much Hebrew you already know."

I thought about Ronnie. She sat for hours each day listening without comprehending to teachers and classmates. Then at home, she had to share her tiny room with Tamara, who continued to show little respect for her privacy and her possessions. Yet the hardships seemed palliative; she was less moody and dull. That was certainly true: life in Israel was too hectic and demanding to afford the luxury of growing dull.

▲   ▲   ▲

On Hapisga, in the empty lot near the bank, next to the shop where the school boys bought their snacks, twine was strung to mark a square. A pickup truck delivered large palm fronds which were heaped within the twine boundary. A man tried to sell me some fronds, but I smiled and shook my head.

The day before Yom Kippur, the children had no school and we took them downtown. At the *shuk* and on every street corner we noticed more palm fronds. But our attention was drawn to the tables and stalls decorated with strings of colored lights, with tinsel and stars in metallic colors for sale. Music blared from cassette players.

We walked up King George Street to Hamashbir, the department store. In the plaza in front, crowds milled around temporary stalls. Tamara beelined to a tinsel dealer; Ronnie ran after her.

"What's going on, Ma?" asked Adam. "It looks like Christmas."

Succos in Israel reminded me of Christmas, too—minus the gifts. Israelis adorned their *succahs* the way Christians dressed their trees. They bought the palm fronds to toss over the slat roofs of their booths and hung as much razzle-dazzle as could be crammed on the walls and dangled from the slats. Right after Yom Kippur, we heard hammering every evening as our neighbors constructed their sheds. Within the next few days, wooden walls topped with greenery graced Bayit Vegan's balconies.

The terrace off our living room wasn't a kosher place to build a *succah* because the cement floor of the terrace above us blocked a direct upward view of the sky. But the apartments had been built for observant Jews: the terraces off the kitchens were staggered, jutting several feet one way or the other beyond the ones upstairs. On our kitchen terrace, a metal framework already existed from earlier years. We hung a sheet from this to create our walls and stuck some branches and twigs the kids picked up on the street on top. We pinned Rosh Hashanah cards and Tamara's school art projects to the cloth walls.

It was a pleasant *succah*, but we lacked a table. The kitchen table was hinged to the wall. The dining table was too large. Discarded in a lot behind our building, Adam found a rusty, twisted ironing board and convinced us it would serve. Jeff and I stationed ourselves at either end, trying to stabilize the thing while we ate. We had a near disaster when I made chicken soup: we lost two bowls, but no one got scalded.

▲   ▲   ▲

Shortly after all the holidays were over and we had taken down the *succah*, Tamara's teacher Rivka told me with a shooing of her hands that I was no longer needed in the *gan*. The next day, I showed up with Jeff at the *ulpan* in Beit Hakerem.

The teacher smiled broadly and spoke slowly: "*Boker tov. Ani Sarah. Ma shmech?*"

"*Baruch Hashem,*" I replied, thinking she'd asked me how I was. I thought I was very clever, answering something more indigenous than a simple "*tov.*"

Some people snickered. "*Lo, lo. Ma shmech?*" Sarah repeated.

"*Mish-mosh?*" I asked, and the whole class laughed.

She repeated herself until I understood. She wanted my name. When I introduced myself, she said, "Shalom, Sintia."

"Sin-ti-a," I said, carefully imitating her pronunciation of my name.

The dozen other students laughed again, and I decided I was going to enjoy myself.

The *ulpan* was taught on the theory that we should learn Hebrew the way we learned our mother tongue: through listening and repeating. There were no translations, no writing. Sarah scolded me when she caught me scribbling phonetically spelled vocabulary words and their English equivalent in a small notebook. She wanted us to manifest an ear for the harsh, guttural language as though we were developmentally still in infancy, as though we had yet to learn the more abstract but useful tools of alphabets and visual symbolic representation.

At first I balked at the reversion to a childlike way of learning, but in fact I was already accustomed to the method: after my weeks in the *gan*, at the *makolet* (where I learned "*halav*" was milk, "*beytsim*" were eggs, and "*lechem*" was bread), and in the streets of Jerusalem, *ulpan* was easy.

Years before, I had been a serious but mediocre student. Now I became the class clown and soon earned the honor of being the teacher's pet. I opened my mouth often, uninhibited by the foolish sounds I uttered, and was rewarded by receiving a lot of attention and encouragement. I learned quickly. Even Jeff, with his previous exposure to the language, came to me for help with his Hebrew.

I also enjoyed the *ulpan* because so many people there were hungry to speak English. I developed warm acquaintances with retired Europeans who'd decided to settle where their pensions would go further, and tourists, usually from America, coming to Hebrew lessons while their spouses studied at Hebrew University or worked at temporary assignments in the area. Our heads ached from concentration, our throats felt raw from the pronunciations. At the break, what I'd learned to call *hafsekah*, we tumbled joyfully into the lounge, where with facility we filled our classmates in on those details of our lives we'd tried so hard to express earlier in Hebrew. Having to use Hebrew was analogous to those amusement park games with levers or dials to operate the claw on the other side of the glass. One tried clumsily to hook a good prize, the effort and frustration enormous and the success rate small. Always there was the temptation to reach over the glass barrier and snag something gracefully with a dexterous hand. English was the dexterous hand. During the break, we cheated.

▲    ▲    ▲

Life settled into a rhythm. The first thing each morning, I did the laundry. I became brave enough to hang the sheets and towels out on the cables beyond the balcony wall, but every time I dropped a clothespin—and could count the seconds before I heard it hit the ground below—I felt overcome with vertigo. Peering over the edge, I thought, How long would it take for me to hit bottom?

After walking Tamara to *gan*, I went to *ulpan* or, on the days we had no class, to the greater language lab of the streets of the city. Communicating like a child made me feel girlish. I imagined myself young, lively, and precocious as I smilingly made my way among the indulgent natives. Or maybe what rejuvenated me was the idealism implicit in our being in the Promised Land. I reverted to a more youthful frame of mind, that blessed belief that anything was possible which more typically embraces people sometime after the years of adolescent impotence and before the onset of adult cynicism. The smile was genuine. I was truly happy as I scrambled over rocky hillsides and explored my exotic surroundings.

Afternoons were quiet. From two to four, the whole city rested. After feeding the kids their midday meal, I sat at the dining table and wrote letters. Or I read *The Jerusalem Post*, or a hard-to-get novel in English. (There was a public library in the center where our *ulpan* met, but it cost us thousands of shekels for a year's membership, and our family was allowed to take out only three books at a time. The whole English collection barely filled four bookcases. I treasured the books I'd brought from America, often taking down one volume or another to savor a few pages of well-written prose.) Often I napped, recuperating from my morning's mental and physical exertions, a nod to the waning stamina of my middle-aged body.

Evenings were more challenging: making something edible for dinner out of the peculiar groceries, sharing in the familial interchange around the table, helping Adam with homework and listening to Ronnie whining.

On the two nights a week he taught his class, Jeff came home after eight. Those evenings were hard on me, in part because I had to be both parents to the children at dinner, in part because I too missed their daddy, but also because when he did return, he sat at the kitchen table half asleep, indifferent to the light supper I served him, too tired to respond to my questions, barely able to produce the hug and kiss required before the children would go to bed.

Jeff complained about the teaching. His students also were tired after a long day, and they had limited patience for his English. They couldn't afford to buy textbooks and were too casual about attending class. Sometimes in the middle of his lecture, a friend of a student would barge into the classroom to ask the student a question. Jeff came home hurt that the students didn't take his class more seriously; he was annoyed with himself for loosing his temper. "Don't they have the least concept of respect? Of common courtesy?"

*Shabbat* was still my hardest day. During the week, I began to feel more self-confident. I began to nurture a belief that I would eventually acclimate to my foreign home. But I was always deflated when I entered a synagogue and couldn't follow the service. Though sermons weren't given during the morning prayers, sometimes a man would present a Torah lesson on Saturday afternoon. These too were inaccessible to me because of my ignorance of Hebrew. I felt religiously thwarted. The other days of the week, I imagined a spirituality in the air; I sensed God's presence in even the most mundane activities, in the most ordinary places. A flowering weed growing out of a crumbling stone wall represented the abundance of His life-giving energy. The leathery Arab woman balancing a bundle on her head showed God's strength. The warm sun was His benevolence. But on Saturday, I couldn't find Him. He abandoned me to the meaningless service taking place beyond the thick curtain of the *mehitzah*.

▲   ▲   ▲

"Ma, I have a bellyache," Ronnie whispered to me when I went in to wake her one morning.

"What is it?" I asked, sharing her hushed tones. "Are you getting your period?"

She shook her head and sat up, hunching over her crumpled blankets. "No, it's not like that. It's really low down, like a cramp, just by my backside."

"Can you go to school?" I placed my palm on her forehead; she felt normal.

"Yeah, I guess so." She stretched and climbed out of bed.

"Good. Maybe you'll feel better if you move around."

She seemed fine all day but woke me during the night. "Ma," she whispered in the dark of my bedroom. "It's really bad."

I got up and went with her into the bathroom. I squinted in the light. "Where exactly does it hurt?"

"My backside. It's all itchy and sore."

I rubbed my eyes. "You want me to take a look?"

She shook her head.

"What did you eat? Maybe you're allergic to something." I tried to remember what I served for supper: only grilled cheese sandwiches and salad.

"After school I go with some of the girls for falafel. You think?"

"Ha, that's probably it. That stuff's terribly spicy." How could she eat that poison? Deep-fried balls of ground chickpeas. The smell from the falafel stands was nauseating. "Where do you get the money?"

"From my allowance. They're only two hundred shekels each and we share them."

"Well, cut it out. I need my sleep." And I lumbered back to bed.

Ronnie continued to suffer. On another night, I again found myself in the bright bathroom rubbing sleep out of my eyes. She swore she hadn't eaten any more falafel. "I hope you didn't pick up dysentery. Those places are never too clean. Do you have diarrhea?"

"No."

Adam interrupted our late-night conference. Rubbing his head, his eyes opened slits, he marched past us to the toilet and pulled down his pajama bottoms.

"Adam!" Ronnie shrieked. She turned away in embarrassment.

"Oh!" He opened his eyes and scratched some more. Before he pulled his pajamas up again, I could see scratches on his buttocks. "Hey, Ma, my rear end's killing me."

The following afternoon, I took all the children to the doctor. His office was in his apartment and, like so many interiors in Jerusalem, had a somewhat stark and shabby look. In the waiting room, which was also his living room, the cover on the couch was torn, the pastel walls were in bad need of paint, the picture books stacked on the formica end table had broken bindings and ripped, crayoned pages, and the plastic toys were encrusted with bits of dried food. Dr. Yaniv's white jacket was stained and missing a button, but his smile was kindly.

"Probably pinworm," he told me. "All the kids get it. I'll give you some pills. Does the little one take pills? I can give her a liquid."

"She seems to be fine," I said. Tamara hadn't complained of rectal discomfort.

"Yes, a liquid?" he repeated. "Your husband and you should take four pills, and the big girl, eh, let's say three. How much do you weigh?" he asked Ronnie. "About fifty kilo? Yes, let's give her three. The boy, two. The little one I will give the liquid. Five cc's. Take the medicine just before bed and first thing in the morning. I'll give you enough to repeat in a week after the eggs hatch."

"Why do my husband and I have to take the pills?" I asked.

"What, you want liquid too?" He laughed.

"No, I was just wondering why we need to take anything. We don't have any worms."

"Worms are very contagious. You can wait until you have symptoms, but by then you will probably have reinfected the children. Better to treat the whole family together. Remember to keep your hands very clean, especially under the fingernails."

The medicine came in small flasks with labels all in Hebrew. I asked the pharmacist, "Are you sure this is for pinworm?"

"What is the problem?" she asked me. She had a receiver tucked between chin and shoulder and held a pen and pad. As she spoke Hebrew into the phone, she picked at chipped nail polish on the thumb grasping the pen. Her eyes scanned the bottle I held and she nodded, careful not to dislodge the receiver.

The only reassurance I had was that, after downing the small pink pills, the children began to sleep well again.

▲   ▲   ▲

The psychologist called. I still dreaded talking on the phone, where I had no facial expression nor gesture to augment the limited, mispronounced oral vocabulary. Ruti spoke reasonably good English: she was the one who had been away until after the holidays. "I am afraid I have to tell you to remove Tamara from the *gan*," she informed me.

"What?" The thought of having to give up my morning freedom was unbearable. Besides, I thought Tamara was doing well. When I brought her in the morning, several children greeted her and helped her hang up her lunch bag. She always seemed willing to go to school, and the *ganenet* always smiled blandly at me. There was no indication of any problem.

"It is not working out," Ruti stated.

"Why? What's the problem?"

"Rivka has not told you?"

"No, she hasn't said anything to me." How could she? She spoke no English.

"Well, it is a problem when Tamara has behavior which is not acceptable," Ruti said.

"What behavior?" I pressed.

"It is the loud noises. It is very disturbing."

"She makes loud noises?"

"Yes. Rivka has not told you?"

"No. What sort of noise?"

"A loud shouting noise, I think." She demonstrated: "'Uh! uh!' It is no good. The teacher says she cannot have Tamara in the *gan*."

"When does she make the noise?" I asked.

"Especially during *rekooz*. You know what is *rekooz*? When they sit around in a circle and have a lesson? I am very sorry it is not working out."

"During the lesson, Tamara makes a loud noise?" I remembered how she and her classmates fidgeted in their seats.

"Sometimes more than once. It is very disturbing."

"Does Rivka tell her to stop?"

"I do not think so."

"Has anyone told her to stop?"

"No. It is no good. She must be taken from the *gan*."

"They take her out of class?" I asked, still unclear.

"You mean out of the classroom? No. No one has taken her out. They do not know what to do. This is why I call. We must take her now from the *gan*. It is too difficult for Rivka. She cannot handle."

"Let me first talk to Tamara. I'll tell her to stop making the noise."

"You can tell her?"

"Yes, of course. I'll tell her to stop." Did Ruti doubt Tamara's ability to comprehend?

"This is a possibility. Maybe it will help. I don't know."

"We can at least try," I said.

"Yes. Perhaps. But if she make it again, she must be removed."

"Yes, I understand. But otherwise she's doing well, isn't she? She seems to like school."

"I have observed her. She does well, considering her handicaps."

"Good. I'll speak to her and then she can stay in the *gan*."

I found Tamara in her room building a wall with her blocks. "That's very nice, Tamara."

"See, Mommy. A house."

"Very good." I sat down on her cot and she climbed into my lap. "Tamara, when you're at school, do you make a loud noise?"

"Noise?"

"A loud noise?" I repeated.

"Uh!" she shouted, then giggled.

"Why do you do that?"

"'Cause I want to." This was her standard answer to "why" questions. She smiled, then grunted again.

"What does Rivka do?"

"*Mora* Rivka."

"*Mora* Rivka," I corrected myself. In Israel, the informality of the first name was amended slightly by an addition of the title "teacher." "What does *Mora* Rivka do?"

She shrugged.

"Does she get angry?"

Another shrug. She looked worried.

"What do the other children do?" I asked.

"Laugh." She smiled broadly, obviously pleased with herself.

No doubt they found amusing the distraction which livened up the boring period. No wonder she kept doing it: her classmates reinforced the unacceptable behavior with their laughter. Like me, Tamara had resorted to being the class clown. How much better I understood Tamara, now that I shared her wide-eyed naïveté in a bewildering environment. But she had to stop the disturbance. I tried to look stern. "Tamara, listen to me very carefully: if you make the loud noise again, they won't let you go to school. Do you understand?"

She nodded.

"Do you like going to school?"

She nodded.

"Are you going to make the loud noise again?"

She nodded.

"No! Don't make the loud noise anymore. Okay?"

She nodded.

I hoped for the best.

▲   ▲   ▲

It was late fall. On a day we had no *ulpan*, I came out of the *makolet* down the steep driveway off Hapisga. Dangling from my wrists were plastic bags with handles, heavy with bags of milk and cups of yogurt and an unwrapped bread. In addition, on an open cardboard tray between my hands, I carefully held thirty eggs. I walked gingerly, afraid any one of the many irregularities in the sidewalk could unbalance me enough to lose the eggs.

When people moaned that life was hard in Israel, I immediately thought of grocery shopping. I likened myself to a displaced primitive trying to forage new terrain, worrying which leaves and roots had unpleasant taste or poisonous side-effect, forever searching to find something flavorful and nourishing in the unknown and, upon finding foodstuffs, struggling to convey the goods to the home camp.

By the path leading off Hapisga to the girls' school and the Hida, a road crew was ripping up a portion of the street. One burly man sat in the cab of a power shovel; another supervised as more men, filthy and unkempt, filled large wheelbarrows and pushed them to a spot where they dumped the chopped up tarmac and loosened earth.

I cautiously picked my way through the workmen. As I was about to turn into the path, I heard the foreman shout, "Hallo, hallo, hallo!"

I looked up just in time to see a boy, no older than sixteen and struggling to push a full wheelbarrow, unsteadied by a clod of dirt in line with his front wheel. The barrow tipped sideways and dumped half its load in the middle of the sidewalk by my feet.

The foreman ran toward him, shouting in Arabic and looking fierce. The boy cowered as though he expected the other to strike him, then set down the wheelbarrow and tried to scoop up the rubble on the pavement with his hands, furtively eyeing his supervisor. The large man shouted instructions at the boy. Then with a disgusted snort, the man turned his back on him and walked away.

Afraid of seeming too interested in the rough-looking road crew, I quickly turned the corner and hurried down the path. But I couldn't shake the image of the boy. He looked so soft, so uncalloused, so out of place among the older, stockier, hardened men. I wondered why he wasn't in school. Moreover, he was beautiful, like the dark negative of a classic marble statue, his facial features perfect, his body lean and well proportioned under his blue jeans and black turtleneck sweater. I wondered why he wasn't spotted by a talent scout and made a model or a movie star. Had no one else noticed the striking, dirt-smudged face?

Until the road was repaired and the crew moved on, I looked for him; I surreptitiously observed him every time I walked past the site, which was quite often, as I took Tamara back and forth to school that way. Within the week, he grew strong enough to push the wheelbarrow unswervingly, and his jeans became shiny black over the thighs, but he still looked too sweet to be subjected to such hard labor.

# Fourteen

A mother stopped me one morning as I dropped Tamara off at kindergarten. "We making a group *yom-huledet* at the *gan*. You will want to join us?"

"What is this?"

"Rivka tell me Tamara make her birt'day this mont'. Also my Yossi and two others. We wish to make only one party. Is enough: the childrens don't need so much parties. Rivka say she wishes only just one a mont'."

"You want to make a group birthday party at school?"

"*Ken*. You want?" She tucked loose curls under her kerchief.

"Yes, okay."

"So, is good. Give me your telephone and I will call to tell you what you must do. Twelve Detsember is good for you? Rivka wishes *Yom Reve'i*, is day when music teacher come."

I calculated *Yom Reve'i*, the fourth day of the week, to be Thursday when it was actually Wednesday. It didn't matter: I had Hebrew lessons both days. "Oh, I go to *ulpan* that day," I told her.

She frowned. "So which is more important?"

After several phone calls from this woman, I began to appreciate just how important kindergarten birthday parties were. As the last year the children celebrated in school, the kindergarten birthday party had to outdo all other parties. The classroom was decorated with floral arrangements and paper chains; the four children with December birthdays were crowned with more flowers looped into a headdress of pipecleaners and silver foil. The cake took the shape of a steam engine pulling three iced cars.

I was requested to provide sixty sandwiches with faces. Tomato paste mixed with *g'vina levan*—soft white cheese readily available in the *makolet* —made the pink base on which I placed slivers of red pepper for mouths and olives cut in half for eyes.

The significance of having the music teacher present became apparent the day of the festivities. She provided the entertainment. She accompanied the songs on her accordion and led the dances, which further glorified the four December-born. I stood awkwardly at Tamara's side as rings of five-year-olds pranced around us, chirping lively paeans. A chair was brought and Tamara told to sit down. Then children grabbed the chair legs and hoisted her into the air six times as she clung to me for balance.

The other three birthday children grew quite puffed up about themselves, ordering friends and parents around, pouting and parading. Tamara responded to all the boisterous well-wishers by clutching my hand and smiling tentatively around the thumb she sucked. At lunch, several children rushed for the honor of sitting by her. Remembering her first day in the class, I found this amusing. But it wasn't only because this day she was "famous" and special. For the past couple of weeks, I'd noticed a growing acceptance of her, even an affection toward her.

When it was time to take her home, several boys and girls hugged her warmly, chattering birthday greetings. As we approached the classroom door, everyone called, "Bye-bye, Tamara." She turned to wave back before walking out to the schoolyard.

▲   ▲   ▲

Bayit Vegan's ritual bath was on the far edge of the neighborhood—beyond the boys' school, down a dark footpath, through a deserted playground, and finally down stone stairs. Jeff worried about me, but I felt safe walking alone, even though it was an hour past sunset.

The *mikvah* had been built recently. Utilitarian rather than attractive, it boasted several baths for immersions and twenty preparation rooms. In contrast to the dark outside, the building was filled with light and activity. Wigged women gossiped in the small lounge waiting until a preparation room opened up. Once the bathing and scrubbing were completed in an individual compartment, a buzzer was pressed to call one of several *mikvah* ladies. How different from the small *mikvah* in Tucson, which was used by no more than fifteen women in a month.

In December my buzz brought an attendant fastidious in her inspection. When she checked my toes, she found some bit of callus which displeased her and, using the cuticle scissors she kept in her apron pocket, she removed a bit of live skin with the dead.

Nor did my initial immersion meet her approval: she said my elbow brushed the side of the tank. On the next try, the top of my head remained above the surface. By the time she was satisfied, my throat was sore from swallowing chlorinated water.

A full year had passed since my miscarriage. The *mikvah* always made me think of reproduction.

My foot ached as I walked back home—up the stairs, through the shadowed playground, between the tall pines which loomed above the narrow path. I wondered whether I should be frightened. I heard footsteps approaching from behind. A young man in black coat and hat passed me without a word. No, unlike in Tucson or in New York, here I had no fear of walking in lonely dark places. For all the insecurity of Israel as a state, I felt no trepidation walking within its borders. No one advised us to change our ways; they all did the same. Still, perhaps I was foolhardy. Perhaps I trusted too much in God.

The air was chilly, especially where I'd been unsuccessful in drying my damp hair and in my ears. After letting myself into our apartment, I sat a long time over the tea Jeff prepared for me, tired from the brisk walk and irritable because of my throbbing toe.

"What's the matter, Cyn?" Jeff asked. "It's okay. If you're not in the mood tonight, it can wait until tomorrow. I'm a little tired myself."

▲   ▲   ▲

"We've been having a pretty cold winter," Naomi Danziger wrote from Tucson. "We've had to turn on the heat almost every evening for a week now, but it still gets up to about the 70's during the day." I longed to be in Tucson, where the daytime sun was warm and heating was cheap and effective.

Naomi's handwriting scrawled illegibly over the page, but even missing a word here and there, I found the ease of comprehension a treat. Her letter brought to mind the faces of old acquaintances, impossible people up close but from this distance, the subjects of sentimental daydreams. I recalled unnosy women, good-natured men. Ed Zlotnick, always ready to help out. Delicious *kiddushes* every Saturday after services. I pictured Naomi's husband, standing tall and earnest at the front of the synagogue, delivering a lucid sermon and trying to keep peace between the silly old men. Bundled in bulky sweaters, I thought of sitting in the dry, baking sunlight that used to stream through our family room window in the winter. Naomi didn't know anything when it came to being cold.

We shivered. We had trouble sleeping at night because we were so chilly. Getting out of bed in the morning took courage, and I often found Tamara cuddled in Ronnie's arms when I went in to wake them. In the afternoon, Ronnie marched around the apartment wrapped in the ugly afghan, stirring up dust where it dragged behind her. I found it more comfortable to sit around in my winter jacket.

When we complained to our Israeli neighbors about the cold radiators, they explained by asking us for tens of thousands of shekels to pay our share of the monthly expense for heating oil. Who could afford to live on an Israeli salary? Neither could our neighbors. To conserve resources and keep the heating bills from rising into the hundreds of thousands, the furnace was turned on only three hours each day.

What little heat came up was shared with the clean laundry. When it was still clammy after days of hanging on our bathroom balcony clotheslines, we draped it over the radiators, where it molded to their contours and stiffened.

Hypothermia gave rise to lethargy and depression. Once again, I viewed everything in Israel as difficult and queer.

But then I reminded myself why I had come. We were living in the land God promised to our forefathers. We were living in a Jewish state. There was no sign of Christmas: in fact, on December 25, the children went to school and I ran my usual errands, never realizing the significance of the date until the evening. But always being cold made me edgy.

▲    ▲    ▲

Growing tired of hearing me nag that he should find work in the desert where it was warm, Jeff arranged to visit the Ben Gurion University in Beer Sheva. I insisted on joining him, which meant Tamara came, too, since I wouldn't be home in time to pick her up when school let out. Ronnie invited herself to go after school to a classmate's house, and our neighbor Rivka agreed to feed and watch Adam for the afternoon.

Reminiscent of our first days in Jerusalem, Jeff, Tamara, and I boarded the bus across the street as soon as the older children had left for the day. We got off at the main Egged bus station and joined the confusion. Soldiers on leave or on duty milled through the crowd. Trim youths with colorful backpacks checked maps and schedules. Squat men and women were weighed down with their parcels and their worries. I hoped I no longer looked like a tourist but wasn't anxious to become like these others. I too carried a plastic basket with sandwiches, oranges, cups and a jar of water. Diapers and a clean pair of small pants were stuffed into my shoulder bag. I wondered, though, if I could avoid whatever pinched their mouths and creased their brows.

Holding Tamara's hand, I stood on a winding line which began at the Beer Sheva sign while Jeff waited at the ticket window. Tamara's large, dark eyes scanned the scene apprehensively as she chewed on her thumb. Perhaps I should have let her go to school, but I didn't feel comfortable to impose her on anyone for the afternoon.

Jeff returned, looking distracted as he calculated how much the ticket agent cheated him. Suddenly he brightened and announced he hadn't been cheated after all. The people behind me scowled when I allowed him in line.

The bus arrived. Like a great earthworm pulling toward its head, the line moved forward and bunched at the door to the coach. Several people ran up alongside the metal barrier that separated our line from the general thoroughfare, climbed over it, and cut in ahead of us. As I stepped back to accommodate the new people, it was my turn to feel annoyed. "It isn't fair," I told their backs. "Why don't you go to the end of the line like everyone else." From behind, we were shoved forward, until we were pressed up against the offensive ones. We inched along, wondering if we'd reach the door only to be informed the bus was full.

Surprisingly, everyone on the line eventually did fit into the bus, though I was forced to hold Tamara on my lap. The man sitting next to me smelled of dust and old clothes and panted asthmatically. Jeff couldn't persuade him to take a different seat, so we were separated for the trip.

The bus took the slightly longer route via Kiryat Gat, but we were told the more direct trip through Hebron was hillier and just as slow. The man beside me sat squarely, with his bag on the floor between his feet. Tamara eyed him cautiously and imitated his shallow breathing, but he paid no attention to her. She turned to look out the window. The scenery was dull and barren, but I liked it because it fed my nostalgia for Arizona. As the bus bumped and rumbled along, we nibbled on the food in my basket. I carefully poured Tamara a little water in a plastic cup. My skirt grew sticky and wrinkled from Tamara's squirming.

Close to noon, we arrived at the Beer Sheva bus depot. The Negev sunlight made us squint, the glare bouncing off cement buildings and pavement. For the first time since winter began, I felt warm enough. I started to sweat and took off my jacket, then helped Tamara remove hers. After shifting the contents of the basket, I stuffed the bulky outer garments in with the remaining food.

Jeff stepped off the bus and joined us under an awning. "How did it go?" he asked. "Let me have a sandwich; I'm starved. Sorry you were stuck with Tam the whole way."

I pulled a bag out from under the jackets and handed it to him. "We don't have much time," I said.

"I saw the place as we were coming into town, about a mile or so back," he said, his mouth full. He continued after swallowing. "Why don't I go over there myself and you and Tam can amuse yourselves." He flipped his hand palm up to check his watch. "We should meet back here at two-thirty. That gives us almost three hours. What do you say?"

"Okay." I had looked forward to spending the day with him. But with constraints on our time and energy, it made sense for me to explore the city while he looked into employment possibilities.

He took another bite, then smiled awkwardly with his mouth full. Waving goodbye, he turned to find his way.

"Daddy, Daddy," Tamara called after him, reaching her arms in his direction.

He returned and leaned down to give her a hug and kiss.

"I go with you," she begged.

"No, you go with Mommy. I'll see you later."

"We could come with you," I suggested halfheartedly, anticipating the boredom of sitting around in offices waiting while Jeff talked to university professors and administrators.

He frowned. He shared my distaste for this plan, though for his own reasons. "She'll be too distracting. We won't be able to do any serious talking."

"Come, Tamara," I insisted. I took her hand and led her away, carrying the basket in my other hand.

"Two-thirty," Jeff called, and I nodded without turning around.

The open market was close by. It was a scaled-down version of Mehane Yehuda. The dryness made the market seem cleaner: flies and germs need moisture to breed. I bought Tamara a pair of yellow-framed sunglasses from a toy vendor, and a bunch of bananas in the next aisle (forgetting the tithe on produce). With the glasses sitting awkwardly on her bridgeless nose, Tamara stared at the Bedouin women dressed in black, ankle-length gowns embroidered in bright colors. Some balanced full baskets on top of their scarf-covered heads.

From the market, we walked through the downtown area. The narrow streets of small, dusty, sun-bleached stone buildings had a tired appearance. We looked into the showcase windows of the one department store and shared a fruit drink sold from an open stand.

A few blocks farther, we found the small compound which housed a museum of archeological artifacts from the area. We were the only visitors there. Off the museum courtyard was the entrance to a tower. I made the mistake of taking Tamara up the endless spiral staircase leading to an observation balcony. At the top, we stepped out to view the city. Vertigo threatened to overtake me when Tamara tossed her sunglasses over the railing.

"No, no! Bad girl!" I hoped no one was standing in the street below. Could I be sued for negligence leading to personal injury? My American mentality: Israelis weren't so litigious. Still, I didn't want anyone hurt.

Going down the unlit stone stairs was difficult. "Carry me," Tamara said, standing at the narrow end of a steep step.

"Here," I said, pulling her out toward the broader side of the stone. Holding her hand and standing two steps below her, I gently guided her down, nervous myself about missing my footing. When we finally emerged back into the sunny courtyard, my knees ached from the tension of our trip down.

We walked all around the outer wall of the museum but couldn't find the sunglasses. "S'gone," Tamara said with a sigh.

A man was walking by across the empty street.

"Excuse me," I called to him. "Can you tell me the time? *Ma sha'a?*"

He stopped and checked his watch. "One and twenty minutes," he called back.

"Thanks. *Toda.*" I decided to head back toward the bus station.

Tamara was tired. She stopped and squatted; I pulled her to standing. Half a block later, she stopped again. I tugged her along. When she squatted a third time and whimpered, I hoisted her onto my hip and carried her along with the basket and my bag. Across a main street, youths sat on their knapsacks by a stone structure reputed to be Abraham's well. I wanted to examine the ancient stones but was too weary to walk one step out of my way. I put Tamara down. She made the last couple of blocks on foot, stopping only one more time—and then I wanted to stop too—to admire the brightly colored, hand-knit socks a Bedouin woman was displaying on a black cloth spread on the sidewalk.

It was two by the time we got to the bus station. I took Tamara to the not-quite-clean ladies' room and changed her diaper after using the toilet myself. We came out and looked for a bench to sit down on.

"Cindy! Hey, Cyn!" Jeff ran up to us waving.

"Daddy!"

"Hi, Tam. You have a good time today?"

"Glasses gone," she reported sadly.

"Huh?" He turned his attention back to me. "Look, I think we can still make that bus if we run," he said, pointing to a lone coach at the other end of the terminal. He scooped up Tamara and I chased after him.

As we were approaching, the bus driver closed his door. "Oh, no," Jeff moaned loudly, his breath heaving out of him from running with Tamara's added weight. He stumbled against the side of the bus and thumped his fist against a window.

The driver opened for us. We clambered on, full of gratitude. "*Toda, toda raba!*" we said, panting.

The bus was half empty and we found seats together. The driver closed the door again, but he didn't pull out for another five minutes. He was only trying to conserve his air conditioning.

On the bumpy road leading away from the desert, I tried not to doze off as I listened to Jeff's description of the university. The heat and the long walk, and the lengthy bus ride made me yawn. Before I nodded off, I heard Jeff say, "I'm not sure I'd like a job there. It's a moot point, though: they have no openings."

Beer Sheva wasn't Tucson, so I didn't feel too bad. It was definitely warm there, but as I pulled on my jacket in the Jerusalem bus station, I looked around at the crowds and the activity and felt I'd returned to civilization. It surprised me that I regarded Jerusalem as home, that I already found the exotic city comfortably familiar, at least by comparison.

▲   ▲   ▲

As we came out of services one Friday evening, we saw a man pushing aside the barricade that blocked Hapisga from traffic on the sabbath. He got back into his car and was about to drive out when a group of men from our congregation surrounded him. There were shouting and banging of fists on the car hood, but at last the men parted and let the car pass. "He shouldn't live in a religious neighborhood if he wants to drive on *Shabbat*," someone commented to us.

Zvi, a man we knew from synagogue, walked over. "He know when he move to this area it is *doti*," he said in agreement. He shook his head. "What can you do?" He shrugged. "Never mind. The reason I am coming over to you is to ask you to come to us tomorrow."

"Thank you," said Jeff. "I think we're free. Cindy?"

"Yes, that would be very nice," I said.

"Good. So you will come."

"What time?" Jeff asked.

"About twelve, twelve and a half. After your dinner. You know where we live? Right over there on the small street coming off of Hapisga. Number eleven. We are in flat *daled*."

"Eleven, *daled*," Jeff repeated. "We'll see you then. No, what am I saying? God willing, we'll see you before then—at morning services."

"Good. *Shabbat shalom*."

After lunch Saturday, we put on winter jackets and boots again and went out into a cold rain. We were soaked by the time we climbed the stairs to their apartment.

"Come in. Welcome. *Shabbat shalom*," Zvi's wife Dina said as she opened the door. Numerous children ran past. Our hosts had four children, including a girl in the kindergarten next door to Tamara's. "You want to play?" Dina asked our three. "Go. Join them."

Ronnie looked miserable. She was thirteen, too old to run with juveniles. Dina noticed. She whispered something to Ronnie which elicited a smile and nod. Ronnie walked off purposefully in the children's wake. As she took my wet coat, Dina said quietly, "I have sent your daughter to talk to my niece, she is staying with us this *Shabbat*. This year she go here to Michlalah, a lovely girl." (Michlalah was the girls' teaching seminary closeby JCT.)

Two other couples were already sitting in the living room.

"Sorry we're late," Jeff said as we entered.

"Late? No, you are not late," Zvi called. "You don't want to be a Yecky."

"What's that?" I asked.

Zvi addressed the men sitting with him at the dining table. "What is a Yecky?" They laughed. To me he explained, "The Germans are Yeckies. You know: always *bediyuk*, on the dot. You say, 'Come to us at three,' and you know they will be here at five minutes until three."

I admired punctuality but made no comment.

Jeff joined the men around the table. I sat down between the other women on the couch. It was a small but attractive room, with a colorful napless area rug over the standard stone tiles, and modern Danish furniture. A vase of anemones sat in the middle of the coffee table.

"Hello. I am named Suri," said the woman on my left, offering me her hand to shake. Like our hostess and me, she was bareheaded. The fourth woman wore a beret.

"I'm Cynthia."

"Pleased to meet."

Dina handed me a plate with wedges from two cakes. "You drink Nescafé or tea?" she asked.

"Tea is fine." Israeli instant coffee tasted like chickory to me.

"You only speak English?" asked the woman on my right. The sequins on her sweater made a rustling noise.

"*Ani medeberit Ivrit*," I bragged.

The women chuckled. It was obvious by my halting accent that I couldn't speak much more Hebrew than that.

"You have a flat near here?" asked the woman named Suri.

"Yes, on Rehov Bayit Vegan."

"Ah." She nodded. "How much you are paying?"

"Four hundred dollars a month."

"So much? It is very large?"

"Not really. We have three bedrooms, a living room—"

"How many square meters?"

"I don't know."

"They are asking too much." She frowned and shook her head. "You should have ask me. I find you one cheaper. And what your husband does?"

"He's teaching at the Jerusalem College of Technology."

"Down the hill? Yes, I know this place. How much they pay him?"

"It's different every month."

"This is because of *inflatsia*."

"Inflation," Dina translated, handing me my tea.

"But approximately how much?" Suri persisted.

I was used to having Israelis ask me these direct personal questions. Jeff told me I should answer "too much" to the one about the rent and "too little" to the other, but my inquisitors were always too forceful for me to successfully evade them. I capitulated. Sooner or later she would get the information she wanted. "I don't know. About seven hundred dollars."

Suri nodded. "This is not bad."

It was considered good pay, seven hundred dollars a month after taxes. This came out to less than nine thousand dollars a year. What would we do without our American dollars? But it was nerve-racking to watch this reservoir dwindling, especially when we had no way of replenishing it.

"How long you will stay in Israel?" asked the other woman.

"No, we're here permanently. *Ani olah hadasha*," I added, gaining their nods of approval.

"It is good you push yourself to speak Hebrew," Dina observed. She settled in a chair and took a sip from her cup.

"But then how we practice our English?" asked Suri.

We all laughed. But in spite of their exertions to speak in English for me, they reverted to the language which came more comfortably to them. "Ach, we forget," apologized Dina. "Sintia, we was just speaking about a girl we know."

"Malka, pass me this," said Suri, pointing to a bowl of nuts on the table. Before tossing cashews and filberts into her mouth, Suri told me, "She used to live in my house. She is married now a few years to a *schwartze*."

"A *schwartze*?" I was surprised. My in-laws used the word to refer to the race of people who infringed on their Brooklyn neighborhood. Good *schwartzes* were janitors or house maids; bad ones were youths who hung out on corners and intimidated them with brazen stares as they walked home from the A&P. Sheila's husband Chad had been brown enough to be called "practically a *schwartze*." "Where did she meet him?" I asked.

"Right here. His people live on the other end of Bayit Vegan."

"Really?" I hadn't seen any dark-skinned people in the neighborhood. I tried to think if I'd seen any blacks at all since coming to Israel.

"So she wears covering her hair all the time," Suri continued her report. "And thick stockings and the sleeves always long, even on the hottest day, even in a *hamsin*."

"She should wear already a veil too, maybe," suggested Malka.

"We were just in Beer Sheva," I said. "How do the Bedouin women wear those long black dresses in that heat?"

"The Bedouin do not bother me," Suri stated. "They keep to themself."

"You know what is the *hamsin*?" Dina asked me. "The very hot, choking desert wind, comes from the east in late August? You cannot breathe on account of the hot, and the air is thick with yellow."

The woman on my right said to Dina, "I must lay down. I cannot even move when is the *hamsin*."

"Yes, Malka, I likewise," agreed Suri. "And I must to close all the shutters and still is dust over everything." Like children ecstatic over a crippling snowstorm, the women delighted in Jerusalem's one climatic affliction. "You haven't been here yet a summer?" she asked me. "Ah, so you don't know everything yet. Ha ha, you will see."

"Oh." I nodded.

"So how many children she has already?" asked Malka, adjusting her beret.

"She married five years already," said Suri. "So how many you think?"

"Five," the other two women guessed.

"No, four actually," Suri corrected them. "But another one on the way."

"This is the problem with the *schwartzes*," said Dina. "They are populating as fast as the Arabs. You see them more all the time. Soon they are taking over the Knesset."

"And they don't serve in the army," complained Malka. "If at least all the young men would serve in the army."

"They say is against their belief," said Suri. "Ha! They just want to stay behind so they get head start on making the babies."

Dina said, "In Me'a Shaarim they are throwing stones at the Egged buses."

"Ah, but is because the advertisement in the shelters," said Suri.

"The Egged is stupid, really," Dina granted. "What they think of? To put by Me'a Shaarim advertisement of women in bikini."

Me'a Shaarim was an ultra-Orthodox neighborhood. "Oh!" I said. "By *schwartzes* you mean Chasidim."

"Yes, the black coats," said Dina. "Chasidim, Haredi. What do you think?"

"People with black skin."

She laughed. "No, those are the Et'iopians. They too are problem. They are being brought secretly to an absorption center somewhere in the Negev?" she asked Suri.

"Yes, in Dimona, I think," Suri answered. "A friend of ours is working at the center. Israel sneak them out of Africa and bring them there, bus loads in the dead of night. They have nothing but the clothings on their back. They all of them must be deloused. Some never before have seen running water from a faucet."

"You think they are really Jews?" asked Malka.

"The Chief Rabbis says yes," said Dina, "so we have to take them in."

"But they are so small, and with the dark skin," said Malka, patting down the sequins on her bosom.

"So? And what about the Moroccans? And the Yemenite? We had to take them too."

"And see the problems we has with them now?" Malka pointed out. "They say in Tel Aviv the Sfardim have gangs and it is no longer safe to walk in some places."

"They don't understand about laws," Dina stated.

"They have an Arab mentality," Suri agreed.

"And what about the Russian immigrants?" asked Dina.

"Ah, the doctors from Russia," said Suri. "They are all coming here saying they are doctors. A woman I know went to one, she is lucky to be alive."

"They don't have the same standards," Dina suggested.

"What do you mean?" Suri asked. "You believe they are all doctors? How can one check?"

"They must have a certificate?"

"In Russian? You can maybe read Russian?"

Dina turned to me. "Your little girl, I notice she too have a darker skin."

I nodded.

"How is this? I see you are not dark. Your husband, he is not dark."

"She's adopted."

Malka asked Suri, "What means this?"

"She was born to different parents," I explained.

"Ah!"

"But she is Jewish?" Suri wanted to know.

"Oh yes. Absolutely."

"Her parents were Sfardi?"

I shook my head.

They all stopped to drink. Afraid they were formulating further questions, I began: "A man tried to drive through the barricade on Hapisga last night."

"Maybe it was not yet candlelight," Malka suggested.

"No, Zvi told me," said Dina. "He said it happen after services."

"*Shabbat* starts so early in the winter."

"Still. He lives here. He should keep track," Dina insisted.

"The *lo-doti* hate us, you know," said Malka. "They want to have football and movies on *Shabbat*."

"So let them move to Tel Aviv," Suri said.

Dina turned to me and smiled sadly. "You know, is true, Sintia, that Israel exist only thanks to her enemies. If all the Arabs would make peace, what would happen then? The only thing what save Israel is the bigger hate surrounding us."

# Fifteen

"What's for dinner, Ma?" Ronnie asked as she sauntered into the kitchen.

"Scrambled eggs," I reported as I cracked another shell.

"Scrambled eggs! That's breakfast."

"When was the last time we had scrambled eggs for breakfast?" I asked.

"I don't know. On Sunday mornings in Tucson, when we didn't have to run to school. I hate going to school on Sunday. It isn't fair, having to go to school six days a week."

"But you have a lot of holidays, and your day is shorter here," I said.

She wrinkled her nose. "Dad has a class tonight, doesn't he? You wouldn't serve him scrambled eggs for dinner."

Adam joined us. "I'm starving. When are we gonna eat?"

"Don't get your hopes up," Ronnie advised him. "We're having scrambled eggs."

"So? It's better than that creepy lentil stuff Mom made last night."

"In Tucson we used to have chicken or hamburgers or lamb chops every night," Ronnie complained.

"In Tucson," I pointed out, "meat was cheaper and your father's paycheck was fatter."

"No it wasn't," Ronnie argued. "Feig's meat was twice as expensive as the nonkosher stuff they sold in the supermarket. Here we don't pay extra to get kosher: all the meat is kosher."

"The meat here is roughly the same price as the kosher meat in Tucson," I informed her. "But it's a lot more expensive than all other food here. How many Israelis do you know who eat meat every night? It's probably not even healthy to eat so much meat." I wiped my hands on the dish towel. "Why don't you slice some bread, Ronnie?" Peripherally, I saw her tongue extend beyond her lips as she went for the loaf and the serrated knife.

I had spent an hour that morning at the Psychology Bureau talking to Ruti. She told me Tamara should attend a special school, and I attempted to convince her that Tamara should stay in the local kindergarten. As I beat the eggs, I ruminated on Ruti's comment, "You have taken on a great deal in a short time. First, to adopt a retarded child and then to come to live in Israel. Life is very hard here. You are under much stress. This must make you feel angry. You are depressed and resentful." When I denied these emotions, she told me I wasn't being honest with myself.

Preoccupied with these thoughts, I brought the eggs to the stove. As I poured them into the frying pan, they sizzled. The sound made me flinch.

▲    ▲    ▲

"Tamara, pick up your dirty clothing and put it in the hamper," I scolded from the doorway.

"I tired, Mommy. I go to sleep." Grinning, she climbed into her bed.

"No, Tamara. First pick up your clothing."

She remained in bed.

"Tamara!"

"No!"

Ronnie came in. "I'll do it, Mom," she offered.

"No, Tamara has to do it," I said with irritation, failing to acknowledge Ronnie's generosity.

"Well, sor-ry," Ronnie said, rolling her eyes before making an about-face and leaving.

Ignoring Ronnie's theatrics, I walked to the bed, grabbed Tamara by the arm, and yanked her to her feet.

"Ow!" She began crying. "Bad Mommy. You hurt me. Go away. I want my other mommy." She tried to slap me with her free hand.

Still gripping her arm, I forced her to lean over and touch her crumpled shirt. She splayed her fingers, refusing to grasp the garment. "Pick it up!" I growled. She complied, then changed her mind and dropped it again. As I spanked her, I heard Jeff's voice over Tamara's screams.

"Daddy's home," Adam called.

"What's going on?" Jeff asked, coming to a stop at the door to the room still wearing his outer clothing and carrying his briefcase. He leaned wearily against the doorjamb and opened his winter jacket.

I straightened to look at him. "She has to pick up her clothing before she goes to bed," I insisted.

His look seemed to say, Is it worth the trouble? I was in no mood to be bucked and returned a look of stoniness. He sighed. After placing his bag on the floor, he walked over to Tamara. "Mommy's angry at you. You should listen to her when she tells you to do something. Come on. Let's pick up the clothing. You want me to help you?" Together they piled the things on her bed; then Jeff folded them and put them away in the drawers.

He followed me into the kitchen, where I started cracking more eggs for his supper.

"What's the matter?" he asked gently. "Did I do something wrong?"

"The clothing was dirty," I stated as I beat the eggs.

▲     ▲     ▲

We were introduced to someone at our synagogue who had a younger brother who was retarded. The woman warned us against the city-run special schools. "They do nothing but baby-sit, and not so good, at that. I once went to pick up my brother and there was another boy who was putting something in the ear of a girl. The teacher paid no attention."

"What do you recommend?" Jeff asked.

"I hear now they have a very good school for younger children near Me'a Shaarim. It's Haredi, but I don't think you have to be Haredi to send your child."

"What's Haredi?"

"The ultra-Orthodox. You know."

Jeff and I went to visit the school. It was located in a low white building on an unpaved alley. The classrooms were bright and pleasant, the office cramped and dark, no more than a large closet. The director, an imposing man in a long coat which matched his dark, curly beard, made us feel welcome. He called in one of his teachers to act as translator.

We talked about Tamara, about coming to live in Israel, about Ruti. The teacher explained that this school, too, had to comply with the Psychology Bureau recommendations, but their own psychologist could make a request if he felt the school suited Tamara's needs. After a brief tour of the facilities, we set up an appointment for Tamara to meet with their psychologist.

▲     ▲     ▲

Ronnie and Adam left for school, and, on cue, Tamara hung her lunch bag around her neck and started for the door.

"No, wait, Tamara," I called from the bathroom, my mouth full of toothpaste.

"Come, Mommy. Time to go to school."

I joined her at the door. "No, Tamara, we don't have to leave yet," I said. "Remember I told you that today we're going to visit a different school?"

"I go to *my* school," she insisted.

I glanced at my watch. Even accounting for the half-hour bus ride, it was too early to leave. "Okay, Tamara. Let me just finish getting dressed and we'll go."

Out on the street, she again balked when instead of hiking up the hill to the Hida, I led her across the street to the bus stop. "No, no! Go to school!"

"Yes, we are going to school, only a new school, just for today."

The pleasure of riding in the bus distracted her. But when we stepped down in an unfamiliar neighborhood, she remembered her misgivings. As we approached the low white building, we saw handicapped children being helped off a small school bus. Tamara tugged a lock of her straight hair as she eyed them. "Let's go home," she announced.

"See all the nice children," I coaxed her, pushing her through the gate.

There was no one at the office, so we walked down the corridor of classrooms. Tamara looked warily into a sunny room with whitewashed walls and colorful toys laid out on a low table. A young woman rolled a boy in a wheelchair to the table and called for three other boys to take seats. The boy in the wheelchair sat in an awkward posture, with his neck craned forward and his head tilted back. The others had the flattened features of Down syndrome. I wondered if Tamara recognized herself in their faces.

The woman saw us and pointed down the hall, directing us in Hebrew. When I turned around, I saw the teacher who had met with us in the office the previous week. She told me where to find the psychologist.

Yitzhak welcomed us into a small, dark space containing a desk and two chairs. Speaking English fluently, he excused himself to find a chair for Tamara. I noticed that plaster was crumbling away from the wall and fluffs of mildew grew from the damp holes.

When he returned, Tamara climbed onto the folding chair and narrowed her eyes on him.

"Good morning," he tried without success. "Would you like to see my book?" He held up a battered picture book. Still no response from Tamara. "You don't want to talk to me yet? Okay. Maybe I'll talk to *Imma* first. Do you call her *Imma*?"

"Mommy," I suggested.

"Shall I talk to Mommy?" he asked her.

Tamara held her hard, silent stare.

I tried to answer Yitzhak's questions candidly, but I was cautious, remembering Ruti's betrayal when I was open with her. I didn't want to be accused again of harboring resentment and anger. As it was, I spoke too much: I sensed Tamara's annoyance with our discussion about her. She unzipped her lunch bag and took out her sandwich, then deliberately pinched pieces off the crust and threw them on the floor. "Tamara, stop that!" I scolded. My cheeks grew warm. "She's never done that before," I apologized to the man.

Maintaining his calm voice, he asked Tamara, "What are you doing?"

"That," she said, repeating the act.

"You're ripping the bread and throwing it down?" he asked.

"Yes." She smiled, obviously pleased with herself.

"Why do you do this?"

"'Cause I want to."

"I see." He nodded. "Is it fun?"

She shrugged.

"Are you hungry?"

"No."

"Put away your lunch, then," he said.

She put the sandwich back in her bag.

I leaned to pick up crumbs, but Yitzhak waved impatiently for me to stop.

"Good," he said. "Can you zip the bag closed?"

She showed him she could.

"Very good. Now let's play a game."

"No."

Ignoring the "no," he described the game: he would touch an object, and she had to name it. He pointed to the book.

Tamara clamped her mouth shut.

"Go on. Say book."

"Say book," she teased.

"Good. Now what is this?" He held up his pen.

She shrugged and shook her head.

"This is a pencil. Say pencil."

"Say pencil."

"Good. What is this?" He pointed to his desk. After a pause, he instructed her: "This is a table."

"Table."

"Very good. How about this?"

"Chair."

"Excellent. Now this?" He reached over and touched the tip of her nose.

She giggled. "Nose."

"Right. How about this?" He brought his finger back to his own nose.

"Nose."

"Are you sure?"

"Yes."

"But I thought you said this was a nose." Leaning close, he touched hers again.

She touched her nose and his nose, saying, "Nose, nose."

"We both have noses, don't we," he agreed.

She got down from her chair and picked up a folded black umbrella she found in a corner. "Umbrella," she stated.

"Right. What do we do with an umbrella?"

"I don't know."

"Sure you do. We open it up. When do we use it?"

"I don't know."

"Well, for instance, would we use it today?"

"Yes." She was smiling.

"Yes? Look outside my window, Tamara."

She glanced at the small pane. In spite of the streaks of dirt, blue sky shone through. "Yes, need umbrella."

"You're being silly. When do we need an umbrella? When it's raining out. It isn't raining."

"Yes it is."

Tamara refused to stack blocks, complete a puzzle, or identify pictures for Yitzhak. Though he said he believed me when I insisted she could do these things, he indicated that he wasn't sure she belonged in his school. "I can't emphasize enough the importance of behavior and cooperation. IQ is one thing, but in order for an education to be suitable, a child has to be willing to learn."

"She behaves very well in the *gan*," I protested.

"Well, what can I say?" His raised eyebrows implied he found that hard to believe. "I'm not saying she shouldn't go here, I just think we have to carefully consider what is best for all parties concerned. Let's see what the *Sherut Psychologie* recommends, and I will present my findings to our governing board."

I couldn't believe a special school would hesitate to accept Tamara, a capable child, who had adapted so well to a change of parents and two drastic changes in environment, and who had successfully integrated in classes of normal children both in Tucson and here.

Tamara was defiant and melancholy the rest of the day. She sat in a corner of her room, sucking her thumb and pulling her hair. Then she picked up a block and turned it over and over in her hands. When I tried to comfort her, she shouted "no" and threw the block at me, grazing my cheek. I grabbed her and spanked her, then sat her in my lap and held her close. "What's bothering you, Tamara?" I asked, rocking her in my arms.

When I took her to school the following morning, she hung back, sulking when her classmates greeted her enthusiastically. In Hebrew, they asked where she'd been, whether she'd been sick. She seemed angry at them, as though they were somehow responsible for the previous day's visit to the special school.

Was it possible that she understood she had a handicap? I realized she must, she had to be aware she was different, that she couldn't do what her peers did. She must have known Yitzhak and I were talking about her and her limitations. I thought back to the time I told her she couldn't make the loud noise in school anymore. In how many other ways had she exerted herself to control her behavior, suppress her impulses to conform to what was socially acceptable in her class? Visiting the special school must have made her feel like a failure, as though all her efforts to fit in at the kindergarten had not been enough.

Two little girls, each with an arm around her, finally persuaded her to join them in the dress-up corner. She began to thaw, to forgive them for their imagined rejection. As I watched from the classroom door, the girls fussed over her, draping colorful rags around her shoulders, hugging and petting her. The corners of her mouth began to twitch, and then she grabbed a ratty wig off one girl's head. The three shrieked with delight at this surprise.

I went home and called Yitzhak. I told him I didn't want to send Tamara to his school.

## Sixteen

The incessant shrieks and giggling of the girls in the apartment induced me to join Jeff on a sabbath walk. That and the hope of warming up in the afternoon sun. "It's actually nicer outside than in," I commented as I stepped beyond the entry, but perhaps I was sweating from the three-flight descent to the street. People told us of the new high-rise hotels downtown that had elevators programmed on Saturdays to operate continually, automatically stopping at each floor, so Orthodox guests could get upstairs to their rooms without violating the *Shabbat*. But our elevator wasn't so sophisticated; none of us could use it.

There were many people out walking. With the neighborhood streets closed to traffic, families and friends strolled down the middle of Rehov Bayit Vegan, skirting around boys playing tag, girls jumping rope. Some of the families had as many as ten children, all the girls in identical dresses of varying sizes, all the boys in dark suits. Adam ignored us as we walked past him. I wondered what damage the wild game would do to his one pair of synagogue pants.

"You think Tam's all right upstairs?" Jeff asked as he unzipped his winter jacket. Maybe it was the stone tile floors that made the apartment as chilly as a cave. The air outside felt balmy.

"Ronnie's there."

"Yeah, but she's busy with Batya."

I shared his misgivings. Ronnie's recent friendship had the intensity of a death grip. When Batya no longer cared for her previous girlfriend, she latched onto Ronnie, who was lonely enough to welcome amity from anyone. Everyone else was ignored when the two were together. "I wish she weren't so enamored of Batya. What does she see in her?"

"She speaks English," Jeff stated.

"Not very well."

"Better than anyone else in Ron's class." He waved to a man and woman walking toward us.

"Who's that?" I whispered. The middle-aged woman emphasized her overripe beauty with an excess of bright cosmetics. Her homely companion had aged more gently; there was a pleasant softness to his features.

"Prof Litansky from the college. Ya'acov. What's his wife's name?"

"Oh my goodness, I should remember." I started going through the alphabet. "P" seemed to have some significance. "*Shabbat shalom*," I greeted them as they approached. Penina, that sounded right. "*Ma shlomech*, Penina?"

"*Tov, toda, aval ani* Pertsa," she replied with a sneer.

I flushed, embarrassed I'd called her by the wrong name.

She rattled off a good deal more Hebrew and grinned at my bewilderment. "What?" she cajoled. "You've been here so long and don't speak Hebrew yet? I thought you were an intelligent woman." She chuckled with amusement, then turned on Jeff. "What about you? You by now of course *medaber Ivrit*, no?"

"*Me'at, me'at*," he replied not altogether accurately. "*Le'at, le'at*"—little by little—was the stock answer to questions about learning Hebrew.

She leaned toward him. Batting mascaraed eyelashes and holding her hand beside her mouth to exclude me, she imparted a boisterous aside in Hebrew followed by raucous laughter.

I doubt Jeff understood more than three or four words of her comment, but he chuckled along. Professor Litansky was very influential at the Jerusalem College of Technology, and Jeff certainly didn't want to slight his wife, even when it was obvious she was having fun at my expense.

Ya'acov Litansky smiled kindly at me. "How are you doing? Are you beginning to feel somewhat settled here?"

"Yes."

"That is good."

His wife interrupted to remind him of an appointment.

"Ah! We must go," he apologized. "We know of three new babies born this week. We are off to wish a *mazel tov*." Then he added, "We must have you for dinner some time."

"Thank you," I said, not that I expected the invitation to materialize.

"*Shabbat shalom*," Jeff called as they departed. We continued in the other direction. When they were beyond earshot, he said, "I don't know what I'm going to do about next year."

"You mean your job?"

"I don't think the college has the money to keep me on, and now I'm worried about Tam too. Come, let's sit down."

We had reached a park. After settling on a bench, I asked, "What's bothering you, Jeff?"

"I think it's becoming evident that that psychologist is going to place Tam in a special school next fall."

"We could just refuse, couldn't we?" Ruti was a strong-willed woman; I didn't look forward to standing up to her.

"Well, we certainly should try, but I doubt we'll be successful," Jeff predicted.

"Why not? We're her parents."

"Have you had any success convincing her up 'til now?"

"Maybe she's right," I said. "Maybe Tamara would be better off in a special school."

"Do you really think that, Cyn?"

"I don't know. Maybe if she were in a special school, she'd be toilet trained by now. Some DS kids are already reading at age six."

Jeff turned to look at me. "Do you really believe that, that she'd be doing better in one of their monkey houses? She's doing so well in the regular classroom. Do you really think she'd be better off with a bunch of kids who drool and rock in their chairs all day?" His broad brow bunched up with tension. He obviously wanted me to agree with him.

I couldn't do it. Things he said irked me. "Wait a minute: I didn't see any drooling and rocking at the school we visited."

"Well, you know what I mean," he qualified. "You can't tell me those kids looked normal."

"Neither does Tamara," I shot back.

"But she's not as bad as them," he insisted.

As a child, I'd been cautioned by my liberal father to be wary of references to "them." Lumping people in groups and holding them at arm's length led to generalizations which in turn led to prejudice. On a fundamental level, I railed at Jeff's prejudice; a more measured evaluation of his comments pointed to the justification of his not wanting Tamara lumped with a group and segregated.

"Tam didn't like those kids, either," he pressed. "She could tell they were different."

My exasperation burst forth. "How can we expect people to accept Tamara when we view other retarded children negatively? If we don't want our kid to play with retarded kids, why should we expect other people to let their kids play with our retarded kid? Why should the children here in the *gan* play with Tamara when Tamara, who's retarded herself, thinks she's too good to play with a handicapped kid?"

Jeff was thoughtful. "I don't think *any* kids should be sent to special schools," he said, changing his tack. "I'd like to see them all mainstreamed."

I rejected his sweeping condemnation of special education. "In a regular classroom, they wouldn't get the extra attention and instruction they need."

"We're back to that?" he asked. "You really think Tamara would learn more in one of those places? In a place where one kid sticks things in another kid's ear?"

"I can't believe they're really like that. No parent would put a child in such a situation. Anyway, we wouldn't send her to something like that. The one we visited was very caring."

"All right, even that one. Would she be better there?"

"I don't know," I admitted. "Maybe she would if she had the right attitude. The psychologist there, that Yitzhak, indicated he didn't think she'd benefit from the school because she was so uncooperative. But if we could get her over her rejection of the place, it looked like the other kids were doing well there." I turned to him. "Didn't you think so? You thought it was a pretty nice place, didn't you? Otherwise we wouldn't have even considered it."

He slouched down on the bench and watched two children on a see-saw. "Anyway, Tam didn't like it. I think she should go to a place she wants to go to."

"But realistically, where will she go next year? This year is fine, but is she really ready to go into first grade next fall? You've seen what those classrooms are like: no toys, no decorations, just a bunch of desks in a dreary room. She couldn't sit there all day listening to a teacher drone on in Hebrew."

"Why can't she repeat kindergarten?" he suggested.

"Yeah, and what about the year after that?" I pushed.

"We can worry then."

I sighed. I wished the problem would go away. If we hadn't adopted Tamara, we wouldn't be worrying about schools. But as difficult as our complex life was, when I imagined it without the complication of Tamara, it seemed too flat and simple. Maybe Ruti was right: we did seem to take on a lot of challenges. But wasn't that what life was all about? Stretching to meet one's responsibilities, pushing oneself to do a little more? The alternative was to shrink and stagnate, to become a smaller person. That's what I'd been doing in Tucson. Life was too easy there, too complacent. It was becoming meaningless and stale. Acknowledging the breadth Tamara added to our lives, the texture and richness she brought, I felt a surge of affection for her. Suddenly I wished we hadn't left her behind in the apartment with Ronnie; I wanted her with us, so that I could grab her in my arms and squeeze her tightly to me. She was worth a fight. "I'll go talk to Ruti again," I said with determination. "Why don't you come with me this time? Maybe if we outnumber her, she'll buckle under."

All the creases fell out of Jeff's forehead and he pulled his sensuous mouth into a smile. "At least I don't have to fight you!" Regardless of being in public, he leaned to kiss me, but I pushed away, peripherally aware of the other people in the park.

▲    ▲    ▲

My muddy stockings felt clammy on my feet, and I shifted in my seat. The overhead lighting spilled weakly onto the neat stack of old picture books, the dolls with stained, faded faces, the cracks in the plastic-covered chairs, and the chips and scuffs on the legs of Ruti's desk. The air smelled of wet raincoats.

Jeff reiterated our desire to keep Tamara in a regular classroom. Ruti insisted we were too emotionally involved with Tamara to decide objectively what was best for her.

"Of course we're emotionally involved," Jeff exploded. "On the contrary, that's why we're the ones who should choose for her. We of all people want what's best for her. All you're interested in is your damned statistics. That and filling your damned special schools. If all the handicapped kids were mainstreamed, you'd be out of a job, wouldn't you?"

Ignoring Jeff's outburst, Ruti continued to outline her long-range plans for Tamara. "Even if it were permissible for her to repeat kindergarten, which it is not in this case, what do you suggest? That she repeat kindergarten indefinitely? Because I can assure you, she will never be ready to go into a normal first grade class. You are unable to be realistic about her."

"I'm very realistic," Jeff maintained. "I'm realistic enough to see she won't do well in your special schools. As her parents and legal guardians, we request that you consider our wishes."

"I have considered your wishes, but then I must do what I know from my years of training and experience."

Jeff gathered up his coat and got to his feet. "Come on, Cyn. We're wasting our time." He glared at Ruti as he stomped out.

Ruti called to me before I reached the door.

Reflexively, I stopped and turned, instantly regretting the lack of resolve my action implied.

"Sintia, you are more reasonable," she beckoned softly.

You're counting on me to be the conciliatory female, aren't you? I thought, my own rage growing. Though I wavered in my conviction about Tamara's schooling, I wouldn't be coerced into betraying my husband.

"It is often this way," she was saying. "Fathers find more difficulty in loving imperfect children, so they must not allow themselves to see the imperfections."

"Cynthia, are you coming?" Jeff growled behind me.

"My husband and I have been more than reasonable," I stated coldly, then began to heat up. "It is you who are stubborn and unreasonable. I have come here how many times and tried to explain to you what we want for Tamara—"

"You don't owe her any more explanations," Jeff interrupted.

I tried to make my kitten face look as ferocious as a lion's, then turned my back on Ruti's enigmatic smile.

Jeff grabbed my wrist and dragged me to the office of the woman in charge. Flouting courtesy, he swung open the door and marched in.

She was on the phone.

"I want to talk to you," Jeff demanded.

"*Rega ehad*," she said into the receiver, then smiled at Jeff. "Please to wait outside. I will see you in one minute."

"We'll wait right here." Jeff helped himself to a seat.

She raised her eyebrows, then returned to her call.

As she rattled on in Hebrew, I had an opportunity to contemplate whether Jeff's angry assertiveness would bring results. I tended to doubt it. But then again, my diplomacy had accomplished nothing. What troubled me more was that Jeff normally exhibited an easy-going temperament: his anger was indicative of a deeper frustration than being crossed by Ruti. I thought of other symptoms of his recent agitated state: fatigue, impatience, insomnia. Why couldn't he relax and adapt to Israel? Why couldn't he be more accommodating? I knew I should be more sympathetic, but his gloominess irritated me. I feared its underlying threat.

The woman hung up, then yanked down the waist of her shirt before turning her attention to us. "What can I do for you?" she asked cheerfully.

Jeff had calmed down. "Sorry I barged in here like that. It's just that I'm so—" His eyes scanned the room as though he hoped to find the word he was looking for. "We were just talking to Ruti about our daughter Tamara, and I—" Unable to express himself, he shook his head, squeezed shut his tearing eyes, and swallowed. When he opened his eyes again, he looked a little better.

I was glad to see he had regained his self-control. The important thing was that we were in Israel; kept in perspective, these bureaucratic games were just small hurdles in our adjustment to living in our homeland. I sat quietly as he again described our objectives in raising Tamara and our abortive interview with Ruti.

Her eyes were sympathetic. "I am very sorry you have had this misunderstanding with the psychologist. I will speak with her, and I am sure we can work this out."

"Good." Jeff relaxed.

"However, I must remind you that I hold Ruti in high opinion. I am sure she will explain to my satisfaction her reasons for her recommendations."

Jeff winced. "What are you saying?" he cried out. "That after all we've just explained, you're still going to follow her recommendations?"

"I did not say that," the woman corrected. "I only say I must listen to her just as I have listen to you." When she smiled, her lips looked greasy. "That is only fair, no?"

"But you expect to agree with her," Jeff surmised.

The woman nodded. "I never before have had to override her decision."

"But this is a special case. Tamara is doing so well in the regular *gan*. You yourself placed her there."

"That is correct," she stated, unmoved. "I am very happy to see it has work out so well." She leaned back in her chair and clasped her hands over her broad middle.

Jeff looked ready to cry. "Come," I said softly, rising to my feet. I gently prodded him out of his chair and led him through the door.

▲   ▲   ▲

In *ulpan* the next day, Jeff slouched in his seat, focusing on his pen and refusing to participate. I was up to my usual clowning, joking that in Hebrew, "*me*" meant "who," "*hoo*" meant "he," and "*he*" meant "she," but my amusement was diminished by the sullen man to my left. At the break, our teacher Sarah approached him.

"What is the matter, Yosef?"

"What difference does it make? You can't do anything about it." He continued to stare at the pen he played with.

"You are having some trouble?"

He finally looked up at her. "It's not right. These psychologists think they know better than everyone. I'm not going to let them push me around. I'm not going to let them decide my family's future."

"What is this? What do the psychologists say?"

"That my daughter, who's doing fine in the regular class, should really be in a special program."

She registered surprise and concern. "She is not keeping up with the other childrens? She is perhaps having trouble with the Hebrew?"

"She has Down syndrome," I supplied. When Sarah didn't understand this, I added, "Mongoloid."

The outdated name brought recognition, undoubtedly conjuring up all the outdated misconceptions and prejudices. "Then she should be in a special school," she said. "It is for the best. Why do you not want this special program for her? They will not charge you for this. In Israel, the state pay for this."

"No, it's not for the best," Jeff corrected. He got up and left the room, left the building.

He never returned to the *ulpan*. I felt like a traitor each day I showed up without him.

## Seventeen

"*Boker tov*," I greeted Jeff and Adam, the first two at the breakfast table.

They didn't return my smile. Jeff turned back to Adam and asked, "Why do you think they do that?"

Adam stared at the bread and cheese on the plate in front of him. We often ate this for breakfast; prepared cereal was too expensive. "I don't know. They say 'cause I'm American."

"What!"

"That's what they say."

"What's the matter?" I asked, sitting down with my cup of coffee.

"Adam's been having trouble with the boys at school," Jeff explained. "He says they're giving him a hard time."

"They hit me, too," he added.

"Who does?" I asked.

"Some kids at school. They throw their orange peels at me and stuff."

"Why?"

"I don't know," Adam insisted.

Too many questions came to mind. Was Adam provoking the boys? How was he responding? What did the teacher do?

Jeff got in a question before I had a chance: "Does the teacher know what's going on?"

"Yeah, I guess so, some of the time. I mean, sometimes she's right there when they start in on me."

"Doesn't she do anything?" I asked.

He shrugged, then picked at the cheese, breaking off a small piece and rolling it between his fingers. "Not much. Sometimes she tells them to be quiet and go back to their seats."

"What about your friends? Don't they stick up for you, or are they too chicken to get involved?"

"I don't have any friends." He slunk down in his chair and watched his fingers rolling the cheese.

"What do you mean? You have lots of friends," I said. "You're always going down to play with them."

"No one from my class. Just some baby kids who live around here."

"What about Ari?"

"We're not too friendly anymore."

Ronnie led Tamara into the kitchen. At once annoyed and relieved by the distraction, I jumped up to slice them some bread. "Are you doing anything to irritate the other boys?" I asked from the cutting board.

"No, Ma. I'm just sitting there minding my own business, and then someone whispers, 'Adam, Adam.'" He stressed the second syllable of his name the way the Israelis did. "And when I turn around, I get hit by a spit wad."

"Pass the milk, please," Ronnie requested.

"And then what happens?"

"Nothing. The other kids laugh, the teacher tells them to shut up and then continues the lesson like nothing's happened."

"Do you get mad? Sometimes kids like to tease someone they can get a rise out of," I said, still looking to find a motivation.

"I don't do anything."

"Maybe you have to stand up to them," Jeff suggested alternatively. "Maybe they're testing you."

"I do that, too. At lunch recess, they're throwing their garbage at me, right? and I turn around and tell them, 'Will ya cut it out?' They don't, so I got up and walked up to this one guy, a big, tough kid, ya know? and I gave him a good shove."

"Good," Jeff said.

I cringed. I hated thinking of my kid getting into fist fights. "Then what happened?" I asked.

He flicked the cheese ball across the table.

"Ma! That landed in my milk," Ronnie complained. "No wonder no one likes you. You're disgusting." She carried her glass to the sink and emptied it, then washed it with exaggerated care. Finally, she returned to the table. "Batya says everyone picks on you because you're American."

"See?" Adam said.

"But you're American too," I pointed out.

"Yeah," Ronnie agreed, "but I'm a girl."

Baffled, I shook my head.

Jeff flipped his wrist to check the time. "It's getting late. You better eat up or you'll be late for school. We can talk more this evening."

"I told you, Dad: I don't wanna go to school." I had a feeling the discussion had come full circle.

"I know, but staying home won't solve anything." Jeff squeezed Adam at the shoulder and the two got up from the table, Adam having eaten nothing. "Oh, I almost forgot to mention," Jeff addressed me as he set his cup down by the sink. "Prof Litansky invited us for the Friday night after this. I told him we'll come. Okay?"

▲     ▲     ▲

That afternoon, when I got back from picking up Tamara from *gan*, an official-looking letter addressed to Jeff was in the mailbox. I took it upstairs and handed it to him.

He was sitting at the dining table with his books open, taking notes for his class that night. "What's this?" Ripping open the envelope he pulled out something with a government seal on the letterhead. Neither he nor I could make out the typed Hebrew.

"Let me see, Dad," offered Adam, just home. For the moment, he seemed unperturbed by the peril he presumably endured in school. He sounded out some of the words. "This is from the Army. It says you have to report for duty."

"What!"

"Here, let me," Ronnie said, coming in and grabbing it from him. After a minute of study, she handed it back to Jeff. "He's right, Dad. Something about *Melu'im*."

"The reserves?"

"I think so."

"Let me ask Rivka across the hall," I suggested.

Rivka understood the letter but couldn't translate it for us.

"*Melu'im*?" I asked her.

"*Ma? Lo.*" She shook her head.

Jeff took the letter, considerably wrinkled by now, to JCT later that afternoon. "It's true," he reported over the phone. "I'm supposed to register with my local reserves unit."

"My God, what will you do?" The telephone jack slipped and the line went dead. I fiddled with it, trying to reconnect. "Hello? Jeff?"

"What happened? Stupid phone. What I said was, Yorachim Ben-Yonah, the administrative assistant here, told me to ignore it."

"Shouldn't you write back saying it's a mistake?"

"Nah. He said I could but that it wouldn't do any good. He said I should be prepared to get a lot more letters ordering me to report for duty, but I should just ignore them."

"Are you sure? Oh dear, what would I do if you got drafted?"

The phone disconnected. When I jiggled the jack, I got a dial tone.

▲     ▲     ▲

"I don't get something," Adam said at dinner.

"What?" I asked.

"Why do we say 'forefathers?'"

"You know, dummy: Avraham, Yitzhak, and Ya'acov," said Ronnie.

"I know," he whined. "But what do they mean: forefathers?"

"Because every Jew can trace himself back to them," I suggested.

"Yeah, but why are they called that?"

"Well, they're really our great-great-great-whatever-grandfathers."

"I know that. But forefathers? There only are three of them."

Even speaking English could get complicated.

"You are so stupid," said Ronnie.

"Stupid," Tamara echoed, giggling.

"Shut up, you retard," Adam said to Tamara, then slapped his hand over his mouth. "Sorry," he mumbled.

▲ ▲ ▲

Ronnie began to come home late each day, and then she'd show up with Batya. Batya was an attractive girl, slight, with shoulder-length brown hair and braces. Ronnie tried to get her own fly-away hair to hang smoothly like Batya's. The two of them would tie up the bathroom as they played a teenaged version of "beauty parlor." They applied hair-glop they'd bought after school, then emerged sporting different styles, some more successful than others but always identical. More and more, Ronnie was looking like her friend. She started to dress like her, with her blouse untucked and her socks rolled in a particular way. She told me her teeth were crooked and pointed to one which was slightly out of alignment. I knew it was just that she wanted braces too.

▲ ▲ ▲

I met Dina in the crazy store down the street. I was buying diapers and another tub of "choco," which I liked to eat off a spoon when no one was looking.

"So, how are you?" she asked.

"Okay."

"My Dorit says she sees your girl in the other kindergarten."

"Yes. Both classes go out to the yard together, don't they."

"It is too bad your girl is not in Dorit's class. The *ganenet* is much better."

"Rivka seems okay."

Dina shook her head and frowned. "But anyway you should insist already that she be taken out of this class. By now what is their excuse for not providing the special education?"

"Oh, we don't want her in special ed. We think she's doing very well in the regular *gan*."

"How can that be? There is too many childrens in this class. And the *ganenet* pay no attention, especially Rivka. Your girl she is better to go in a special class."

"I don't know," I said. "She's learning how to pray, and I think she's beginning to understand a little Hebrew."

"Yes, Dorit says she talk all the time now Hebrew."

"And the other children like her."

"This I know, but is very unusual. They are very rough childrens in this class."

"But they're nice to Tamara," I said.

"Yes, I know. I have seen when I come to bring Dorit in the morning. Israeli childrens are not usual so gentle. I see them with Tamara, they are very good to her. I am amazing."

I tried not to laugh. Yes, you are amazing, I thought. I said, "So it's good Tamara's in the class. She brings out the best in the other children."

"Yes, maybe it is good for the others, but is not fair for your girl. She would be better in a special class."

▲  ▲  ▲

"Ma, I think I got them again," Ronnie grumbled when I went in to wake her one morning.

"What?"

"You know, the worms."

"Oh brother! What's the matter? You have trouble sleeping again?"

"Mm. Look." She pointed to Tamara, who was lying on her side, her hand down the back of her diaper, scratching in her sleep.

"I guess we go visit Dr. Yaniv this afternoon."

He seemed happy to see us. "Did the pills I gave you last time work?"

"I'm not sure. The kids seemed better but now they're complaining again."

"Ach, this is not uncommon. Another child has them, he scratches himself, he doesn't wash carefully, he plays with your child, your child doesn't wash before he puts his hands in his mouth, and there you have it: anal-oral infection. I will give you a double dose this time; that way you can medicate yourself when they recur."

"Maybe you should give Batya some pills too," I suggested to Ronnie as we walked to the pharmacy.

"Really, Mom!" She rolled her eyes. "What am I supposed to do? Go up to her and say, 'Do you happen to have an itchy behind?' Really."

"She'll just give them back to you again," I warned.

▲  ▲  ▲

Tamara watched the long shadow of her swinging arm wave into the middle of Rehov Bayit Vegan as we walked to the synagogue the Litanskys preferred. I glanced at Adam. In the waning light, his black eye looked like a smudge of dirt. Ronnie's skirt was too short, but so was Jeff's paycheck; the prices went up faster than the adjustment of his salary, and the dollars wouldn't last forever if I kept spending them to buy clothing. Still, I wished Ronnie had put on something more acceptable. Pertsa Litansky would surely fault me for my daughter's immodest hem.

Ya'acov Litansky met us in the street and led the way up the alley to the *shul*.

I was the only married woman behind the *mehitzah*. All the wives were home setting out the Friday evening meal. Girls dressed in clean white blouses scowled at me as I climbed past them to three empty chairs. When I was settled, Tamara lay her head on my lap and fell asleep.

It came time to stand for the silent *Amidah*. Unwilling to disturb Tamara, I remained seated.

"Ma," Ronnie coached me.

"I can't," I whispered. "Tamara's fallen asleep."

Ronnie sighed and cast her eyes upward. I watched her pray. She performed all the little rituals with serious concentration: the three steps backward and three steps forward, the bending of the knees and bowing, the staccato rocking as she murmured rapidly in Hebrew, turning the pages in her book. Except that her knees stuck out, she could pass for one of the Israeli girls. I noticed she'd tucked in her blouse. Was it that she'd decided to conform to the style dictated by these new girls, or was it universally accepted in Bayit Vegan that the "casual look" was not appropriate on *Shabbat*?

Services finished. I woke Tamara and brushed at the wrinkles in my skirt. Lifting the sleepy girl on her shoulder, Ronnie followed me out into the dusk.

"There they are," Jeff said.

As we approached them, Ya'acov called, "*Shabbat shalom*," before turning his back and leading Jeff and Adam toward his house.

I could hear Ronnie panting. "Put Tamara down," I said. "She's too heavy."

Tamara didn't like the idea. "Up! Up! Carry me!" she begged Ronnie.

Ya'acov's dark coat disappeared around a bend. "Come on," I said. "Let's catch up with them."

They were waiting at an unlit entry. "Where were you?" Jeff asked.

His impatience irked me. Why didn't he help with Tamara? It must have been Ya'acov's presence which made Jeff tense. Was he that anxious to make a good impression? And if so, didn't he realize being irritated with his wife reflected badly on him?

We walked up flights of stairs. Tamara, holding my hand and Ronnie's, made slow progress. We could hear the receding echo of the men's footsteps.

The light from an open doorway fell on a landing. "Ah, here you are. *Shabbat shalom*." Pertsa's red lips were drawn back to show all her teeth. "*B'rucha haba'a*," she welcomed me.

In the living room, Tamara scurried over to a black-lacquered wall
unit full of leather-bound books, crystal and silver, a collection of
menorahs, and dolls in Israeli costumes. She just missed colliding with the
large table covered with white linen and heavy china. We squeezed between table and couch to take our places for *kiddush*. After the wine, we
all had to squeeze back out to get to the kitchen, where we ritually
washed our hands in preparation for eating challah.

"Mommy, sit next to me," Tamara called as we returned to the
table. I held my finger to my lips, reminding her to remain silent until
after the blessing over the bread, worrying that the Litanskys would fault
us with not teaching Tamara properly.

The men talked about physics throughout the meal. Jeff behaved like
a doctoral student with his thesis advisor, instead of an established
scientist who had students of his own. "Oh, yes, of course you're right,"
he said whenever Ya'acov disagreed with him. Trying to distance myself
from his obsequiousness, I concentrated on the prodigious portions
heaped on my plate.

I ate too much; I had to loosen my belt. Pertsa grinned across the
table. Embarrassed, I said, "You cook too well."

"Yes, I know," she agreed. "So, tell me: how does your boy come to
have a black eye?"

I wondered how truthful I should be. Was it diplomatic to complain
about Israeli children? "A boy in school punched him."

"Just like that? For no reason?"

"'Cause I'm American," Adam informed her.

She nodded. "Yes, Ya'acov, too. He came here from Russia when he
was a small boy. He also had to learn to use his fists."

"But I thought the Israelis want new immigrants," I said.

"Yes, we want them, and we need them." She shrugged. "But then
the boys must prove they belong, that they are tough."

"I spoke to his teacher about it," I said.

"So what good did it do you, no?" she guessed.

"I know. All she said was, 'Yes, I saw the boys hit him. What can
you do? He is American.'"

"This is the way it is."

"But I'm not American," Adam insisted. "I'm Israeli now. I told
them that, too, but it doesn't do any good."

She ran her fingers through the hair growing down his neck. "It is
really too bad. I promise you it will be better. They will accept you in
time. My sons, too, had to earn acceptance. After each sabbatical, they
had to come back and show they were still tough. It has to do with the
universal conscription. All you boys are being raised to be soldiers. You
must prove to your comrades you can be counted on. Unfortunately, the
way your friends learn if they can count on you is by testing you in this
unpleasant way. Like hazing in a fraternity. Once you have proven

yourself, then things will get better." She turned back to me. "So, it is not so easy to come to live in Israel."

I wondered why I had disliked her. She seemed like the most empathic Israeli I knew.

▲   ▲   ▲

Tuesday afternoon, Pertsa called. "*Shalom*, Sintia. *Ma shlomech?*"

"*Tov, toda.* And you?

"*Baruch Hashem.* I am calling because I have two tickets to the concert at the Jerusalem Theater this evening. Ya'acov can't make it after all. So you will come with me?"

"I have to ask Jeff."

"Pooey! I'm not inviting him. Just the ladies' night out. He will baby-sit."

Her audacity made me smile. "What time?"

"Eight o'clock. I will pick you up a little after seven. Parking is terrible over there. This way we will have time for a cup of coffee."

"Oh, but Jeff has a class this evening. He doesn't get home 'til well after seven."

"So you can't leave the children for five minutes? If there is a problem, they can't knock on the neighbor's door?"

"I guess so." I pitied Jeff, coming home exhausted and then having to deal with putting the kids to sleep. "Look, Pertsa, let me just give Jeff a call and then I'll get back to you."

"You are crazy to hesitate even for a minute. The *symphonica* tickets are absolutely impossible to get. He will manage without you this once, I am sure."

"Okay."

"Good. Meet me downstairs at seven."

I immediately called Jeff, but he wasn't in. It was close to five when I finally reached him. "Jeff, sweetheart, I've been trying to get you all afternoon."

"Why? I was in the lab all day. I just stopped in to get my notes for class. Is anything wrong?"

"Not really. Pertsa Litansky wants me to go to a concert with her, and I just wanted to make sure you don't mind baby-sitting."

"Of course not. Look, I have to run. We can discuss it this evening."

"Well, no, we can't."

"What's the problem?"

"Jeff, it's tonight."

"What's tonight?"

"Pay attention. I know you're in a hurry to get to class. The concert's tonight."

"Tonight! Couldn't she give you a little notice?"

"You know how she is."

He grunted. "Do you want to go?"

"Yeah, I think so." I didn't mention that I couldn't easily back out at this point. "It might help matters for you at the college," I added with false altruism.

"Okay, so tell her you'll go. I'll see you later."

"Jeff, don't hang up yet." I could feel his impatience. "I may have to leave before you get home. But the kids'll be all right alone for a few minutes. I'll ask Rivka across the hall to keep an eye on them."

"Okay, okay. I really have to run. It's fine. Have a good time."

In the next two hours, I rushed around getting the kids' dinner and checking with Rivka and finding something nice to wear and giving Ronnie instructions.

"Ma, I'm old enough to baby-sit. Why d'ya have to ask Rivka to stop in?"

"She's a nice woman. She won't bother you."

"She always smells of onions."

"All right, all right," I said, throwing my keys and wallet into a patent leather clutch. "Daddy'll be home soon. Help him out. He'll be tired."

Out on the landing, before the elevator arrived, I could hear Ronnie telling Adam she was in charge and he'd better do his homework. He shouted back that she should mind her own business. The elevator came. I hesitated, wondering if I ought to go back into the apartment to quiet the kids down. I glanced at my watch; it was 7:05, so I went directly into the elevator.

I stood in the terraced garden a good ten minutes before a small white car pulled to a stop at the curb. Perhaps to Pertsa, a quarter of an hour constituted "a little after seven," because she didn't apologize for keeping me waiting. She sped along the winding, hilly roads, my nervousness of the past few hours increasing as I considered the flimsy door latch and the lack of a seatbelt. I gripped the dashboard, afraid at every turn I'd be flung out into the night. As we crossed the unpopulated valley south of Hebrew University, the speedometer needle inched toward 75. I averted my eyes, staring at my right foot braking reflexively against the floorboard.

"Have you been to the Israel Museum yet?" she asked.

"Not yet." Through the window beyond her, I glimpsed the landmark Menorah in front of the Knesset. Who had time for sightseeing? Daily existence consumed all our energy.

In Rehavia, the traffic forced her to slow down, and, as I calmed, I realized Israel was on the metric system and 75 kph was not even 50 mph.

The concert was only fair, but by the time Pertsa drove me home, I'd developed a fondness for her, a tolerance bordering on amusement for her blunt and brash ways.

It was midnight and the streets were deserted, yet the empty darkness around buildings and plants seemed alive with magic. As I let myself out of her car, I thanked her again for taking me to the concert.

"So?" she said. "And what are friends for?"

# Eighteen

His restlessness woke me. I could make out a dark hulk sitting on the edge of the bed. "Jeff?" I whispered.

The shape moved. "Oh, sorry, Cyn. I didn't mean to wake you."

"What's the matter?"

"Nothing. Go back to sleep."

"Stop worrying so much. You'd feel better if you'd get a good night's sleep." I groped to find his hand.

"How can I not worry? I can't find a job. I've written or called every place I can think of. I've schlepped all over the place to meet with these guys and try to talk them into offering me something. I don't know what more to do."

"Something will show up. Maybe JCT will find some funds."

"They really don't have it. And the guy at Israeli Aircraft said I need to know Hebrew, and the Technion has nothing. Industry's a real sweat. They expect you to put in twelve-hour days, and anyway, they all look like they're on the verge of bankruptcy."

"You've got to learn Hebrew anyway. Why don't you try another *ulpan*? Take an intensive one over the summer."

"I can't learn Hebrew."

"Sure you can. If I can learn, anyone can."

"And what about Tamara? They're not gonna let her go to the kindergarten next year."

"Maybe you'll get a job in a town where they will. We'll get out of the clutches of these psychologists and everything'll be fine."

"Besides, even if I got a job, the inflation will kill us. You see how the Israelis go on shopping sprees as soon as they get their paycheck? They're running to buy stuff before the prices go up again. There's no incentive to save your shekels because they become worthless in no time."

"But our dollars are worth more and more," I pointed out.

"Not really. Not with the prices skyrocketing. Besides, we can't keep cashing in the dollars or we'll go broke."

"We'll have no savings, that's all. We'll be like the Israelis."

"Don't be naive, Cyn. We can't live like that. What if we needed money for something? What if we wanted to buy a house, or a car? What if we wanted to fly back to America to visit? Of course we need our savings."

I thought a minute. Somehow thousands of people here were living a middle-class existence without anything extra in the bank. How did they manage? "Aren't there government-subsidized mortgages?"

"Yeah, and how are we supposed to pay mortgage payments when we can't even afford to cover food and clothing now?"

"But we wouldn't have to pay rent."

"But we would have to buy appliances and furniture, and who knows what other expenses there are? Property taxes? I don't know."

"So we won't buy a house. We'll stay in this apartment."

"Until the owners want it back. They bought it for their daughter. When she gets married and leaves home, out we go." His sigh stirred air currents. He continued, "Another thing I'm worried about is the half-salary we've been getting from UA."

"I know: this is something else we won't be getting after this year."

"Worse than that, Cyn. Technically, if you don't come back after a sabbatical, they're entitled to ask for that money back."

"That doesn't sound right. How can they do that?"

"I don't know if they will, but legally they can. Technically, you get a sabbatical in order to 'maintain and enhance your competency in your field,' or some such jargon. They pay you because you're supposed to be a bigger big-shot when you get back. But if you don't come back, they can claim back their misspent funds. It's sort of a contractual agreement: we pay you to study and interact with your colleagues so when you return, you can do your job better for us."

In the quiet, I could hear the ticking of the alarm clock. "That's a lot of money to pay back," I said finally.

"Roughly twenty thou."

I thought some more. In an emergency, I'd part with the bracelet, but to suggest this now as an answer to our money problems seemed disadvantageous. Liquidating the diamonds was somehow tantamount to dissolving our marriage. The bracelet had taken on meaning beyond its monetary value.

I remembered something else. "There's always Tamara's trust fund," I mentioned.

"I don't feel right about touching that. What if, God forbid, something were to happen to us? What if she suddenly needed another heart operation?"

"We have insurance."

"You know what I mean. It's not our money."

"As soon as we're more settled, I'll take a job too," I offered. "That ought to help. I can teach English. All the Israelis want to learn English."

He sighed. "Are you happy here?"

The question cheered me up. Yes, yes, of course I was glad to be in our homeland. "I walk down the street smiling and saying to myself, '*Lama ani same'ach? Ani same'ach ki ani b'eretz Yisroel.*'"

"What in the world does that mean?"

"Why am I happy? I'm happy because I'm in Israel."

"That's good," he said, squeezing my hand. Then he lay down and pretended to go back to sleep, but I could see the wetness of his open eyes glowing in the dark.

▲   ▲   ▲

In the morning, I reminded him that our anniversary was in a few days. "Why don't we find a baby-sitter and go out?" I suggested.

"More money you want to spend?" Jeff protested.

"I'm old enough to baby-sit," Ronnie said. "I'm almost fourteen."

I laughed. "You're right. But what about Adam? Can you two be trusted to get along while we're out?" I turned to Jeff. "Come on. It'll do us good to get out for a change."

He was looking at a calendar. "Wait a minute. How can we go out? March fifteenth falls on a Friday. We can't go out on Shabbas."

"After dinner, we'll go out for a walk. Come on, Jeff. We really should celebrate."

"Yeah. We'll go out for a walk."

But after dinner Friday, he begged off, saying he was too exhausted to make it down all the stairs.

Ronnie had organized Adam: he was clearing the table as she got Tamara ready for bed.

"Aren't you going?" she asked when I came into the girls' bedroom to say good night to Tamara.

"Your father's tired." I fingered my bracelet, shifting it around my wrist.

"But you've got to. It's your anniversary."

"Maybe another night. Can we take a raincheck on your baby-sitting services?"

"Sure, Mom. You look tired too. Go to bed. I'll clean up."

"Thanks, Ronnie."

Jeff was already in his pajamas when I crossed the hall into our room. "I'm sorry, Cyn. I'm just so wiped out lately."

"Don't worry about it, Jeff. Ronnie said she'll baby-sit another night. We'll go out some time when you're not so tired." I started undressing, slipping off my shoes, removing my jewelry. Jeff climbed into bed. He was soon asleep.

▲   ▲   ▲

I welcomed spring, the warming of the old stones. The air had a new texture: it was pregnant with something sweet and soft. It made me feel tender and giddy.

But it seemed to have another effect on our neighbors: the wives of Bayit Vegan heralded the season by embarking on extensive cleaning. Every rug was rolled up and carried out to be hung over a balcony railing, where it was beaten and aired. Every cupboard and cabinet was emptied and wiped clean, then all the removed contents shaken and dusted. Every pocket and pocketbook was turned inside out and inspected; lint was picked from every seam. Ronnie came home from school with instructions to go through all our books and wipe off each page. I told her she was crazy, but she insisted that otherwise we might inadvertently be in possession of a crumb of *chumetz*—leavened bread—when Passover came.

On a top shelf in the kitchen, I came across the Litanskys' dishes, the ones which had contained our first meal eaten in Israel. I invited Pertsa to come over for a cup of coffee on a morning I didn't have *ulpan*.

She said she couldn't come because she was too busy, but why didn't I come over to her house?

"Okay. You know, I still have your plates. I'll bring them over with me."

"What plates? Oh no, I have no place to put them right now. Do you mind putting them away with your *chumetz* things? You'll return them to me after *Pesach*."

When I arrived, I could see she also was in the throes of pre-Passover madness. The curtains were down and the cushions of her couch were scattered. As we talked, she scraped the cracks between the leaves of her dining table with a paring knife. The faded kerchief tied around her head contrasted with her ever brightly made-up face.

"I don't suppose we'll be able to have anyone over during the week of *Pesach*," I commented to Jeff that evening.

He looked up from *The Jerusalem Post*. "What's the matter now?"

"I'm too lazy. Our house just won't be *chumetz*-free enough."

One day, in imitation of all the people around me, I opened the windows to air out the apartment. As I slopped water over the floor tiles, a bird flew in, checking our rooms for a good nesting place. The foreign creature flapping overhead made my scalp prickle. In Greek tragedies, seers read omens in birds' behavior: what did this one portend? Swinging the mop handle around my head, I shooed it back outside and shut all the windows again.

But despite my refusal to clean so rigorously for Passover, I felt poignantly the significance of the festival commemorating the exodus from Egypt. We too had left our Goshen. God brought us with a strong hand and an outstretched arm into the land He promised our forefathers. Our "next year in Jerusalem" had come. My eyes lingered on the Judean Hills; I breathed in the mixed aroma of Israel.

Then one day as I ran from my *ulpan* to pick up Tamara at the kindergarten, I passed the road crew that had repaired Hapisga the previous fall. I quickly scanned the group in search of the beautiful Arab boy. I was shocked when I found him. His jeans and black turtleneck were no more tattered than to be expected after so many months of rough use. His features were still classic, perfect. But his face had lost all its childish softness and warmth. His eyes looked fierce, his mouth mean. What cruelty had he experienced beyond the hard labor? Would his future ever hold more than long, arduous days? He glanced at me and I cringed because I felt his unfocused hatred.

But why should he hate me? What had I done to him? It was his crude co-workers, his abrasive foreman who had roughened him. Is our desire to belong to our own people so great that we are unwilling to blame our brothers? Must we always deflect our loathing outward, beyond the clan which offers some security and an identity? The boy hated me for no greater reason than that I was a Jew living in Bayit Vegan, the "house and garden" district where he spilled his sweat.

For many days afterward, I took Tamara home a round-about way so we wouldn't have to pass him again.

▲    ▲    ▲

We heard reports on the radio: Stones were thrown at buses carrying Jews from their jobs in Tel Aviv to their homes in settlement towns near Nablus. IDF soldiers captured terrorists near the Lebanon border. Homemade bombs blew up cars in the West Bank. And what did Israeli soldiers do to control the situation? I didn't want to think too much about this. I pretended the West Bank—which abutted my city—was as remote as Vietnam had been when I lived in New York.

I dismissed my uneasiness with rationalization: terrorists forfeited all rights to be treated with humanity.

But I was surrounded by terrorists and their offspring. In the 1940's, Jews had performed acts of terror against the British who then ruled the land. Not that the British were equitable governors. But what was it about this piece of property that aroused such a strong desire for possession that civilized people were driven to treachery?

As we sat down to our seder, I was forced to see many parallels between the Passover story and the present Arab situation in Israel. After the Six Day War in '67, the Arabs newly under Israeli occupation lived better than they had before. They were given electricity, plumbing, education, and steady work. So too Pharaoh welcomed Joseph's family; at first our ancestors lived very well in Egypt. But as the Hebrews prospered, the Egyptians became fearful. The Hebrews' birth rate alarmed them, just as the Israelis now worried that the Arabs' growing population would overtake theirs.

How were the Israelis now treating the non-Jews within their borders? Pharaoh dealt with his foreigners by suppression and hard labor. These methods backfired: the striving for freedom from slavery brought Jacob's twelve tribes together. Their oppression bound them into an entity. The Arabs in modern Israel also did hard labor, and there were reports of infringements of human rights in the West Bank and Gaza. And in the 1980's, disparate groups among the Arabs were uniting.

But there were important differences as well. The ancient Hebrews were not allowed to leave, they were forced into bondage; the Palestinians *chose* to remain in occupied territory and refugee camps, they chose to work for Israeli employers. Thousands of years ago, the Israelites in Egypt were meek. It took God to punish the overlords with plagues. On the other hand, of the Arabs there were those who did not timidly wait for redemption. They were rising up to strike out at the Zionists. For this reason, the Israelis viewed the Arabs themselves as a plague.

Millenia ago, God heard the cries of the Israelite slaves and promised "to make of them a great nation." Would God hear the Arabs' cries? Would He also make them a nation? But God, I reminded Him, You gave this land to us. If the Palestinians are destined for nationhood, don't You think You could find them a different corner of the Middle East?

▲   ▲   ▲

At least once a week there was a knock on the door around dinner time. It was always someone holding a charity box and asking (in Hebrew) for a donation. I'd ask in English what it was for and was usually told it was to support a yeshiva or an orphanage. For the orphans I'd find spare change in my purse. For the yeshivas I was less generous: didn't the government support all schools?

One time, two young men came asking me to contribute money for their sister's wedding. The nerve of them, I thought. Let her have a less elaborate reception. They told me it was a very big *mitzvah* to help buy a bride's wedding feast. Why should I contribute to festivities I wasn't even invited to attend! Did they think I was so rich I could afford to underwrite their *simcha*? But then I worried, What if years from now, we can't afford to make a wedding feast for Ronnie? Will Adam have to go around begging from our neighbors? I found a couple of coins in my pocket and gave it to them. Was this how Israelis without any savings managed?

Another time it was an old woman. She was tiny and stooped under layers of faded garments. "*T'sedakah, t'sedakah,*" she said, making the coins already collected jangle in the metal can. She pointed to the slot and smiled encouragingly.

"What is it for?" I asked.

"*T'sedakah,*" she repeated, again shaking the can.

"Charity for what?"

She said something in Hebrew.

"I'm sorry. I don't understand you."

I was just about to close the door on her when the elevator stopped at our floor and Jeff emerged, home from his class.

The woman turned to him and shook her can. "*T'sedakah*," she said hopefully.

"Oh, sure," he said, immediately putting down his briefcase, pulling out his wallet, and removing several bills. "Here." He tried to stuff the notes into the slim slot; failing, he handed them to her.

"*Toda, toda raba*," she said, followed by a spouting of verbiage which undoubtedly recommended him to Heaven.

"*Toda* to you," he rejoined. He held open the door of the elevator for her.

In a minute, I heard her on the fourth floor, shaking her can and requesting *t'sedakah*.

"What's the matter?" he asked me after he came in and closed the door.

"She didn't tell me what it was for," I said.

"Who knows?" He didn't seem to care. He carried his books into the living room.

I followed him. "How do you know she's not keeping the money for herself?" I asked.

He shrugged. "Looks like she could use it."

"I thought you were worried about our finances. We can't afford to support every little old lady who knocks on our door."

"It's okay, Cyn. God forbid I should ever be too poor to give *t'sedakah*."

▲   ▲   ▲

A Friday afternoon in May, we were all home getting ready for *Shabbat* when the director of the Psychology Bureau called. "Mrs. Rott, I have a very good news. We are fortunate to have now an opening for your daughter in an excellent program."

"Where is this?"

I didn't catch the Hebrew name. In English, she continued, "It is in Talpiot, not so far from you. Of course, the bus will take her."

"The bus?"

"Yes, of course: you are entitled to the school bus. It will pick her up at your door."

At this point, Jeff, who'd been listening with his head against mine, grabbed the receiver from me. "What exactly do you have in mind?" he asked.

Presumably she told him.

"I thought we made it very clear we're not sending her to any of your special programs," he said.

I put my head against his and heard her explain that he was welcome to appeal their decision.

"How do we do that?"

"You make an appeal and it is heard by the court. I must have you understand, however, that it is customary for the court to weigh more heavily the professional recommendations."

"In other words, you're saying we'll lose."

"How am I to know? But, yes, it is usually so."

Jeff cranked his mouth to the side as he scratched his beard under his chin. "All right," he said. "We'll keep her home."

"How do you mean?" she asked.

"We won't send her to your special school. If she can't go to the school we want, she won't go to any school."

"She won't go to any school? Surely you know this is not the best for your daughter."

"It's better than sending her to one of your schools."

"No school at all? No, this we cannot allow."

"What do you mean?" Jeff challenged her. "I'll do what I damn please."

"No, no, I am afraid I must tell you you are mistaken. Every child in Israel must go to school. It is the law. If you are keeping her home, you break the law. You will be put in jail."

Jeff began to pace furiously, taking the receiver out of earshot. "Now you're threatening me with jail? I never heard of such a thing. What are you, the Gestapo or something?"

He stopped pacing. After a pause in which he listened to her reply, he said very carefully, "Let's get one thing straight: you will not force me to do anything with my child that I don't wholeheartedly approve of. Do you understand? Good. No, wait, let me finish. I will not go to jail. I still have my American passport. If what you tell me is true, and if you still insist on stubbornly holding to your decision, I'll pack my bags and take my daughter back to Tucson, where I can send her to any damn school I please. Do you understand? Am I making myself clear?"

Again he waited for her response. Again he spoke: "Then I am to understand that you still will not change your mind, even if it means you are forcing a Jewish family to leave Israel?"

I glanced into the living room at the children. Adam and Ronnie stared wide-eyed at me, their expressions frozen. I imagined I could see their ears stretching forward, straining to hear the crucial conversation.

"Yes, you are forcing me," Jeff said. "I want you to understand that, that it is you who are causing a family to leave." After a moment, he replaced the receiver in its cradle.

# Nineteen

I was unreasonably miserable; there was no rational cause for my despondency. I could easily list all the things that were wrong with our life in Israel: Tamara's schooling, Jeff's inability to find a secure job, Adam's hazing, the isolation and vulnerability resulting from our ignorance of Hebrew, outrageous inflation, the precarious government, the disquieting and unsolvable Arab issue, the inadequate heating in the winter, the unnerving birds flying in every time I opened a window, the irascible and erratic personalities of our acquaintances, the enervating day-to-day living. But for all the exhaustion borne of climbing hills and stairs, chasing buses, elbowing through crowds in pursuit of our daily bread, for all the frustrations encountered in shops and post office, government bureaus and synagogue, I was compensated by an unfathomable source of energy. For all our worries and fears, big and small, I found the strength to cope. It were as though the exigencies of our Israeli existence tapped the wellspring of my own personal Fountain of Youth. I had never felt so stimulated, so invigorated, so strong and capable of meeting every challenge. Something was very right with my being in Israel: I felt I was home at last, even though this home was too foreign, too exotic for me to ever assimilate. I rejoiced in the beauty of the simplest pleasures; it was a gift to be able to open my eyes, to draw a breath. I couldn't bear the thought of leaving.

On the other side of the seesaw was Jeff, who, once he had verbalized the possibility of returning to the States, seized the idea. Suddenly he was free. He could once again laugh and enjoy life, because he'd found his escape. To thwart this hope, I would damn him to despair. I was caught in the eternal triangle, forced to choose one love or the other, because if I chose to stay in Israel, I would surely lose Jeff: either he'd leave without me or he'd lose his sanity. He could not stay in Israel and remain himself. There was too much stress; something had to give under the pressure.

What gave was me, my sacrificed dream. I was angry at Tamara for becoming the reason Jeff chose to leave, angry at Jeff for using Tamara. But I realized Tamara's school placement was only a small part of Jeff's distress. If the psychologists had been pliant, Jeff would have placed some other worthy cause between us and our staying in Israel. Seeing how desperately Jeff wanted to leave, I couldn't voice my own devastation. I was unable to express the unhappiness his decision caused me.

He asked, "How do you feel, Cyn? I know how much you wanted to come here. If you really want to stay, maybe...but I don't know how. Don't you agree with me the situation is untenable?"

I replied, "I guess you're right," suppressing my anger and disappointment. I reiterated all the problems with our existence in Israel, trying to convince myself of their import, and I pretended that I agreed with him. I wasn't willing to sacrifice him, neither his mind nor his body. I wanted both his sanity and his proximity. But I hated him for forcing me to choose.

▲  ▲  ▲

The children made adjustments to our change in plans. Adam, of course, was greatly relieved. He was tired of walking home from school with eyes in the back of his head, ever alert to an attack from the rear. As the spring ripened, he began skipping school altogether. Neither Jeff nor I scolded him for his truancy. A sense of security was a child's birthright, and if he felt safer away from his classmates, we weren't willing to force him to face his cowardice. His acceptance by them was no longer worth the battle.

Tamara, with no comprehension beyond the immediacy of each day, had no complaints about our shifted direction, but Ronnie was at first very resistant. How could she live without Batya? We were so unfair to drag her across the world and, just when she was finally happy, drag her back again. Batya, after grieving with Ronnie over their imminent separation, set out to find a new friend. So as not to prolong her own agony any longer, she ignored Ronnie during the last weeks of school, except to the extent that divulging Ronnie's many confidences enhanced her status with potential new attachments. Thus thanks to Batya's disloyalty, Ronnie came to favor our departure.

Sarah, my *ulpan* teacher, didn't hesitate to tell me we were making a terrible mistake. "Where else can a Jew live and be all the time Jewish, without always thinking about the non-Jew, without thinking when will be the next pogrom?"

I nodded.

"It is your husband Yosef, no?" she guessed. "He refuse to adjust. He never get used to here."

I didn't answer.

"Then you must insist," she stated. "Eventually he will get used."

"I can't."

"Such a shame," she said. "You are my best pupil."

The Litanskys were surprisingly supportive. I had expected Pertsa, strong-willed and blunt, to also insist we stay. That first night in Israel, by the food she'd left for us, wasn't there a note saying "welcome home"? Instead, she expressed sorrow that it hadn't worked out, and sympathy. "I know, I know," she consoled me. "It isn't easy. Life here is very hard. You mustn't feel guilty to leave." She pointed to the bag of dishes I was finally returning. "I wish my plates could remain in your cabinet. That way I'd always know where they are and I'd also know where you are."

I told her the woman at the Psychology Bureau said we could be put in jail over Tamara's schooling.

"Pooey." She laughed it off. "In jail? They cannot do that."

"You don't think so?" I was less certain. "Anyway, that she even said such a thing is bad enough. Imagine, threatening us that way!"

"Yes, it is bad. Obviously she is a stupid and unpleasant woman. But she is not the only reason you leave."

"But I don't want to go," I protested.

"Yes, I know. But you must go with your husband. A man needs work. He feels he is nothing without his work. You must stand beside him; he needs you now more than ever."

I accepted her advice as sound, though I resented it. Would an American woman tell me I should give up my own fulfillment for my husband's sense of self worth? But my marriage to him was also part of my fulfillment. Something had to be compromised.

And then there was another thing which added to my unhappiness: a feeling of failure. We had failed to make it, we had failed to accomplish what we'd set out to do. People came from all over the world to settle in Israel, and they stayed, even under much greater adversity. I felt we hadn't tried long enough, hard enough. Wasn't the dream of a Jewish homeland greater than the petty ego-gratification of the individual? Jeff would never receive the Nobel prize for his obscure research in optics. Was it that important to him to get a job in physics? We could live on a kibbutz, we could pick oranges. Somehow, if our commitment were strong enough, we could find ways to feed and clothe ourselves, we could bend a bit in our expectations. Did it make that much difference which school Tamara went to? But our commitment wasn't deep enough; we hadn't sincerely turned our allegiance over to Israel. By taking a sabbatical from the University of Arizona instead of quitting outright, Jeff had an all-too-convenient alternative when the psychologists got to him. The boys in Adam's class were right: we were still Americans. For all our idealism, we still clung to our American comforts and freedoms.

▲    ▲    ▲

We bought plane tickets—one-way tickets—to America for early July, then made preparations to leave. I wept into the possessions I crammed back into our luggage. When we were coming to live in Israel as new immigrants, we'd been allowed three suitcases per ticket; now our status had been devalued and we were allowed only two. So we were forced to leave a bit of ourselves behind. I filled the most battered bags with discards and left them downstairs by the garbage bins. Although my neighbors were annoyed with the swarm of ragpickers they attracted, I was glad to know our old things weren't going to waste.

I dragged, the marvelous resources of energy suddenly spent. Jeff had to do everything, visit government bureaus, the bank; I complained of vague infirmities which interfered with my activity. Of course, the same reason which enervated me energized Jeff. He hurried to complete each transaction which brought him closer to leaving.

We had to pay an exit tax: all Israelis, and we with our A-1 visas, were required to pay hundreds of thousands of shekels each time they left the country. Professors Jeff knew had to recalculate whether it was worth it to go overseas to earn American dollars for the summer. Some decided to go without their families. At the same time, the Israeli government was publicly criticizing the Soviet Union for the "ransom" it required of the emigrating Jews, but they refused to see any parallel between the Russians and themselves.

And the amount kept going up, usually overnight: there was a story in the news of travelers stranded at Ben Gurion Airport because their morning flight left before opening time at the bank where they had to pay the increment. Jeff initially paid $250 per person; before we left, he had to add another $50 for each of us.

Jeff added the exit tax to the things he hated about Israel. "What if we couldn't come up with the fifteen hundred dollars?" he fumed. "It's disgusting, having to buy your way out of a country. It's a police state once they start interfering with your freedom of movement. And how do you like this? I can't convert my shekels back into dollars." Not that we had so many shekels left. But he bristled at being restricted. "I hate controlled currencies."

At the last minute, he felt like sightseeing. We no longer had the rest of our lives to explore the country, and it was a way to spend our Israeli money. "I'm not coming back here. No point leaving anything in the bank, where it'll depreciate to nothing with inflation anyway." (By now, the exchange rate was a thousand shekels to a dollar. We'd experienced 300% inflation in less than a year.)

I dropped the *ulpan*. We kept the kids out of school and took buses to Haifa, to the beach in Tel Aviv. After touring all Jerusalem's major attractions, we visited the minor ones: the village of Eyn Kerem with its convents, the Mt. Scopus campus of Hebrew University with its panoramic views. We entered the Old City through the Damascus Gate and explored the Moslem Quarter, our excitement heightened by our defiance in the face of perceived danger. Once again safe at home, we swore we weren't scared. We praised the Arab shopkeepers with their ingratiating smiles, the benign indifference of the robe-and-scarf draped men pushing through the narrow alleys. It was true: Jeff's and Adam's skullcaps drew more overt hostility in the non-religious Jewish neighborhoods of Tel Aviv.

▲    ▲    ▲

The last couple of weeks in Israel, Jeff was crazed with fear we wouldn't make it out. A series of strikes placed themselves between us and the airport. A taxi-drivers' strike was followed by a threatened gasoline-station strike. (Jeff bought a ten-liter jerry jug and filled it at a petrol pump so the taxi driver, once again working, couldn't refuse to drive us to Lod for lack of fuel.) Then the truckers went on strike. They demonstrated by blocking the main highways with their vehicles. Another raise in the exit tax was rumored. Fearful we too would be prevented from boarding our early-morning plane and then be unable to get five seats on another flight during the summer tourist season, Jeff traded our tickets for those on a flight leaving in late June. His paranoia reminded me of my fear the previous summer that we wouldn't get to Israel, that some catastrophe would stand in the way of our arriving here. How ironic that after surmounting all my imagined hurdles and finally arriving in Israel, we now worried we wouldn't be able to depart.

Jeff also feared he might be prevented from leaving by the government. "Maybe they'll say we came under false pretenses. Maybe they'll say we have to repay all we owe them before we can board the plane." He started adding large sums on his calculator: the salary he'd been paid by a grant for new immigrants, the new-immigrant income tax rebates, subsidies toward our plane tickets to Israel and our rent. "What about the free ride from Lod to Jerusalem when we first arrived?" Jeff suggested. Concluding we didn't have that much money, he decided to change his story. "No, no," he told all acquaintances, assuming anyone might be connected with the government. "Where'd you get that idea? We aren't going back permanently. We're just going for the summer vacation. Cynthia misses her parents. We're just going back for a visit."

I resented being used in his ruse. But, I comforted myself, maybe he'll be forced to make good on his promises. Maybe the lies will somehow come true. Maybe we will return.

▲    ▲    ▲

The morning of our departure arrived. Before dawn, Jeff dragged all the suitcases into the elevator and down to the entry as I dressed Tamara, checked through the apartment again, and herded the children out. We stood in the dark waiting for the cab. Jeff was agitated, fearful the taxi driver had overslept, worried we'd miss our flight, but I was grateful for the few extra minutes in which to absorb my parting impressions—the white stones, a whiff of jasmine, the stillness of the cool air, the predawn chirping of the birds in the pines, and my sadness. Stretching to remember everything this last time was much like seeing it initially: my perceptions were clear and fresh, stripped of the coating of repeated experience which reduces even the spectacular to banality. All the months of walking through the entry disappeared, and I was once again seeing it for the first time upon our arrival to this mysterious land, flutters in my stomach, the excitement of the unknown.

The taxi was only five minutes late, and it had a full tank of gas, though the driver was happy to receive the gift of the jerry jug, which he stashed in his trunk before confronting our ten fifty-pound bags. He was a powerful man: he threw our bulging suitcases up onto the luggage rack on the roof of the cab while Jeff rummaged through the trunk in search of rope to tie them down. I sat half-dozing in the backseat with the children. Stealing away in the night was not what I wanted to remember about Israel.

On the road to the airport, I twisted around once to look out the rear window. The Judean Hills stood in silhouette against the lightening sky.

# Part III.  B'Galoot (In Exile)

# Twenty

Memory has a way of editing. All the awkward constructions, misplaced modifiers, redundancies, and vagaries are subtly cleaned up until, with time, one can only recall a greatly improved version, a rarefication of what actually was, a masterfully composed fiction. Knowing this, I feared returning to Tucson, which in Israel had taken on an Eden-like attraction: a place where the sun always shone in a cloudless blue sky, where the landscape was uncluttered with claustrophobic life, where on a whim one plucked an orange from laden trees. Time ticked by leisurely, allowing hours of sitting on a veranda sipping suntea, that mellow infusion slowly brewed by solar heat in a glass jar set outside. Lazing in the shade near a pool, one watched through tinted glasses small lizards doing push-ups on a stucco wall. The rustle of palm leaves suggested the breeze stirring them: one imagined its whisper skimming over warm skin. Living in Jerusalem, I renounced this Heaven on Earth, proclaiming the paradise deadening. But on the long flight westward, I worried I'd be disappointed, that I'd find forgotten filth or poverty, ugliness and hustle, like weeds which my memory had yanked out by the roots and tossed away but in reality still proliferated.

And so I was dazzled by the beauty of Tucson upon our arrival. The airport was no longer quaint: the glitz of chrome and glass and endless new carpeting were in blatant contrast with the airport we had left behind the day before. The car we rented looked too large, the roads too broad and smooth. How peculiar to interpret each sign at a glance, to understand every overheard conversation. I'd expected culture shock going to a foreign land, but I was surprised at how strong it was on our return to the familiar. I felt a bit like Gulliver, who, returning from his stay with the giants of Brobdingnag, found Englishmen diminutive. Tucson had hardly changed, but how different it looked from my new perspective!

In the first week, as we slept off our jetlag in a hotel, drove the rented car in search of housing, called on old friends, shopped in Lucky supermarket, I was overwhelmed with how pleasant everything was—the air-conditioned, well-maintained environment, the ordered, easy life, the polite people, the breathtaking mountain views. If Tucson living amounted to dull, unrelenting satisfaction, I was tired enough, physically and emotionally, to embrace this sweet death with open arms. I wept guilty tears over my disloyalty to Israel; then, in a futile attempt to preserve my own integrity, I blamed Jeff for my desertion.

"This time, I'd like a house with a swimming pool," I specified. "And with a formal dining room. Also, Ronnie is getting older. She should have a room of her own." If Jeff could leave Israel in search of comfort, I would insist on nothing short of ostentation. As a realtor walked us through a modest home, I talked of redoing the kitchen, calling in a landscaper, adding a bathroom.

Later, sitting under the hotel olive trees in the twilight, Jeff complained. "Look, Cyn, let's be realistic. Sure, the money's better here than there, but I'm still only making assoc prof pay. That doesn't exactly put us in the millionaire bracket. And our savings took a beating going to Israel. The airfare alone cost us thousands."

But I held onto the idea that our new life in Tucson had to be much better than in Jerusalem, than our previous time in Tucson, to justify abandoning the Zionist dream. None of the houses within walking distance of the Young Israel Synagogue pleased me. They were small and old, with cracks in the tile kitchen counters and water stains on the ceiling. Unwilling to compromise, we were forced to take temporary shelter in an apartment.

We had to go as far as Old Spanish Trail, at the eastern limits of the city, to find one with three bedrooms. I liked living so far out. The Santa Catalina Mountains in the north, the Rincon range to the east, seemed close enough to touch, incredibly clear against the brilliant sky, their crevices casting cobalt shadows on their pinkish flanks. Arizona's mountains looked so new and raw compared to the worn, softly rounded Judean Hills.

Two-level buildings surrounded a central courtyard, with its swimming pool, playground, and patio shaded by palms and eucalyptus. Arizona had houses cheap enough that anyone with steady work could afford the mortgage, so apartments were filled with the elderly, the poor, and those too unstable to make a commitment to a major purchase.

The other children in the complex received our three without hesitation; even Tamara was accepted. Sitting with preschoolers behind the swings, she was offered plastic cups which she filled with smooth gravel. From the moment he finished breakfast each day, Adam was outside with a clutch of children—both boys and girls—playing ball or tag in the courtyard, swimming, or sliding down the steep walls of the wash behind the complex. Ronnie and two adolescent sisters spent hours listening to rock music while polishing their nails and fixing their hair.

(Of interest: in our first days back in Tucson, Ronnie staunchly refused to go swimming in the hotel pool, claiming no Bayit Vegan girl would so obscenely expose her body in public. But within a day of meeting her new friends at the complex, she was pulling on her bathing suit and running out to have a swim with them. Arizona-in-July heat had conspired with the waning influence of her remote Orthodox peers, the proximity of girls with different attitudes and values.)

In the evening, I joined the mothers, returned from work, sitting on the patio smoking and chatting. They, too, were unquestioningly accepting. That I was a woman was reason enough to trust and talk to me. Their simplicity, their lack of conspiratorial gossip or catty machinations, was refreshing, though I harbored a snobbish belief that their uncomplicated approach stemmed from an inferiority. I supposed them unable to grasp more complex relationships. Most of them were divorced.

The few men in residence were uneducated; they drove tow trucks or made pizza or put up billboards for a living. In order to socialize, Jeff suppressed his identity—"Oh, yeah, I work over at the U," he'd admit casually. Maybe they thought he worked on grounds or maintenance.

I had to laugh at myself: by striving to enter the luxury class, I'd forced us into joining this working-class world instead. But America is truly a land of plenty, I mused, that the lower class takes for granted living better than the Litanskys, than the senior professor at a Jerusalem college. These semiliterate people accepted without marvel the 17-cubic-foot refrigerator, dishwasher, wall-to-wall carpeting, and thermostat-controlled air-conditioning included in the rent. They thought nothing of the two bathrooms in their apartment, the pool at their doorstep, their old but commodious cars which they filled up with gas without a second thought.

We had not one piece of furniture, only the contents of ten large suitcases and our carry-on bags. We slept on the floor until we could buy beds; a neighbor lent us a card table until we purchased a dinette from the Salvation Army. On the floor against the wall, we stacked our books, which the post office began delivering to Jeff's university office and he brought home by threes and fours each day. "Why do you need all those books?" Adam's new friends asked. They couldn't understand why we had books in the absence of a couch and chairs, a television. Our regard for books: was that all that differentiated us from our neighbors?

▲   ▲   ▲

The most radical change in our life was the inability to walk to synagogue on Saturday. On weekdays, Jeff stopped at Young Israel on his way to the University to help make morning *minyan*. But we no longer attended *Shabbat* services. I had no contact with organized religion. I no longer prayed.

I'd make little slips. Forgetting it was Friday night, I switched off the bathroom light. I put milk in my coffee too soon after a meat meal. I took a drink of water before I remembered it was the fast day of Tisha B'Av.

I started questioning why I was observant at all. I'd been raised in a nonreligious home; it was only after meeting Jeff that I agreed to follow all these rules. Why should I have changed? Was it in a flush of newlywed unity that I submitted to Jeff's wishes? If he could drag me from Israel, I no longer felt bound to practice his religion. The rituals seemed as foreign as my absurd infatuation with the Promised Land. I wanted to shed them. I wanted to be an American. Like Esau, I despised my birthright. It set me apart, it stood in the way of my total assimilation. I only wanted to fit in with the uncomplicated women chatting on the patio.

To think, Gentiles actually envied Jews because we were the Chosen People! Did they know what we were chosen for? God picked us to be His *servants*. What an honor! Whereas the non-Jew only had to keep seven laws relating to common human decency to be considered righteous, Jews were required to observe 613 commandments. Every aspect of a Jew's life was regulated. And the only visible reward was the gift of the *Shabbat*, our taste of life in the hereafter. But even this was messed up because there was so much we couldn't do on it, and, if you lived close to a synagogue, you spent half the day there saying prayers. Some day of rest!

Closing my eyes against the Saturday afternoon glare, I lay back on my chaise lounge, listened to Brenda describing the women whose hair she permed for a living, and held my glass out to Kathy, who refilled it from the gallon jar of suntea.

That summer, God abandoned me. He ceased to exist for me. I turned my back on Israel, on Judaism. I died spiritually.

# Twenty-One

For the High Holy Days, we stayed in the International Plaza Hotel on Speedway and Campbell, putting us within walking distance of the synagogue. Unable to cook in the room, or spend money in a restaurant (assuming there were a kosher one), we were dependent on the hospitality of various congregants for our meals. For each dinner we ate at someone's house, we had to pay by hearing "I told you so."

On Tuesday, the second day of the new year, we were eating at the Fishers'. Before we'd finished the gefilte fish, Ed Zlotnick, also a guest for lunch, started in. "So. You didn't believe me when I told you the Israelis just love American Jews, especially when they stay on this side of the Atlantic."

"I kept telling them I'm an Israeli, but they kept telling me they were gonna beat me up anyway," Adam related with relish. "Tell him, Dad. Tell him about my black eye."

Ed shook his head. "That bad, huh? You're a pretty tough kid yourself, Adam. Did you show them your fists?"

"Yeah, but there were a lot of them and I didn't have anybody on my side."

Catching my eye, Ed commented, "It's got now so the boys act out their parents' antipathy. That's really bad. I thought at least your kids would have it easy. All that propaganda about how Israel is such a great place to raise children."

"Speaking of kids in Israel, how's your daughter doing?" Marty asked Ed.

"Okay. She'll be finishing up after this year."

Melanie stood to collect the fish plates. "After that, watch out, Ed. As I remember, she was a knockout. She'll probably sink her claws into some gorgeous Sabra."

"No way. She's really intent on her career, and doctors do lousy in Israel, they're a dime a dozen. No, she'll be coming back, do her residencies here. I don't think she has any plans to set up house. Certainly not in Israel."

"Not to change the subject," I said, "but where are the Danzigers? Jeff told me that they've moved. What happened? Where'd they go?"

"He was offered the pulpit of a more prosperous congregation somewhere in the mid-West," Melanie said. "It came up pretty suddenly. I
guess it's a step up for them. We couldn't afford to pay him very much,
and he's got a growing family. You know Naomi's expecting again?"

"No, really? This would be number four."

"Yup."

"Too bad they're not still living here," Ronnie said. "I love to baby-
sit new babies."

"Me too," echoed Valerie, the Fishers' twelve-year-old. "I love
babies."

"How old's the oldest one?" I asked.

"Five? Six maybe?" She shrugged. "Anyhow, now Marty's busy on
the search committee looking for a new rabbi."

I missed Naomi. When she wrote to us in Israel, she gained the
status of friend. One small consolation during our preparations to return
to Tucson was that I could pursue that friendship. Now she was out of
reach.

Ed handed Melanie his plate and small fork, then turned his attention back to Jeff. "So, Professor Roth, what besides Adam's black eye
made you come back?"

Each time we talked about the bureaucracy, the inflation, and all the
difficulties we had with integrating, I felt guilty, as though I'd committed
an infidelity. My betrayal of Israel seemed to have a reflexive effect,
hurting me deeply. Because our friends encouraged me to inflict these
wounds, I hated them.

"Do you know," Jeff was saying, "that when we first got to Israel
just a year ago, the exchange rate was three hundred shekels to the
dollar."

"Three hundred and fifty," I corrected him.

"No it wasn't. Three hundred."

"It doesn't matter," Marty interrupted. "So what's the point?"

"I'm sure it was three hundred, but Cyn probably knows better. In
any case, I never knew how much they were going to pay me. Each
month, my paycheck was different. It had to be adjusted to keep up with
the inflation."

"That's not so bad then," Marty said. "At least they were willing to
adjust the amount."

"Yeah, except they were always a bit behind the present exchange
rate. I was always getting a little less than I should. Not that I know how
anybody could live on that salary, even without the inflation. Do you
know, by the time we left in June, they were up to a thousand shekels to
the dollar? Even if the dollar was standing still, and we all know it isn't,
that's a three hundred percent increase."

"Pretty steep," Ed agreed.

"By now it's probably doubled again."

"No, as a matter of fact," Ed said. "As a matter of fact, the economy is completely under control. The exchange rate is still a thousand per dollar."

"Incredible. What did they do?"

"I don't know. They hold it down artificially, I guess. In any case, the shekel's finally stable."

"Incredible."

Jeff didn't look happy the Israelis had their economy under control. I could understand that. This news made me resentful too, as though the rampant inflation before was an aberration especially meant to try us. And my self-loathing increased as well, because I saw it as a test we'd failed. If we'd stayed a little longer, would things have settled down? Maybe a job would have shown up too, and in a town where Tamara could have fit into the educational system. What was the word Israelis were always saying? *Savlenoot.* We lacked patience.

Nothing was quite the same as before, and I was annoyed with the weather for being so indifferent to my mood, angry at the sun for shining in such a clear blue sky. I was annoyed that we were all sitting around the Fishers' big dining table in their comfortable brick ranch house, behaving as though nothing had happened, as though we'd never really been away. Everything was fine, everything was *kol beseder.* Israel was a far-off place that we should get sentimental over but never take too seriously.

▲   ▲   ▲

It was hard to sit through the long services. It had been months, a different lifetime, since I'd been to services. In Israel, they rarely ran more than an hour and a half. Though I'd missed the singing there, now Mr. Schneider's cantorial flourishes irked me. Come on, get on with it, I thought. Bored and uninterested, I passed the time gossiping with the other women in my section, making frequent trips to the ladies' room, and taking Tamara out for walks around the block.

"Go school?" she suggested on one of our circuits. She had returned to Second Street School after Labor Day.

"Not today, Tamara. It's Yom Kippur."

"Yes. Come!" She tugged on my hand.

We were only two blocks away. "Okay. But just for a minute. We can't stay. We have to get back to synagogue."

It being an ordinary Wednesday morning for the rest of the world, we found everyone at the school engaged in their usual activities. How different from Israel, where everything stopped on Rosh Hashanah and Yom Kippur.

"Hey, Tam-Tam," called one of the teachers. "Don't you look nice all dressed up."

Tamara was wearing one of her crinolined, lacy creations. She'd barely grown since her parents purchased her wardrobe. Had memory of mother and father endured as well as the garment, or had Jeff and I totally replaced them? When we got back to the apartment that night, I would show her pictures of Chad and Sheila to help keep their memory alive.

Breaking loose, she ran to the sandbox. I was anxious for the dress. "Come, Tamara. Time to go back."

As we walked along Tucson Boulevard, crossing Hawthorne, I heard a rumble and looked to the west. Though it was still bright and clear where we were, off in the distance I saw a large cloud with a gray haze of rain falling beneath it. "Look, Tamara. It's raining over there."

She looked at the finger I pointed with. I gently turned her head in the right direction but she still seemed to be looking elsewhere. She seemed focused on the sunlight. Her impish grin reflected in her eyes, and she said, "Uh-oh, Mommy. Need an umbrella."

Once again in synagogue, my mind wandered from the page in the prayer book. Around me, people beat their fists against their breasts as they asked God to forgive them for a long list of transgressions. Instead, I reproached Him: why didn't You help make things work out for us in Israel? Then I laughed at myself for talking to Someone I no longer believe in.

▲     ▲     ▲

Ronnie disturbed my last sip of coffee. "Ma, I can't find my bus pass. I looked everywhere."

"What were you wearing yesterday? Did you check your pockets?"

"Oh, wait, here it is!" She pulled it out of a textbook where it was keeping her place. "Bye, Ma. I'll be home the regular time." She slammed out of the apartment. She seemed to be adjusting well to her first year of high school.

Jeff had already left, taking Tamara with him. Our routine was for him to park near the synagogue, drop her off at Second Street after services, and then walk the half mile to the Optical Sciences Building, saving the monthly University parking fee. In the afternoon, I would pick her up. Though the bus service wasn't bad, we'd already acquired two second-hand cars. Adam walked to Steele Elementary with the other kids from the complex.

I refilled my cup and leafed through a magazine Brenda had lent me. It was a castoff from the beauty salon, with pages ripped out and pictures of hairdos circled. I couldn't find the end of the story I was reading.

I flipped the periodical closed, poured the tepid coffee down the drain, and went to shower and dress. Then I drove to the Park Mall, where I wandered through the air-conditioned maze, nearly empty of shoppers because who besides me had her weekday morning free? Maybe it's time I find a job, I thought, but lacked the motivation to inquire in a shop with a "help wanted" sign in the window. I rationalized that with my college degree, I should look for something more challenging than "sales clerk," though it probably would be an improvement over my Kopy Kat job. But I was overcome with inertia.

After buying a box of chocolates at Fanny Farmer (were they kosher? did I care?) and a booklet of puzzles at Revco's, I drove home. I searched for a sharpened pencil while the glass pot refilled in our new coffee maker. Then, with steaming mug and candy close at hand, I settled down at the dinette to solve half the crosswords in the book.

▲    ▲    ▲

"You still doing that, Mom?" Adam asked when he came in for dinner.

"Let me just finish this up." I filled in the last couple of letters. "What is it, Adam?"

"What are we having?" He glanced over to the stove. "Hamburgers! Yum. Hey, Mom, why are you always doing those things? Is that the same one you were doing before when I got home from school?"

"No, I finished that one a while ago."

"Let me see that book." He riffled through the pages. The newsprint was bumpy like seersucker where my pencil had made its impression. "Wow, you did a lot of them, didn't you. You must be pretty good."

▲    ▲    ▲

"You have a nice view of the mountains this far out," Mandy commented. She pushed her pink-lensed glasses up on her nose and smiled at me. (No mountain was visible from our apartment door, unless she was referring to me.) "Gee, it's great to see you again. I sort of thought, when you left last year—selling the house and everything—I figured we'd never see you again."

She and Ned had been our neighbors when we lived on Ninth Street. I felt funny starting up again with old acquaintances: only a year before, I'd turned my back on them without a second thought.

"Come in," said Jeff. He brought a couple of kitchen chairs into the living room so we could sit. The Petersens settled on our lone couch. "Can I get you something to drink? A coke? Some juice?"

"Haven't you found anything reasonable yet?" asked Ned. "We'd love to have you back in the neighborhood."

"Have you looked at the house on Fourth near Plumer?" asked his wife. "It's been on the market a while now. It looks beautiful from the outside."

"We've been swamped, getting back into the swing of things again, the school term and all," Jeff apologized. "We really should start looking again."

I didn't really care anymore. Driving to pick up Tamara from school each day was a nuisance, but if we moved near the synagogue, Jeff would expect me to join him for Shabbas services. I was just as happy to spend my Saturdays by the pool.

▲    ▲    ▲

Jeff punched numbers into his calculator and scribbled on a yellow pad. I placed his refilled mug on the table and sat down. "Yeah, I think we can do it," he said.

"How do you feel about it?" I asked.

"Yeah, it's a nice house. Good location. The yard's a mess, but I guess we can fix it up. What is that thing back there? An old boat? Maybe we can write the offer contingent on their getting rid of the junk."

"Adam would like the boat."

"What's he gonna do with a boat? There's no water around here. I doubt it would float, anyway."

"It makes a nice climbing toy," I suggested.

"Look: you like the house? Let's make a bid on it. We'll worry about the boat later. Splintery old thing. I wonder how much you have to pay to get someone to cart it off."

In the twenty-four hours our offer was pending, I was too excited to sleep. I lay awake imagining how I'd decorate the living room, which bedroom I'd give to each child, mentally shifting furniture and hanging pictures. I sketched floor plans and made lists of what we'd need.

The realtor called the following afternoon. "I have good news," she started. "They feel your offer's just a little lower than they want, but I think we can put this thing together."

"Oh."

"They made a counter-offer. If you're free, I could come over this evening after your husband gets home, and we can discuss our next move."

After hanging up, I called Jeff, but he was in a class, so I left word with the department secretary. When he didn't show up at his usual time, I grew nervous. Hadn't he got my message? Where was he?

He finally walked in, steamed up and sweaty from sitting in traffic.

"Good, I'm glad you're here. The realtor is due any minute. If you hurry, you have just enough time to wash up and change your shirt."

"What! I was just going for a swim. You didn't tell me she was coming."

"I tried to reach you. I left a message with Jennine."

"Well I never got it. You really should have checked with me first."

Why was he being so peevish? Why, after how many years of marriage, did he still require the formality of advance notice on all our arrangements?

"Anyway, what's with the house? Did they accept our offer?"

"They want a little more."

"No! I hope you told her that. I think we made a very fair offer. The house has been sitting on the market for a long time. They obviously aren't willing to accept what it's worth."

"Jeff, calm down. There's the realtor now." I went to open the door.

Her visit was fruitless. Jeff insisted we couldn't afford to make a higher offer. I was embarrassed about his intransigence and the smell of his sweat. She left us bickering over how much we could afford while the kids whined for their dinner.

As we undressed for bed, Jeff's eyes settled on my hips. Was he calculating their increasing girth?

I quickly pulled down my nightgown.

He collected his dirty underwear and carried it to the bathroom hamper. I felt a pat on the backside as he passed. In Israel he'd been too tired, but now he was back to his old appetites. Maybe he found the greater surface area of my flesh even more enticing, though I certainly didn't. I didn't think my flabbiness was very attractive at all. My body felt muffled with fat, my mind edgy with caffeine.

He returned from the bathroom and offered me one of his particularly engaging, lopsided grins. "Hey, Cyn, I'm sorry about the house. Don't feel bad about it. There'll be other houses."

All night his breath was like a loose strand of hair blowing across my cheek.

▲   ▲   ▲

Jeff's parents came for their annual visit at the end of October. That they hadn't come the previous year didn't throw off this pattern; it was only a hiccup, a small interruption in the norm. They seemed not to notice the redecorated airport nor the absence of the children, who had stayed home to leave enough seats in the car. They showed only a moment's bewilderment when we drove them to the apartment instead of our old house on Ninth Street.

At the apartment, Adam and Ronnie greeted their grandparents enthusiastically. I found Tamara in the small kitchen, where she was building with her blocks on the linoleum.

"Tamara, take your blocks out of the kitchen," I scolded her. "Why aren't you allowed to play in here?"

She looked up at me and stuck out her lower lip.

"Because I could trip when I'm holding a pot of hot water or a sharp knife," I supplied.

With her eyes and pout still focused on me, she swung blindly at her tower, toppling it.

"Come, I'll help you clean up." I knelt to gather the blocks into their carton. "Grandma and Grandpa are here. You want to say hello to them?"

"No." She was still glaring at me.

"Are you angry with me?"

"No."

"Good. Then help me clean up. Then we'll go say hello to Grandma and Grandpa."

I lifted the filled box and stood. Taking Tamara in my free hand, I yanked her to her feet and led her to the living room, where my in-laws sat on either end of the new couch, each examining various Israeli artifacts the children presented.

"See, Grandma, this is my *machberit*," said Ronnie, handing over the small, brown notebook. "Open it up. See. It's full of Hebrew."

"Tamara wants to show Grandma something, too," I said.

Ronnie turned to us; the old woman blinked at the exotic girl.

"You want to show Grandma your Gali sneakers?" I prompted Tamara. Gali was the Israeli equivalent of Nike or Reebok. Everyone there wore Gali sneakers. Even the Orthodox women in their long skirts and kerchiefs wore lace-up running shoes.

A thumb thrust deep in her mouth, Tamara lifted her foot.

"Tell Grandma where we bought them."

She removed her thumb. "Israel."

"Sheila's child," the woman muttered.

On an impulse, I put down the box and lifted Tamara onto my mother-in-law's lap. Throughout their two-week stay, I would thrust Tamara on our guests, forcing them to accept the girl who was their grandchild twice over, who was both their daughter's child and now their son's.

An interesting relationship developed. Tamara often held back, shy of the withdrawn pair. Or perhaps she felt she couldn't compete with her verbal siblings. But I sensed in the old couple a growing fondness toward her. Maybe they appreciated her slow, quiet ways. Her rhythm, her cautious approach to life, mirrored theirs.

We pressed our guests to take our bedroom—Jeff would sleep on a borrowed cot in Adam's room, I could easily share Tamara's bed—but they staunchly refused, using our new couch and the cot set up in the living room. Toward the end of their visit, Tamara would come out to them there early each morning. She'd bring a stuffed bunny or a book with her and keep them company as they finished dressing and folded the blankets.

As always, they were totally unobtrusive. At first I feared I'd have no solitude, but they left me each day for walks along Old Spanish Trail. They sat for hours in the warm sun on the patio. Thus I had the privacy to eat my chocolates and do my puzzles. I was growing to be like them: cut off, treasuring my isolation.

▲   ▲   ▲

"What are your plans for today?" Jeff asked one morning in November.

"Oh, I don't know. Why?"

"Well, if you're going shopping, I noticed we're getting low on coffee filters."

"Oh, okay. I'll pick some up." I was glad for an excuse to go where I could buy more sweets.

Jeff looked at me quizzically. "Are you okay?"

"Uh-huh. Why?"

"You seem sort of—I don't know—quiet lately. You making friends here? Are you happy?"

"Uh-huh."

"Good." He smiled enigmatically. "Tam," he called. "Time to go to school."

I was annoyed with him that he didn't see I'd lied to him. Obviously I couldn't be "okay" if all I did was sit around all day stuffing my face and filling up an endless supply of puzzle books.

Was Jeff deliberately refusing to see my silent protest, my half-dead existence? Was he afraid of what would come out if he probed too deeply, or did he simply not care? What had happened to my involved, sensitive husband, the man who used to make me laugh, who cried over the lost pregnancy? Where was the Jeff who bought the beautiful bracelet I hid in my dresser? Even Adam was more perceptive. "Why do you do those, Mom?" he'd asked. "You spend all that time writing in the words and then, when you finally finish them all, you just throw the book out. What's the point of that?"

Had Jeff's experience in Israel made him callous? Or did he also suffer the humiliation of our failure, the loss of our greatest dream? Was his smile his own way of lying?

But I wouldn't talk to him about it. Suppressing whatever it was that was wrong with me took up too much of my energy.

▲   ▲   ▲

"Mrs. Roth! So you're back from Israel." Dr. Freedman's jovial voice was loud, and he was slow to shut the door. Why must he announce my business to the whole office?

"Hello, doctor."

Glancing at the chart in his hand, he said, "Ah-ha! Is this weight gain significant?"

I glowered. I didn't need him to tell me about my significant weight gain.

"Want to talk?" he asked more gently.

Sitting on the edge of the examination table, crinkling in the paper gown, I felt vulnerable. Tears came from nowhere.

He handed me a tissue and patted my upper arm, then brought over the molded-plastic chair and sat down, attentive but unobtrusive.

"I'm sorry," I said when I'd finished crying.

"It's okay." He waited for me to say more.

"I just seem so tired all the time. I have no energy. I drag around and can't get anything done. I still haven't unpacked everything. It's such a mess. And my nose is always stuffed, and I have this mild headache sometimes. I get out of breath a lot of the time, too. Sometimes I have dizzy spells. And look at this: see, on the side of my nose? Don't you think I'm a little old to be getting pimples? But this whitehead doesn't seem to want to go away. I've had it for weeks already. And you see here behind my ear? All of a sudden I'm getting boils." I looked down at my bare feet. "And, um, I can't seem to get interested in sex. Why is that? I want to, but then nothing happens. I'd rather go to sleep."

He nodded sympathetically. "You getting along all right with your husband?"

"Yes. It's just that everything's so flat. Nothing can excite me. Nothing has any taste."

"Hmm. Let's run some tests. Check your hemoglobin count, your thyroid. There are any number of reasons for you to be having these symptoms. You're not on any medication, are you? What about the weight? Let's see: seventeen pounds since spring eighty-four. Israeli food fattening? A lot of starch, I bet."

"No, I've gained it all since we got back."

"What have you been eating?"

I sighed. I was too embarrassed to mention the chocolates. Besides, then he'd blame all my symptoms on them. "I eat all right. Probably too much, and I could use more exercise. I have been drinking too much coffee."

"But it hasn't been doing much good, has it, from what you're saying. You're still tired." He scratched his scalp. "Let's take a look at you now and we'll get you back in a week when we have the test results."

As I lay down on the table and he pulled on his latex glove, he asked, "Didn't work out in Israel, huh? They say life's very hard over there. Where were you? Haifa?"

"No, Jerusalem."

"I don't know why I had you going to Haifa. Just relax now. I thought your husband was working at the Technion."

"No, Jerusalem College of Technology."

"I don't know that one."

"It's a small place. It's only been in existence a few years. They didn't have the money to offer Jeff anything permanent."

"That's too bad. What's he doing now?"

"He's back at the University. He'd taken a leave."

"Lucky. How are the kids taking it? You have a boy and a girl, don't you?"

My head jerked up from the table. "I must not have seen you since my sister-in-law died."

"Whoa! When did this happen?"

"She and her husband were killed in a car crash just before we were supposed to leave. We adopted their daughter."

He leaned back against the counter and peeled off the glove. "I'm trying to remember: you told me about your niece, didn't you?" He wrinkled his brow.

"She has Down syndrome."

"Ah, that's it." He nodded slowly. "How's it working out?" He came to the side of the table and began kneading my breasts.

"Okay. She's a cute kid."

"Yeah, they're very lovable. How old is she now?"

"Six. Almost seven."

"She speak at all? Aren't they teaching these kids sign language nowadays?"

"She talks so we haven't bothered. She even picked up some Hebrew over there."

"Really? That's great. You can sit up now." He offered his hand and pulled me up.

"Thanks. She's in the primary class at Second Street School now and she's learning to write." Actually, while her classmates wrote, she scribbled, but some of her scrawl resembled letters.

"That's wonderful. She must be one of the good ones. I've heard some of them even go on to college."

I resented his use of "these kids," as though she weren't as much an individual as anyone else. What did he mean by "good ones"? Would he call less capable kids "bad"? Anyway, I wasn't so sure Tamara could be classified as "good," seeing as she was still in diapers.

But then I softened. Dr. Freedman was trying to be kind. I accepted his comments in that spirit.

When I returned the following week, he told me all the tests came back negative and that I was healthy. "Then why am I feeling so lousy?" I asked.

We were in his office. He put down his pen and gazed across the large desk. "I think, Mrs. Roth, that you're depressed."

"Depressed?"

"Yes."

"Why?"

"About Israel. Here you'd finally fulfilled your lifetime dream, and then it didn't work out. You feel let down."

"But we've been back for months already. I've already accepted everything. There were so many things that were bad there: we couldn't speak the language, and Jeff couldn't find a job, and they're all crazy, and the money was crazy. Everyone had said, 'It'll be hard for you but at least it's great for the children,' like we were making a noble sacrifice for the sake of the kids. But they were wrong—it was lousy for the children, too. It wasn't good for any of us."

"That may be what you believe here"—he tapped his forehead—"but I don't think you've resolved anything here." He placed his hand on his chest.

My eyes stung and I felt in my pockets for a tissue. "But I wouldn't want to go back," I insisted.

He was silent.

"I have this daydream," I admitted quietly, "that Jeff dies and I take the kids back to live on a kibbutz."

He nodded.

"I don't really want Jeff to die."

"Of course not." After a pause, he said, "It was his idea to leave, wasn't it?"

"I wanted to give it more time. But I don't think the end result would have been different."

"No," he agreed. "Look, at least you gave it a try. That's more than most people ever do. How many people spend their whole life saying, 'Someday I'm going to—whatever.' At least you actually went ahead and did it."

"Yeah, I guess so."

"I don't think there's anything wrong with your feeling depressed right now. I mean, I wouldn't suggest counseling, or even an antidepressant, unless you begin to feel much worse. Not necessary. There's a direct correlation between what you're feeling and what you've experienced. It's like the death of someone very dear to you. It's quite normal to feel a bit sad."

"I'm grieving?" I dabbed at my eyes.

"Yes, you could say that."

I stood up. "Thank you, Dr. Freedman." I was grateful to him for putting into words my sorrow, for legitimizing my despondency.

The doctor reached to shake my hand. It felt funny: in Israel, I'd gotten out of the habit of any casual physical contact with men.

The late autumn sun bounced off the blacktop parking lot, making me squint. But then the taut muscles of my face relaxed into a smile.

## Twenty-Two

Hanging a name on my symptoms brought relief, but it didn't cure my depression. It was like finding the proper label to stick on a file of random correspondence: though the intrinsic interrelatedness was now clear, the letters still had to be dealt with—read, answered, thrown out or saved. I didn't feel up to sorting through my messy folder, so I wasted my days drinking coffee and thumbing through magazines. Crosswords were my greatest intellectual challenge, and I rationalized that my time-wasting was okay because I was "recovering" and needed my rest. I felt profoundly empty; I stuffed food into myself in a feeble attempt to fill the void.

How dull I was. Even the manifestations of my unhappiness were boring. I didn't get drunk, I didn't snort cocaine. I didn't do anything reckless. Even when my car was the only one on the road, I didn't speed. My wrists remained unscathed by razor blades. I didn't beat my children; I hadn't even taken a swing at Jeff. My promiscuity went no further than half-hearted daydreams which lacked the potency to arouse me. My only vices were indolence and gluttony.

I still thought of leaving Jeff. During my long hours alone during the day, I pictured myself becoming a barroom floozy, or hiking alone in the Rincon Mountains. Both ideas terrified me. I was too plump and middle-aged to be anything but ridiculous in the first role, vulnerable in the latter.

I imagined myself in love with Dr. Freedman, the man who understood me. Had his probing and prodding of my most intimate anatomy given rise to his intuition regarding my innermost feelings? No, he wouldn't work as a daydream lover: his repeated clinical examinations of me in real life stood in the way of any romantic fantasy. I tried imagining a return to Israel, where I'd find a bilingual native—a dark, curly-haired Sabra looking macho in his army fatigues—who could forever bridge the gap between me and my perplexing homeland. Jeff, who'd linked me to my Jewish heritage, failed as my liaison to Zion. Now what I needed was someone who could help me navigate through the bureaucracy and cultural differences to a point where I'd feel comfortably a part of life there.

But even my fantasies were unsatisfying: I couldn't abandon reality enough to disencumber myself of maternal entanglements. Where are my children through all this? I kept thinking. Would I leave them with the deserted husband? No, I couldn't: nuisance that they were, I'd miss them too much.

And then there was the problem of Jeff: in spite of my resentment, I couldn't emotionally divorce myself from him. He still was my greatest love. I would think of the little things about him that irked me—the small bulge of belly above his belt, the strong odor of his perspiration when he first walked in after work each evening, the way he picked his teeth after dinner. Everything that I claimed to find obnoxious in him, that I used as a wedge between us, became endearing in my reveries. I'd despair of ever again smelling his strong tang, of having him grab my backside with familiarity, of nagging him about leaving his shoes where I could trip on them. How perverse: I'd weep over my loss as though it were real.

My perversity became even more convoluted. I began to worry that if anything were to happen to Jeff, I'd drop even the outward trappings of Jewish practice. I was afraid I'd drift away, never again going to synagogue, no longer keeping kosher, driving and shopping and running errands on Saturday. If I gave all that up, it would be as though the past fifteen years were a sham. All my adult life would amount to nothing, a silly joke. It frightened me to forfeit all those years.

Thus I drifted into winter, into 1986, into apathetically agreeing on the purchase of a tiny tumble-down house three blocks from synagogue.

▲   ▲   ▲

"Wake up, lazy bones."

"Oh, Jeff, it's Saturday." I rolled onto my belly and bunched the pillow around my head.

"Come on, Cyn!" He yanked the covers off me. "It's seven forty-five already. Services begin at nine. That's why we bought this house—so we could go to shul. Or did you forget?"

"Yeah, yeah. Just a minute." I opened my eyelid just enough to see him go through the door, cross the narrow hall, and enter the girls' room. I heard him growl, Tamara shriek and giggle, Ronnie whine, "Oh, Daddy!" I rolled out of bed.

One good thing about the house was that we didn't have to run out and buy a lot to decorate it. Our meager collection of beds, dinette, and couch completely filled the cubicles. There was something womblike and comforting about small rooms: placing furniture was a lot like solving a crossword puzzle—only one solution fit. I didn't like to think there were choices; they made me fret whether I'd chosen correctly.

In the few days we'd lived in the house, I could already see the good of our move. Adam was happily reunited with old friends at Sam Hughes Elementary a few blocks away. Paco and Darren and J.J. once again traipsed through my house, helping themselves to bananas and glasses of milk. The other boys had grown in our absence; they now towered over Adam, who was still short and round with baby fat.

Even closer than Sam Hughes was Second Street School; holding Tamara's pudgy hand, I led her there and back over the packed dust, past palo verdes and mesquites, desert broom and creosote bush. Ronnie still rode the bus out to Rincon High, but it was a shorter ride, and in the opposite direction. Now she rode into the rising sun each morning. Jeff walked to work. I walked to Rincon Market on Sixth, where I replenished our supply of milk and bread and fruit.

On the evening of our move, Ronnie agreed to watch Tamara so Jeff and I could step out. We wandered over to UA and ended up across campus at the music department's weekly concert. How nice to once again live closeby to Tucson's main source of "culture." I hadn't been to a live performance since Pertsa took me to the symphony. I watched the percussionist. A person could dissipate a lot of anger banging on drums.

Before picking Tamara up from school on Friday, I walked to the Himmel Library and took out a pile of books. Somehow, those books gave me strength. I felt more capable and alert as I strolled back through the park. The great trees, dormant and bare except for the clusters of mistletoe in their loftiest branches, lifted my spirits.

But now I was expected to go to synagogue.

Jeff was helping me with the clasp of my bracelet. "Maybe I'll go back to school next fall," I surprised myself by saying.

"That's a great idea, Cyn. What were you thinking of taking?"

"Well, my bachelor's in English lit isn't doing me much good. Maybe I could take some business courses, or library science, or...." Too many choices. I felt confused.

"I'll bring home a catalog if you'll remind me on Monday."

"Thanks."

"Cynthia?" He lifted up my chin so that I looked at him.

"Uh-huh?"

"You know, we got this house cheap. We have a steady income and very few expenses, except maybe to repair the stucco." He grinned. "With a guaranteed roof over our heads and two passable cars, what else do we need? Some groceries and a few rags to put on? We really don't have to worry about money anymore. You know that, don't you?"

"Yes?" What was he getting at?

"So you should take classes that really interest you. You don't have to worry about getting a good job. If you just want to be a college bum the rest of your life, it's okay with me." He stroked my cheek, tempting me to purr.

Instead, I broke away and laughed. "I'll be thirty-nine this year," I commented. It wasn't really a non sequitur. How odd it would be, going back to school. How strange to sit in a classroom of college students again. To be around all that youthful idealism.

At breakfast, I suggested Jeff go on with Adam and Ronnie to synagogue. "There's no point in me getting Tamara there so early. She can't
sit through the whole thing."

"Okay. What time did you plan on coming?"

"Maybe ten, ten-thirty."

"Okay," he said while chewing his cereal. "Don't be any later. They
finish by half-past eleven."

Jeff gulped down his coffee. "Adam, you ready to go? Put away your
brush, Ronnie. Your hair is beautiful. Come. Let's get there on time."

I spent the next hour reading a library book while Tamara sang to
herself.

When we arrived at synagogue, someone was reading aloud a prayer
in English: "...bless the State of Israel which marks the dawn of our
deliverance. Shield it beneath the wings of Thy love; spread over it Thy
tabernacle of peace...." A tabernacle is a *succah*, I reflected, and everyone
knows a *succah*'s roof is full of holes. No wonder Israel had a hard time,
with us asking God for such flimsy protection.

I left Tamara with Ronnie and went back to the kitchen to offer my
help setting out the *kiddush*. There were gefilte fish balls and pickled
herring to arrange with toothpicks on glass plates, and cake to cut up, and
large containers of Seven-Up to set out. By the time I returned to the
girls, Cantor Schneider was leading the "Adon Olam." I congratulated
myself on my timing.

Tamara was singing along.

"Where were you?" Ronnie whispered.

"Helping with the *kiddush*."

"Oh." She frowned.

The service concluded with the song. I smiled and wished good
Shabbas to the few other women in my section, then, with the girls,
joined Jeff and Adam and said hello to the men.

"It's good to have you back with us again," I was told repeatedly.

▲   ▲   ▲

That afternoon, we took a stroll to our old house several blocks
away. It felt funny walking along Ninth Street again. We stopped to chat
with the Petersens, who were out gardening in their front yard.

Ned leaned on his hoe and wiped the sweat off his face. "Hey, we're
real glad to have you back in the area."

"We have to get you guys over for drinks one of these days," Mandy
said.

We continued down the block to our former home. The new
owners weren't in. It was probably just as well: when he saw the garish
shade of green they'd painted the trim, Adam said "Ew!" loud enough to
be heard in the next block.

"It's not our house anymore," Jeff lectured him. "It's none of our business what color they paint it."

"Our house!" Recognizing the place where she'd lived only a short time, Tamara headed up the driveway.

Ronnie ran up after her calling, "Come back here." Seeing Ronnie under the carport gave me a jolt. With the old, familiar surroundings as a frame of reference, it was obvious how much taller she'd grown.

▲   ▲   ▲

"What's that?" I mumbled early one morning.

Tamara was singing loudly in the kitchen. There was silence. Then she started again. I could make out "*modeh ani.*" Where had I heard that before? Oh yes, I remembered.

Jeff lay on his back with his eyes open, his elbows jutting out from either side of his head. "You hear that? I'm impressed. She knows the whole thing."

"She learned it in *gan*. They used to recite it each morning."

"Yeah. You're supposed to teach little Jewish kids to say it first thing in the morning. So anyway that's one thing good about Israel, teaching Tam what I should've taught her." He grimaced. "I'm not such a good Jew, am I? Neglecting the proper training of my kids." He scratched his chest, then under his chin. "Which reminds me: you know, we should start looking into getting Ad prepared for his bar mitzvah. Don't kid yourself, it's not that far off."

"He won't be thirteen for another year."

"Exactly. You think he can learn everything in a year?"

"He knows a lot of Hebrew."

"Yeah, good thing too. But he still has to learn his Haftorah. Maybe he could do some of the Torah reading."

"Who'll teach him?"

"I'll ask around shul. One of those old men should be willing to earn a little money. How much you think we should pay?"

Tamara marched into our room. She carried a stuffed animal against her shoulder. In her other hand she held open a small book. Pretending to read, she chanted the psalm of David we sang on Saturdays while the Torah was carried back to the Ark. Obviously the doll was supposed to represent the Torah scroll. Children mimic the adult world by playing house, school, doctor; she was imitating what she'd seen on Shabbas.

▲   ▲   ▲

I did an experiment. I opened the refrigerator and took out the chicken wing and thigh left from the previous night's dinner. Careful not to put flesh near my dairy dishes, I placed them on a paper plate. Then

I took out a glass and filled it with milk. I sat down to my lunch.

Why was I so nervous? Before I met Jeff, I'd often eaten chicken and milk products at the same meal. I used to eat lobster, cheeseburgers, ham and swiss on rye. I'd put sour cream on the baked potato I ate with my steak. Bacon-lettuce-and-tomato sandwiches were a favorite. Fried oysters, cheese-and-meat casseroles, chocolate cream pie after pork chops, chicken ala king, beef stroganoff....

Which fork should I use? Never mind: I picked it up in my hands. My teeth sank into the thigh. I loved cold chicken. I ripped off large chunks of cooked muscle, then nibbled the bones clean. Satisfied, I sat back in my chair and wiped my mouth with a paper napkin.

I was thirsty. Empire kosher chickens always made me thirsty. It was all the salt they used to draw the blood out of the flesh. I stared at the milk. It looked so white. I ran a finger against the glass. It felt cool. My mouth felt dry.

The house was quiet. "Come on, you coward," I challenged myself. I wrapped my fingers around the glass. Ridiculous dietary laws: they had nothing to do with reality. After staring at the white liquid close up, I shut my eyes and tipped it to my lips.

It tasted surprisingly delicious—sweet, rich. Overwhelmed with thirst, my sip grew to something greedier. I swallowed large gulps, tilting the glass up to speed the flow. When it was empty, I stuck my tongue out inside the wall of the glass, searching out the last drop.

So there.

A gurgling came from my throat and I burped. It left a bad taste. I burped again, and then a queasiness clutched my stomach. Nausea made my ears ring. I bolted from the table and ran for the bathroom. But then I calmed myself and swallowed it all back down. Throughout the afternoon, I imagined the chicken and milk at war in my gut.

▲    ▲    ▲

Stepping out of the shower, I looked at myself. In the apartment, we didn't have a full-length mirror, sparing me the horror of what I was becoming. But our house had one embedded in the bathroom door. The teardrops of old paint blemishing the glass did little to hide my size or shape. My reflection was pale and large. Even my face was swollen, my pointy chin and high cheek bones softened the way rocks and bushes look after a snowfall. My small nose was all but lost. I used to look kittenish. "Fat cat!" I yelled at my image.

I went to an Overeaters Anonymous meeting. It was okay. The people there were friendly and warm. They made me feel welcome. The trouble was they kept talking about their Higher Power: how He had helped them, how when they let Him into their lives, He took away their compulsion to eat.

I was too angry at God to have faith in Him. If He did exist, if I could still believe in Him, I'd end up arguing with Him. I'd shout, "Why all these false starts? All these wrong moves? You stick a baby in my womb and then kill it. Because of You I drag myself halfway around the world and then You let it not work out, so we're back here again. Why are You doing this? What do You want from me?"

The people at the meeting talked about counting their blessings.

Sure, I thought. One thing was for sure. Life was a struggle, no matter what. Even when I used to let God into my life, it was hard.

A woman across the room said, "I used to have everything—a good husband, a nice home and my health—but I wasn't satisfied. I cheated on my husband and hit the booze, and then I ate myself into a size eighteen. God gave me an easy life, but I wasn't satisfied, so I complicated it."

I decided she had it backwards: I had an easy life until God complicated it.

The meeting was held in a church. It ended with the Lord's Prayer. We stood in a circle holding hands and they recited, "Our Father, Who art in Heaven." The woman on my right had bony fingers adorned with lots of rings. One ring had twisted around. Instead of joining their chant, I concentrated on the pain inflicted by the gem pressing into my palm.

▲　　▲　　▲

A postcard came from my sister. She was vacationing in the Bahamas. "How nice," I commented to Jeff. "She might have come here, you know. When was the last time our kids saw their aunt? In fact, she's never even met her newest niece." Thinking of her thin, tan form on a sunny beach, I banged the silverware tray onto its shelf and slammed the cabinet door shut.

"Come on, Cyn," said Jeff. "So what would you do if she came to Tucson? You two never got along."

"Doesn't she feel any familial ties at all?"

"Evidently not. Look, stop worrying about it, will you?"

"I just can't see how the two of us could have been raised in the same home yet turn out to be so different."

"Maybe she's thinking the same thing. She's probably wondering how her sister could be such a religious fanatic. She probably can't figure out how the Cindy she grew up with could be keeping kosher and going to shul each week. To her, you're probably a very strange character."

"Thanks!" A strange character, that about summed it up.

"Hey, Cyn, forget about your sister for a minute and look what else came in the mail. This showed up at work today."

"What's that?"

"Somebody forwarded our year-end statement from Bank Leumi."

"Only a couple of months late." I looked at the envelope with our

Bayit Vegan address crossed out and the University of Arizona inked in.

"It probably sat around for a while. Someone must have given it to Litansky. He's the only one who would know where to find me."

I hadn't written to Pertsa or anyone else in Israel. It was too painful.

He pulled out the statement and unfolded it. The page was crammed with small Hebrew letters and lots of numbers.

I was amazed. "We still have money in our account?"

"Yeah. It seems the college continued to deposit my salary over the summer—see these figures? six hundred eighty-nine thousand et cetera, that's for June, and six ninety-three, July, seven hundred whatever for August. I forgot they hired me for a full year. Also, the government continued to deposit our monthly child allowance. But what's even more interesting is this. See this? All the numbers change."

"They changed their minds and withdrew all the money they'd given us," I guessed.

"Sort of looks that way, doesn't it. I couldn't figure any of it out so I called up this Israeli prof in the UA aggie school and he told me he'd stop by and have a look. His name is Shlomo Levi, by the way. We really should have him and his wife over some time. The guy's a riot. You should hear the blast he let out about the Israeli economy."

"What did he say?"

"When he saw this mess, he just started laughing. It seems before, when we'd been in Israel, we were dealing with the bad old shekels. Now everything's been changed to the new improved shekels. I guess no one could deal with the unwieldy numbers. Anyway, the bottom line is that one new shekel equals a thousand old shekels."

"So the shekel's now worth a dollar?"

"Roughly."

"And we have a couple of thousand dollars' worth of shekels in Bank Leumi?"

"Yeah. Which we can't touch."

"Unless we go back to Israel. We can spend them there." I grinned. I didn't know whether to take myself seriously.

▲    ▲    ▲

March was unusually cold. The Santa Catalinas looked flat and distant—ripped construction paper against a sky of rubbed charcoal. There were flurries and heavy rain and gusts. Hanging from eaves and under ramadas, ceramic cowbells and chimes made of pottery or beaten metal clanked and jangled. The schoolyard flagpole became a one-note flute, producing an eerie, ringing whistle when wind blew down its long hollow. Gray filaments were tugged from chimneys. Whiffs of the sour-smelling smoke mixed with the stench of tar being used to repair a neighbor's roof.

But as we shivered in our winter jackets, we heard the call of birds, creatures with more faith in the changing of seasons. Trees and bushes began to green, their new leaves fluttering like a nervous audience applauding the blustery weather. Airborne was the subtle tantalizing promise of citrus blossoms not yet opened. When the wind blew, we glimpsed the small white fists peeking behind the foliage.

Toward the end of the month, my parents visited. My mother couldn't restrain herself from mentioning that I'd "put on a little weight," as if I might not have been aware of it myself. She couldn't even wait until we'd left the airport. It was practically the first thing she said, right after "hello." Then she criticized the house. "Oh, Cindy, this is a come down. I thought you were going to buy something nicer when you got back. What happened?" After only one night in our crowded house, they asked the use of one of our idle cars. They found a cheap motel room out by I-10.

I noticed with irritation that they ignored Tamara. Unlike with my in-laws, I had no success getting them to accept her. When I tried to push her on them, they squirmed. I had thought they would dote on her to prove how open-minded they were.

Tamara was fascinated by my mother's beauty marks. She pressed her stubby finger against each brown spot on the back of my mother's hands and arms, then reached for the ones on her neck and cheeks.

"Please get off my lap, now, dear," my mother requested in her stilted voice.

"Dad, why don't you read Tamara a book," I suggested.

"Okay," said my father. "I was just going to play a game of chess with Ronnie. I'll read to her after I finish."

Tamara was slow, but she wasn't stupid. She avoided them, finding solitary occupations to amuse herself. I found her in her room, singing, crayoning, showing her stuffed bunny pictures in her books.

It was harder for me to avoid my parents. The weather wasn't conducive to sightseeing or sunbathing, and I didn't have the excuse of going to work. Every morning, they appeared on our doorstep.

What was it about them that bothered me so much? After all, I could accept Jeff's parents, and they were far more boorish. Of course I never fully appreciated my connection to my in-laws; their behavior had no bearing on me. But my own parents had to be perfect. I wanted them to be extravagant in their tolerance because this interest in the welfare of others, regardless of background or beliefs, was the value they instilled in me that I most cherished.

But they were never really so broad as to embrace all humanity, at least when it came to me. No doubt religious practices I espoused when I married Jeff troubled them. If I was annoyed they weren't perfect, they seemed disappointed I failed to live by their ideal. Hadn't they also taught me, along with "love thy neighbor," that rituals were atavistic and that organized religions separated people? Each theology presented itself as the only right way and scorned the infidels who refused to accept its teachings. They cited the Crusades, the Inquisition, the modern-day unrest in India and Ireland and Lebanon, as senseless violence perpetrated in the name of God. I agreed with them, but then how to explain Jeff, a deeply religious man, who was more generous with both his money and his love than either of them?

▲    ▲    ▲

They hadn't realized when they picked dates for their trip to Tucson that Purim fell within the time of their stay. The Fast of Esther took them by surprise. "What do you mean, you're not eating?" my mother asked at lunchtime. "Are you on some sort of crazy diet?"

"No. It's a religious fast. We can eat again this evening."

"Listen, Cindy," my father said, "maybe your mom and I will go out for lunch."

"You can eat here," I said.

"No." My mother shook her head.

My dad smirked. "We don't want to interfere with your *mishegas*."

I found irony in his use of Yiddish to put down Judaism.

That evening we went to synagogue to hear the reading of the Megillah. My parents wanted to do something else—escape to a movie, spend the evening watching TV in the motel room—but Ronnie and Adam prevailed. "Come with us!" Ronnie insisted. She wore a plastic flowerpot on her head, and rosebuds made from satin ribbons were pinned to her blouse. "Purim is the best. Everyone wears costumes, and whenever they say Haman's name, you have to shout and stamp your feet."

"Why?" asked my mother.

"Because he's the bad guy who wanted to kill all the Jews in Persia," Adam explained. In a loosened necktie and Jeff's old jacket, he was supposed to be a bum.

My mother looked aghast. Here were her grandchildren, engaged in some sort of primitive voodoo.

There was a larger crowd than usual at Young Israel. A lot of people who couldn't be bothered the rest of the year thought it was fun to show up on Purim.

Tamara grew excited with the activity and high spirits in the synagogue. She wore a silverfoil crown Ronnie made for her. "I Queen Esther," she told anyone who asked. But then the reading began. Each time Haman's name was mentioned, the roar of "boos" and thunder of stamping feet scared her.

Suddenly concerned about the child, my mother made a sour face and shook her head. "You should really take her out," she said. "They're too wild."

Suddenly conscientious, I pointed out that I was required to hear the whole Megillah.

"Look at her," my mother said.

Tamara was sucking her thumb and pulling her fine hair. Drying tears streaked her cheeks. At that moment, Cantor Schneider called out, "Haman," and the boisterous congregants drowned out Tamara's shrieks. Looking pathetic, she reached her arms to me.

I lifted her, hugged her, soothed her. "Listen, Ma, why don't you take her home for me. Here's the key."

She shook her head.

"Go on, Ma. I can tell you don't want to stay either."

"I feel a little unsure of myself with her," she admitted. "I don't understand what she's saying." She spoke in clipped, carefully enunciated words, as though demonstrating how she wished to be spoken to.

"That didn't stop you from baby-sitting for Ronnie when she was a year old," I said.

My mother reluctantly took the key and stood. "Come, Tamara," she said in her false voice.

Tamara wouldn't go to her, clinging instead to me.

"Never mind, Ma. Sit down."

She sighed.

Tamara dealt with her fear by falling asleep in my arms. She stirred and moaned with each rise of the din, but then settled back into somnolence. I refused to talk to my mother, forcing myself to concentrate on the story of Esther. I could understand every few words of the Hebrew. Of course, I already knew the story.

Before my parents headed back east, I had become scrupulously observant, just to push it in their faces. How absurd I was: a fat, middle-aged woman still acting out her adolescent rebellion against her parents. It gave me pleasure to see their discomfort. I started reciting blessings before I ate fruit, before I drank water, upon gazing on the mountains. "Blessed art Thou, Lord our God, King of the Universe, Who created great wonders." I didn't even know if I had the standard form. I pretended to know what I was doing. I pretended to be pious.

# Twenty-Three

There were no unfinished crossword puzzles in the house, and I'd already read all my library books; I planned to exchange them for others before picking up Tamara from school. Standing by the bookcase looking for something to fill the morning, I noticed the small red volume Jeff had bought me years before. This was not Jane Austen's best, but the pleasure of the leather binding, the ribbon bookmark dangling from the spine, the feel of the slim book in my palm, made me think it should be retitled *Sense and Sensibility—and Sensuousness*. There was more to the experience of reading than scanning words.

The phone rang and I slipped the ribbon between the pages, not because I really cared about keeping my place—I was only browsing—but because I enjoyed sliding my finger along the satin.

"Hi. Good. I got you in. Hope I didn't catch you at a bad time. It seem's like everybody's running, running, including myself, what with *Pesach* cleaning and all the shopping and what-have-you."

"What can I do for you?" I could tell it was Roberta Grossman, wife of the new rabbi, though she forgot to identify herself. The English major in me itched to edit her characteristic wordiness.

"I was wondering: are you free tomorrow afternoon to help with a *tahara*?"

"Sure. What's that?"

"I just got a call from Handmakers, you know, the Jewish nursing home. Did you know Betsy Singer? They tell me she used to be the president of the sisterhood."

"No, I don't remember her."

"No? Well anyway, it must have been a long time ago, since she's been at Handmakers for I think they said something like ten years. They called to say she's just passed on."

"That's too bad."

"Yeah, well, but sometimes it's a blessing. You know, when they've just been sitting around in a home that many years. Anyway, what we have to do is prepare her for burial. What we need is preferably four women. Well, I guess if we had to, we could do it with three, but the bodies are usually heavy and hard to handle. Also, we want to get done quickly because of the Shabbas coming up. By the way, what time is sun-set tomorrow, do you know? I have to look that up. Anyway, what we have to do is we wash her, then pour water over her as a final ritual bath, instead of the *mikvah*, since obviously she can't do that herself. Then we dress her in a shroud and that's it, I think. It's called a *tahara* because we're making her clean for burial. Do you think you could help us out?"

I felt a little queasy.

"My husband wants to bury her by three," she continued. "Maybe we could meet at one? What do you think? It shouldn't take more than an hour."

"Okay," I said tentatively. I'd have to arrange for Tamara to stay late at school. Adam could visit a friend until I got home.

"Are you sure? I'll tell you right now it isn't pretty. But it's a very big *mitzvah*."

"Okay, I'll do it," I said definitely before I could change my mind. What was I scared of, after all I'd been through? I'd already encountered death. I was half dead myself.

▲     ▲     ▲

I turned off Speedway onto Oracle. As I drove north, the sky grew dark with clouds. By the time I turned into the parking lot at Evergreen Cemetery, hail tapped loudly on the car roof. I had to make a run for the mortuary door, trying not to slip on the ice balls littering the pavement.

We looked out of place, like the cleaning crew who couldn't find the back door, standing in the solemn, formal entry wearing button-down cardigans over wet cotton dresses, with sodden kerchiefs tied around our heads. Roberta came in carrying a bag of towels and plastic buckets. She was an easy-going woman of impressive proportions, both in height and breadth. Even with my added poundage, I felt small next to her.

One of the discreet morticians, who wore the only dark suits I ever saw in Tucson, quickly ushered the four of us through a door to a maze of antiseptically spotless halls and eventually into a large room resembling a high school science lab. "Do you have everything you need?" he asked, and when Roberta nodded, he left and quietly shut the door.

The other two women and I stood there, glancing furtively at the sheet-covered lump on the metal table. Calm Roberta put down her buckets and began emptying their contents—a booklet, a bottle full of sand, a broken plate, scissors, washcloths—along a counter.

Marlene pulled a pair of latex gloves from her handbag. "Roberta, is it all right for me to wear these?"

The rabbi's wife drew back her lips into something kinder than a sneer. "I guess so. It's preferable not to, but if you'd feel more comfort-able, I guess it's all right."

"What did she die of?" asked Ellen, the fourth woman.

"You know, I don't know. I didn't think to ask them, and I don't remember them saying. I guess just old age. She must have been very old."

"How old?" Ellen and I said almost together. I felt jumpy. Ellen smiled awkwardly at me.

"I'm not sure. In her late eighties, maybe?"

Eying Marlene's gloves, I wondered aloud: "Do you think we can catch anything from...?" I tapered off, unsure whether to address Betsy as "her." Somehow, this pronoun seemed wrong for the inanimate body before us.

"I don't think so," Roberta answered. "I used to do these all the time in Queens, and I never heard of anyone catching anything. Of course, we'll wash thoroughly when we're through, and I guess maybe you should shower when you get home. You'll be showering anyway for Shabbas." She shrugged, obviously indifferent to germs.

I contemplated leaving but couldn't bring myself to abandon the others. My social cowardice was greater than my repugnance: courage to remain arose from a fear of offending my acquaintances.

"So." Roberta picked up the booklet and checked the order of the procedure. "Why don't you all wash your hands now and then we can begin. We have a lot to do and not that much time." She glanced at her watch.

We filed over to the sink, relieved momentarily from the intense concentration we had focused on the covered body. Using pitchers, we poured water over one hand and then the other, back and forth, as though we were preparing to partake of challah and a festive meal, instead of the gruesome ritual that awaited us. I lingered by the garbage pail, carefully drying between my fingers and around each cuticle before reluctantly dropping in the paper towel.

I followed the others to the table with the body. Marlene pulled on her gloves and fussed to fit them snugly around each knuckle and manicured fingernail. "I promised my husband." She grinned apologetically. Her husband was a doctor.

"Are you ready?" Roberta asked. She lifted a corner of the sheet. "We want to respect the body, so out of modesty we'll try to keep the sheet on, only exposing the part we're working on." She peeked under the sheet. "Oh, good, we're in luck. She's not so bad." She folded back the cloth, exposing the head.

I'd never seen a dead person before. It was hard to say what was so horrifying about that first look. Having never met Betsy Singer in life, I had no basis for comparison, but she really didn't look bad. In fact, in spite of the shriveled skin and sunken eyesockets of old age, I could see she had well-proportioned features and good bone structure, a decidedly handsome face and beautiful gray eyes. But I'd never been repulsed by monsters, or locales so alien as to resemble nothing familiar. It was those creatures and situations that diverged only slightly from the accustomed that chilled me: the mutilation of one fleshy finger of a shopkeeper on Ben Yehuda Street nauseated me much more than the metal hooks of a prosthesis, the cries of cats in our backyard, sounding like the wails of an infant, seemed more sinister than shrieks of horror-film ghouls. Gallons of blood out of context did nothing to make my flesh crawl, but Iris Murdoch's description of a drop of blood like a tear by the corner of an eye gave me nightmares long after reading one of her novels.

What was so terrible about Betsy was that she was almost human but not quite. There was something subtly—but seriously—amiss. It looked as though she were made of wax, only worse, because she was more lifelike than anything at Madame Tussaud's. Her skin was truly skin, her eyes were *not* glass. The bulges and nodules in her neck were not the art of a sculptor carving from the outside inward, but the parts of her body—the veins, the sinew, the larynx—that over the years had worked their way gradually through layers of fat and flesh outward to the surface, until now their form pressed against the last barrier, the sagging membrane of the skin. She was too real. The only thing she lacked was life, but oh, what a vast shortcoming! Those gray eyes, staring at nothingness beyond the acoustical tile ceiling, the wavy yellow-white hair framing her high cheeks, the lovely lips that formed no kiss nor grin nor curse.

I'm not sure whether I gasped, whether I actually stepped back, but I shrank inside. I perceived a drawing away, a growing distance between myself and the lifeless head.

Roberta's voice pulled me out of my swoon, instructing me to wet a washcloth and gently wipe the crust of dried tears out of the corners of the eyes. Robotlike, with the juices of my own life-essence carefully protected and sealed away in some secret, distant part of me, I proceeded with the *tahara*, dabbing around the mouth, into the nostrils that refused to stir with a breath. I had a vague awareness of the other women stationed at the right hand and foot, Roberta looming at the left hand, but my concentration was narrowed on the minutiae of each individual wrinkle and pore. I was careful to keep my small white cloth between my live flesh and the dead flesh I was cleaning, buffering me from direct contact. As though across miles, I heard Roberta ask me to save any loose hairs to be placed later in the foot of the coffin at the other end of the room, and I was forced to pick off a couple of silvery strands sticking to the washcloth and put them on a paper towel. But that was the closest I came to touching anything.

Then, as I poked carefully into the hole of the right ear, I noticed the tip of the lobe jiggle. I jumped back and stifled the scream that rose to fill my throat. Looking up, I stared blindly at the far wall, at a poster with instructions on embalming hanging there, charting in blue and red all the veins and arteries of a human figure. The ringing in my ears subsided, replaced by the syncopated dripping of the water in the sink. I became aware of a faint odor but disregarded it. Perhaps it was me, my sweat, the excretion of my fear.

Roberta glanced up from the hand she held in hers, the stiff fingers separate and curling toward the ceiling. "You all right, Cynthia?"

I nodded; I couldn't talk.

"You want to step out in the hall for a minute? Get a little fresh air?" she suggested.

I shuffled woodenly to the door, opened it, and breathed in. A door at the end of the hall opened to the outside, and a fresh, damp breeze blew the smell of ozone and wet earth to my feverish face. The animated thrumming of the downpour outside, the hail now melting into giant raindrops before striking the ground, seemed to wake me from a trance. I felt a return of my involuntary functions, sucking in greedy breaths as though I had ceased respiration back in the room. My stomach rumbled. My body made me realize that as deadening as my months of depression had been, I wasn't yet as dead as Betsy Singer. I went back to my task.

The odor was more pronounced after the fresh air of the hall. It reminded me of something, but I couldn't say what. All I knew was that I didn't like it, that I associated it with something nasty.

Roberta turned and smiled at me and I smiled back. I felt better, as though, now that I had confronted the worst, I was inured to the morbid for life. "Why don't you come work on this foot now," she said. I noticed the sheet had been replaced over the head.

"Okay." I stationed myself next to the comfortably large, secure rabbi's wife and lifted the bottom corner of the sheet. The smell increased warningly, but I still couldn't identify it. Dirty feet, I thought.

The heel and ankle were wrapped in gauze. "What do I do now?"

She lowered the heavy arm onto the metal table and joined me. "Hmm. I wonder why they did that. I guess we should remove it and take a look." She walked to the counter to get the scissors and then cut through a layer of gauze, carefully peeling a little back. "Maybe there's a sore under there. If it's too bloody, I guess we'll have to leave it, but it would be nice to remove everything to do a proper job. Make sure you save any gauze that has dried blood on it, just like with the hair. Here, you wanna do this?"

I silenced my objection, taking the end of the gauze and pulling away a couple of inches. When I came to where it continued under the heel, I couldn't proceed without lifting the foot. How I wished I too had a pair of latex gloves! Swallowing the bitter-tasting saliva in my mouth— and imagining I was swallowing the contaminated air with it—I braced myself for my first direct contact with the dead flesh. Gingerly, tentatively, I slipped my right hand palm upward under the back of the knee. The skin was velvety soft and profoundly cold. Not just room temperature cool, but icy. "Roberta," I uttered in a small voice, "why is she so cold?"

"I think they kept her refrigerated overnight. How are you doing with that?"

I lifted, but lifting the knee didn't raise the foot. The heel squeaked against the metal table as it moved.

I shifted my hand under the thin calf, the muscle flabby at the thawed surface and frozen hard deeper inside. The leg of the little woman was very heavy. When the heel hovered an inch from the table top, I quickly tugged away the gauze caught under it before having to let the leg drop. The foulness grew even more perceptible. I noticed an edge of what looked like a dark bruise where I'd exposed some of the heel. "How do you think she did that?" I wondered, barely audible, as much to myself as to my three companions. "Funny place to bang yourself."

I unwrapped the gauze another turn and lifted the calf again. Something about that semifrozen white flesh made me think of a raw chicken leg. That association, accompanied by what the additional exposure revealed—like an extra clue on The Concentration Game: I could hear Hugh Downs of my childhood, as I lay in bed, home sick from school, my head aching, my stomach churning, trying to distract myself by watching my parents' portable TV rolled in from their room, Hugh Downs' voice saying, "Can you tell us, for five hundred dollars and the game, what it says?"—as the darkened skin came away with the bandage, I suddenly knew what I smelled. Rotten chicken. Like the time I bought it anyway, even though it looked a little funny, something, the plastic bag, somehow it didn't look right, and then when it defrosted, the overpoweringly revolting stench. I stared at the rotting ankle and felt stunned by a dizzy, nauseating shock.

Marlene looked up. "Phew!"

"Does it smell a little in here?" Roberta asked. "Ellen, you finished with that hand? Why don't you go prop open the door?"

"What is it?" persisted Marlene.

Their voices spun around me, but I had retreated somewhere deep within a hidden cavity, frozen and numb. Then a niggling disgusting thought entered my hollowness: had I touched it, had I touched the blackness? The tips of my fingers prickled with angry sensation, and I stared at them and imagined them shriveling with leprosy.

Roberta was saying something: "...better wrap that up again."

I vaguely remember lifting the calf again so she could tie new gauze around the foot. Then I stumbled to the sink, where like Lady MacBeth I frantically scrubbed invisible spots. Nobody else seemed to mind; they continued with the torso as though they encountered gangrene every day.

I felt my mortality closing in on me. I kept thinking, I'm going to die, someday I'm going to die. Someday I too will be subjected to this final mortification, living women uncovering all the secrets of my dead body, discovering little faults and asymmetries, the kinky hair that grows from a mole, the roll of puckered fat, the pimple on my thigh. There was no escape from this last indignation. Blindly, my head spinning, I staggered outside.

The rain was less violent; whereas before it revived me, now its soft rhythm calmed me. I stood there a long time before I noticed Marlene. "You can't ever be the same after this, can you?" she said, as soft and soothing as the rain. "This is just one of those things you do that you're never the same after, isn't it?" I nodded and followed her back into the room.

They needed my help to roll the body over onto its side to wash the back. Then, saying prayers, we poured pitchers of water over the face, the body, the arms and legs. "*Tahara he, tahara he*"—she is cleansed, she is purified. The water ran down the table to a drain between the feet.

We dried the body with big white clean towels. Somehow everything was different: Betsy Singer's body was pure and clean. I no longer feared its taint. I rubbed her delicate skin tenderly, almost lovingly, her hand and arm and armpit. I gently lifted her breast to wipe under it. My towel softly stroked her face dry. Would someone bathe me when I died? Would someone swallow her revulsion to perform my last rites? I imagined Betsy Singer's soul hovering in the room, already less tormented now that her body was prepared. I sensed the ease, and I relaxed into that cushion of peacefulness. I felt the special bond that follows any positive physical intimacy.

Roberta unwrapped the clean white linen shroud, and I helped to slip it on, feeling like I was dressing a giant helpless infant, *my* infant somehow because I had somehow adopted her, given birth to her, helped her through a passage to another world, just as babies slid into this world bathed in pure amniotic waters. There was the spiritual elation I had previously known after arduously expelling a slippery infant from my womb. And like all my offspring, especially my adopted daughter, she had taught me something, she had brought me to a new understanding: None of us knew when we'd die. The only thing we could be certain of was that, at least for now, we were alive. I was still living.

It was nearly three o'clock. As gracefully as possible, we lifted Betsy into the coffin. We placed sand from the land of Israel in her hands and eyes—so that she could hold and behold the Land in her final resting place. We placed broken crockery on her mouth and eyelids, tied a cloth over her face, wrapped the white sheet around her, and fit the lid into place. There was a final prayer to ask her soul forgiveness for having offended her body. I knew I had, but I also knew she forgave me. We washed up and helped Roberta collect all the damp towels and washcloths into her green plastic bag. I offered to help carry out the buckets, and Marlene and Ellen said goodbye and left.

The rain had stopped. Off in the western sky, the sun was peering out at the glistening wet world from under the cover of thick gray clouds. All the greens of the trees around the mortuary looked vibrant and healthy; the hard, parched, buff-colored dirt had become soft, chocolatey brown. Everything that held water sparkled—the leaves, the cars in the parking lot, the puddles. Birds chirruped and darted. I was dazzled by how incredibly beautiful and alive everything looked.

As we walked to the car, drowning snails crunching under our feet, Roberta sifted through a dozen keys on a ring to find the one that unlocked her trunk. After making some room for me to put the buckets in, she asked, "How are you doing now?"

"I'm fine. Really." I meant it.

"You'll be okay?"

"I think so."

"No nightmares?"

I grinned reassuringly up at her. In spite of her temperament and constitution, there were strain and fatigue in her face.

"I really appreciate your coming," she said, "what with it being *erev* Shabbas and all. Thanks again."

"Thanks for asking me. I really mean it."

She slammed close the trunk and found the key to her car door. "I better get going. Good Shabbas. I'll see you tomorrow in synagogue."

I stepped over puddles to my car, absent-mindedly picking at the grittiness under my nails, then flicking away the grains of sand.

# Twenty-Four

April came and the weather warmed. I warmed too. Like icy numb extremities which prickle as they thaw, I experienced a sharpened awareness of the sensate world. How ironic that I had feared touching dead flesh: it was this tactile connection which renewed my feeling and brought me back to life.

Of course it helped that the desert was bursting with spring. Chinaberry trees covered themselves in tiny white petals outlined in lavender. The mesquites dangled yellow catkins which Tamara called caterpillars, and palo verdes produced simple blooms resembling butterflies. Thorny ocotillos, normally ugly eight-foot tall sticks, now waved red plumes like pennants. Humming birds dipped their beaks into the vermilion bells sent up on stalks by aloe vera, and along the ground, fuzzy pale green-gray weeds opened delicate flowers the color of apricots.

All the orange blossoms unfurled simultaneously, in a crescendo, so that the air was heavy with their pollen. Even the bees got drunk. They overindulged. Then, too laden to fly back to their hives, they staggered on the ground. Tamara got stung when she stroked the furry insects.

▲    ▲    ▲

How like jasmine the citrus smelled! The small waxy flower even looked like jasmine. After hanging out the laundry one morning, I sat on the cement steps leading down from the back door, inhaling nectar and dreaming of the sun on old white stones. The southern Arizona sky approximated the blue over Jerusalem, but there the illusion ended. I'm in love, I thought. Not with Dr. Freedman, or my prototype Sabra, but with a place. Tears of longing filled my eyes. My arms ached with emptiness. But even if I were there, how could I embrace my love?

My mind wandered Jerusalem's streets. They ran like terraces, tracing the contours of the hills. Vines and weeds growing on ancient walls shaded my path, yet the warm air glinted with light. I climbed a hundred stone steps from one street to the next. At the top, I looked down over hills of baked earth with outcroppings of great white rocks and veined with green along the wadis. On a slope in the distance nestled

a village of bleached mud houses—like Tamara's block structures, haphazard and precarious though they had endured a century.

History vibrated throughout the landscape, a fourth dimension
shimmering like the ripples of heated air that rise off the desert floor. In
every direction, it overlaid the view with the countless lives of all ages,
all those who at other times shared the same terrain. Every particle, every
void within each atom, was saturated with souls, with dreams, with the
eyes that over millenia had beheld this land. This handful of dirt: how
many people had trod on it, tilled it, brushed it from their garments?

My mental journey took me to the bustle of the *shuk*, the congestion
of Jaffa Road where it nears King George. Noise and activity swirled
around me. Odors strong enough to taste tingled on my palate: rotting
fruit, onions, spicy falafel, old clothes, sweat, perfume.

The streets and alleys were filled with people arrayed in exotic costumes. A group of bearded Armenian priests, austere and elegant in black
gowns and high rimless hats, walked past Muslims dressed in striped,
looser robes and flowing headscarves. Bedouin women wearing long,
embroidered dresses balanced baskets of pomegranates like heavy crowns.
There were nuns in gray habits, their modesty contrasting with Israeli
girl-soldiers in khaki miniskirts and anklets. Hard-faced women in chic,
bright-colored knits pretended to ignore the smiles of men with hairy,
muscular legs extending below shorts, with hairy chests exposed at their
open collars. Wearing frock coats and knickers, their sidelocks twisted
tightly around their ears, Chasidim leaned forward to keep pace with
their rapid feet; their wives in bouffant wigs and calf-length skirts,
pushing strollers full of babies and bundles, stopped on the sidewalk to
exchange greetings. Waddling along in old shoes stretched over bunions,
short, grizzly men in dirty knit caps breathed garlic into the fetid
atmosphere. Buxom hags draped in dark cottons, paisley kerchiefs knotted
under their chins, pressed against me, their heat weighing on me. Humanity from all the world, from every nation, crushed into the small space.

Their babble enveloped me. Voices rich with unintelligible words
formed languages I never learned. Arabic, melodic and rolling and full of
w's and soft j's, wiped against my face like large sticky hand-shaped
figleaves. There came the counterpoint of Hebrew: gutturals and strong
vowels spoken with arrogance. The harshness of the sounds, the brashness
of the manner, brought a grin to my face. I felt indulgent: a mother who
slaps her son for impertinence, all the while trying to suppress the pride
and admiration she feels for his boldness.

I walked again through Jaffa Gate into the Old City. Swarthy men
in embroidered caps, dark trousers, and wool sweaters sat out on the
pavement on leather stools sipping strong coffee from small cups. One
signaled for a refill from the man with an enormous brass urn strapped
to his back.

I followed a rag-clad boy leading a donkey hitched to a wagon. The beast strained to pull the large, spoked wheels up steps paved into the narrow street, hooves slipping on the stone worn smooth by centuries of sandals. Alleys wound between close walls broken only by low doorways. Each rough gate led to someone's home. Did people really dwell here? What would it be like to live within the walled city?

Abruptly, the irregular walls ended. Through an aperture was a sun-blanched plaza, uncanny within the crowded maze of walls. The large open space contained nothing but hard light. Around this space spun confusion and disorder, but here was quiet. All movement stopped. Time stopped. This was the center of the world, the eye of the storm, a vortex weirdly still amidst the turmoil.

Across the space, the Kotel rose to the sky. This wall was older than the others—older than the wall built by Suleiman the Turk around the city's perimeter, older than any of the houses and warrens, the excavated Roman ruins near the Dung Gate, older than the Church of the Holy Sepulchre or El Aqsa Mosque erected on the Temple Mount. Dry weeds grew out of its chinks. Irreverent pigeons nested in its crags. *Hakotel Hama'aravi*: the Western Wall, our holiest place.

Drawn to the ancient rampart, I traversed the plaza. The relentless sun baked down on me. It was too bright; my eyelids closed against the glare. I moved slowly, pushing against the resistance of so great an energy.

At last I stood before the massive boulders that rose straight up out of sight. I stood within the narrow margin of shade they cast and leaned my forehead against the cool stone.

*Are You here, God? Is this where I must come to find You?*

▲    ▲    ▲

In a swoon, I fell from my perch on the back doorstep, landing hard on the packed dust of Tucson, Arizona. In my jolt back to reality, I found another reality: that I would always stand beside the Kotel, that I need only reach within my heart, into my thoughts, to touch God.

Our solar system is not the center of the galaxy, and our galaxy is far from the center of the Universe, yet God blessed the Earth with abundance and beauty. So too did He create this farflung bit of desert in the southwest United States, remote though it is. He could be in Heaven, or in the Promised Land of Israel, but He is also here, with me, wherever I am.

# Twenty-Five

The sun was so bright, my eyes blinked protectively away from that portion of the sky. There was no moisture in Tucson's atmosphere to diffuse the radiant heat; where the rays reached was markedly hotter than where they were blocked. I was always aware of how the shadows fell. During the winter, I avoided them, choosing instead to walk where it was warm. Now I sought out the shade.

Tamara went to Second Street School right through the summer. Under a parachute draped to shade the sandbox, she sat for hours in a puddle created by generous doses of water. Before she left each afternoon, someone had to hose her down. Her clothing dried within the time of our short walk home.

Adam went to Sports-O-Rama at the University all morning. After lunch, he disappeared again, out bike riding or off to a movie or miniature golf with his friends. We bought him a season's bus pass and he moved independently. I felt a little sad that he no longer needed me to drive him to these places.

Ronnie, now fifteen, developed a crush on a life guard at Himmel Park Pool. She signed up for junior lifesaving lessons and spent all day in the water, only leaving when the afternoon thunder rumbling in the distance forced the pool's closure. She ran home wrapped in a towel. Then, her bathing suit dripping on the floor, she joined Tamara and me at the living room window to watch the spectacular lightning. A cathartic downpour followed, flooding the yards, flushing mud and leaves into the stream in the gutter, and washing the heat from the day. Within an hour, the storm passed. The evening sun painted the scurrying clouds salmon and pink and slate. Soon a rainbow appeared in the eastern sky. I rarely remembered to say the blessings for all these phenomena, but surely God knew the awe that was in my heart.

Jeff spent his days doing research at the University. In the evenings, we left Ronnie to baby-sit and walked to Bobb's Dobbs for a beer, or as far as Bentley's for espresso. Strolling down the cool night streets was as refreshing as the quaff at our destination. Crickets scampered over the ground, leaping when we stepped too close; in the dark around houses, black widows reposed on their sticky webs. Taking these opportunities when the children couldn't interrupt, Jeff chattered excitedly about his successes in the lab. I thought to myself, He might as well be talking Greek—or Hebrew. All I understood about optics was that it had something to do with light and seeing. I'd squeeze his hand, making him chuckle. "Am I boring you? All right, I'll talk about something else."

Though I continued to feel a tender sorrow about our absence from Israel, I no longer blamed Jeff. I was glad I never vented my fury at him for tearing me from the place. Once I had accommodated to my physical distance from Jerusalem, it was easier to mend our relationship, since there had never been an actual breach. At least I still had Jeff. Sometimes I was overcome with an urge to stop on the dark street and kiss him as if we were young lovers.

When everyone else had left for their daytime activities, instead of sitting in the house eating, I went out for walks. Mesquite seed pods skittled underfoot, sounding like diamond-back rattle snakes. I passed a house where an attempt had been made to create a lawn. All the strips of sod had dried out, looking like so many welcome mats laid end-to-end across the yard. Along Third Street half-naked joggers ran, the women's backsides jiggling below the edge of their running shorts, the men's bare backs reddening like roasting turkeys. Fools, I thought under my wide-brimmed straw hat. They'll all get skin cancer...if their hearts don't give out first.

My mind wandered philosophically as my feet carried me around the neighborhood. I wondered if the people I met on my meanderings longed for their ancestral lands. Did the Hispanics miss Mexico or Spain? The man with the long straight black hair sitting at the bus stop: would he really be willing to return to tribal life? The Petersens weren't venturing back to Scandinavia, blacks didn't move back to Africa, Asians seemed to be settling in. People whose forefathers hailed from Ireland, Germany, Italy, made tours to the Old Country, but then they came back here. America was a land full of displaced people; it was one big refugee camp. The problem was, "homelands" only looked desirable from a distance, from a romanticized, nostalgic perspective. What if the Palestinians had a homeland? What if they had the homeland they sought: all of what is Israel plus a bit of Jordan thrown in for good measure? After the rejoicing, would they still be happy? Would each Palestinian-in-exile return to the arid acre his father had plowed? Would the Palestinians then live in peace and contentment?

This made me sigh. I still missed Israel. I had made such an effort to be there, I invested so much—financially, yes, and physically too, but it was the emotional and the spiritual investment I made which left me bankrupt when we departed. But I was coming into another inheritance; I was discovering the wealth of the land where I now made my home. In the glaring Tucson sunshine, life seemed more precious for its frustrating futility. Our greatest efforts are insignificant against the order of the cosmos, yet all the more reason to treasure what small riches we have.

▲   ▲   ▲

On Saturday, October 4, 1986, the first day of the year 5747, we made our way to synagogue. From a telephone wire, a mocking bird regaled us with his repertoire of melodies. The mountains looked crisp in the bright daylight. Every pebble on our path cast a miniature shadow.

Adam tested the durability of his new pants by leaping up onto our neighbors' retaining wall, then balancing along the top until he reached the corner. Though he had just entered junior high, he was still our irresponsible young dreamer. It was hard to believe the rite of passage of his bar mitzvah the following spring would transform him into a man.

Ronnie and Tamara walked ahead of me, one as tall as my eyebrows, the other still waist-high. Both were wearing new dresses. Ronnie seemed to outgrow her clothing every few months. Tamara's development was more subtle; she was tiny compared to other seven-year-olds. Yet the frilly dresses her first parents bought her had finally become too snug. She looked less babyish without puffy sleeves and big bows, and without the bulk of a diaper under her skirt. The staff at Second Street School had put training pants on her, and Tamara managed to keep them dry most of the time. Perhaps I hadn't been pushy enough. But then again, perhaps she just hadn't been ready.

Beside me strolled Jeff. His new white satin Rosh Hashanah *kippah* was as shiny as his balding scalp. He wore his white prayer shawl draped neatly on his shoulders. Like folded angel wings, I thought. The fringes resembled exotic feathers. I smiled to myself, imagining him spreading the cloth wings and flying off to perform some good deed.

I straightened the bodice of my dress. It wasn't new, but I felt good in it, pleased to be able to once again fit into my old clothing. The fat was gradually melting away. "I was thinking about maybe going for my masters," I said to Jeff.

"Sure," he replied. "Why not? You're enjoying your class, aren't you."

I nodded. I had enrolled in an English literature class after all. I still liked good books.

▲   ▲   ▲

Blowing the shofar is forbidden on the sabbath. The next day, Sunday, the second day of Rosh Hashanah, we were all the more anxious to hear it.

The congregation stood poised, waiting for the call of the ram's horn to repent, to return to God.

Jeff tapped Adam and Tamara on the back and they ran to join the other children clustered around the *bimah*. Ronnie stood quietly by my side.

Mr. Liebowitz handed Cantor Schneider the shofar. The twisted cone was translucent and glowed with the natural polish sweaty palms had applied over the years. The cantor blew hard but no sound came forth. As tension built throughout the synagogue, he wiped his lips, he wiped the mouthpiece, and tried again. Halfway through the aspiration there was the splutter of spittle followed by the primordial blare.

Relief seeped into me. Let it be a good year, I prayed.